# MARINES NEVER CRY

## BECOMING A MAN WHEN IT MATTERED

Timothy C. Hall

BANYAN · TREE · PRESS

BANYAN TREE PRESS

*Marines Never Cry: Becoming a Man When it Mattered*

ISBN: 978-1-936449-95-8

Library of Congress Control Number: 2017930460

Cover Design and Interior Layout: Ronda Taylor, www.rondataylor.com

Banyan Tree Press

# Praise for *Marines Never Cry* ...

*Marines Never Cry* is a compelling account of a youth who strives to mature in the most challenging place possible ... the Marine Corps and a confused, deadly war with the fears and frustration of mortal combat. There, his ideals and core beliefs are sorely tested and found wanting at times. Throughout the book, he has reason to cry when he loses those closest to him, but he doesn't. Tim Hall gives us a Vietnam equivalent of Catch 22 with his capacity to personalize not only his war, but also the unique life and experiences that molded this young man.

— Bob Fischer, Colonel USMC (Ret),
Senior Advisor to 6th Bn., South Vietnamese Marines, Vietnam 1966-1968
Author of *Guerrilla Grunt, Covan* and co-author of *The Miracle Workers of South Boulder Road*

---

In Vietnam, we Marines learned quickly that war never goes well or as planned. Tim Hall brings that "lesson learned" home to a new generation of readers who have no idea what transpired fifty years ago, in a faraway Southeast Asian country. Through his main character, Zeke Hammond, an all-American kid from rural roots, Tim weaves actual tales of intrigue, levity, and danger that most people have never experienced or even thought of in their entire lives. He did change names to protect both the innocent and guilty alike. In this book, Tim aptly records United States Marines going about their daily routines of boredom and toil, of events both good and bad and the untimely dangerous exploits of Marines, who "never cry" until the war is over. Tim's poignant book takes place in the mid 1960's during one of America's longest and costliest wars. Very well done, brother Tim!

— Grady T. Birdsong, Corporal, USMC
1st Bn., 27th Marines; 2nd Bn., 9th Marines, Vietnam 1968-1969
Author of *A Fortunate Passage* and co-author of *The Miracle Workers of South Boulder Road*

*Marines Never Cry* paints a good picture of how things were for truck drivers in Vietnam, particularly those who convoyed into dangerous places like An Hoa. I know because I was a grunt in that area, specifically Operation Allen Brook at Go Noi. You'll find my name referenced several times in the book, *Every Marine: 1968 Vietnam; A Battle for Go Noi Island*. I know first-hand what those truckers experienced when they drove those big ass trucks—BATs, as Tim calls them—through what was called "Indian Country" to bring us the ammo and everything else we needed to fight the war. God bless the truckers; they're the unsung heroes of Vietnam.

— Wesley S. Love, Sergeant, USMC
3rd Bn. 27th Marines, Vietnam, 1968

# DEDICATION

M*arines Never Cry* is dedicated to the truck drivers of the Vietnam War. It is the story of Zeke Hammond, a Baby Boomer, who joined the Marine Corps and drove a 26-wheeler in the DaNang area and on convoys into "Indian Country" where danger lurked around every corner. Truck drivers in Vietnam, regardless of their branch of service, were the unsung heroes of the war. They risked life and limb in support of American and allied operations against Viet Cong insurgents and North Vietnamese Army regulars, bringing food, water, ammo and supplies – often under fire – to far-flung base camps and skirmish lines.

*Marines Never Cry* also gives the reader a tragicomic glimpse of what it was like for rank-and-file Marines behind the scenes and off-camera, so to speak, both in Vietnam and on the home front. While in Vietnam, the people closest to him either died or were killed. Hammond has countless brushes with death in Vietnam and extraordinary life-changing moments after he came home and confronted his fiancé's killer and a gang of vandals that ravaged the family farm.

*Marines Never Cry* is a work of fiction, but is inspired by true events and crafted to portray the thoughts, emotions and actions of real people in the context of the Vietnam War in 1966 and 1967. Where appropriate, names and other potentially identifying information have been changed. While some of the language, actions, thoughts or references may be jarring to some readers, it is a story that will make you laugh, cry, get mad ... and appreciate another side of the Vietnam coin.

# ACKNOWLEDGMENTS

Thanks to my wife, Shirley, not only for her insight and skills in helping me write this book, but also for her patience and support during the time it took to bring the story to fruition.

Thanks to my beta readers—those authors who edited, critiqued and strengthened my story—specifically, Karen Douglass, 1st Lieutenant, USAF; Dr. Fred Baker; Laurel McHargue, U.S. Military Academy graduate, Class of 1983; Bob Fischer, Colonel, USMC (Ret.), Senior Advisor to the South Vietnam Marine Corps; and Grady Birdsong, Corporal, USMC, 1/27 and 2/9, Vietnam.

Thanks to Dan Guenther, Captain, USMC, Third Amphibian Tractor Bn., Vietnam and recipient of the Bronze Star with Combat "V" (for valor), for being a role model through his many wonderful books, his sometimes sobering stories about Vietnam, for his writing advice and for helping me better understand the perspective of an officer who brought the fight to the enemy at An Hoa, Arizona Territory and Dodge City.

Thanks to Les Kennedy, Lieutenant Colonel, USA (ret.), recipient of the Distinguished Service Cross, for helping me gain an understanding of the amazing accomplishments of the Green Berets in Vietnam and an appreciation for what it takes to be a true warrior.

Thanks to Carolann Walters for naming the protagonist.

Thanks to my publisher, Banyan Tree Press/Hugo House Publishers, Ltd, specifically Dr. Patricia Ross for being a mentor, taskmaster and friend.

Last but not least, thanks to the members of the Colorado Association of Independent Publishers for their support, encouragement and friendship and their passion to write and help others do the same.

I had the occasion to quote a line from a few songs that were popular during the time Zeke Hammond was in Vietnam to amplify a point or emotion. I would like to acknowledge those artists, specifically: Cher, *Bang Bang (My Baby Shot Me Down)*, Imperial, 1966; Glenn Yarbrough, *Baby the Rain Must Fall*, RCA Victor, January 1965; Paul Simon, *I am a Rock*, Columbia, December 1965; Herman's Hermits, *There's a Kind of Hush*, De Lane Lea Studios, January 1967; The Animals, *We Gotta Get out of this Place*, Columbia Graphophone, July 1965; and Jimi Hendrix, *Hey, Joe*, Polydor, October 1966.

Reggie Thompson, we never wrote our management book. You died too early. We were brothers once ... and young. You were an inspiration.

# CONTENTS

# PROLOGUE

Some have said it just wasn't my time.

Bullshit. I don't believe in that crap. Life is a lottery. God watches from a distance and lets nature take its course.

I subscribe to the Hank Williams School of Predestination reflected in one of his songs, *I'll Never Get Out of this World Alive,* and that's as deep as it gets for me. Besides, the "it wasn't his time" crap sounds like predestination where anything that happens or doesn't happen was "meant to be." That's too glib.

I'm Zeke Hammond. My mother, Naomi, married a U.S. Marine back in 1944. She couldn't resist the dress blue uniform and his charming line of bullshit. He cheated on her, big time. They divorced about six months after I was born. I never met him, but he wrote to me a few times when I was in Vietnam. I refer to him as my progenitor rather than father. After they split, I stayed with my mom's parents, Walter and Velma, on their dairy farm in Northeastern Pennsylvania while she went off to college to get her teaching degree.

Years later she married a guy named Midge, and they took me to the South Shore of Long Island to live happily ever after ... but I didn't. I went back to the farm where I belonged to finish out my last couple years of high school and help Walter with the farming. Velma and Walter were the greatest surrogate parents ever and living on a farm was the ultimate high for a thousand reasons. They were poor, but we had everything.

The summer of 1965 was the demarcation point between youth and adulthood for me. It was a wild and crazy time, full of hedonistic pleasures, satisfying work, few responsibilities and virtually no stresses or strains.

When I hear songs from '65, I remember everything—the sights, sounds and smells of youth. It was perfect. I didn't pay any attention to the drums of war beating in a faraway place called Vietnam on the other side of the planet. I didn't know or care about any of that. I met a girl named Sharon and fell madly in love. I was as free as a bird and had it all ... until I didn't.

# —PART I—

# HALCYON DAYS

# AN ODD BEGINNING

---

ZEKE LIKED BEING ODD. HE WISHED HE HAD
A T-SHIRT WITH THAT INSCRIPTION.

---

Zeke spent the first six years of his life and a lot of time thereafter with Walter and Velma on their dairy farm in northeastern Pennsylvania. It was not a very large farm, but sufficient to make a living. Up until Walter stopped farming in the early 1960s, he used a team of white Belgian horses and a 1930 Model D John Deere iron-wheel tractor to spread the manure, mow the hay and plant the corn.

The house was unpainted and uninsulated. They used a coal stove in the kitchen for cooking, which also heated water on a side tank. There was an upright coal stove in the dining and living rooms. The cellar was cold, dark and damp. The upstairs was cold in the winter and hot in the summer. They did not have an indoor toilet and their only running water came down through a series of lead pipes from a hilltop spring above the house about a quarter mile away.

Up until a couple years before Zeke was born, neither the house nor the barns had electricity. The rural electrification program had not yet arrived in that neck of the woods. Walter and Velma used lanterns and candles to light the house and kerosene generators to power the barns. They used a wooden icebox in the cellar to keep the food cold. The roof leaked and the floorboards were uneven or missing. There was no air conditioning either— only window screens and a noisy fan. Washing clothes was time-consuming drudgery. Each week, Velma moved her wringer washer into the kitchen along with the rinse tubs and went at it for an entire day, which included time spent hanging the clothes on the outside lines.

Velma hung fly ribbons from the ceiling just above the kitchen table—maybe two or three at a time. The sticky, stinky ribbons were always filled with flies, mosquitoes and bees that had flown in through open doors and holes in the window screens. The sound of a fly trying to break loose of the ribbon was common during meals. Listening to insects trying to escape from certain death just above his head gave Zeke the willies as he stared at the hapless creatures and slowly chewed his food.

Zeke played in the attic, a dark, scary place that smelled like old wet wood, coal dust, cardboard and sweaty bedding. It contained family treasures, collectibles and junk from the past century and was the home of hundreds of mud wasps that got through the cracks in the roof and the spaces between the slats on the back wall. There was a door on the far end of the attic. His game was to run through the attic and jump out the back door onto the roof of the outhouse below without being stung by a mud wasp. It was Zeke against the wasps and the score was usually tied. No matter how fast he ran, one or two would always get him.

The work was non-stop and living was rudimentary, but Walter and Velma saw their work as satisfying and even fun, not drudgery. They were close to nature and felt close to God. They were probably at or below the poverty level by modern standards, but never wanted for anything of importance. Velma would often say, "we're rich in other ways."

The nearest town was the Borough of Dinglebury, about ten miles away. Zeke was bussed to Dinglebury School for First Grade when he was five years old. Zeke's mom, Naomi, graduated from the same school in 1942, exactly six months after the start of World War II. Dinglebury claimed to have the largest feed mill and the most bars per capita in the Commonwealth of Pennsylvania. Their town logo was a picture of the feed mill with a Gibbons beer bottle overlay. Zeke's best friend in First Grade was a boy named Dex, short for Dexter. Ironically, many years later, Dex would figure prominently in the most traumatic experience of Zeke's life.

Walter and Velma had a gaggle of sisters and brothers, the oldest of whom was born in the 1870s. It was an extended family where everyone

2

cared deeply for each other and showed it. They visited the farm often and always spent the holidays there. They were all Calvinists and Grangers; the women were all active in the Women's Christian Temperance Union. They did not drink alcohol, play cards or dance and lived by the Ten Commandments and Roy Rogers' Riders Rules, a list of prescriptions for being a good citizen. They hunted game, read books, involved themselves in community activities, sang religious songs and loved each other's company. They shared the same way of speaking, the same witticisms, the same mispronunciations and the same rustic accents.

Grandma Velma handled illnesses and accidents like a pro. She was a midwife and fancied herself a doctor of sorts. She knew all kinds of cures—herbal and otherwise—and had a calming, reassuring way about her that instilled confidence in her "patients." She staved off infection with Boric Acid and Witch Hazel, cured bronchial problems with warm Mustard Plasters and took care of anything else with Sal Hepatica, camphor and spirits of niter. Her two mainstays for general ills were Fletcher's Castoria and Dr. Naylor's Udder Balm. Zeke liked the taste of castoria and the smell of udder balm even though the salve was designed to treat cows' udders. Medical doctors were seldom needed.

✪ ✪ ✪

Zeke's progenitor, Dan, was a world-class high school track star. When World War II broke out, he joined the Marine Corps. There was something about a charming, handsome guy in a Marine dress blue uniform with a crazy sense of humor that Naomi found appealing. They were married a couple years after she graduated from high school and they went to live at the Marine Corps base in Cherry Point, North Carolina with the intention of living happily ever after.

After a couple blissful years, the bloom fell off the rose and Dan decided that mating with another woman would be more gratifying than maintaining his marriage. Naomi, pregnant with Zeke at the time, found out about the infidelity and tried to work things out under the condition that Dan stop screwing around. Not only did he refuse Naomi's offer, but he suggested that all three live together under the same roof in a ménage a trios. Dan was way ahead of his time in terms of sexual kinkiness.

When all else failed, Naomi filed charges against him through the Marine Corps for Adultery and Buggery which was considered Conduct Unbecoming a Marine, pursuant to the Uniform Code of Military Justice (UCMJ). Marines sometimes laughed at the idea that there could ever be any conduct "unbecoming a Marine" since Marines were stereotyped as such bad boys, but the UCMJ specifically forbade adultery and buggery, particularly on a military base and particularly when the wife was pregnant. Dan was disciplined and reduced in grade from staff sergeant to buck sergeant. He lost prestige, power, privilege and money.

Naomi divorced Dan a few months later, when Zeke was six months old, refusing child support or any other contact with him forever. Dan married "the other woman," and lived miserably ever after from what Zeke heard, dying prematurely and humiliatingly.

Dan had hurt Zeke's mother badly and there was no forgiving him. Whenever Naomi told Zeke stories about Dan, she would cry. She never got over the hurt and pain. Not ever. Zeke grew up thinking that his "father," whom he knew only through pictures and stories, was a first-class schmuck. But he admired Dan's prowess in track and his status as a Marine and thought maybe he wasn't all bad.

While Zeke was enjoying those halcyon years with his grandparents, Naomi completed college and had gotten a job teaching second grade at a school in New York State, about 50 miles from the farm. She took Zeke there to live with her, but Walter and Velma took him back to the farm on weekends and holidays. Zeke loved his mother, but his roots were on the farm with his grandparents. Weekdays with mom; weekends on the farm. It was the best of all worlds.

Teachers were not paid so well in those days and most worked second jobs to make ends meet. Naomi worked as a waitress at a nearby "dude ranch" designed for city folk to ride horses, morph into cowboys and cowgirls and carouse. The ranch bartender was a second-generation German from New York City nicknamed Midge. He stood about 5' 2" in his yellow cowboy boots, but nobody thought much about his name or his height because he was a charming fellow and full of fun. After a few beers at ranch parties, like clockwork, Midge would morph into a wild man, stripping off his clothes down to a pair of leopard print briefs and doing a provocative little dance to the clapping, whistling and hooting of the ranch guests. Sometimes he'd even dress up as a woman, make-up and all, and do a striptease. He was the life of every party.

In time, Midge and Naomi became more than friends. The infatuation gradually turned to love and, unbeknownst to Zeke, they got married one weekend. It was a quick civil ceremony performed by a small-town Justice of the Peace. After all was said and done, Naomi informed Zeke what had transpired.

"Guess what? Midge and I just got married. We're now husband and wife and Midge is your new dad."

"That's great mom. Hope you guys have a great life together. I guess that means I stay with Gram and Gramp and you two will go live in New York City or something, right?"

"No, you'll be coming to live with us" they said in unison, looking at each other with knowing smiles and loving eyes.

Until then, Midge had been just a nice guy, an indulgent friend who brought Zeke candy and other goodies and took him and his mother to drive-in movies on weekends. Now, overnight, Midge was his stepfather and they would all be migrating to Queens or some other exotic place in downstate New York. He did *not* want to go and he did not return their smile.

"Why me, I'm not marrying him? I want to stay on the farm."

Zeke fired off a few more protestations and even said the word "hell" in the process, not caring about the consequences of using a sinful word in a Calvinist house.

"I won't go. You can beat me or even kill me, but I still won't go."

Naomi did not tolerate backtalk. She ended the conversation by pulling him out of Midge's line of sight and giving him an offer he couldn't refuse. He saw further resistance as futile.

He bid a tearful goodbye to his grandparents, the dogs, cats and his favorite cow, the one he had named Cherry, and slid into the back seat of Midge's Ford Crestliner to begin the four-hour trip to the South Shore of Long Island to begin a new life. It would be a character-building adventure, the likes of which he could never have imagined at the time.

✪ ✪ ✪

Naomi and Midge bought a thirty-year-old house at 240 Central Avenue. It had been advertised as a "handyman special," which was accurate in every way. It was the dumpiest house on the block. The only thing that didn't need repair or replacement was the variegated cream color asbestos shingles that adorned every square inch of the exterior. Midge painted the window frames and the only functioning door a shade of glossy green that shouted, "Gypsies live here." Neighborhood kids made fun of the house and referred to it as "240," a number that became a pejorative. This required Zeke to uphold the family honor by returning insults and firing back epithets of his own. Sometimes those verbal duals would lead to full-blown fights with Zeke and the offending big mouth at each other's throats, literally, brawling in the street. Living at 240 toughened him up in many ways.

Naomi required Zeke to become Catholic to please Midge, a change that his Calvinist grandparents did not like, but accepted. He made the most of it and even became an Altar Boy, mainly because it gave him an edge with Catholic girls. Altar Boys had to memorize prayers in Latin, take part in the Mass, look like cherubs and refrain from drinking the Holy Communion wine.

Zeke convinced his Catholic friends and acquaintances that as an Altar Boy he had the power to intercede with Jesus on their behalf for fifty cents per intercession. He insisted that his intercession was a recognized alternative to going to Confession and was infinitely preferable to being harangued for inconsequential Venial sins and then wasting another half-hour saying prayers by rote as penance. Zeke would put his hand on their heads and recite the Confiteor in Latin, slowly and contritely.

*"Confiteor Deo omnipotenti, beatae Mariae Semper Virgini, beato Michaeli Archangelo..."*

Zeke offered his intercession services to Jewish kids as well, but found out quickly that they didn't believe in Jesus.

Zeke managed to escape from 240 during the summers. As soon as the school year was finished, Midge and Naomi would drop him off at the farm for three whole months. It was like heaven. His grandparents showed unconditional love to him and to all their grandchildren. They rewarded good behavior with many reinforcers, including love and other positive attention, and punished bad behavior by withdrawal of positive reinforcers, principally by showing they were disappointed or hurt. They *never* used corporal punishment; it wasn't their approach to child-rearing.

Naomi and Midge produced a batch of children in rapid succession—Midge Junior, Margaret, Jean, and Madeline, in that order. They were the cutest, smartest most adorable little whippersnappers in the world, at least to Zeke. The last one was born when Zeke was 16. He felt like he was their second father. For fun, Zeke numbered the kids, starting with him as number 1 and ending with Madeline as number 5. As they got older, they all referred to themselves using that birth order number in addition to their names. Naomi said it made her feel like she birthed a litter of puppies rather than children. It was all in fun. Zeke had changed them, fed them, played with them and thanked God for them. He was their *half*-brother, but that didn't seem to enter into the picture.

✪ ✪ ✪

Zeke started out doing fairly well in school on Long Island and even participated in sports. He played Right Tackle on the football team and in Track he was a star. He didn't do so well in Wrestling. He was kicked off the team for administering a bloody "ground-and-pound" to a competitor he thought had intentionally hit him in the groin during a match.

Zeke hung around with a tough crowd of Irish, German, and Italian kids whose primary leisure time interests included drinking beer, wearing flashy clothes, seducing female classmates and going to condemned movies—those banned by the Catholic Church as being violent or risqué. Sometimes they would all go to a Saturday matinée, sit behind a row of girls and have a circle jerk contest, the winner being the one who could ejaculate in the shortest time. The girls' reactions ranged from cries of shock and revulsion to quiet stares of admiration.

Zeke joined The Counts SAC out of Oceanside. SAC meant Social and Athletic Club, a public relations ploy designed to conjure up an image of benign wholesomeness. The Counts' preoccupation was booze, broads and belligerence; no drugs or crazy stuff. Most Counts were badass Italian or Sicilian kids; Zeke was the token Anglo-Saxon. The Counts helped him develop a taste for Italian food, Chianti and Countesses, their female auxiliary. They taught him Italian curse words, including the classic, *va fangu,* to help Zeke fit in. In time, they made him an Honorary Italian and lifelong Count through an initiation process where he was required to drink a bottle of Chianti while humping an obese, but attractive Countess to the beat of the Surfaris' song, *Wipe Out* … in front of the entire membership.

The fun and games ended at the beginning of his junior year. Zeke's relationship with Midge deteriorated, as did his school grades. His mother was powerless to change things. He was caught up in the heady hedonism of suburban Italian gang life and was going downhill fast. His mother suggested that he return to the farm to help his aging Grandparents and get away from the bad influences of Long Island. It was time for a change and Zeke recognized it too. Having lived at the farm during his first six years and weekends, holidays and the better part of summers thereafter, Zeke was more of a son than a grandson to Walter and Velma. They were both happy to have him back where, in their mind, he always belonged and should never have left in the first place.

Zeke's new school was named Cletus O. Wilmore School of Horticulture, Industry and Technology. Most people called it Cletus for short; others used the initials, an abbreviation that wasn't thought through by the school board when it was created. The academics seemed easier at Cletus than they were at his Long Island high school and his grades improved.

Zeke found that Cletus girls were like low hanging fruit—luscious and ripe for the pickin'. He didn't know if this was because of his pompadour hair style or his skin-tight pants. He usually wore black shirts with a flashy colored undershirt underneath. He had high-cut shoes with Cuban heels and pointy toes—very stylish back in New York. He had learned how to dress from his Italian brothers, The Counts. He loved being the center of attention and worked hard to maintain a James Dean bad boy image. It was heady stuff.

It all seemed so cool until Zeke's home room teacher, Mr. Pap, called on him to read the morning prayer, which was standard procedure following the Pledge of Allegiance. He considered telling Mr. Pap that he was Jewish or atheist to get off the hook. Reading from the bible was not compatible with the image he had been trying to project at Cletus. He begrudgingly acquiesced, but decided to make a show of it using hand gestures, voice inflections and suggestive moves to amplify the text. He added words and gave his own interpretation of the parables as he played the part of a born-again preacher.

Mr. Pap and the students were quiet and polite at first until it became clear that this new boy in school was being a sacrilegious clown. The students were laughing and responding with mock "amens" and "hallelujahs". Mr. Pap, a man of some experience, didn't fall into the trap of losing his cool and making him sit down, which is exactly what Zeke was hoping for. He listened patiently until Zeke concluded with "Let me hear an Amen" to which the students responded with a loud resounding collective "AMEN!"

"Thank you, Zeke. That was outstanding. I'll be recommending you to the Theatrical Department. You are a natural. And, by the way, did you know that your namesake, Ezekiel, was a prophet in the Old Testament and his name means "God strengthens" in Hebrew? I'd like you to do some research on Ezekiel and give us a complete report next week."

Cletus teachers didn't overreact to Zeke's antics the way they did at his high school on Long Island. It wasn't as much fun.

There were limits, however. Zeke was suspended from school three days before he was to graduate for "organizing a micturition initiative in violation of school policy." He had talked all the boys in his shop class into urinating in the teacher's waste basket until the whole place smelled like a litter box.

Walter had just recovered from a stroke after he had fallen off a ladder. He lost his speech and the ability to walk or write his name. He had worked hard to regain those abilities through incredible self-discipline and determination. Despite his afflictions, Walter went to the school, defended Zeke in a lawyerly fashion and got him off the hook. The suspension was rescinded and Zeke graduated with only one unflattering comment on his report card. The shop teacher wrote that Zeke might have Oppositional Defiant Disorder, a silly psychological label so broad that it applied to all teenagers in all places and times throughout history. Zeke liked being ODD. If he could have gotten a t-shirt with that inscription, he would have done so.

## 2

# RIVERIA

HE WAS TOO BUSY HAVING FUN. IT WAS THE GOOD LIFE,
AT LEAST FOR THAT BRIEF MOMENT IN TIME.

After high school Zeke stayed on the farm for another year helping Walter and Velma. They were getting up in years. They needed him and he wanted to be there. He took a few college preparatory classes and worked for his uncle haying and loading flagstone. After work, he caroused with a bunch of "rum-dum" friends, as Velma called them. Everything was deliciously carefree.

But the world was changing fast—Martin Luther King had marched on Washington; President Kennedy had been assassinated and there had been a skirmish of some sort between the U.S. and the North Vietnamese in the Gulf of Tonkin a couple months after he graduated. President Johnson ordered the bombing of North Vietnam and landed a U.S. Marine Expeditionary Force on China Beach near DaNang, South Vietnam in March of 1965. Zeke, his rum-dum friends and his fellow Baby Boomers were about to be caught up in a "shitstorm" that had been in the making for a long time and would permutate throughout America forever. But Zeke hadn't been paying attention. He was too busy having fun.

✪ ✪ ✪

Zeke bought a 1956 Buick Century Riviera two-door hardtop. It would come to symbolize the best of times and the worst of times for the rest of his life. He paid $240 for the car, a lot of money in 1965. He convinced his

11

mother to give him a loan telling her that the price tag, 240, was a sign from God that it was the right thing to do. The Riviera was more compact and streamlined than other '56 Buick models. It had a 322 cubic inch "Fireball" engine, a 4-barrel carburetor and dual exhausts. Best of all, it had a good radio with front and back speakers. He replaced the stock mufflers with straight-through steel-packs, which made the car sound more powerful than it was, and added racing stripes. As a final touch, he attached a speaker to the inside of the front grill. People could hear Zeke coming from a mile away.

The Riviera had all the options and creature comforts of the day except one: No rear shock absorbers. Even if Zeke had the money to replace the shocks, the mounts were rusted out and there was no way to fix the problem. Without shocks, the coil springs caused the car to bounce down the road like a Low-Rider even on the best of roads. On dirt roads, the bounces were magnified. At drive-in movies, the exaggerated bouncing was a dead give-away as to what was going on inside the car. The upside of having no shocks was the edge it gave Zeke when drag racing. Upon acceleration, the coil springs compressed and shifted the weight to the rear wheels, which reduced tire spin and gave him a jump on his competitor. Another upside was the way Zeke could make the car "dance" by alternatively accelerating and braking to the sound of the music on the radio. He and his friends traveled the circuit with the Riviera to anywhere there were girls and beer in their hedonistic quest for sex and good times. It was the good life, at least at that moment in time.

# 3

# SHARON

GOOD LORD, YOU LOOK JUST LIKE THAT MOVIE ACTRESS,
SHARON SOMETHING-OR-OTHER.

While cruising down the highway in the Riviera one beautiful spring afternoon, Zeke spotted a couple females hovering around an old station wagon alongside the road. They seemed to need some help. Zeke pulled in behind what looked like an early 1950s Plymouth and came to a stop.

"Need some help?" Zeke said as he walked toward the group.

The older woman put down her tire wrench and looked at Zeke with a big smile. "Sure do. I loosened the lug nuts and was about to jack it up but my daughter, Sharon here, just pulled out the spare and said it was flat too."

Zeke looked toward the girl named Sharon as she looked at him. Their eyes met. "Good Lord, you look just like that movie actress, Sharon something-or-other; Sharon Tate, that's the one. Wow, what a coincidence. And you even have the same first name as her."

Sharon just smiled.

He could not take his eyes off her. Sharon giggled and asked him if anything was wrong, which broke the spell.

"Oh, no. Sorry. I just got something in my eye. Let's take a look at that tire," Zeke replied as he winked at her.

"First of all, do you always loosen the lug nuts before you jack up the car?"

"Of course we do. If you don't do that before you jack up the car, you could push the car off the jack." Zeke smiled and winked at her.

13

"Well, Sharon, I'm Zeke, Zeke Hammond."

"We're the Everlys," she said.

"This is my mother, Helen."

"Wait, let me guess, are you related to the Everly Brothers?"

Helen and Sharon looked at each other in polite amusement. They had heard that line before.

"You know who I mean, don't you—Don and Phil Everly—the Everly Brothers? They made some great music up until a couple years ago."

"I have another brother," said Sharon, "his name is Harley, not Don or Phil. Is there any more information you need before you help us?"

"Oh, yea. Sorry. Yep, sure is flat."

Sharon slapped her forehead lightly as if to say, "no shit, Sherlock."

"Today's your lucky day. I always carry a couple spares in the trunk and the bolt patterns will match. You can use one of mine and give it back when you get your tire fixed."

Zeke switched out the tires in a few minutes. He could feel Sharon's eyes on him as she stood with her arms folded standing behind him watching his muscles stiffen and the veins in his biceps bulge under skin glistening from sweat. It was hot and humid and Zeke was becoming aware that his Jade East cologne was souring as it mingled with his sweat.

He looked at Sharon and saw that she had a smile on her face. He felt like a goofy kid, which in some ways he was. He kept staring at her as he walked backward for a couple of steps and collided with the front fender of his car. They both started laughing. His heart was beating rapidly and he was not thinking right. He was so fixated on her pretty eyes and her movie actress body that he had just made a damn fool of himself. Zeke closed his trunk and fired up the Riviera hoping to impress Sharon. She pretended not to even notice.

Helen offered Zeke some lunch for his trouble.

"Sounds good. Maybe I'll take you up on that if it's okay with Ms. Sharon, here."

"I don't care. Suit yourself," said Sharon.

"I'll take that as a yes."

*This Sharon is a feisty little broad and damn good-looking*, thought Zeke.

As he followed the Everlys down the highway toward their house, he noticed that the spare he had put on Helen's Plymouth was a lot larger than the other tires. It was working, but one side of the car was higher than the other. *Crap. Hope they don't notice*, thought Zeke.

Helen drove about ten miles-per-hour below the speed limit, which drove Zeke nuts. He made a practice of always driving at least ten miles an hour *above* the speed limit. Helen began to slow down and put her left arm out to signal a turn. *Holy crap, that car doesn't have turn signals*, Zeke snickered. Their driveway was a rough dirt road so cratered and uneven that Zeke downshifted to low gear and crawled up the road slowly to avoid excessive bouncing and damaging the undercarriage of his car.

A young guy was sitting on the couch in the living room watching television.

"This is my brother, Harley," said Sharon.

When Harley got up and reached out to shake, Zeke noticed his seriously deformed hand. He hesitated for a moment and Harley laughed.

"Cut off by a train when I was playing on the tracks," he said.

Helen intervened before Harley could go any further. "Not true, Zeke. He was born that way. He's had a bunch of surgeries to try to make the hand normal and we still have more to do."

Harley then opened his shirt to show Zeke his hairless chest. He had an indentation in his sternum the size of a fist. "Heart transplant; had to break my breast bone."

Harley enjoyed creating stories to describe his deformities. He felt he could gauge a person by their reaction to his bullshit. Zeke caught on quickly and responded: "You could use that hole in your chest for an ash tray or to hold a beer."

Harley laughed. "Good idea," he said.

Sharon and Helen just shook their heads.

Before Zeke could sit down, Sharon challenged Zeke to try a trick she had learned. "It's a Yoga thing, I think it's called Backward Bending Wall Walking," she said.

"Some people call it the downward sliding zipper buster," said Harley with a smile.

15

Sharon stood with her back against the wall and put her hands over her head behind her, fingers pointed down.

"Most guys can't do this; it's a girl thing," she said as she proceeded to hand-walk all the way to the floor bending over backwards as she went. When her head touched the floor, she hand-walked all the way back up to a standing position with her feet still planted in the same spot. *What a contortionist. And what a body,* Zeke thought. Her clothes were tight and just enough skin showed to give him an idea of what he was missing.

Zeke was a serious weight lifter and an active athlete in school, but he was not sure if he was agile enough to match Sharon's amazing feat. To his surprise, it was easier than he thought. He slapped hand-over-hand down the wall backwards. About the time his head reached the floor his pants popped open. Ignoring the laughter, he came right back up the wall without moving his feet, but his clothes had fallen apart in the process. Everyone was laughing except Sharon. She looked at Zeke and winked. Zeke was in love.

✪ ✪ ✪

As the days and weeks passed, Zeke and Harley began palling around together. Harley had a great sense of humor and was as adventurous as Zeke. He was very bright and a loyal friend. Zeke visited the Everly house every chance he got. There was always something going on there and he loved being around Sharon. She was one of those girls that would make a guy tingle all over just being in her presence. The feeling was indescribable. She was so pretty, so full of fun and so smart. He thought she walked on water.

One late night Zeke dropped Harley off at the Everly house after drinking, road racing and carousing. As he was walking back to the Riviera, he heard "hey" behind him. His heart stopped. He turned to defend himself and there was Sharon.

"Damn, girl. You scared the shit out of me," said Zeke.

Sharon was dressed in a see-through negligee. She was bare-footed and wearing only panties under her negligee. She had been worried about Zeke knowing he was racing and drinking with her brother. She had snuck out of the house and was waiting for him. The moon beamed down directly on her in a way that made time stop. Zeke became oblivious to his surroundings.

"I was worried. I'd die if anything happened to you," she said, with tears running slowly down her cheeks.

"And I'd die if anything happened to you too," Zeke replied.

He gathered Sharon in his arms, led her to his car and drove quietly and slowly away into the night.

After they consummated their relationship, Zeke gave Sharon his solid gold high school ring. It had a yellow topaz stone. Sharon thought it was beautiful and often said so. She wore it around her neck on a chain as a symbol that she and Zeke were "going steady," a term which meant she was spoken for and they would be soul mates forever.

# 4

# BABY THE RAIN MUST FALL

WHILE THEY HAD BEEN PLAYING,
A SHITSTORM HAD BEEN BREWING ...

The lazy, hazy, crazy days of summer, to borrow a line from Nat King Cole, were flying by. Sharon and Zeke could pack a lot into each day and night, but they could not stop the march of time. It was still August and still hot, but there was a smell in the air and a look in the sky that signaled changes were coming. *The Endless Summer* was just a movie and fall would be coming soon. Sharon and Zeke knew they had something going, something deep and special, and they liked the idea that maybe someday they would get married and perhaps even have some kids and a good life together. Sharon was not too pushy. She knew Zeke was up in the air about his future and did not want to pressure him with talk of marriage, at least not then.

Zeke had thought about college, but after twelve years in school that was not for him. The haying was done and good full-time jobs were hard to find for young people with minimal skills. That area of Northeastern Pennsylvania always seemed to be in a depression. Local jobs just weren't available unless a guy wanted to work in a flagstone quarry or maybe a gas station.

"If I'm going to get a decent job I've got to expand my horizons and commute to Scranton or Binghamton," he told Sharon.

"Scranton?! Yuck! Scranton is the armpit of the state. The culm dumps in that whole Wyoming Valley smell like one giant sulfurous fart and make your eyes water. You should look around in Binghamton, Zeke, maybe

Endicott-Johnson City Shoe Company. I heard they were hiring; it's inside work too; you'd have a roof over your head."

Zeke drove up to E-J Shoes and filled out an application for anything they had. He was instructed to produce a urine sample, which he thought was bizarre and intrusive, especially since a female nurse was standing right behind him tapping her foot impatiently and talking to him. This pressure was inhibiting; he couldn't "go." He scooped some liquid from the urinal, hoping the last guy to use it didn't have some disqualifying disease. Something about the process felt dehumanizing and he decided to show his displeasure. He turned around with his fly open, fully exposed, holding the urine cup.

"Here it is. Come and get it."

As the nurse got close, he dropped the cup on her shoes. She splashed around in the urine puddle cursing and sputtering. He wished he'd had his camera to capture that magic moment.

"I'm all outta pee. Let's do this part later," he said.

A supervisor took Zeke down to the conveyor belt where he would be working as a Box Assembler 1, forming the cardboard boxes that would be used to pack shoes for delivery.

"The job pays $1.50 an hour starting tomorrow at 7 a.m.," said the supervisor with a smile, thinking Zeke would be pleased with the offer.

Zeke drove back home slowly, right at the speed limit, mulling things over and laughing aloud intermittently as he thought of the E-J nurse splashing around in his urine. *Can I live with being a Box Assembler 1? Never had a job title before. Threw hay bales, loaded flagstone, cleaned stables, milked cows, and sheared sheep—men's work. Box Assembler? The guys would have fun with that one; I'd be a laughing stock. A dollar and a half would be okay if the job was closer, but E-J's a long way; I'd net zero after taxes, commuting and time. What would Sharon think about her Leader of the Pack being a box handler?* Sharon sometimes referred to Zeke as Leader of the Pack based on the song by the Shangri-La's a couple years earlier; she saw him that way. By the time he arrived back home he knew E-J Shoes was not going to be in his future.

In March 1965, a bunch of Marines had been sent to the other side of the planet to fight Communist guerillas, called *Cong San Viet Nam*, better known as Viet Cong or VC, in a country Zeke had never heard of—South Vietnam. By April there were more than sixty-thousand American troops in Vietnam. In August, the U.S. had launched a major offensive called Operation Starlight resulting in forty-five Americans dead and more than two hundred wounded. Something big had been happening and was getting bigger by the day. Sharon and Zeke, and virtually everyone they knew, had not been paying attention. While they had been playing, a shitstorm had been brewing that was about to dump on the whole country.

Sitting in the Riviera under a clear evening sky with the full moon overhead, listening to the radio, Sharon and Zeke mused about a world that was becoming more complicated by the minute. Young men were being drafted (involuntarily inducted) into the Armed Forces in increasing numbers to go to Vietnam. Some were enlisting. Others were finding ways to avoid military service by getting married, going to college or claiming Conscientious Objector status, saying they did not believe in war. Sharon was worried.

"Don't worry, Sharon; I'd never allow myself to be drafted and forced to go into the Army or end up in some place I didn't want to be. I would enlist. I'd go into the Marines."

Sharon immediately replied with alarm. "Holy shit, are you kidding?!" He was taken aback; Sharon seldom cursed.

"Well … yes, the Marines. I talked to some recruiters at the high school last year and it's been in the back of my mind. If I stay here what am I gonna do—sling shit on the farm, fuck around with cardboard boxes up at E-J Shoes or do some other menial crap for peasant's wages? Not me. There's gotta be something better in our future and the Marines might be the way to go right now."

"But you're not getting the whole picture, Zeke. My girlfriend's brother is in Vietnam right now. He told her it's not just a conflict or a police action; it's a real war. If you go into the Marines, you'll have to go there and you might get killed. Marines always have the highest casualty rates because they're all nuts. They run *toward* the enemy rather than around them. They take needless chances and never retreat. They're just crazy."

21

"But Sharon, that's why Marines always win. That's the point. First, Marines are the most prestigious branch of the service and the finest fighting force in the world. Second, they have the most awesome uniforms. Third, I want to see if I can do it—if I've got what it takes to be a Marine. There's probably a fourth reason too—my father, or more aptly, my progenitor, was a career Marine. I've seen his pictures and heard lots of stories about him. I guess I have a thing about following in his footsteps even though I never met the guy. I'll add a fifth reason to my list too—I've been hearing a lot about Vietnam. I want to join the Marines so I can help the South Vietnamese people, especially the kids, and keep them from being killed and oppressed by those no-good Communist bastards from North Vietnam and those cockroaches called Viet Cong, or VC. Once I do that and come back, we'll have plenty of time to get married; we'll spend our whole lives together. I've just got to do this thing now, otherwise I'll always see myself as less than a man no matter what else I do in life."

Zeke started singing *Baby the Rain Must Fall,* Glenn Yarbrough's hit single from earlier in the year. The song summed up his philosophy of life at that moment. "Baby the rain must fall. Baby the wind must blow. Wherever my heart leads me, baby I must go ..."

It was as if Yarbrough had written the song with Zeke in mind.

There was silence. Then a smile came over Sharon's face. She knew Zeke wasn't going to change his mind without some form of ultimatum where he'd have to choose between her and the Corps. She wasn't going to put him in that situation.

"Where'd you learn all that patriotic gibberish?"

"It's not gibberish. I need to stand for something, to be somebody and do something important. This is my chance. When I'm an old man in my forties, I want to look back on my youth with pride. If I don't I'll end up like all the other douche bags around here where my only claim to fame will be how much beer I can drink or how far I can blow snot out of one nostril. Can you handle all that?"

"Yea, I can handle all that" she smiled as her hand slid down his leg.

22

"Be serious, Sharon. I mean after hearing all that, do you want to break it off now or do you want to wait for me? I'll understand if you want to bail out. It's not going to be easy if you stick with me."

Sharon clutched Zeke's high school ring hanging from her gold chain then hugged him and started to cry, whispering in his ear how much she loved him and how she would never let him go.

Zeke would have been crushed had she responded otherwise, but he had to make the offer. They spent the rest of the night sealing the deal beneath the full moon, talking and holding on to each other tightly, wondering what the future would bring.

# 5

# BRING IT ON!

I WONDER HOW THIS IS GOING TO TURN OUT. FUCK 'UM.
THEY CAN'T KILL ME, CAN THEY?

The Marine recruiter's office was in the county courthouse in Scranton. Zeke donned his best clothes and prepared the Rivera for the sixty-mile round trip. He packed oil and water for the engine and stowed an extra bald spare tire in the trunk, "just in case." He was on a mission that day and was not going to be derailed by car problems or anything else.

Walter and Velma were ambivalent about his joining the Marines. They were worried about what could happen to him given the situation in Vietnam. At the same time, they were proud that he was volunteering to serve his country, particularly in the Marines. They gave him a nice Calvinist blessing before he took off for Scranton:

"It's in God's hands. Thy will be done," said Velma in her most solemn Calvinist voice.

✪ ✪ ✪

Zeke had forgotten about parking meters, something he never had to deal with out in the countryside. *Parking, like air, should be free*, he thought. *Fuck these people and their meters. If I get a parking ticket or the car gets towed, tough shit. I'll worry about that later.* All he cared about was getting into the courthouse and becoming a Marine—that day. He saw no difference between signing up for the Marines and *being* a Marine. He would soon learn the difference. He trotted up the stone steps to the front door of the

25

courthouse and headed for the Marine recruiter's office. As he walked past Army, Air Force and Navy recruiter's offices, each one called out asking him to enlist in their branch. He ignored them all and never slowed down until he reached the Marines.

Zeke's recruiter was unusually honest. He found out later that some Marine recruiters in other areas were not so honest and were making phony promises to induce young men to enlist. It was astonishing to later learn how many recruits had been promised aviation school if they enlisted for a four-year hitch. Zeke did not need such inducement. He was ready to enlist with no strings attached and no expectations about any job. He just wanted to be a United States Marine

Zeke was offered several enlistment options and chose two years' active duty with four years of reserve time thinking that would be long enough to determine whether he liked being a Marine or not. At the end of two years, he would be free to get out or extend his enlistment depending on the situation at the time. He was also mindful of Sharon's concerns about being away from each other too long. When he signed on the dotted line, he yelled out for all to hear: "Hallelujah, I'm a Marine!"

The recruiter just looked at him and smiled. "See you next month, Zeke. You'll be leaving for Parris Island with Aaron Disaronno, gesturing to a fellow sitting across the room at another desk filling out paperwork. You should get to know him. We'll give you both a nice send-off from the Scranton bus station."

Hearing Zeke yell about being a Marine and then his name mentioned, Aaron walked over to introduce himself. "My name is Disaronno, but people call me Aaron for short," he said holding out his hand to shake.

"Pleased to meet you, Aaron. Does Aaron mean short in Italian or does short mean Aaron? And what is Aaron short for? Is there a longer version of that name?"

Aaron became confused and started to give a potentially long explanation of how Disaronno was an Italian liqueur and what he had meant until Zeke cut him off with a wave of his hand.

"Just kidding, Aaron." *This guy's gonna be entertaining.*

Aaron had dropped out of school and had been digging graves for a living for the past couple of years. He decided he'd had enough of that and enlisted for four years, not planning ahead or negotiating anything special in exchange for that much time. Like Zeke, he was mindlessly exuberant about the possibilities for him in the Marine Corps and was willing to accept whatever came his way. Aaron seemed to be a nice fellow, but admitted that he was clumsy with women and his love life was not healthy. Since they would soon be fellow Marines, Zeke thought he would help him out by fixing him up with a girl he knew. She was called Fat Sue. She was an overweight, unkempt sexpot who enjoyed the attention of men—many men; the more the merrier. Aaron liked her right from the start.

"Aaron, if you insist on vaginal intercourse with Sue, you need to use *two* condoms, one over the other, secured with a rubber band, for extra safety from venereal disease and to be sure she doesn't get knocked up. On the other hand, if you want to avoid all that, it might be better to have anal intercourse with her. Rumor has it, that's her preference anyway. That would be the way to go first time around. If she resists, tell her you're going into the Marines soon and are likely to be killed; it's her patriotic duty to let you explore her poop chute."

Zeke had fabricated all that advice and wished he could have been a fly on the wall to see what they did. He couldn't help himself; it was all in fun.

Aaron fell in love with Fat Sue after their first encounter. Falling in love based on one exchange of bodily fluids was a sign of weakness and inexperience. Sue had told Aaron that he was her "first" and Aaron believed her. He was beholden to Zeke for the introduction and doltishly happy. He wanted to marry her before he left for Parris Island. Zeke was surprised at the instant attraction between the two and suggested to Aaron that he should wait until he came back home on leave in a few months as a test of her fidelity. Aaron reluctantly agreed.

The day came. Sharon and her mom, Helen, picked up Zeke at the farm. Walter and Velma said their solemn goodbyes accompanied by a cryptic reading from the Calvinist *Upper Room* magazine. They were off to pick up Aaron and Fat Sue and then head to Scranton to meet the recruiters at the bus station. Sue's hair looked bigger than ever and she was wearing a double dose of blue eye shadow, rouge and red lipstick. The recruiters, looking dapper in their Marine uniforms with lots of colorful service ribbons pinned to their shirts, greeted everyone. Aaron had gotten a 1950s-style haircut and was wearing his father's suit, which was a bit too large and out of style. Zeke went casual knowing the hair and suit would be removed within twenty-four hours and would not impress anyone.

They would be heading to the Philadelphia Naval Shipyard for "processing" and then on to Marine Corps Recruit Depot (MCRD), Parris Island, South Carolina for basic training. That was a mouthful and the word "depot" made the place sound like a train station so most people just called it PI. Recruits from east of the Mississippi River went to PI for basic training and were referred to as Sand Fleas because PI was built on a swamp and the resident insects crawled into every orifice of the body constantly. Those from west of the Mississippi went to MCRD, San Diego for basic training and were referred to as Hollywood Marines. The training was equally hellacious on both sides of the country.

Sharon was quietly shedding tears. She was proud that her beau was going to be a Marine, but she now followed the news about Vietnam and feared what lay ahead. And she was going to miss him terribly. Fat Sue and Aaron were mauling each other and showing more emotion about their separation than was warranted by the short time they had been together. Aaron's lips were as red as Sue's from all the kissing. The spectacle was amusing and took the edge off the goodbyes, at least for Zeke. Sharon and Zeke kissed goodbye. It was a long, deep, flavorful kiss that left them both a little dizzy. They took one last look at each other before Zeke boarded the bus. When the bus door snapped shut, he knew that everything that had happened up until then was history and a new chapter of life had just begun.

In Philadelphia enlistees were pecker-checked (physically examined), as it was called, and declared either good to go or released as defectives. Those who passed the tests solemnly swore to uphold the constitution and defend the United States against all enemies, foreign or domestic ... so help them, God. For Zeke, swearing allegiance to God, Country and Corps was one of life's magic moments. He would remember it forever.

From Philadelphia, Zeke, Aaron and other newly sworn Marine wannabes flew to Charleston, South Carolina. That was Zeke's and Aaron's first time in an airplane and was a bit unnerving, especially as they encountered turbulence or the pilot made sharp turns or changed altitude. Zeke hummed *Baby the Rain Must Fall* and got through the ordeal like a seasoned traveler. Aaron threw up all over his dad's suit.

After a few hours hanging around the Charleston Airport drinking and bonding, more Marine wannabes arrived at the airport from the northeast and upper Atlantic states. There must have been more than one hundred bright-eyed bushy-tailed go-getters assembled in the waiting areas and lounge. Hours later, they all climbed onto charter buses that would take them on the seventy-five- mile trip from Charleston to PI. Most were quiet and alone with their thoughts as they looked out the windows into the dark night at the Live Oak trees and antebellum houses. It was midnight and still surprisingly hot and humid.

The Ribbon Creek incident came to Zeke's mind where, nine years earlier, a PI Drill Instructor had marched his platoon through a swampy tidal creek resulting in the death of six recruits. He had heard many stories about the brutality of Marine Corps recruit training. For a few moments, he became cold and filled with apprehension. *What the fuck am I doing here? I wonder how this is going to turn out. Fuck 'um. They can't kill me, can they? Bring it on!*

# —PART II—
# THE MARINES

# 6

# PARRIS ISLAND

THE MOST DIFFICULT PART OF BASIC TRAINING FOR ZEKE
WAS LEARNING TO SUPPRESS HIS LAUGHTER.

It started from the moment a Drill Instructor (DI) opened the bus door. The enlistees kept talking and tittering ("grab-assing" in Marine Corps lingo) as if they were on a high school outing. Zeke shut up; Aaron didn't. The DI took a step toward Aaron and gave him a loud resounding slap on the side of his head followed by a combination of insults and orders to "SHUT THE FUCK UP" in a voice so loud it triggered Irritable Bowel Syndrome in every recruit on the bus. There was instant silence.

The DI told everyone to count off by twos such that half the men on the bus were number ones and the other half were number twos.

"Ones are piss; twos are shit. Remember that," yelled the DI.

"That's all you are—nothing but piss and shit until you graduate; that is, *if* you graduate. Nothing more."

"When you get off this bus your walking days are over. From now on, everywhere you go you will run. "Do you understand me?"

No one replied.

"From now on you will all sound off with 'YES SIR' whenever a Drill Instructor asks you a question. Now, do you assholes understand me?"

"YES SIR," they yelled in unison.

"Okay, when you maggots get off the bus—running—you will alternate such that pisses will go through the left door of the barracks and shits will go through the door on the right. Do you understand me?"

"YES SIR," came the deafening response.

Zeke was a one and Aaron was a two, but instead of alternating as instructed, Aaron followed Zeke. He was confused. He couldn't remember whether he was piss or shit. The DI gave Aaron his second loud resounding slap of the day, this one knocking him to the ground and accompanied by more insults.

"What the fuck is wrong with you, private? Do you have shit in your ears? *Por qué no hablas Inglés?* What the fuck is your name?"

"Aaron Disaronno, sir, but you can call me Aaron."

"Did you call me a ewe? That's a female sheep."

"No sir. I said *you*, not ewe."

"Are you calling me a liar?"

"No sir you're not a liar and I didn't call you a ewe, I mean, the Drill Instructor a ewe, I mean whatever the Drill Instructor thinks I did, then I did, but I didn't mean to do it."

Disaronno eh? That's an Italian liqueur. Are you an Italian lick-her? Do you lick pussy?

"No sir."

"Well, why not, are you a queer? You don't like pussy?"

"Yes sir, but not to lick."

"You must be a Gay *Caballero*. I'm going to be watching you. Now get the fuck out of my sight," said the DI, giving him a kick.

*This boot camp stuff is some funny shit. God, it's 3 o'clock in the morning. I don't think we're going to get any sleep. Tomorrow's going to be a long day.*

✪ ✪ ✪

Aaron had gotten a haircut and wore a suit to make a good impression; it wasn't working. He had been smacked twice and kicked once before he even stepped foot into the receiving barracks. When all the recruits were lined up in the barracks, Shits on the port (left) side, Piss on the starboard (right) side, each man standing at attention facing a bunk, the DI yelled at Aaron again.

"You must think you're better than everyone else with that fucking suit. Holy shit, it looks like you puked on your suit! Couldn't handle the plane ride? You didn't even have the courtesy to clean it off. You must be some

34

kind of fucking pig. Do you see anyone else here wearing a suit with puke on it ... well do you, Private Disaronno?

"No sir."

"You're not a team player are you maggot? You wanted to be different and stand out like you're better than the rest of us didn't you?"

"Yes sir, I mean no sir," Aaron yelled.

"Well which is it—yes or no, Dapper Dan?" When the DI yelled, his spittle flew directly into Aaron's face.

"I don't know sir."

The harassment that Aaron and all other recruits received was part of the screening process to separate the wheat from the chaff—to screen *in* the strong and weed *out* the weak, or "non-hackers" as the DIs called them. The theory was, if a recruit couldn't handle the verbal harassment and the physical and mental rigors of training then he wouldn't be able to handle combat, which could cost him his life and the lives of other Marines.

"You better get your shit together, Private Disaronno, or you'll never be a Marine. Maybe you should have joined the Army. With that haircut and suit, you look like Army material."

"Yes sir" replied Aaron, "sorry sir."

"Sorry?! Never apologize mister; it's a sign of weakness. John Wayne said that and they're words to live by."

Instead of shutting up, Aaron did it again. "Yes sir. I'm sorry for saying 'sorry' sir."

The DI just shook his head and said aloud for all to hear, "Holy shit, this guy has a major malfunction."

When the DI moved away, Zeke whispered to Aaron, "I told you not to waste a buck and a half on that dopey haircut!"

The next recruit in line, a fellow from Ohio, had brought a loaded .22 caliber pistol. The DIs confiscated the pistol and worked him over verbally, punctuated with a few slaps that resounded throughout the barracks.

"You must be a killer bee. Brought your little stinger to kill the Cong?" asked the DI mockingly.

"Sir, what's a Cong sir?"

"Cong means Viet Cong, the VC, the goblins we're gonna train you to kill. There's also the NVA, the North Vietnamese Army. We don't worry much about what they're called. They're all the same to us—goblins. Communist goblins. Boy, didn't you do any research about all this shit before you signed up?"

"Yes sir. I want to carry my pistol with me to Vietnam to kill Cong and NVA, I mean goblins, for God, Country and Corps."

"I like your line of bullshit, recruit; it impresses the hell out of me. We'll see how tough you are with real weapons. This pea shooter is now the property of the United States Marine Corps and you are in deep shit for violating the Geneva Convention rules which says you can't use pea shooters to kill Communists!"

Another fellow brought a bunch of books. A second DI dumped them on the floor of the barracks and yelled: "Where the fuck did you get the idea you'd have time to read this shit? The only thing you're going to be reading at Parris Island is the *Marine Corps Guidebook.*"

Zeke took a mild rebuke for looking like a Beatle with his long hair. He knew he was asking for trouble, but could not resist: "Which Beatle, sir?"

Zeke hoped the DI would say Paul McCartney and would warm up to him. He still did not get the seriousness of where he was and with whom he was dealing. It was not high school anymore.

Without reply, the DI hit him solidly in the solar plexus.

"You will never speak at Parris Island again, not ever, except to say 'yes sir' or 'no sir.' If I hear you say anything other than that, I will kick you in the ass as hard as I can with these size twelves," he said, pointing to his boots.

"Is that understood?"

"Yes sir. I understand," at which point the DI kicked him squarely in the rear end. The toe of his boot made slight contact with his low-hanging fruit and it hurt like hell.

"You went over your word quota just then, smart-ass. Think about it."

This went on for more than an hour as the DIs inspected everyone's belongings and gave the recruits their first taste of how things were going to be at PI. What the DIs yelled and how they yelled it were so funny that Zeke thought he was going to bust a gut to keep from laughing. Not being able to laugh made things all the funnier. *I've gotta tune this shit out or I'm going to pass out from trying not to laugh and I'll be in big-time trouble.*

Zeke and Aaron were assigned to one of four platoons in Company S, Third Recruit Training Battalion. Training unfolded along the lines of the movie *Full Metal Jacket* minus the "Private Pyle" subplot. A defective such as Pyle would have been weeded out immediately. Each platoon was staffed with a Senior Drill Instructor and two assistants, typically sergeants, but sometimes corporals.

Once the recruits were issued their utilities (work uniforms) they were ordered to stand at attention in front of their racks (bunk beds) as the Senior DI went down the line hitting everyone he thought did not look like a Marine. When he came to Aaron, he noticed a pen in his front pocket. Without warning, the Senior DI hit him squarely in the pocket with a Karate chop, the purpose of which was to break the pen and discipline Aaron for being out of uniform. Aaron fell to the floor, holding his chest in pain. On the surface, this seemed cruel, which it probably was, but for Zeke it was hilarious—not the chop, *per se,* but how it was done and what the SDI said. Zeke almost choked trying to keep a straight face.

Platoons were allowed one trip to the Post Exchange during basic training to replenish shaving supplies, boot polish and so forth. While there, a recruit named Knutt tried to sneak a soda and got caught. Sweets of any kind (candy, cookies, pastries, gum or soda pop) were called pogey bait and were forbidden during basic training, even if received in the mail from home. It seemed as though everything and everyone went silent while Private Knutt's quarter looped through the machine's nooks and crannies. The cup noisily dropped from the dispenser and filled with 7-Up. Eighty recruits and the three drill instructors looked at Private Knutt in disbelief. His blatant violation of rules and the code of Marine self-discipline infuriated them. The Senior DI called a standing "School Circle" around Knutt, right there in public. When the School Circle opened, Knutt was standing at attention with a bloody nose and the empty paper soda cup sticking out of his mouth.

School Circle was a term used in basic training meaning that all recruits were to make a mad dash to the DI, drop to a cross-legged position sitting tightly bunched around him in a circle, stare at him with catatonic expressions and pay undivided attention to what he had to say. School Circle was also a signal to gather around a recruit for a beating by a DI for disciplinary purposes, as was the case with Private Knutt. For regular Marines, it meant a group problem-solving situation and could be called by any Marine in the unit at any time assuming there was a good reason for doing so.

For two days, Private Knutt was seen walking out of step ten yards behind the platoon with the paper cup in his mouth as a symbol of his status as a shitbird, a miserable defective mope in the language of the Marine Corps; a *persona non grata*. Zeke could hardly see straight from suppressing laughter every time the platoon fell into formation, especially when a DI would say something to Knutt and he would have to respond through the cup without dropping it from his mouth. During one of those conversations between Knutt and a DI, Zeke burst out with a loud laugh that made the entire platoon start to chuckle.

"Private Hammond, do you think that's funny?"

"No sir."

"Then why did you laugh? What the fuck is so funny?"

"You are sir."

"Wrong answer, asshole. "Get down for pushups—one fucking million of them. Ready, begin…"

A hundred or so pushups later, Zeke was ordered back into line. He wasn't laughing anymore.

✪ ✪ ✪

A couple weeks into recruit training, the Senior DI was replaced with an overweight, heavy drinking, chain-smoking fellow with a long, convoluted ethnic name. He told the platoon to call him Staff Sergeant Biff or *sir*. He was an old guy to the recruits, probably mid-to-late thirties. He spoke with a colorful Southern twang and bragged about how much he drank and smoked, implying it was all part of being a Marine. He also taught the platoon how to curse, Marine Corps style, by inserting profanity between syllables or words: "I'll guaran-goddamn-tee you, holy fuckin' shit" and so forth.

Biff was fair and reasonable. If the platoon screwed up, he had a unique way of making everyone feel ashamed and determined to try harder. Instead of hitting, he would lay a guilt trip on the recruits and punish them by leading a long-distance run in full combat gear, chanting cadence with rifles at Port Arms. He could run for miles and wore them out. It was astonishing how fit he was for a guy with a Body Mass Index higher than his age.

✪ ✪ ✪

Care and Cleaning of the Colt M1911 pistol class took place outside on wooden bleachers after the noon meal. M1911 was shorthand for the Colt Model M1911 .45 Caliber semi-automatic pistol. Even though it was the fall season, the average temperature in the shade was 85 degrees with humidity levels in the nineties. It was draining, particularly after eating, which made it difficult to stay alert. Biff directed each recruit to sit on the bleachers at attention with heels locked together and feet spread at a 45-degree angle. He called it "sitting at attention." Recruits were told to remain in this position throughout class and there would be no nodding off, no matter how tired or hot they were.

While class was being conducted, another DI would walk around behind the bleachers to assess compliance. If he spotted feet not positioned properly or some other transgression, he would grab the offending recruit's ankles and drag him down backwards through the seats and out to the ground with a bang, crash and a surprised yell. To Zeke, that was the funniest thing he had yet witnessed at Parris Island. One minute the recruit was sitting there; the next minute he would drop out of sight as though he fell into quicksand. Those yanked from the bleachers were required to do Jumping Jacks until they dropped.

Some things were not so funny. The platoon was "gigged" (faulted) during a command inspection because one of the recruits, an Italian guy from Boston named Al Berghetti, had a five-o'clock shadow and it was only 10:00 in the morning. Biff assumed that Berghetti had not shaved properly and made him dry shave while running in place with a bucket over his head as punishment. In truth, Berghetti was born with a 5 o'clock shadow and always looked like a bum no matter how hard he shaved and scraped his face. It was torture for Al, particularly when one of the DIs tripped him just as he was running the razor under his chin.

By far the most stimulating basic training activity at Parris Island was the Confidence Course, particularly the Slide for Life, which entailed shinning down a cable high above a pond filled with smelly green slime. Halfway down the cable the recruit was required to swing under the cable, relock his legs and shinny the rest of the way upside down, head first. It took strength, stamina and courage to execute the Slide for Life properly, especially if a recruit had a fear of heights.

Aaron positioned himself on the forty-foot platform leaned over to grab the cable and fell, screaming in a high pitch like a girl all the way down as he splashed head first into the slime pond. The recruits applauded and laughed as the DIs yelled and cursed at Aaron for being such a klutz. Zeke fell to the ground laughing so hard he could hardly breathe. When Aaron emerged from the quagmire, he looked like a creature from a horror movie, covered from head to toe with unidentifiable vegetation and swamp goo. Biff gave the recruits a pass for Clapping and Laughing Without Permission, a violation of the UCMJ, because he and the other two DIs were laughing too.

Rifle qualification meant shooting at two hundred, three hundred and five hundred yards in the standing, sitting and prone positions, respectively, and attaining a score that corresponded to Marksman, Sharpshooter or Expert—without tripods, sandbags or similar aids used by other branches of the service. It was, and still is, the most challenging rifle qualification venue in the Armed Forces. Zeke's claim to fame at Parris Island was the distinction of being one of only a handful of recruits to qualify with the M14 rifle out of four platoons in Company S, each platoon consisting of approximately eighty recruits each—over three hundred guys.

The DIs made it clear that anyone who did not attain at least a Marksman level score was unqualified to be a Marine and would be considered "lower than whale shit, and that's at the bottom of the ocean," according to Biff.

"War is a game of Survival of the Fittest. Those of you who do not attain a minimum level of proficiency by obtaining the Marksman Badge are not fit to be Marines and will probably be the first ones to die in combat and that's how it should be. If you cannot qualify with the M14, you have no right to reproduce and pollute the gene pool with weakness and incompetence. Is that understood?" bellowed Biff.

"Aye, Aye sir," yelled the recruits in response.

Zeke turned to Aaron with a smile and whispered, "that means you."

Company S force-marched—a pace that was almost a run—several miles to the rifle range on the far side of Parris Island on a day when hurricane winds were so strong that some targets blew off the holders. Anything that was not nailed down blew away or flapped in the breeze at a ninety-degree angle. It was very difficult to keep the rifle steady and maintain a proper sight picture. Dirt and sand was flying everywhere and it was hard to see the targets or hear instructions from the DIs and range officers. In peacetime, the range would have been closed and qualifications postponed until the storm passed, but recruits had to be moved through training quicker than usual to fill the manpower needs of the escalating Vietnam "police action," as it was called at the time. No changes in schedules were permitted, come hell or high water.

Because of the weather conditions, most of the three-hundred recruits failed to qualify at all. Their shooting scores never reached the level of Marksman. Normally, qualifications would conform to a Bell Curve with a few Experts at the high end, a few unqualified at the low end and everyone else falling somewhere in the range of Marksman or Sharpshooter, but not that day. There were *no* Experts, only one Sharpshooter and only a handful of Marksmen. No more than 10 percent qualified. Zeke was among that 10 percent. The remaining 270 recruits, including Aaron, failed to qualify and were "not fit to be Marines," at least according to Biff. Zeke and his fellow elite Marksmen had their "Fifteen Minutes of Fame" that day.

Later in the squad bay, Zeke whispered to Aaron, "Well there it is. You failed. That means you can't reproduce children until you qualify. Biff said so. I'll tell Fat Sue what happened."

Zeke was just kidding—"busting balls"—as the saying went. He didn't realize how badly Aaron felt or how he might react. Aaron jumped up and threw his entire footlocker at Zeke who dodged out of the way just in time. The contents exploded all over the squad bay with a loud noise, almost like a car accident. All three Drill Instructors were on the scene in a flash.

"What the fuck is going on in here?" yelled Biff.

"Sir, I had an accident, sir," replied Aaron in perfect form, standing at attention and saying "sir" before and after his reply.

One of the Drill Instructor's punched Aaron in the stomach and when he doubled over gave him a backhand in the face. The one-two hits knocked him to the floor. "There is no such thing as an accident in the Marine Corps—only negligence by shitbirds. Accident is a word used by weaklings to excuse being fucked up. Do you understand me?"

"Yes sir" Aaron yelled loudly as he jumped back to his feet at attention.

By that point in basic training, Aaron must have set a record for the number of times he was hit, kicked or berated. If there had been a Drubbing medal, it would have been his.

Zeke, Aaron and the other 298 young men of Company S, Third Battalion, MCRD, Parris Island marched across the Parade grounds in their dress green uniforms to the sounds of *Semper Fidelis*, the *Marines' Hymn,* and *The Star-Spangled Banner.* It was a splendid ceremony. The commanding general made an inspiring speech and reminded the graduates that the United States Marine Corps was the crème de la crème of the World's military, after which he officially pronounced them Marines.

The *Marines' Hymn* sounded again and the company marched away with precision and élan. Parents and family members had traveled long distances to witness the rite-of-passage. They were proud and happy. They didn't want to think about how many of those marching before them would be dead within a year.

✪ ✪ ✪

When they returned to the squad bay, they changed out of their dress green uniforms into their utilities and formed a School Circle around Staff Sergeant Biff.

"Well graduates, you passed the toughest test of your lives. You are now United States Marines. Welcome to the Corps!"

Every recruit in the platoon let out a bloodcurdling growl. Marines in 1965 did not use the battle cry "Oorah" or its variants; they growled instead. It was the Marine battle cry. It gave them strength and intimidated opponents. Biff smiled and growled back in response.

"Ten percent of the men that started out with us eight weeks ago didn't make it. They were non-hackers and we sent them home. They should get credit for trying, but they were not good enough to be Marines. Ten percent is the average. That's where our expression 'there's always that ten percent' comes from. I expect that percentage to double given that most of the next round of recruits will be draftees."

The platoon cat-called and booed in response.

"Yea, that's right, fucking *draftees*. Because of Vietnam, the government decided to bring people into the Corps that don't want to be here, which goes against our basic principles. Draftees have to be dragged kicking and screaming into the Armed Forces. They wouldn't go into any service, let alone the Marine Corps, without being forced. But we'll adapt and overcome and I'm sure there'll be some good apples in the bunch."

"From Parris Island, you will join the Infantry Training Regiment, also known as ITR, at Camp Geiger which is part of Camp Lejeune. After that, you will go to your Military Occupational Specialty school. Your MOS is the job the Marine Corps has assigned to you based on the paperwork you completed and tests you took, keeping in mind that the needs of the Corps took precedence. In other words, you'll go anywhere and do anything the Corps wants you to do regardless of aptitude, preference or whatever the hell your recruiter might have promised you. After that, most of you will go to Jungle Warfare Training then on to Vietnam.

If you go to Vietnam, you are at risk of dying a premature death. You could be wounded, contract some exotic disease or be captured and tortured by the enemy. You knew or should have known that before you signed up, so don't piss and moan or worry about it; embrace it as a real Marine should. Just remember what you have learned here at Parris Island: The Marine Corps has been around for 190 years. You are all part of a brotherhood, not only with each other, but with all Marines who came before you and all who will follow you. Regardless of race, creed, or color—or whether they're fuckin' draftees—we are *one*. We are United States Marines!"

Without prompting, the entire platoon jumped to their feet and growled as one, louder than ever before. This was the greatest moment of their young lives and one they would remember as long as they lived.

Zeke and his cohorts had expected orders for Vietnam immediately after completing boot camp. They had not gotten the memo, so to speak, about MOS school, infantry training, or Jungle Warfare Training before setting foot in Vietnam. Zeke was disappointed. *I can shoot. What else do I need to know? By the time I get through with all this training bullshit, the war will be over. What's the use of being a Marine without a war?*

✪ ✪ ✪

Zeke received an MOS of 3531—truck driver. He was not pleased. He had not joined the Marine Corps to drive trucks. He could have stayed in Pennsylvania and done that as a civilian, he thought. He wanted to be an 0311—an infantryman—landing on the shores of Guadalcanal, humping up Mt. Suribachi under fire or pushing the Red Chinese back across the 38th Parallel just like they did in *Guadalcanal Diary, The Sands of Iwo Jima* and *Pork Chop Hill.*

Zeke had written on his application to join the Marines, under the category of skills and abilities, that he had driven trucks and tractors on the farm. Apparently, Zeke's skills matched the Corps' needs so that was that. Zeke had also noted on his application that he had killed many woodchucks at long range with his Marlin .22 caliber rifle. Only a few weeks earlier, right there at PI, he was one of only a handful that had qualified with the M14. *Why hadn't those facts been considered? Why wasn't I selected to be a sniper or something more befitting? This is nuts.*

Aaron also received a 3531 MOS but, unlike Zeke, he was happy.

"Why are you happy about being a truck driver? You could have married Fat Sue and drove a truck back home for a living. Aaron, this is bullshit. This isn't why we joined the Corps is it?"

Aaron thought about it for a minute and replied in a voice that sounded like it was on 33⅓ RPM and should have been on 45. He was trying to sound philosophical, but he sounded drunk. "If the Marine Corps wants me to be a truck driver, then so be it. Who am I to complain? It must be God's will. He has a plan for me."

Zeke burst out laughing. "What makes you think God even includes you in his thoughts, let alone has a 'plan' for *you*? Once you started sodomizing Fat Sue, God ripped up your plan and wrote you off, you dumb shit."

Aaron slowly realized that Zeke was just busting balls and cracked a smile as his mind shifted from God's plan to sodomy. "Truth is, Zeke, she says she won't do it the normal way until we're married."

They both laughed and enjoyed having on-base liberty for the rest of the day. Zeke felt good. Making it through Parris Island gave him a natural high. He felt different about himself. He had gained weight, gotten stronger, sharpened his mind and built more self-confidence. He hoped the feeling would last forever.

# 7

# SPLIBS AND CHUCKS

The next morning before first light, Company S bid adieu to PI and boarded busses for the 5-hour journey to Camp Geiger, part of the 2nd Marine Division at Camp Lejeune in North Carolina. There they would join the Infantry Training Regiment (ITR) where newly minted Marines were taught the tactics and weaponry needed for combat. Every Marine, regardless of MOS, was considered, first and foremost, an infantryman and had to meet rigorous shooting standards with his rifle as well as the M60 machine gun, rocket launcher, M79 grenade launcher, light anti-tank weapons, the M1911 .45 caliber semi-automatic pistol—even a flamethrower. Zeke and his cohorts practiced arming and disarming land mines, throwing hand grenades, using bayonets and crawling through live machine gun fire as land mines exploded all around them.

Using hand grenades was the first item on the training agenda. When Zeke entered the open cinder block bay to practice pulling the pin and throwing properly, the instructor, a corporal, told him to look around at the walls and notice where the shrapnel had hit.

"Not long ago a trainee got discombobulated and blew his own ass up right here in this bay. Blood and guts were everywhere. We hosed it off and painted over it. One less shitbird to worry about. He would have died in 'Nam anyway, most likely."

Those disrespectful words made Zeke nervous and angry at the same. *One less shitbird?! What kind of Marine would say that about another*

*Marine who had such a horrible accident? Oh yea, no such thing as an accident; only negligence.* It was his own fault in the corporal's eyes. Zeke pulled the pin and hurtled his grenade far over the top of the bay, straight-arm, further than anyone in the class had yet thrown. He turned and looked straight into the instructor's eyes.

"No shitbirds in my family."

The instructor detected insolence in Zeke's words and ordered him out of the bay and back in line with the others. Zeke shook his head in disgust.

"Been to Vietnam yet, corporal?"

"No, not yet ..."

The corporal was about to say more, but Zeke cut him off in disgust with a wave of his hand and walked back to his group.

Next on the agenda was how to deal with tear gas. Trainees were marched in groups of twelve into a large shed. Instructors had gas masks; trainees did not. They were told they could not leave the shed until they sang the entire first verse of the *Marines' Hymn* after the gas was released. Tear Gas reminded Zeke of the outhouse at the farm in the summer—eyes watered and nose hairs burned, but small sips of air and breathing through the mouth made it tolerable.

Aaron was one of the twelve guys in Zeke's group and in less than a minute after the gas was released Aaron panicked and bolted toward the locked exit door. One of the instructors grabbed him by his utility jacket and flipped him on the floor. That was probably the fifteenth time Aaron had been knocked on his ass by a training NCO since he stepped off the bus at Parris Island. Aaron's demonstration of weakness cost the whole group another three minutes in the shed coughing, tearing and spitting from the powerful chemicals. This time, the trainees were ordered to sing the second verse of the *Marines' Hymn*. Everyone knew the first verse; no one remembered the second verse. The sound of the disjointed singing-while-choking was hilarious. Aaron's lapse of self-control was held up for ridicule and used to illustrate that panicking under stress could cost lives in combat.

Zeke's favorite weapons were the flamethrower, although it was hot to use, and the machine gun, despite how it hurt his ear drums. He loved the M79 grenade launcher—a small single-shot, shoulder-fired, break-action weapon that could lob a 40 mm round four hundred yards or so. He wished he could get one for hunting woodchucks back on the farm. He would be able to destroy a whole colony of those critters with one shot.

✪ ✪ ✪

Something insidious happened almost the moment the new Marines got off the bus at Camp Geiger. At Parris Island, recruits had been told there was only one color in the Corps—Marine Corps green. Apparently, that message had not sunk in with many of the black Marines. They self-segregated and clustered in separate areas of their respective barracks. Zeke had made friends with black recruits at Parris Island and now those same Marines wanted nothing to do with him. It was disappointing and hurtful. He liked all the guys regardless of color and it pissed him off that they were acting as if all whites were bad guys or something. It was equally disconcerting to see some whites behave badly in response to this self-segregation.

Blacks were called splibs and whites were called chucks. The derivation of the terms was unknown and seemed to be inoffensive and acceptable when referring to race. There were several petty thefts of chucks' property by a few splibs and a couple of fistfights between the most pugnacious among them. For the majority who did not take racial differences seriously, either out of ignorance or apathy, self-segregation by black Marines and their seemingly unwarranted hostility toward white Marines ran counter to everything they had all been taught about teamwork and brotherhood.

Most chucks didn't know or care why splibs were being such jerks and began to see them as whiners, shirkers and second class Marines—not because of race, but because of behavior. Zeke was generally aware of the civil rights issues of the day, but he never expected to see those issues carry over into the Marine Corps, especially not the way they were unfolding. It did not bode well.

✪ ✪ ✪

From the first day of ITR, Zeke took note of Recon training going on about halfway between the chow hall and his squad bay. Reconnaissance

Marines, a.k.a., Recons, were the *crème de la crème* of the Corps. They were the Marine's version of the Army's Special Forces or the Navy's SEALs. Marine Recons had to parachute, conduct underwater operations, scout deep into enemy territory and often engage in deadly combat, sometimes hand-to-hand. They were assigned the most challenging, dangerous and adventurous missions of any group in the Marines.

When he could, Zeke would stop to watch the Recons practice parachute landing falls and train. He was impressed. Zeke thought about brazenly approaching the Recon instructor and asking for his help in transferring into his unit. The only thing that made him hesitate was the aquaphobia he had acquired from Drown Proofing classes at Parris Island where recruits learned how to stay afloat in the water, fully clothed, for at least one hour. Struggling recruits were screamed at and beaten with fiberglass rescue poles as they flopped around and sucked water into their lungs trying to get the hang of it. Now, just the smell of chlorine triggered Irritable Bowel Syndrome. Zeke thought he would pass on the Recon experience and stick with truck driving.

During ITR Zeke was selected for night guard duty at the base ammunition depot. He and the three other guards had to qualify with a 12-gauge pump-action shotgun. Zeke had shot his grandfather's double-barrel 12-gauge countless times growing on the farm and had no problem with the recoil or hitting his mark. What took getting use to with the Marine pump-action was chambering one shell after another by retracting a slide and pushing it back in place. *Wait till I tell Gramp about this. We'll have to get one of these pump actions when I get back home.*

Zeke felt that guarding the ammo dump was a great responsibility and loved the idea of carrying a shotgun. It was unique and intimidating. He was very conscientious and rehearsed various maneuvers and positions if it became necessary to confront an intruder. The guards were told that Recon Marines would be checking their diligence so they had better be on the alert and ready for action at all times. It was part of Recon training to see if they could sneak up on the guards and catch them sleeping or not minding their post properly.

Several nights went by without incident until the Sergeant of the Guard, a fat, slack-eyed corporal with five years in grade, paid a visit. As Zeke was making his rounds protecting the ammo and looking out for Recons, he spotted movement. He thought the figure might be a Recon Marine or an intruder so he assumed the role of tracker rather than tracked. He moved to concealment then inched his way toward the spot where he had last seen the figure, keeping his eyes peeled to detect any additional movement. As he inched toward the guard shack, he spied the figure squatting down with his back to Zeke.

Ignoring the "Halt, who goes there" routine, which was Standard Operating Procedure, Zeke shouted with his best command voice: "Make one move and I'll blow your fucking head off. Put your hands on your head and don't turn around. Get down with your face in the dirt. Do it NOW!"

The figure was wearing Marine Corps utilities; Zeke assumed he had caught a Recon.

"One false move and "I'll shoot you in the ass and blow your shit all over creation. Now identify yourself, cocksucker!"

"I'm Corporal Kallen, Sergeant of the Guard, you asshole. You're going to jail for this" he replied.

*Oh, shit. Well, what the fuck. In for a dime, in for a dollar.*

"If you're a corporal, how could you be *Sergeant* of the Guard?"

"Corporals can be Sergeants of the Guard even if they're not really sergeants," replied Kallen.

"You expect me to believe that babble? Turn over you sack of shit and let me see your face." With that, the figure turned over on his back.

"You're not a Marine. You're too fat to be a Marine you lyin' fuck stick," said Zeke, pointing the shotgun at Kallen's groin.

"Don't shoot for God's sake! Check my identification card! Call MP headquarters! Please ... just don't shoot me," pleaded Kallen.

"Okay, get on your feet. Let me see your ID card. Throw it over to me and keep your distance. My finger's on the trigger." Zeke knew the game was almost over, but was milking it for all it was worth.

"Okay, Corporal Kallen, I'm sorry about the confusion. Next time, announce your presence; there would be a lot less rigmarole. You could be on the receiving end of some serious buckshot sneaking around here at night."

Kallen told Zeke to stand at attention and present arms then grabbed the shotgun out of his hands and brought it down with a crack on Zeke's right clavicle. Striking another Marine in that context was a court martial offense but, obviously, Kallen didn't care. Zeke was more angry than hurt.

It was a painful hit, but Zeke did not flinch. He did not want to give Kallen the satisfaction. Kallen called Zeke down every which way, but his epithets and threats paled in comparison to those received at Parris Island. Despite the painful blow to his shoulder, Zeke could not hold back his laughter thinking about what he had put Kallen through. His smirk turned into a smile then to laughter. It was contagious. Kallen started to smile and finally saw the humor in the whole thing. As he departed, he made a salute-like gesture.

"Carry on, private."

Zeke replied returning a faux salute. *That guy has a sense of humor. He should be a real sergeant,* thought Zeke, rubbing his clavicle.

✪ ✪ ✪

The graduation from ITR was unceremonious. There were clichés about the Marine Corps and infantry training and the awarding of the private first class (PFC) stripe to four Marines who had stood out during ITR, one of whom was Aaron. Aaron was a nice guy with a winning smile and had the ability to engage in the most vacuous conversations about any topic. He was also obsequious—an ass-kisser. It paid off. Aaron's platoon sergeant took a liking to him and recommended him for promotion from Private to PFC. Zeke knew Aaron's history at Parris Island and ITR; he had done nothing to deserve a promotion. In truth, Zeke felt that Aaron should have been screened *out* of the Corps after all his screw-ups, capped by his failure to qualify with the M14. Zeke liked Aaron in some ways, but that promotion without merit drove a wedge between them. It also concerned him that the Marine Corps rewarded personality over performance. Zeke was young and naïve.

## 8

# MONSTER TRUCKS

MONTFORD POINT NEGLECTED TO TEACH THE "TOP 10"
THINGS TRUCKERS WOULD NEED TO KNOW IN VIETNAM.

Montford Point was the home of the 2nd Marine Division's Motor Transport School where Marines learned to drive M54s, the original monster trucks of the day. The M54 was the Corps' primary heavy truck, rated to carry five tons off-road and ten tons on a highway. A fully loaded M54 could also pull a long flatbed trailer filled to the sky with tons of materiel—food, ammo, supplies, equipment and such. Although the engine could generate 224 horsepower, it was governed for a top speed of 52 miles-per-hour. However, by removing the speed governor in the engine, any speed limit law in America could be broken.

The M54 had a dual range transmission (high and low) with six gears— five forward and one reverse. In High range, it could be driven on good roads and highways. Low range was for muddy trails, swamps and hauling extreme loads up long steep hills. Since there were six gears in High range and six gears in Low range, the truck had the moniker "six by" or 6 x 6.

Zeke, Aaron and 23 other Marines were assigned to Montford Point after ITR. They drove through swamps and deep water using special equipment to keep the engine dry and the exhaust above water line. After that, they learned how to extricate from deep mud using sophisticated winching. The winch on the front of the truck weighed over seven hundred pounds and could pull a load weighing as much as the truck—about twenty thousand pounds.

The training at Montford Point was good, basic Cold War stuff. In time, it would become clear that the Montford Point school of Marine Corps truck driving was behind the times. It neglected to teach the "Top 10" tactics for driving and surviving in Vietnam at the wheel of such a big target, specifically:

- Best protocols for defensive rifle carry in the cab;
- Shooting or throwing grenades effectively while driving;
- Minimizing damage from land mines;
- Using the truck for cover and concealment during a firefight;
- Avoiding collisions with civilians, bicycle riders and water buffalo;
- Dealing with an enemy that uses grappling hooks to steal cargo off moving trucks;
- Deterring kids from putting hand grenades in the 78-gallon fuel tanks;
- Keeping Marine passengers civil and in line while driving through populated areas;
- Dealing with impromptu roadblocks by prostitutes squatting in the middle of the road; and
- Using the truck as a weapon if all else fails.

Twenty of the twenty five Marines in the class had passed the written, oral and tactical driving tests and were issued military driver's licenses; the other five were given a new MOS—0311, Basic Riflemen, and sent to the 6th Marine Regiment. Failure had consequences. Instead of riding in style, those five would soon be walking through the jungle in Vietnam with a shortened life expectancy.

# 9

# HOMEWARD BOUND

---

SHE SCREAMED AND JUMPED INTO HIS ARMS MAKING QUITE A
SCENE. IT WAS EMBARRASSING ... BUT DELIGHTFUL.

---

The Monster Truck class was given leave and orders to report to their next duty station when they returned—2nd Motor Transport Battalion located in yet another part of Camp Lejeune. Zeke and Aaron went home together. After all they had been through, they fundamentally cared about each other and were brother Marines.

When they arrived in Scranton, the whole Disaronno family was there to pick them up—all eight of them, in their 1959 pink and gray Chevy station wagon. Fat Sue had come along too, wearing a very large dress and intense makeup, ready for action. On the way home from Scranton, Aaron became a bit ostentatious about his PFC stripe and made a remark about Zeke still being a private.

Zeke smugly looked at Aaron while tapping his Marksman shooting badge and replied in a whisper that only Aaron could hear, "I wouldn't trade this badge for your stripe. Remember, those who can't shoot aren't real Marines."

That comment ended further allusions to rank.

✪ ✪ ✪

While Zeke was away, his grandfather, Walter had bought a 1959 Buick LeSabre. *Wow, a new used car; only six years old and such a deal,* Zeke thought. He could not wait to see it. Walter opened the barn door slowly with a big smile on his face. He loved this new car and hoped Zeke would like it too.

"Holy shit," Zeke exclaimed with a furrowed brow.

The LeSabre was a pea green four-door sedan with a yellow and green interior that reminded Zeke of the colorful omelets they served at the Dinglebury restaurant. Zeke thought the style was sharp, figuratively and literally (the tail fins could hurt you If you bumped into them), but the color was not something he would have picked … and would have never thought existed.

Zeke caught himself before he made any sarcastic comments. He did not want to hurt his grandfather's feelings and really did appreciate the effort he had made to get a good car for him to use while he was home on leave. Zeke took a deep breath and forced a demeanor change from astonished ambivalence to gratitude.

"Gramp, I love the color. It's Marine Corps green; just perfect! And who would want a 2-door hardtop? Four-door sedans are much more practical."

Both Walter and Velma were beaming. They had gone through a lot with Zeke since he returned to live with them three years earlier. For a while, he seemed incorrigible and beyond redemption. Now they were proud of him. Their grandson was a Marine! They could not say enough about how great he looked in his dress greens with the National Defense Ribbon and the Marksman badge.

Zeke drove the LeSabre down to the Dinglebury Diner to meet Sharon. She was waiting when he came in. She looked great. She screamed like a little girl and jumped into his arms making quite a scene. It was embarrassing … but delightful. He loved how demonstrative she was.

"You know that song by Simon and Garfunkel, *Homeward Bound*? Whenever I heard it, I thought of you. Now I'm here. It's been a *long* time; at least it feels that way."

Sharon was all over Zeke, almost afraid to let go fearing he would disappear again. When things settled down, Zeke asked her if she wanted to see the new car.

"I bought a limousine just for us," he said with a smile.

"Limousine? You bought a limousine?"

"Well, not really. Gramp traded for this knowing we'd need a car. Wasn't that nice of him? He's great," said Zeke, knowing the car was not hip in any way.

"Oh my God," said Sharon, "it's ... well, beautiful. Sharp tailfins, literally. Marine Corps green, no less. It must be over twenty feet long. Are the seats comfortable?"

A knowing smile came over Zeke's face.

✪ ✪ ✪

Within what seemed like a blink of an eye, Zeke and Aaron's leave was over. Sharon and Fat Sue were tearful, but proud of their Marines as they bid them goodbye.

*"Au revoir mon amour"* said Zeke, blowing Sharon a kiss as they departed.

Zeke liked to use the few French words and phrases to impress her. "Goodbye my love" sounded better in French. Aaron and Sue jammed their tongues down each other's throats and slobbered a bit, as was their custom, and off they went to Scranton to catch the southbound bus back to Camp Lejeune. On the way, Zeke couldn't resist asking Aaron how he fared with his girlfriend.

"Well, what about Fat Sue?"

"What about her?"

"Back side or front side?"

"Both ... equally."

"Wow, that means she loves you. I assume you two will be getting married, right?"

"Yea, maybe next time I come home on leave."

"Congratulations, brother."

"Well Zeke, are you going to tell me about you and Sharon?"

"Fuck no. It's none of your business. Besides, we don't even have sex. We consider it vulgar and demeaning. We've taken a vow of abstinence."

Zeke and Aaron started laughing and gave each other a high five while growling *"Semper Fi; Do or Die."*

57

Zeke and Aaron had gone through PI, ITR and Motor Transport School together and would still be together at their first permanent duty station, 2nd Motor Transport Battalion. They had become close despite the petty squabbles and tricks that Zeke played on Aaron. It was helpful to both of them to be able to talk to about the girls, home, and the friends, places and things they had in common, including the daunting Marine Corps experiences they had shared thus far. There would be many more daunting experiences ahead.

# 10

# ROUGH RIDERS OF SANTO DOMINGO

---

THE THOUGHT OF MISSING OUT ON VIETNAM MADE HIM SICK TO HIS STOMACH AND ANGRY AT THE CORPS.

---

Second Motor Transport Battalion had indirectly participated in military operations in Santo Domingo, the capitol of the Dominican Republic, in the spring of 1965. The Dominican Republic action was small and limited and the only action 2nd Motors experienced was sitting in their trucks on board the ship bouncing up and down with the waves in the Caribbean Sea. Shots were exchanged, Marines quickly prevailed and 2nd Motors returned to Camp Lejeune to grow cobwebs. With tongue-in-cheek, because of the rough sea waves, they nicknamed themselves the Rough Riders of Santo Domingo, a name that stuck.

Second Motors' Rough Riders platoon sergeant resembled Master Sergeant Bilko from the Fifties television series *You'll Never Get Rich.* Coincidently, 2nd Motors seemed to operate like Bilko's motor pool. There was little to do except for make-work which freed up time to grab-ass, listen to music, play cards, wash trucks that were already clean, tighten nuts that were already tight and work on engines that didn't need to be worked on because the trucks seldom moved. But if there was another flare-up in the Dominican Republic, 2nd Motors' Rough Riders would again be ready to wait off shore on Navy ships with their sparkling trucks, spit-shined boots, starched covers and unfired rifles.

Every day Zeke and his platoon would march from their air-conditioned brick barracks to the motor pool led by Corporal Buck, a big old country boy from West Virginia. Buck was a Marine with nothing to prove because he had "been there; done that." He had already served a thirteen-month tour of duty in Vietnam. Zeke did not know why the military called the time in Vietnam a "tour." Tour sounded like a casual understatement and conjured up the image of a sightseeing trip or a vacation. Buck wore jungle boots and spoke matter-of-factly about Vietnam without obvious embellishment. The guys in the platoon saw his jungle boots as a status symbol, something they would all soon proudly wear, they hoped, just like Buck.

In a few weeks, many of Zeke's cohorts, including Aaron, received orders to "FMF-WESTPAC, Ground Forces," military-speak for Fleet Marine Force-Western Pacific, a sanitized way of saying Vietnam. Zeke began to worry about being overlooked and perhaps remaining with Sgt. Bilko at Camp Lejeune forever. *Why am I not being shipped out with them? Aaron and I joined at the same time and should go to Vietnam at the same time. How can I ever face my family and friends—and Sharon—if I stay here?* Zeke worked himself up into quite a lather. He was ready to fight and, if necessary, die for his country. It was a family tradition. The thought of missing out on Vietnam made him sick to his stomach and angry at the Corps.

Zeke "pissed and moaned" to Sergeant Bilko about the prospect of remaining at Lejeune and missing the action in Vietnam. Bilko was an old salt who had served in the Korean War with the 7th Marine Regiment. He had received twelve medals and ribbons, including the Purple Heart, during his 22 years in the Corps.

"Be careful what you ask for, Marine, you just might get it—and if you do, that is, if you get to Vietnam—you'd better have your head and ass wired together if you want to get back in one piece. You young pups think war is fun and games and the good guys always win. Not so. It's not like the movies."

With that, Bilko opened his utility shirt to reveal a deep, horrible looking scar that ran diagonally across his chest to his stomach.

"Red Chinese bayonet," he said.

*That won't happen to me; I'm a truck driver. Besides, he probably got that in a bar fight and he's just trying to bullshit me. Fuck him!*

Within a couple weeks, Zeke's orders for WESTPAC arrived. At last, he was going to get his jungle boots. As he looked over his orders, he thought of a book he had read in high school about a soldier in World War I—*Johnny Got His Gun* by Dalton Trumbo. He remembered how the main character, Joe Bonham, ended up—almost a vegetable. *Screw it. It's an antiwar book. Trumbo was a fucking Communist and the story was not even true. Get your head out of your ass, Hammond.*

# 11

# WHAT WOULD JIM BOWIE DO?

THERE IS SOMETHING ABOUT A KNIFE
THAT INSTILLS A DEEP, PRIMAL FEAR.

In preparation for Vietnam, Zeke went to Jacksonville, a few miles from Camp Lejeune, and purchased a Bowie knife. The weapon was 16 inches long from stem to stern, unsheathed, with a fine white bone handle. Those who saw it drew an audible breath of amazement and appreciation at the size, beauty and artisanship and perhaps because of its Freudian symbolism. Zeke arranged to meet Sharon in New York City while in leave for some partying and touring, after which they would take the train out to Long Island to meet his family at 240 and then head off for Camp Pendleton for Jungle Warfare Training.

Zeke thought of The City as a den of iniquity and a potentially dangerous place where Troglodytes, as he called them, represented 51 percent of the population. He did not like the idea of going there, but he knew the other 49 percent were peaceable and The City had some wonderful things to see. As a precaution, he strapped the Bowie knife on his left side with the handle under his armpit and the blade extending down his torso. The knife made him feel more confident if Trogs mistook him and Sharon for easy targets. He didn't really think he'd have to use it. Just the sight of the massive tool would be a deterrent to Trogs, he assumed. It concerned Zeke that he would have some explaining to do to the police *and* the Marine Corps if he was caught carrying a concealed weapon, especially one that audacious, but he felt the trade-off was worth the risk. He was Crocodile Dundee long before the movie.

The evening was fun and uneventful except for the hooker who asked Zeke if he wanted a date despite walking hand-in-hand with Sharon. He replied to the hooker that she smelled like cow shit and made the "gag-me" sign with his thumb and fingers. They laughed and kept walking while the nasty whore sputtered unintelligible epithets. Her pimp overheard the exchange and directed some undecipherable street jive toward Zeke in a challenging voice. Zeke turned, walked toward the pimp and casually opened his jacket to display the Bowie. The pimp stared with wide eyes at the giant knife. There is something about a knife that instills a deep, primal fear. No more words were exchanged.

✪ ✪ ✪

The house next door to 240 belonged to Zeke's step-Aunt, a second-generation Irish lass named Lena. Her family had emigrated from Ireland and her first language was Gaelic. The only thing more entertaining than hearing her talk, especially after she had a few drinks, was hearing her yell in Gaelic with a Brooklyn accent. When they arrived at 240 from their New York adventure, Zeke persuaded Sharon to go next door to Aunt Lena's to "test out her bed." Sharon was nervous.

"How can we just go over there like that? Isn't anyone around?"

"Naw, it's all dark. I'll turn on their stereo and play some LPs while we stretch out in her bed. I'll make us a couple of drinks too. They have lots of booze over there. It's okay. She won't mind."

"She won't mind wrinkled sheets?"

"There won't be any traces. I'll put her pillow under your butt," at which point they broke out laughing thinking about Lena laying her head, perhaps face first, on that pillow the next day.

They tiptoed over to Aunt Lena's, unlocked the back door and walked silently to the bedroom in the dark. Sharon pulled back the covers of Lena's bed and they both got naked. As the fireworks began, Lena popped out of the bathroom where she had been getting ready for bed.

"*DIA ÁR SÁBHÁ!*," she exclaimed loudly in Gaelic which, loosely translated, meant WTF? Lena was just as startled as Zeke and Sharon. Lena dropped the water glass she was carrying as Zeke and Sharon covered their nakedness. Lena pointed at them and they pointed at her. After a moment of awkward silence, the three of them started to snicker. This quickly evolved into nervous laughter. After they got recombobulated, Lena invited Zeke and Sharon to sit down with her and share a glass of harsh-tasting low-end brandy. A couple of glasses and some great conversation later, Lena announced that she was going next door to 240 and would be back in a couple hours.

"You two can stay here for a while," she said with her lilting brogue and a knowing smile.

✪ ✪ ✪

The next morning, Sharon, Naomi and the siblings—the urchins, as he called them—ages three through ten, took Zeke to JFK Airport to board a Boeing 707 to Los Angeles, the first leg of his journey to Camp Pendleton in San Diego County, California. Midge didn't come; he was working. The kids were young and did not understand the seriousness of what was happening. Naomi did. So did Sharon. Zeke was detached from the present and focused on the future. He was already in Vietnam in his mind. He heard the song, *Bang, Bang,* by Cher on the car radio. It was a silly song, but some of the words resonated and stuck with him forever: *Bang, bang, you shot me down. Bang, bang, I hit the ground. Bang, bang that awful sound ...*

Zeke also thought about his conversation with Sharon a few days earlier where he again raised the issue of whether he and Sharon should continue their relationship. They had talked about that issue nine months earlier before he went to Parris Island and they needed to talk about it again, considering the amount of time he would be gone and especially given his destination. Zeke had no doubt he would return from Parris Island; he wasn't so sure about Vietnam. He was willing to spare her all the drama that was about to unfold if that was what she wanted. Sharon wanted no part of it and was offended that he had brought it up again. She promised to be true and wait for him, forever if need be. That was exactly what Zeke wanted to hear.

After they shook hands and kissed to seal the deal, Zeke began to think that her acquiescence had come too easy and felt the need to punctuate the conversation with stronger words. As he was kissing her ear and caressing her blond hair, he whispered softly, "Okay. You're committed. You had your chance. Now you're stuck with me forever. And oh, by the way, if anyone tries to put the hit on you when I'm gone, tell them your boyfriend's a crazy Marine with a big Bowie knife and to leave you alone."

Sharon looked shocked.

"Just kidding, just kidding," said Zeke.

They both laughed and hugged each other again.

Zeke was not a violent person, but he could say shockingly violent things sometimes to make a point as he stared at a person with cold, x-ray eyes. It was an effective means of non-verbal intimidation in most situations. Sharon had grown accustomed to Zeke's ways, but sometimes what he'd say and how he'd say it would take the air out of the room, figuratively speaking. She knew how to redirect him when he got off on a tangent like that.

"Let's get married when you come back from Vietnam, she whispered. "We'll have a baby Zeke or a baby Sharon."

She had worked out the details in her mind. It would give them both something to look forward to—to live for—as the days and months passed. She described how pretty the little girl would be. Zeke laughed and talked about how handsome and strong the little boy would be. He nodded his head in agreement and gave her a big hug. Sharon cried and squealed with happiness.

✪ ✪ ✪

A voice came over the loudspeaker that jarred Zeke back to the present. "TWA Flight 240 to LA is now boarding at Gate 12."

The irony of the flight number made him frown and smile alternatively. He paused for a moment, standing almost at attention. He was wearing his Marine dress greens adorned with his National Defense Ribbon and Sharpshooter Badge. Sharon was impressed. Once again, Zeke said his goodbyes to his mom and the urchins. He gave Sharon a protracted hug and kiss.

As he walked over to the gate to board the plane he didn't want to look back. *Okay, one last look. I may never see them again.* He looked back at everyone standing there with forlorn looks and blew them all a kiss. He mouthed the words "I love you" to Sharon and gave her a "thumb's up" gesture. She was trying to be stoic, but was tearing up. Zeke would have teared up too but it was unbecoming for a Marine to show emotion, particularly in public. As he was about to turn to enter the plane, Sharon ran to him and threw her arms around him for the last time.

# 12

# SURVIVAL, ESCAPE, RESISTANCE AND EVASION

---

FOCUSED, DISCIPLINED ANGER TRUMPS FEAR.

---

The MP at the entrance to Camp Pendleton told Zeke that he was "out of uniform." *Could the bullshit really be starting this quickly?* Zeke was wearing dress greens, the uniform of the day at Camp Lejeune on the east coast, his last duty station. To Zeke's chagrin, the MP was wearing khakis, obviously the uniform of the day at Camp Pendleton there on the west coast.

"I didn't get the memo corporal," he replied with a good-natured smile and his hands clasped together as if in prayer pretending he was requesting forgiveness for his "sin." Zeke's taxi driver stuck up for him. "I brung lots of these boys through the gate wearing greens and there ain't been no problem before."

That driver knew the score. He knew that Marines were coming to Pendleton from all parts of the country on their way to Vietnam. He also knew that some of these same Marines would not be coming back in one piece or not coming back at all. He did not hide his annoyance at the MP for being a ball-buster.

The tight-jawed MP reluctantly motioned them through the gate with the admonition that Zeke should get his "private ass" into the proper uniform ASAP or he'd "be standing tall in front of the man." That was an unsubtle way of telling Zeke to don khakis or he would have to explain his transgression to his commanding officer.

Doing a little research later, Zeke found he had done nothing wrong. Under the circumstances, he had not violated any regulations. The MP either didn't know the protocol or was just busting balls.

Zeke was assigned to 2nd Replacement Battalion, Unit 240 (U240). *Why does the number 240 keep coming up in my life? Is this good or bad? What the hell does it mean?*

The first order of business for Marines assigned to the Replacement Battalion was to dye their white skivvies green in the barracks washing machines. They had to purchase the dye with their own money, which gave them something to bitch about right from the start. First, the color was not a military green; it was Peter Pan green. Second, they wondered why there was not enough money in the Department of Defense budget to issue dark green undies instead of having to "buy and dye" themselves. It was humorous and undignified at the same time. Third, this begged the question about WTF they would be doing running around Vietnam in their underwear such that it had to be dyed green.

Once everyone's underwear was sufficiently green, U240 was taken to an area within Camp Pendleton with the improbable name Las Pulgas, meaning "Those Fleas" in Spanish for Survival, Escape, Resistance, and Evasion (SERE) school, a.k.a. Jungle Warfare Training. Marines force-marched, shot all kinds of weapons, learned how to handle explosives, detect booby traps, and escaped and evaded "enemies," played by Recon Marines. They participated in countless war games, day and night.

U240 was "gung ho" every step of the way until the Easter Bunny incident. It was the afternoon of April 10th, Easter Sunday. The Marines watched intently while a slack-eyed instructor killed a cute domesticated rabbit and a rattlesnake to demonstrate how to kill and prepare food to live off the land. The rabbit killer, a leathery old staff sergeant with a gravelly voice who looked like he had been around since the Battle of Chapultepec, had given the rabbit a Karate chop and then skinned it while it was still alive. The Marines were audibly repulsed. Zeke yelled out in a muffled voice, "Killing a bunny on Easter Sunday is a Mortal Sin!"

This caused tittering through the group. Marines were reputed to be "underpaid, oversexed, professional killers" as they use to say with pride, but they had a soft spot for kids and animals. A few of the guys mumbled something about skinning the instructor and eating him rather than the Easter bunny.

✪ ✪ ✪

Prisoner of War (POW) training was part of SERE school; it was conducted by the British Marines. U240 referred to them as BMs. The double-entendre was intended. Marine reservists, dressed in black uniforms, played the role of enemy captors. Each Reservist had a large red star on his black helmet to signify that he was a CMF—a Communist MF. Rank-and-file Marines did not respect reservists. They were perceived to have taken the easy way out by enlisting for only six months of active duty, which effectively precluded them from going to Vietnam.

After a lecture by BM Captain Oakley, U240 was surrounded and "captured" by the CMFs and trotted off to a compound built to resemble an NVA prison camp. U240 had been trained to intentionally spread out the line on the way to the compound so that one or two men could subtly jump off the road and escape at a blind spot or curve. One of the U240 captives forgot the "subtly" part and jumped off the road before the line had been sufficiently stretched, before there was any real opportunity to escape. He was pounced on by the CMFs and physically and verbally abused with great fanfare and lots of blank gunfire into the air.

Zeke laughed aloud—as much at the stupidity of the escapee as at the CMFs' response. It was a hilarious scene and he could not suppress the laugh. As punishment for laughing, a CMF poured a canteen of water over Zeke's head, threw dirt on him and gave him a couple slaps in the back of the head. It was worth the laugh. Had the situation been real both the line jumper and Zeke would have suffered serious consequences, possibly death.

Upon arrival at the POW camp, sergeants of various stripes and officers were separated from the rank-and-file and marched out of sight—probably to the club for beers, it was said. Captives were selected at random to be water-boarded, hung on poles facing the sun, Lakota Sundance style, stuffed into coffin-like boxes below the ground, partially buried, and generally abused, physically and mentally. Those who were selected for water boarding and who refused to give information beyond name, rank and serial number were held under water until they were close to drowning.

It was all humorous to Zeke until the CMFs came for him. He had been sitting on a rickety wooden table inside the compound and it collapsed. The noise and Zeke's cursing attracted attention and he was dragged off to the water torture trough. Zeke would rather have been hung out to dry in the sun or beaten rather than deal with water. Just the idea of being submerged in water brought back memories of Drown Proofing at Parris Island and scared the hell out of him.

The CMFs tied Zeke's hands and feet and submerged his entire body. Each time he was unresponsive to a question, a CMF would shove him back under water and then pull his head out of the water at the last minute, just before he passed out. He thought his lungs would burst and he was going to die. It was the scariest and most physically painful thing he had ever experienced. After the fifth or sixth iteration, he remembered the saying he had learned in ITR: focused, disciplined anger trumps fear. Anger replaced fear as he cursed and spit water into the CMFs' faces each time they pulled his head out of the water. The yelling attracted Captain Oakley's attention. Oakley watched the proceedings for a few minutes and was impressed by Zeke's resistance, then ordered him to be released.

In a mild Cockney accent, Oakley tried to give Zeke some brutally honest advice: "Hammond, you've got a strong spirit and you didn't break, which I respect, but you lost control; you got mad. Cursing and spitting at your captors would have gotten you killed in a real POW situation and it wouldn't have been a pretty death."

After a moment of reflection, Zeke snapped back with a borderline insolent response: "Well captain, then I would have died happy."

"My word, you American Marines are even crazier than we British Marines. And you're a salty young man who must learn the hard way."

"Captain, I must ask you this: What if I didn't have any information to give the enemy?"

"Wouldn't matter, chap, they wouldn't believe you. Fake it. Make up stuff. Just die with honor and say nothing to hurt your fellow Marines or compromise your country's mission. Don't ever behave like some of those U.S. Army POWs did during the Korean War; they gave information to the enemy freely and were killed anyway. That's why we're doing this—to make sure what happened in Korea doesn't happen in Vietnam."

*I would keep my mouth shut to the end and die with honor,* he thought. He just knew that's how he'd go out if captured and that was fine with him.

"Now get back to that table you broke, Marine, and see if you can repair it."

Zeke squished back across the POW yard with his boots full of water and his utilities soaking wet. He was one pissed off Marine at that point and thought he'd like to kill one of those CMFs that water-boarded him as he saw them grab another Marine to water board—this time a guy with an MOS of 5537, saxophone player, the most unlikely person in U240 to become a POW. Zeke yelled to the sax player, "Tell them to fuck themselves and spit water in their faces; they hate that!"

The training was so well choreographed by the captors, so real, so painful, and so maddening that U240 began to see themselves as POWs for real and began to resist, big time. The senior corporal got on his feet and started doing Jumping Jack calisthenics. The entire unit followed suit yelling out cadence calls at the top of their lungs to drown out the propaganda being broadcast from speakers hung around the compound. When that corporal was dragged away by the CMFs, the next senior man immediately took over to lead the Jumping Jack resistance movement. It was beautiful to see the chain of command executed in perfect Marine Corps fashion all the way down to Senior PFC as CMFs kept removing the leaders.

Captain Oakley moved to quell the resistance. As he reached out to grab one of the Marines by the collar, the Marine turned and gave Oakley a wallop that knocked the beret off his head and sent him flying. The entire unit smelled blood and seized the opportunity to charge the main gate growling, yelling like banshees, and carrying the huge iron pot full of water that had been sitting in the middle of the compound. U240 was going to batter down the gate and administer some payback to the CMFs.

The wide-eyed CMFs shot blanks into the air at the same time they were yelling, "stop or I'll shoot," oblivious to the fact that they had already started shooting. The pot-carriers doused the CMFs with water then used the iron pot to batter down the gate. In a flash of temporary insanity, the guys in U240 were going to kill every CMF as if they were NVA. It was real. Everyone could feel it.

Captain Oakley took out his pistol and added to the debacle by firing three or four rounds into the air—real bullets, not training blanks—and regained control of the situation just in time to stop the donnybrook. Oakley put the entire group in a giant School Circle and made a slow, deliberate speech. He was angry.

"I am surprised and disappointed. I thought American Marines had more self-discipline. I was mistaken. I will not ask who that man was that hit me or who led this riot, but you should know that had this been a real POW camp and you had rebelled like that, you would be lying in a pool of your own blood right now. That would have been all the excuse the NVA needed to waste your dumb asses. Not one of you would have survived."

The guys later joked that the NVA might have killed a few of them, but the Marines would have killed the guards and had a better chance of survival by taking action when they had the chance. No remorse. They were still green, just like their skivvies … and naïve.

The last exercise at Pendleton was Drown Proofing, writ large—a feet-first jump from a seemingly mile-high diving board into a flaming pool of water, fully clothed and in low-light conditions. Apparently, Marines needed to know how to jump into the ocean from the height of a ship's deck and swim underwater some distance to clear the fire that had been sparked by gunfire from an enemy ship. Since most Marines would be going to Vietnam by plane, that exercise seemed frivolous to most of the rank-and-file. Jumping into the Pacific Ocean from a ship would surely be deadly and sharks would eat those who survived the jump anyway. It was a World War II thing in the minds of the young Marines and they did not see the value of the exercise.

The diving board was high, the water was deep and the flames were intense and widespread. For those with a fear of heights, water or fire it was the sum of all fears. Zeke had been Drown-Proofed, and water-boarded. *Enough already!* At first, he thought he'd figure out a way to leave the pool area pretending he'd already jumped, but he had second thoughts. He could not live with himself if he passed up the exercise. He replaced fear with anger as he aggressively worked his way up the ladder. As he stood at the end of the diving board looking down into the flames, he let out with a loud growl and jumped. It was a long way down. He pierced through the fire at high speed, landing feet first at the bottom of the pool. He pulled himself to the surface and doggie paddled out to safety without help from the Recon Marines swirling around in the water ready to drag out non-hackers. Once again, focused, disciplined anger trumped fear.

✪ ✪ ✪

A couple days before departure to WESTPAC, a master sergeant who could have doubled for Richard Simmons of *Sergeant Preston of the Yukon* fame, called for personal weapons to be turned in. He reminded everyone that such weapons were not permitted in combat, per the Geneva and Hague Conventions, the UCMJ and anything else that came to his mind. Combatants could only kill each other with *approved* weapons and ammunition. He added that failure to comply would have dire consequences. Zeke showed his Jacksonville Bowie knife to the master sergeant and asked imploringly if there were any exceptions.

"You've gotta be shitin' me, Marine. Did I say there were exceptions? No! Now take that goddamned sword to the Battalion Armory, get it tagged and sent home or your ass will be in the wringer."

Sergeant Preston of the Yukon would never have talked like that. Zeke was pissed. He was to leave for Vietnam unarmed.

✪ ✪ ✪

That evening U240 was given liberty. Since Camp Pendleton was so close to Mexico, many of the Marines headed for Tijuana. They were warned that if they were thrown in jail by Mexican authorities or otherwise failed to show up the next morning, they would be guilty of "Missing Movement" and would be considered deserters. Every day Zeke seemed to learn a new and interesting Marine Corps term that could be used in a stand-up comedy routine. He joked about the term Missing Movement and began using it to describe constipation, sexual issues, bad dancing or anything else that came to mind.

Marines in U240 were old enough to go to war but none were old enough to drink adult beverages in the State of California because they were all under 21 years of age. In 1966 that also made them too young to vote. Barry McGuire had summed it up well in his song, *Eve of Destruction*, nine months earlier. Most of the guys did not want to take the chance of "Missing Movement," and decided to stay on base in the barracks with Mary Palmer and her Five Sisters, a crude expression for self-stimulation.

In Mexico, there were no age limits on anything. Zeke and four Marines headed to Tijuana. They slugged back tequila, watched a woman named *Fan-Fan la Tulipe*, "do" a mule, had a *ménage a cinco* with a dark-haired senorita named *Rojo Grande*, sang along with Mariachis and broke a pool stick across the face of a wise ass who muttered something in Spanish that didn't sound flattering. Zeke and his compadres rejoined U240 with an hour to spare, ready to go to Vietnam.

## 13

# BE A MAN!

---

"VAYA CON DIOS. GO WITH GOD, MY DEAREST SON."

---

The next day U240 was bussed to Marine Corps Air Station - El Toro in Orange County, California. They would fly to Vietnam with stops in Hawaii, Wake Island and Okinawa. Each stop represented yet another frustrating delay in mixing it up with the enemy. A couple months earlier Zeke began to feel that training and paperwork processing had become ends in themselves and the war would be over by the time he got there. Now it looked like things were finally coming together and he would soon be in Vietnam. He thought, with luck, he might meet up with some of his buds from PI, ITR or Montford Point who were already in Vietnam. He hoped to see Aaron who had gone to Vietnam a month earlier and was driving trucks around a place called Chu Lai.

U240 Marines were told to make their last phone calls to parents and loved ones because "it might be the last time you ever talk to them." Zeke had been so preoccupied with himself and his training that he had not re-flected much about those closest to him—Sharon and his family. He made one call and that was to Velma and Walter. Walter talked to him as the grandfather he had always been: upbeat, supportive, confident and loving. He expressed his pride in Zeke and his mission and said he would be wait-ing for his letters. He thought he heard his grandfather crying, but quickly dismissed the idea. Walter never cried in front of people.

"Zeke, I've always seen you as my own son. I have loved you more than life itself. I'm praying that you'll come back to us."

"I love you too, Gramp. I use to call you dad when I was little. You're the only father I ever really had. Stay well. I'll be okay."

With that, they said their final goodbyes. They had never expressed their love for each other in words; only with deeds … until then.

Zeke felt good. Gramp's words had pumped him up and he was happy. During training, the instructors would say, "Look at the man to your left; look at the man to your right. In six months one of you will be *dead*." That line had been used so many times it lost its shock value. However, that evening, it resonated. He had acted as if he was about to enter some high school competition and after the game he would come back home and everything would be the same.

*God, please let me see all of them again. Don't let this be the last time.*

About sun-up the next morning U240 lifted off from El Toro. Zeke looked out the window in a trance as the plane ascended. As the plane leveled out at its designated cruising altitude, Zeke opened the letters from home he had received the day before. Between preparations for departure and the trip to Tijuana, he had not had time to read them. The first letter was from his mother.

"*Vaya con Dios*—go with God, my dearest son. PS: I'll rattle the beads for you every day."

Rattling the beads was a borderline sacrilegious way of referring to praying the Catholic rosary. It conjured up a funny image and made him smile, which was just what he needed at that moment. Walter had equally powerful words: "Now son, you have a dirty job to do. Above all *be a man* and do what you've been trained to do. God willing, we will be here when you come back. Don't worry about your grandmother and me; we've lived our 'three score and ten' and then some, as the bible says. Just take care of yourself and come back to your mother alive."

Walter had lived through the Spanish-American War, the first and second world wars, the Korean War, the Cold War and the First Indochina war. He was a student of history and understood the personal, historical and political nature of war. He had been following the Vietnam situation since it began to gain momentum in the early 1960s when it was referred to as the Second Indochina War. He knew his grandson was stepping into a mess.

The next day Walter called Zeke's mom to remind her that he had purchased a three-plot burial site many years earlier and offered the third plot for Zeke if he was killed. He would be buried at home next to his grandparents in the same cemetery where so many of his ancestors were resting. The image of Zeke lying under the ground in that cemetery made Naomi numb. The time had come and she knew she had to face reality. Like so many other parents of those heading into harm's way, she cried at the possibility of never seeing her son alive again.

After five hours or so, the plane landed in Hawaii for refueling, then on to sparsely populated Wake Island, twenty-three hundred miles west of Hawaii, for more fuel and some fresh air. Wake is a three square mile possession of the United States located in the middle of the Pacific Ocean. It is one of the most isolated islands in the world. Zeke wondered what it would be like to be stationed on Wake. Claustrophobic, he guessed. The tropical smell and feel of the air was new to him. He had never been further west than Susquehanna County before he joined the Marine Corps. He was seeing exotic places just like his recruiter had promised and he liked it.

In a couple hours, U240 left Wake Island headed for Okinawa. Sitting across from Zeke was a sergeant named Garcia from Del Rio, Texas. He had already served two thirteen-month tours in Vietnam as a Grunt and had received a Purple Heart for a hand-to-hand scrape with an NVA soldier who knew how to wield a bayonet. Garcia said he shot him 8 times with his M1911. He was headed for his third tour with only four months of active duty remaining on his four-year enlistment.

"I know I'm not gonna make it this time," he said.

Zeke listened to his story and nodded his head with interest and empathy. There was nothing to say. The Marines say, "Attitude is Everything" as a guide for survival. With his fatalistic attitude, Garcia was a dead man walking.

# 14

# LUCKY ĐỐNG

THE 10-ĐỐNG PIECE WAS HIS "LUCK," FOR MARINES A
TERM WITH DEEP MEANING BEYOND THE ORDINARY.

Okinawa, a.k.a., "the Rock," located between the East China Sea and
the Philippine Sea, is the capital of the Ryukyu Islands and was one
of the bloodiest battlegrounds of the Pacific during World War II. The Rock
was the final stop for Marines on their way to Vietnam.

Soon after arrival at Okinawa, U240 was "processed." A splib sergeant
with Corbeau printed on his name tag was one of the processors and was
extraordinarily abusive to Marines as they passed by his table with paperwork in hand. Corbeau made remarks about what their girlfriends or wives
would be doing at home with other guys while they were in Vietnam. Corbeau yelled, cursed and acted like a Drill Instructor for no apparent reason
other than pure meanness. He didn't discriminate; he meted out abuse to
everyone regardless of race or ethnicity.

Corbeau also used the tired old line about how one out of three Marines
would be killed in Vietnam and then proceeded to point to every third guy
in line with his finger gun yelling "bang, you're dead." Corbeau should have
had his ass kicked, but as a paperwork processor, he held a position of power
by virtue of his rank and the option to handle or mishandle paperwork as
he chose. There was nothing to do but grin and bear it like basic recruits
instead of combat-trained Marines about to put their lives on the line.

A Marine standing next to Zeke who looked like he had some seniority
whispered, "An asshole like that could end up KIA in the 'Nam."

Zeke looked at him with surprise. "KIA—killed in action? How so?

The Marine, who had already spent a tour in Vietnam, shrugged. "Just sayin' how things work in the real world, that's all. A nasty MF like that would be wasted by his own men."

"What do you mean, "wasted?""

The Marine ran his finger across his throat. *"Giêt chêt!"*

"Do you mean cut his throat? Murder him?"

"You really are naïve, Hammond," the Marine replied as he walked away.

*Murder a fellow Marine? Zeke thought. Nah. Can't happen; not in the Marine Corps.*

The poem Zeke learned in high school French, *The Fox and the Crow*, came to mind: *Maître Corbeau, sur un arbre perché (*Mister Crow, perched in a tree) ... and started to smile to himself. When he got to Corbeau's processing station Zeke bantered with him. He was careful to maintain a smile and use double entendres and ambiguities to maintain plausible deniability in case Corbeau was smart enough to detect Zeke's passive aggression and sarcasm. Corbeau told Zeke to step out of line and come with him.

"Where to, Sergeant Corbeau?"

"I been lookin' for a driver and I think you'll do. You'll be drivin' around the island makin' deliveries. Who knows, if I likes you, maybe I'll keep your ass outta the 'Nam."

*Oh for God's sake, what next?*

"Sergeant, I *want* to go to Vietnam. You wouldn't be doing me any favors keeping me here. That's why I joined the Marine Corps—to keep the South Vietnamese from getting fucked over by those Commie goblin MFs."

Corbeau just smiled and shook his head.

"Ain't gonna happen right now. You need to knock off the backtalk or you'll be on mess duty peelin' spuds instead of drivin.' You dig?"

Corbeau directed Zeke to his new home, a Quonset hut occupied solely by a pudgy PFC who was passing time waiting to turn 18, which would happen in a few weeks. He had gone through all the preliminaries—basic training, ITR and SERE, but was not old quite old enough to be in Vietnam. Zeke had not realized until then that men could not be "in country"—in Vietnam—until they reached their 18th birthday. Zeke called the PFC "Teen" since he was boot (junior) to Zeke, both in the Corps and in life.

"Well, Teen, we're in the same boat. We're stuck on The Rock for a while longer. Might's well make the best of it. You can be my tour guide and I'll take you around if you need a lift anywhere. I'm gonna be a driver and we can help each other out."

Zeke was assigned to drive a Marine Corps version of a UPS truck hither and yon. Driving such a preposterous vehicle after being trained on the M54 at Montford Point was embarrassing. It was also embarrassing not knowing where he was going and having no map, but he muddled through. He enjoyed the radio, blasting rock and roll at full tilt with the sliding door open as he sped all around the island. Zeke got to see a lot of Okinawa by being a driver and was starting to enjoy the experience.

Zeke let Teen ride around with him and took him places. Teen introduced Zeke to the night life. One afternoon they decided to stop at a "Sugar Shack" in Koza (now Okinawa City). Sugar Shack was subtler and more pleasing to the ear than "whore house." Apparently, the term came into vogue after Jimmy Gilmer and the Fireballs released a pop tune by that name three years earlier in 1963.

There were three Marines already sitting in the anteroom drinking Pussy Willows—warm Sake and Coca-Cola—awaiting their turns. They were about the same age as Zeke, but looked like old men. They seemed friendly enough so Zeke struck up a conversation. They had been part of the 9th Marine Amphibious Brigade, the first Marine Corps combat unit in Vietnam. They had landed at China Beach, Vietnam in March 1965 and were returning home.

The more they drank the more they loosened up and felt at liberty to share their gut-wrenching experiences. Zeke needed to hear their stories and they appreciated his listening. By the time their turns came, their sexual urges had dissipated because of the serious talk and number of Pussy Willows. They chose instead to keep drinking and talking. The tales these Marines spun were sobering. The Sugar Shack lost money that night.

Zeke's brief sojourn on The Rock was cut short after about two weeks when he was told he would be joining the next batch of replacements heading to Vietnam. He had no idea why he was chosen to stay and drive in the first place or why the sudden change of venue was ordered. He bid Teen adieu and wished him a memorable 18th birthday, laughing with him about how he would probably be shipped to Vietnam by Special Delivery five minutes after he turned 18. They vowed to keep in touch.

Zeke heard that Teen drowned soon after arriving in Vietnam. He would never see his 19th birthday. *How could anyone drown in Vietnam? Rice paddies weren't that deep were they? What the hell was he doing, swimming in a river or something? Wonder if he'd passed Drown Proofing?* It was a mystery. Zeke was deeply pained by Teen's death; he was the first Marine he knew personally to die in Vietnam. He could visualize a military representative driving to Teen's house and telling his parents the bad news. Then he thought of that same scenario taking place all over America, literally by the thousands. Zeke went into a deep funk. Simon and Garfunkel's song played repeatedly in his head for days: *I am a rock. I am an island ... and a rock feels no pain. And an island never cries.*

Zeke hooked up with his new Vietnam-bound unit and marched with them to a warehouse where each man was given a large box in which to put dress uniforms, civilian clothes and other worldly possessions—stuff they carried in their sea bags, but would not need in Vietnam. Each Marine sealed his respective box and addressed it to his next of kin or most appropriate friend or lover. Survivors could pick up their boxes in thirteen months on the return trip. For those killed or wounded ... well, that was the reason for the address label. This sobering moment generated some dark humor. Some just stared at the sealed box in silence.

Later, Zeke was sitting on the sand waiting his turn to be "processed" for what seemed like the tenth time since first receiving his orders for WESTPAC. It was hotter than blue blazes and he was roasting in the sun sitting on white sand with no shade. But unnecessary pain and discomfort made Marines stronger, they said. "Pain is Weakness Leaving the Body" was one of the Marines' many slogans. He leaned back and felt something buried in the sand. It was a 10-Đồng Vietnamese coin, fancifully inscribed with the words *Việt Nam Cộng Hoà* (Republic of Vietnam). The date of the coin was 1964, the first year the 10-Đồng piece was added to Vietnamese currency. It was also the year Zeke graduated from high school and the year President Johnson used the Gulf of Tonkin incident to escalate the conflict in Vietnam. Zeke concluded that the coin was placed there by his Guardian Angel and decided to wear it on a chain around his neck. The 10-Đồng piece was going to be his "luck," for Marines a term that went much deeper than the ordinary definition of the word.

That evening Zeke and his cohorts boarded a cargo plane with their sea bags slung over their shoulders. Weapons and other equipment would be issued when they got to Vietnam. The seats consisted of canvas webbing and constructed at a ninety-degree angle so that each man sat upright, almost at attention. The urinal tubes were located between seats every twenty feet and about even with the shoulder of the men sitting on either side of the tube's opening. Adjacent Marines diverted their eyes when the tube was in use or they would have been urinated on or worse.

Soon after takeoff, Zeke slipped out of his uncomfortable seat at the back of the plane and curled up on the mountain of sea bags piled directly behind him in the tail. He dozed off with the sound of the aircraft's four engines buzzing loudly in his ears. It was one-hundred-decibel "white noise." He fell into peaceful sleep clutching the good luck coin around his neck.

After an hour or so in the air, the plane began to shake and vibrate as it penetrated clear air turbulence. The turbulence was moderate to severe in aviation terms and did not subside. Zeke felt the aircraft making a high G-force banking turn. When the plane rolled out, the engines did not sound right and the flight seemed even rougher. This was worrisome. *Almost* getting to Vietnam would not count for anything, just like *almost* joining the Marine Corps. "Almost" doesn't count except in love and horseshoes, as Zeke remembered the quaint saying used by family elders.

An hour later the Marines were told to prepare for landing ... back in Okinawa. Apparently, there had been a serious problem. The pilot had declared an emergency and was directed to return to the Rock for repair. At that point, Zeke didn't know or even care whether he would get to Vietnam. There had been so many obstacles and delays that he decided not to worry about it anymore. As his mom, Naomi would say: *Que sera, sera* or, translated into Marine vernacular, fuck it!

After a couple hours on the hot tarmac in the humid night with no water or food, resting on their sea bags, the Marines were abruptly ordered to their feet and back onto the same plane in which they had already flown halfway to Vietnam and back. *Good God, this is the part where the aircraft malfunctions and we crash into the ocean. That Drown Proofing shit at Parris Island and fire diving at Pendleton might come in handy after all.*

Five hours of uneventful flight later the plane began its descent, approaching from the east over the South China Sea until it entered the DaNang Tactical Control Area. It then descended rapidly at a steep angle. The interior and exterior lights were turned off and the pilots ordered silence—as if the VC couldn't see or hear the plane in the dark and as if they could hear talking on the plane. Hundreds of men had been killed on their first day in Vietnam, a few by enemy sniper fire on final approach to the airport before the wheels touched the ground. In theory, the aerobatic maneuvers made it harder for a VC sniper to hit his mark.

"Welcome to Vietnam" came a voice over the plane's public address system.

Zeke had arrived … at last.

# —PART III—

# VIETNAM

## 15

# GOOD MORNING VIETNAM

---

THE SMELL WAS SO STRONG ZEKE COULD ALMOST TASTE IT.

---

It was May, the first month of summer in Vietnam. The average temperature during that month averaged ninety degrees with debilitating humidity. Even though it was dawn, getting off the plane was like walking into a sauna. The sweat darkened the Marines' Peter Pan green underwear and it seeped through their utilities. Within a half-hour, they looked like they had been swimming with their clothes on.

Zeke and his fellow passengers were again "processed" and told where to go to be picked up by someone from their respective units. Zeke was assigned to Heavy Platoon near DaNang. He wondered if "heavy" referred to the weight of the truck or the loads they carried or pulled. *That's a macho sounding name for a platoon. Beats the hell out of being in the light platoon. Maybe everyone in Heavy Platoon is overweight,* he thought, laughing aloud. He sat under a lone tree and waited, taking in the sights, sounds and smells. *So, this is Vietnam.* He had no apprehensions or regrets. He was just unbelievably hot and sweaty, more so than he had ever been in his life.

While waiting, Zeke heard music coming from a nearby radio. Then he heard "GOOD MORNING VIETNAM" followed by a catchy jingle. It was Adrian Cronauer, the voice of Armed Forces Radio's Dawn Buster morning show.

"Today, we salute the 8th Tactical Bomb Squadron."

The salute was followed by another song—*Baby, the Rain Must Fall.* That song was a year and eighty-five hundred miles old, but it got his juices flowing again despite being dehydrated, tired, and hungry. *Thank you, Glen*

*Yarborough,* he thought as he clutched his 10-Đồng coin and looked up at the morning sky. *Lord, give me strength.*

A tight-jawed corporal showed up in a covered military pick-up to take Zeke to his new unit. He immediately scolded Zeke for having rolled up his sleeves in the ninety-degree heat and 100 percent humidity. *Oh no, don't tell me there are assholes even here!* The corporal looked fresh and was hardly sweating, obviously acclimated to the heat. From Zeke's perspective, with few exceptions, corporals were among the most neurotic Marines in the Corps. They were no longer part of the rank-and-file and were junior NCOs—low-level supervisors in the civilian world. They were generally intoxicated with their newly found power and had to be handled with kid gloves.

They rolled through the entrance to Heavy Platoon under a banner that exclaimed Vietnam Welcomes the U.S. Marine Corps. Above the banner was a yellow flag with three horizontal red stripes—the flag of the Republic of South Vietnam.

"Nice welcome sign. Looks like they appreciate our being here. Check out those kids waving at us. They must really like Americans."

"Don't be fooled by their shit-eatin' grins and pathetic little faces" replied the corporal. "They'd drop a grenade in your gas tank or toss one through your truck window in a heartbeat. They're looking for food, begging for money, selling shit or pimping their sisters or mothers."

With that, Zeke and the corporal began to talk. By the time they arrived at Heavy Platoon headquarters the corporal seemed like a normal guy despite his rank.

✪ ✪ ✪

After checking in and being processed, Zeke was told he would be driving M54s, the same trucks he had been trained on at Montford Point. He was issued his equipment, which included a cot with half the canvas missing and a mosquito net with no poles to hold the netting off his body. That night he slept with his back on the cot and his butt resting on sandbags with the net draped over him like a blanket. Between the mosquito attacks, the sandbags and the stifling heat, Zeke got little sleep that first night. It was common for Marines with seniority in Vietnam to test newbies (new guys) to get a sense of them. Apparently, Zeke's was the "half-assed cot test." It was like being a Pledge in a fraternity; he needed to take everything they dished out with stoic acceptance and friendly banter until he understood the lay of the land.

On his first full day in Vietnam, Zeke was assigned to the ultimate shit detail, figuratively and literally—pulling tubs filled with floating feces and urine from under the 5-seat outhouses, stirring kerosene into the mixture and setting it on fire. When the fire burned out and the tub cooled, the elixir was dumped into a shallow hole and covered with dirt. The smell was so strong Zeke could almost taste it. There were no masks or gloves to help sanitize the process. It was a primal experience.

"Why the hell don't they get Vietnamese to handle this shit? After all, that's the least these people could do for us for saving them from Communism," Zeke exclaimed loudly.

"Hey guys, see this stir stick? We should form a rock group and name it The Shit Sticks," at which point he and his fellow burners started doing impressions of guitar playing with their stir sticks.

"You guys look like you're having a lot of fun," yelled a sergeant as he approached them with a pout on his face. They must have had a class on pouting in NCO school since they all seemed to have that same demeanor.

"Sergeant, is there any job shittier than this in the Marine Corps, pardon the pun?"

Zeke was careful to ask the question with a smile to avoid the impression that he was not perfectly happy burning excrement for a living.

"I see your name is Hammond" the sergeant replied looking at Zeke's name printed on his shirt.

"In answer to your question, Hammond, ever hear the expression 'Shit rolls downhill? Well that should explain everything to you. And no, this isn't the shittiest job in the Marine Corps, pardon your stupid pun. That job would be picking up the dead and their body parts after a firefight and loading that pile of human slurry onto the back of one of our trucks. That mess looks and smells worse than anything you're dealing with now, so stop whining and get with the program."

Zeke and the Shit Sticks resumed their slave-like demeanors and said nothing more.

# 16

# DAY TRIPPIN'

---

THE HARDEST PART OF DAY TRIPPIN' LOCALLY WAS
NOT RUNNING INTO PEDESTRIANS AND WATER BUFFALO.

---

Zeke was assigned to the day shift—what they called "Day Trippers."
The motor pool was most active during the daytime hours, from
dawn to dusk; it was invigorating. Low-flying helicopters were routine.
Periodically the sounds of artillery and gunfire could be heard off in the
distance. They were constant reminders that there was a war going on and
Marine infantry brothers were out there in the bush somewhere, not far
away, killing or being killed.

The M54 trucks were not the clean and polished versions he had driven
back at Montford Point and Camp Lejeune. Heavy Platoon's trucks were
banged up, draped with sandbags for protection, missing their tailgates and,
in some cases, missing their windows and canvas tops. The trucks were
perpetually covered with a layer of dirt, inside and out. They were coming
and going all the time around the clock.

Each morning Day Trippers would amble to the motor pool to stand in
formation for daily briefings and assignments presided over by the Company
commander, Captain Tennille, a first ("top") sergeant named Singer and a
gaggle of other NCOs he'd get to know in time. Singer was an unpleasant
little man who walked around with his mouth open most of the time as if
he could not breathe through his nose. He always seemed to be frowning
and angry looking.

Formation was much like a police roll call. Topics ranged from mundane
updates to general operating issues such as convoy assignments; status of

trucks damaged in the field from land mines, shrapnel and sniper rounds; reports of VC activity in the area; requests for volunteers for various duties and, once in a while, with baited breath and bowed head, identification of truckers KIA or WIA, wounded in action. Truckers were regularly reminded that hamlets and villages were off limits to American Nationals and there was to be no contact with Charlotte the Harlot, a generic term for South Vietnamese prostitutes. Marines were reminded in graphic terms about Black Syphilis and how Charlotte might be a VC and have wedged razor blades in her *labia majora* to cripple a Marine and put him out of the fight. These were painfully true stories designed to encourage abstinence.

Black Syphilis was a generic term for a virulent, incurable form of venereal disease, contracted by having "unprotected sex" in that part of the world with notoriously unhygienic women. Marines who contracted it were sent to Clark Air Base in The Philippines, to die a miserable death. They were classified as "Died Not as a Result of Hostile Action" along with those that had succumbed to accidents, illnesses, and suicides while in Vietnam. The thought of Black Syphilis gave Marines pause in planning their sexual activities, but the razor-blades-in-the-labia majora warning became just a source of jokes and dark humor. Zeke told everyone a tall tale about how he once knew an Italian girl by the name of Labia Majora and she had no hidden razor blades. This sparked a round of laughter and equally smutty jokes.

Truck drivers were sitting ducks. They drove large, noisy machines, which attracted attention. It was easy for the enemy to just shoot at a gas tank or tire to create havoc. It was almost as easy to pick off a driver whose weapon was mounted in the cab and cumbersome to access quickly. With practice, placing the weapon in just the right position, a driver could return fire immediately while driving. Another occupational hazard was avoiding crossing paths with pedestrians, motorbikes and water buffalo, but it happened, usually by accident; occasionally on purpose, it was said.

Land mines and random shots from the shadows took truckers' lives, but infrequently, at least close to the DaNang area. The situation became much worse the further Day Trippers traveled from the relative security of the DaNang area into the countryside, particularly on convoys to the hinterlands of Vietnam. While some areas were clearly more dangerous than others, there were no boundaries on where the war began and ended. Death could come at any time, any place and in many gruesome ways.

✪ ✪ ✪

Zeke made friends with a salty private who had been in the Corps for five years including some time in the Portsmouth Naval Prison in Maine. He was called "The Old Prive." Most Marines referred to him as TOP. He had long hair for a Marine and a military service number beginning with 19, which represented significant seniority. TOP was in the tenth month of his second Tour in Vietnam and wore his cover compressed at a "don't fuck with me" angle. Zeke felt that TOP was the "go to" guy to get the skinny (information). *This guy's spent more time in Vietnam than most of us have spent in the Corps. He should know a thing or two regardless of his rank.*

TOP cautioned that running over a Vietnamese person—adult or child— or a water buffalo could buy a lot of trouble and cost the government a lot of money. The U.S. made large financial settlements to families who lost their kin under the tires of an American military truck. He gave some good advice on how to handle large crowds on busy streets and roads.

"The first way to keep Gooks away from your truck is to backfire your engine. We call it 'Light 'Um Up' because it sounds like a shotgun and blows flame and soot out the tailpipe. It's pretty impressive."

"TOP, you used the word 'Gook.' What's a Gook?"

"Man, you don't know nothin' do you? A Gook is a Vietnamese man, woman or child regardless of whose side they're on. You can call them Slopes, Slant-eyed MFs, Luke the Gook or anything else that comes to mind."

"Okay, so tell me more about backfiring. I thought Light 'Um Up meant to shoot someone."

"The truckers' version of the expression don't mean the same as it does with the Grunts," replied TOP. "Our version is less dramatic and it's really funny to watch 'um hit the deck and scatter. If that don't work you give them a nudge with the front bumper and beep the horn. Same for water buffalo or anything else that might be in your way. Escalate at will."

Zeke did not like what he was hearing. *Surely he's kidding me,* he thought. *God almighty, if that's what's going on and that's how these people are regarded they probably don't care much for Americans.*

"They never taught us crap like that at Montford Point. So how do you do all that?"

"You just downshift, wind up the RPMs, flip off the magneto switch for a couple seconds and then flip it back on. The longer you wait before switching it back on the louder the noise and the larger the flame out the exhaust pipe. It sounds like a grenade going off and every Gook in the area will drop their shit and belly-down on the ground or *di-di* for dear life. If they're close to the exhaust they might get a face full of soot and they'll think they've been shot. They're a jumpy bunch and it's a sure fire way, pardon the pun, to clear your path. By the way, *di-di* means get out, high-ankle, run away, just so you know."

TOP was laughing with delight, obviously replaying in his mind the many times he had played Light 'Um Up.

"I see you're not laughing, Mr. goody two-shoes," said TOP. You look like you got a problem with that. Well after you're here in 'Nam a while I'll bet you'll grow up and see things a little differently."

"Fuck yourself, TOP," Zeke replied, "we're supposed to be helping these people not harassing them. You're creating enemies when you do that shit and some Marine that didn't do anything wrong will pay the price.

Zeke was noticing a lot of contempt for the Vietnamese on the part of the Marines who had been in country for a while. It didn't make sense to him given what the mission was supposed to be—to help the South Vietnamese people remain free and safe from Communist aggression by North Vietnam by winning their hearts and minds. Zeke understood that Marines suspected every Vietnamese civilian of being an undercover VC or Communist sympathizer, but he did not like the idea of harassing them without knowing for sure. And the idea of deliberately running into them or their water buffalo seemed bad. *Marines wouldn't do that,* thought Zeke, *would they?*

"You think that's something," said TOP, "there's another game I invented myself. I call it 'Bean Bag,' like the kid game, except the bag only goes one way."

The trucks had sandbags on the floorboards and fenders to absorb the impact of land mines. A full sandbag weighed 35 pounds, on average, and TOP flung them from his truck at water buffalo, pedestrians, dogs, or anything else he felt like targeting, whenever the spirit moved him. He bragged about waving and smiling at a busload of people and, when they smiled and waved back in response, he tossed a full sandbag at them right through the window.

"One time, there was this old guy boppin' along the road with a pole over his shoulders balancing a bunch of shit dangling from a rope down each end of the pole. He was in my way and wouldn't move so I tossed a bag at him; caught him square in the back. Boy, did he go flyin'."

"Did you kill him? A bag that heavy flying from a moving truck must have done him in, right?"

"All I know is the old fuck just laid there in the road face down with his shit everywhere. Bet he steps out of the way next time," said TOP, laughing.

"You know, TOP, that's murder unless he represented a clear and present danger, which he didn't.

"Who cares? He was probably VC anyway."

Zeke did not laugh.

"Another time, one night when I was runnin' topless through DaNang I roped me a Gook, just like a cowboy ropin' a steer."

"What the hell do you mean, 'topless'?"

"No canvas top over the cab. Didn't they teach you that in Montford Point either?"

"I tied a big knot at the end of one of my cargo ropes, twirled it a few times just like a cowboy and threw it at a goblin ridin' his bike too close to my truck. The rope wrapped around his handlebars. I felt a tug, kinda like a fish on a line. I held onto the rope and just kept drivin'. Sure as shit, I'd snagged the little bastard's bike and pulled it right out from under him. He went flyin'. Can you image what that fuckin' VC thought? I call that game 'going fishing'. You throw out your line and see what you catch," he said, again laughing like a nut case as he told the story.

"What did you do with the bike?"

"I gave it to charity," TOP responded with a laugh.

It was becoming clear to Zeke that some Marines either saw all Vietnamese as the enemy or simply enjoyed beating people down. This seemed cruel to Zeke. He had not been in Vietnam long enough to feel that way and hoped he never would. He started to get angry.

"TOP, why did you do all that shit? Were they VC or NVA?"

"Who cares, replied Prive. I was just having fun. All these cock suckers hate Americans and would kill us in a heartbeat if they had the chance."

"How do you know that"?

"Look it up, newbie, it's in all the books," said TOP sarcastically, growing annoyed with Zeke's questions.

"Look it up where? Zeke knew where the conversation was heading.

"Up your ass," yelled TOP.

Zeke grabbed a half-full sandbag and swung it across TOP's face. The impact almost knocked him out. The bag split and both of them were covered with blood and sand.

"You're right TOP, it *is* fun. Thanks for the lesson," Zeke said with clenched teeth as he walked away.

Zeke assumed that TOP would have no credibility if he decided to press charges for assault and Zeke would have quite a story to tell if TOP pursued the matter. *I can't be seen with this guy. He's a total shitbird and beaucoup dinky dau.*

*Dinky dau* meant crazy in the local vernacular. When preceded by the French word, *beaucoup*, it meant *very* crazy, perhaps mentally ill. That was TOP.

✪ ✪ ✪

When Zeke arrived in Vietnam, Buddhists were burning themselves in downtown DaNang to protest against the South Vietnam government, particularly Premier Nguyen Cao Ky. It had something to do with a conflict between Catholics and Buddhists and some crazy stuff on the part of

Ky who sided with the Catholics and was on a power trip it was said. The spillover from the protests was dangerous, hence the need for a Marine to ride "Shotgun" in the passenger seat as backup in case the rioters turned on the truckers.

Zeke and his Shotgun headed to DaNang to pick up a load from a Navy ship that had just docked in the harbor. As they approached the street that led to the dock, they spied a young man with a shaven head, wrapped in orange chemise, seated cross-legged in the street. He was a Buddhist monk about to self-immolate as part of the protest movement. They watched as the monk soaked his body with gasoline and light a match. There were no cries of agony, just silence ... except for the light wind whipping the flames. The monk sat there for the longest time before he melted. Zeke was struck by the power of mind over matter. That scene that would stick with him forever.

✪ ✪ ✪

Zeke had been writing to his grandparents regularly. He told them about the water buffalo and how they didn't look anything like Holstein cows. He described the beautiful "Technicolor" environment, the rice paddies and the ten salt tablets he was supposed to take each day because of the heat and humidity. He told them about some of the more unpleasant things including the Buddhist protests. Walter enjoyed the letters, but he seemed to be fading. Zeke was worried about him. He told Walter that he'd take over the farm when he got back, implying they'd all live happily ever after once he returned from Vietnam. Zeke was serious. Walter foreshadowed things to come in his response.

"Now Zeke, don't fret about me. You have enough to think about. I'm almost 81 years old and have had a good life. I'm proud of you. Lord willin,' I may be here when you come home. The Marines have trained you well. Just keep your focus, trust in God and be a man, my son."

Exactly two weeks later, Zeke received a letter from his mother.

"Gramp died on May twenty first. People commented that there were more visitors at his funeral than JFK's," referring to President John F. Kennedy.

Zeke was beside himself. He wanted to let go and cry his eyes out in the worst way. But that was out of the question. He was in the company of Marines and there was a war going on. Besides, Gramp had said "be a *man* … you've got a job to do."

# 17

# RULES OF ENGAGEMENT

EVEN THE VC WOULD LAUGH AT THAT ONE;
THEN I'D SHOOT AT THE SOUND OF THE LAUGHTER.

Z eke was pulled off Day Trippin' and transferred to perimeter guard. His job was to walk back and forth from dusk till dawn guarding against enemy incursions with his trusty M14, ready to do or die, as he had been trained. Across the road there was a cluster of Vietnamese houses, businesses and assorted Sugar Shacks referred to collectively as "Dogpatch" from Al Capp's classic newspaper comic strip, *Li'l Abner.* Dogpatches sprung up all over Vietnam as the American presence escalated. Dogpatches, particularly Sugar Shacks, were off limits to Marines, but that order was virtually unenforceable. Forbidding sexual commerce only made its pursuit more stimulating and exciting to the Marines, most whom were in their late teens and early twenties.

Zeke took guard duty seriously, but soon found that the rules of engagement complicated that role. The first night on the perimeter an overweight Marine approached Zeke's position from some distance, huffing and puffing. Zeke could tell it was a Marine even in the dark because of the body profile and starched cover—a Marine cap starched to hold its shape. No self-respecting VC would wear a starched cover. When the Marine came within twenty-five yards or so, Zeke greeted him with a friendly *"Semper Fi,"* as one Marine to another.

"Marine, I'm Staff Sergeant Watkins; I'm the Sergeant-of-the-Guard. I want to know why you didn't challenge me with the proper protocol: 'Halt, who goes there?' I could have been an enemy combatant."

Here they were, making noise about protocol within easy enemy rifle shot and perfectly silhouetted by the moon. They were easy targets if the enemy had been so inclined to take the opportunity. Zeke apologized and told Watkins that he neither challenged nor shot because he identified him by appearance and starched cover. Had there been any doubt, Zeke said, Watkins would have never heard the shot that killed him. Zeke liked to use that line. It was dramatic and took the air out of the room, so to speak.

Watkins was apoplectic, partly because of what he perceived as a salty response from Zeke and partly because he realized he had done a stupid thing by trying to play games with this Marine who could have killed him with impunity under the circumstances.

"What would you do if you received incoming fire from that Dogpatch village across the road?"

"Staff Sergeant, Watkins, I would wait to see the flash from a discharged bullet to determine the origin of the fire, assume the prone position and then unleash a prodigious line of fire at the flash."

It was a trick question.

"Prodigious? Aren't you a fancy talker," replied Watkins. "NO, YOU WILL NOT SHOOT BACK," he yelled. "Didn't anybody tell you the rules of engagement when you got here? If you kill a non-combatant by mistake, Trinh Thi Ngo, a.k.a., Hanoi Hannah, will use it as propaganda. She makes English language broadcasts for North Vietnam directed against American servicemen in South Vietnam. The bitch even reads the names and hometowns of our KIA over the radio. Those bastards use dirty tricks to convince the Vietnamese populace that we are the bad guys and Communism is superior to democracy and freedom. Therefore, you will *not* shoot back. Do you understand that, Marine? Those are the rules of engagement!"

*Engagement? What a silly euphemism. So sanitized. Such bullshit*, Zeke thought.

Instructors at Parris Island, ITR and SERE never mentioned anything about not shooting back at the enemy; just the opposite. Zeke mulled Watkins' words over in his mind as he walked his post. *Not good*, he thought, *not good at all. Next time that fat fuck sneaks up on me, I'll pop illumination and give him the same treatment I gave Kallen back in Lejeune at the ammo dump. Even the VC would laugh at that one; then I'd shoot at the sound of the laughter.*

**✪ ✪ ✪**

A few days later, just as Zeke started another guard shift at dusk, he heard one loud distinct report of a pistol from the Heavy Platoon living area. He immediately took cover and prepared to defend the perimeter, not knowing whether that shot was the beginning of something serious or an accidental discharge. He remembered what Watkins had told him about shooting into Dogpatch, but if this was the real thing, Watkins' rules be damned; it would be *Semper Fi*, Do or Die time. There was no second shot and no assault on the perimeter. Just quiet. It turned out that one of the rank-and-file had shot himself with an M1911 pistol.

Officially, it was reported that the Marine had a negligent discharge while cleaning his weapon. Truth told, he was a shitbird, one of the 'ten percent', and had deliberately shot himself to get out of Vietnam and go home. He was trying to hit the fleshy part of his thigh but misaligned the weapon and hit himself in the ass. He had not been authorized to carry a handgun and was in trouble for that too. He was treated for his injury and no one saw him again. He would probably tell everyone back in the states that he had been wounded in action and buy a Purple Heart.

# 18

# PINK EGGS

---

"WE ASSUME THE MAJORITY ARE VIET CONG OR
VC SYMPATHIZERS. WE TREAT THEM ACCORDINGLY."

---

One early morning Zeke picked up three Marines from a mess hall to take them to replenish food and kitchen supplies for their unit. One Marine got in the cab with Zeke, the other two climbed up onto the bed of the truck. They had brought a large crate of twelve dozen eggs. Zeke wondered why they were bringing eggs, particularly that many, but he did not make an issue of it.

A few miles down the road the two guys in the back started throwing the eggs at any Vietnamese man, woman, child or water buffalo in sight. They threw as hard and as fast as they could. The speed of the truck increased the velocity of the throw and must have caused great pain for those hit in the face or other sensitive places. The number of eggs those guys threw in just seconds was astonishing.

The egging produced a lot of heated yells and gestures from those who were hit or saw what was happening. Some threw stones back at the Marines doing the egging and bloodied them. Zeke yelled at the doofuses to knock it off as he jammed on his brakes sliding to a halt on the dirt road, which sent both of them flying up against the back of the cab. *They must have had a lot of practice,* thought Zeke. There it was—two doofuses *losing* the hearts and minds of the Vietnamese people by assaulting them just for fun.

A flurry of rocks, cans and debris came hurtling through the air, hitting Zeke and the doofuses and breaking the windshield of the truck. The Marine that had been sitting in the cab with Zeke jumped out and opened fire with his M14 in the direction of the stone throwers. Return shots rang out from several hooches. One of the doofuses was dead before he collapsed in the bed of the truck. Blood flew everywhere—into the cab, onto Zeke and all over the eggs, turning the shells pink. Zeke jumped back into the truck and highballed it down the road as fast as the M54 would go, yelling to the two remaining doofuses to provide covering fire until they were out of range. That was a mistake. They indiscriminately emptied their twenty-round magazines into the hooches.

When the skirmish was over, it was officially reported that the Marines had been attacked by the Viet Cong, resulting in one KIA, which then justified the use of deadly force, per the Rules of Engagement. One Marine was dead, two Vietnamese civilians were killed and a child and a water buffalo were injured. There was extensive damage to four hooches and a score of Vietnamese were covered with raw eggs. The American government covered the cost of the injuries and damage and reimbursed the families for the loss of their kin.

Zeke did not understand what was going on. The indiscriminate abuse of the Vietnamese people was shocking. He knew the enemy had infiltrated the populace, but it bothered him that Marines seemed to unleash hell on every Vietnamese person that fit the profile of a Viet Cong or North Vietnamese soldier without really knowing if they were the enemy. They looked like the enemy and that was enough, it seemed. Zeke had no problem with killing goblins, but had a real problem with assuming everyone was the enemy. *What the hell are we even here for? Who are we supposed to be helping?*

Zeke made a point of tracking down the doofus that had been in the cab of the truck with him that day. He seemed to be the ringleader. He wanted to have a sit-down with him and find out what he had been thinking and what was motivating the outrageous treatment of Vietnamese civilians by virtually every Marine he encountered. Corporal Bush was the Marine he was looking for. He worked in food services, which was where he got all the eggs. Bush outranked Zeke and he knew he needed to be careful about pushing the matter too far, but it was important to talk with him.

"Corporal Bush, I'm Zeke Hammond. I was the one who was driving the truck the day we ran into that trouble in the village, or as you call it, the ville, remember?"

"Oh yea, I recognize you. That was a hell of a firefight eh?"

"It was a hell of an egg fight that led to a firefight and people's deaths. I really gotta know … what the hell was that all about? I cannot get it out of my mind. Why did you guys instigate it; was there a tactical reason?" What am I missing here?"

"Well Hammond, since you're a new guy I'll talk to you. If you were not, I'd tell you to go fuck yourself for being so naïve. Here's the poop: we don't know who the enemy is. They dress like everyone else and there is no way to distinguish the good guys from the goblins until they start shooting. So we just assume that the majority of those we see, particularly young men, but sometimes women and children, are Viet Cong or VC sympathizers. We treat them accordingly."

"Okay, Bush, even if you're right, isn't it a war crime to start shit with civilians that way—not distinguishing enemies from friendlies?"

"Hammond, I don't even have to answer any of your questions. Who the fuck are you to be givin' me the Third Degree anyway? Better watch your tone of voice or you'll be cleanin' shitters instead of drivin' trucks."

"Been there, done that, corporal. I only want to know what you're thinking. I want to understand. If you're right, I need to know so I won't be making the wrong assumptions when I'm out in the middle of these people."

"Okay Hammond, I'll tell you a little story. I was a Grunt when I first came to Nam. If you think what *we* do is rough you should see what those VC animals do to our guys and to their own people, including women and children. Theirs is not a noble cause and they're not noble people. College pukes back home think the National Liberation Front and the North Vietnamese bastards are some sort of freedom fighters and we're the oppressors. That's all wrong. Americans don't torture women and rape children; VC and NVA do. Americans don't torture prisoners; VC and NVA do. Those bastards captured one of our guys, a splib dude from Memphis. Good guy. They hung him up on a tree and cut off his dick. They threw it to the dogs. He was screaming and bleeding for a long while until one of our snipers

107

crawled up and put him out of his misery, whacking a couple of those miserable VC cocksuckers in the process. I can still hear his screams. I'll never get it out of my head."

"Okay, Bush, that's awful and I understand what you're saying, but that doesn't explain why you assume *all* Vietnamese are VC and are doing that shit."

"Hammond, I'll leave that up to you to figure out. By the time your tour is done, maybe you'll understand."

"I don't think I want to understand. All this shit is nuts."

"Here's a word of advice, Hammond; don't get captured. Did you ever read about what the English did to heretics and political prisoners back in the 1500s? They disemboweled them. That's right, they cut open their stomachs and pulled out their intestines and fed 'um to the dogs while they were still alive. There's no greater pain that that. That's what VC do to South Vietnamese soldiers *and* civilians. Just imagine what they'll do to you as an American Marine if they get the chance. They'll start by cutting off your nuts and go from there. Are you gettin' the picture?"

"It's complicated," said Zeke. "They never told us about all that shit when we were going through training. We only got the broad strokes—about fighting Communism, freedom and such."

Zeke felt like puking. He thought if he ever even saw such stuff, let alone experienced it, he would go mad. *How could human beings do that do each other? What a world we live in. I guess it's always been that way.*

"Fuckin' A it's complicated," said Bush. This is the *real* world, boy. Now *di-di* on out of here and don't overthink it. Just kill 'um all and let God sort 'um out," he said with a sardonic smile.

## 19

# SLIPPIN' AND SLIDIN'

---

THE TRUCKS WERE A BLOODY MESS AND THE
SCENT ENVELOPED THE MOTOR POOL.

---

Zeke and a few other truckers were sent to a spot near Hill 327 to pick up a stack of VC that had been killed in a firefight with the Grunts. They were to transport the bodies to a gravesite where they would be catalogued by the South Vietnamese military and buried, probably in a mass grave covered with lime.

The sight of dead human beings that looked like they'd been put through a meat grinder was bad enough, but the smell was worse—worse than the decaying woodchucks that Zeke's dog used to leave on the front yard in the sun to ripen back on the farm. Carrion. The Grunts must have really kicked some ass because the dead were piled high and the ground was covered with blood and guts. The only way to deal with the mess was with humor … very dark humor.

After the initial shock wore off, the truckers formed a system where the bodies, or parts thereof, were dragged to two Marines standing by the tailgate. Those two would grab each end of the body, swing it back and forth to build momentum and toss it into the bed of the truck, one after another, all afternoon in the blazing heat. Two or three guys standing in the bed of the truck would arrange the bodies in neat piles to maximize space. This was accomplished without benefit of gloves or masks. The only Marines with gloves were those who got them from home. Zeke was fortunate enough to have a bandana—one of those big red ones that farmers carried in the back pocket of their overalls—to shield his nose from the smell. He had bought it at the hardware store in Dinglebury years ago. He tied it around his nose and mouth as tightly as he could, but his eyes still watered from the evaporating ooze.

The bed of the truck was slippery from all the blood and other fluids and the guys arranging the bodies in the bed of the truck had trouble keeping their balance. One of Zeke's close buddies, Rusty, slipped and fell into the center of the pile. He yelled, screamed, coughed and cursed to high heaven. He was a mess. He was the laughing stock of the work party. Zeke called him a necrophiliac and said he had fallen on purpose for sexual gratification. The comic relief was welcome. Some Marines took pictures of each other with a dead VC or their body parts; they had no qualms. After all, these were the enemy. They were trying to kill Marines and would have tortured and killed the truckers if they had the chance.

After dropping off the bodies at the appointed place and time, the Marines returned to the motor pool. There was no joy in their faces as they parked their trucks. They were covered with remnants of their work and smelled like a blended cocktail of blood, excrement, vomit, and sweat. The Marines thought they'd be contaminated forever and would never get that smell out of their nostrils and their minds.

The trucks were a bloody mess and the scent enveloped the motor pool when they arrived. Top Sergeant Singer happened to be nearby when the trucks rolled in and immediately took personal affront to the sights and smells of war. Singer took every violation of anything personally. He chewed out the drivers for not cleaning the trucks before they returned to the motor pool and for looking and smelling so gross. It was a Catch 22; the only place to wash out the truck beds without being shot at was the motor pool. Captain Tennille became involved and deescalated the situation when he told Top Singer that they should get a picture of themselves with all of us in front of the bloody trucks. It would make for a good war story at the Officers' Club.

## 20

# SPEEDING IN A COMBAT ZONE

"Guilty Without Consideration of Extenuating Circumstances."

Zeke hauled one-hundred pound 155-millimeter artillery projectiles from a multi-acre Ammunition Supply Point (ASP) to the DaNang air base for transshipment to Marine infantry units in the field. Truckers were expected to deliver their loads from ASP to waiting planes "without delay." There were speed limits on most of the roads around the DaNang area— thirty-five miles-per-hour or less, but truckers often found it necessary to exceed the speed limits to get their jobs done. If they were caught speeding by the MPs they would be in serious trouble. The MPs, overseers, monitors and micro-managers of all ranks gave serious work-a-day Marines almost more stress than did the enemy. Truckers had a name for them: Garret Troopers, a term of disparagement borrowed from Barry Sadler's record album, *Ballads of the Green Beret*.

One night Zeke was highballing a load of mortar rounds to a plane that was waiting to resupply a position held by elements of the South Korean Marines' Blue Dragon Brigade in the Central Highlands. The Blue Dragons were knee-deep in the shit, meaning they were involved in heavy combat, and were running low on ammunition. They were in danger of being overrun by the enemy and needed immediate help. Zeke knew that it was a life or death situation and made the twenty-five minute trip from ASP to the air base in less than fifteen minutes.

Zeke was just turning onto the tarmac toward the plane, engines running and ready to go, when an MP Jeep pulled behind him blowing a weak-sounding siren and flashing a little red light. Zeke stopped and walked back to the

Jeep to see what they wanted. It was dark and Zeke did not notice that one of the MPs was a lieutenant. He did not salute until he got close and saw the gold bars on his collar. The lieutenant was annoyed for Zeke's failure to salute quicker and for exceeding the posted speed limit. Zeke tried to talk his way out of the situation.

"Sir, may I remind the lieutenant that it is SOP to *not* salute in a combat zone because that form of public acknowledgement could identify command personnel and draw fire from a sniper?"

Zeke then told the lieutenant about the need for speed to get ammo to the Blue Dragons to help them win a battle with the NVA that was raging at that very moment.

Despite Zeke's protestations and rationale, he was cited for "Speeding in a War Zone While Hauling Hazardous Material" and for "Disrespecting an Officer by Delayed Salute." The citations sounded like something the MPs made up on the spot. During the time it took to cite Zeke, the plane that had been waiting for him took off. They had a partial load and could not wait any longer for Zeke given the intensity of the situation.

Zeke felt strongly that the charges were out of line, especially given the totality of the circumstances. Every driver in Heavy Platoon, even the staff NCOs, agreed. Zeke felt confident that Captain Tennille would agree with him and dismiss the charges with a figurative slap on the wrist and a mild rebuke. When Zeke entered Top Singer's office, Top scrunched up his face in his usual childlike pout and marched Zeke into Tennille's office, counting cadence for the seventeen steps it took to get there. Singer called out "Parade Rest" in a too-loud voice that made Zeke laugh to himself.

Zeke exhibited a contrite, respectful demeanor. He tried to show remorse and demonstrate that he took the matter seriously even though he saw the whole thing as unreasonable and inappropriate. He was naïve. The circumstances did not matter to Captain Tennille or Top Singer. Neither did Zeke's exemplary record in the Corps. To them, everything was black and white; no shades of gray. He was found "Guilty Without Consideration of Extenuating Circumstances."

Zeke put a spin on the ticket and the Office Hours and made jokes about how it probably ruined his chances to become a general. His fellow truckers were as frustrated about the outcome as he was and it dampened Heavy Platoon's morale for a while. In Zeke's mind, the whole affair was just another example of mixed messages about the war. The external enemies were the NVA, the VC and their sympathizers, corrupt South Vietnamese officials, the Soviet Union, Red China and anti-American movie stars. The internal enemies were politicians who created unreasonable Rules of Engagement and a percentage of career Marines that treated their men with utter contempt and disrespect in so many ways and not using common sense in the context of Vietnam. Maybe the war protestors and conscientious objectors back home were right—the Vietnam War was an unnecessarily stressful and untenable situation at many levels.

# 21

# SIAM

After three months in country, Zeke went to Bangkok on R&R, not because he needed to rest and recuperate, which is what the term R&R meant, but because the opportunity arose. He wanted to party with clean women and see Siam, the name that Zeke liked to use instead of the country's modern name, Thailand. He loved the movie, *The King and I,* and wanted to see what it was like since he was on that side of the world anyway and might never have the chance again. He also wanted a tattoo like those on the arms of most Marines at the time. However, his tattoo was going to be *different*—no Eagle, Globe and Anchor, no bulldog with a helmet and certainly no Death before Dishonor; that one required twenty-inch biceps. He wanted a hybrid that reflected the Marine Corps and Vietnam with a patriotic backdrop, something that would be so unique he would have the only one like it in the world.

Marines were encouraged to budget $100 per day for R&R. With Hazardous Duty Pay and Combat Pay added to his regular paycheck, Zeke had saved enough. *Wouldn't it be nice if guys on R&R got a per diem, maybe twenty dollars? It's not like the government doesn't have the money. What a great way to say thank you for not running away to Canada and for volunteering to risk their lives in the cause of freedom and all that jazz.*

Zeke's friend, Aaron, was serving with Heavy Platoon in Chu Lai, sixty miles or so southeast of DaNang. They were doing the same things, but in different areas of operation. Aaron's promotion to PFC in ITR, obsequiously earned, had helped him move ahead. He had recently received a promotion to lance corporal. Zeke was happy for him and called him a "lifer" in jest, suggesting that Aaron might become a career Marine since he had done so well in such a short time.

Aaron and Zeke had written to each other and hoped they could figure out a way to get together in Vietnam or on R&R. There were rules about eligibility for R&R but unit politics played a part in getting approval. Aaron's request was turned down. Zeke was disappointed. Aaron was a douche bag in many respects, but they had gone through a lot together—Parris Island, ITR, Montford Point and Camp Lejeune. They were home-boys of sorts. Zeke missed him.

Zeke wrote to Aaron telling him "I'm gonna drink ten gallons of beer, get a tattoo and boom-boom twenty women," promising to send him a picture of each girl he met. He'd even send Aaron a picture of his new tattoo once the ink dried. Zeke did not see "keeping company" with Charlotte the Harlot as cheating on Sharon. He saw it as simply exchanging body fluids—nothing more than taking care of primal biological needs. *Don't mean nothin'. It's just sex; not love,* he told himself.

Upon arrival in Bangkok, servicemen were given an R&R booklet. On page 2, they were warned to behave themselves or Thailand could withdraw its "invitation" to American servicemen to visit their country. *Fat chance,* thought Zeke. *These people are making a fortune with this R&R gig. War is good for their economy.* The only thing that would stop Thailand, Japan, Malaysia, the Philippines or Australia from being R&R sites was if all the Charlottes went on strike or disappeared.

Zeke selected the Golden Palace Hotel and hooked up with a driver for hire named Urda who chauffeured him around in a quaint little foreign sedan. Urda steered Zeke to the best nightclubs, restaurants and tourist attractions and made sure he had ample female companionship to satisfy his every whim. Urda tried to double as a tour guide, but his command of English was marginal and he was difficult to understand, sometimes giving Zeke a laugh in the middle of one of his explanations.

Zeke placed third in a dance contest, toured the Temple of the Reclining Buddha and visited the Bangkok Zoo where he was pictured with a Boa Constrictor around his neck. He kept company with three different women each day—for breakfast, lunch and dinner—and was having a blast.

Urda drove Zeke to a sleazy out-of-the-way section of Bangkok near a smelly polluted river crowded with sampans. They went up to the second floor of a flimsy building and met a tattoo artist that looked like one of those martial arts movie actors, crazy eyes and all. Zeke selected a template and asked the artist if he could hand print the words "Bangkok" and "Vietnam" on the banner and "U.S. Marines" across the top. The artist went to work. No machines—everything was drawn, colored and printed by hand. After a couple hours, it was done. Zeke thought he was probably the only person out of a global population of over 3.4 billion at that time sporting a tattoo exactly like that.

That night, Urda took him to a bar where he met a nice young woman. They were enjoying drinks and conversation when a fight broke out between three or four Marines who were also on R&R. The nice young woman snuggled up to Zeke and whispered that she didn't like Marines because they were too wild, crazy, loud and crude, or something to that effect, but she liked *him* and suggested they leave. When they got back to the Golden Palace, she spotted Zeke's new tattoo and let out a groan, slapped her forehead and mumbled something in Siamese that did not sound very polite. He went out of his way to prove to her that Marines were not all the same; some were even better.

✪ ✪ ✪

Between rounds of self-indulgence, Zeke did some soul-searching. Driving a truck was honorable work. It was somewhat fulfilling and sometimes dangerous with snipers, land mines and VC seemingly everywhere, but it wasn't exactly what he had in mind when he joined the Marine Corps. He felt that he was missing something. He even felt guilty knowing that Marines just like him were scattered all over the northern part of South Vietnam, out there somewhere fighting the good fight and being killed or wounded. He felt he should be there with them; maybe they needed him.

It also troubled him that he had not encountered leaders that respected the rank-and-file. He felt he was under the thumb of a bunch of old men who had forgotten how to be *real* Marines or did not understand that context is everything and common sense is needed in war. For the most part, he saw them as nothing more than bureaucrats living vicariously off the glory and reputation of brave Marines who had preceded them throughout the Corps' 191-year history.

Zeke was not sure what to do so, just for the hell of it, he solicited Urda's input over a dozen or so Singha beers. Zeke was pleased with Urda's grasp of the situation. *This guy's really got his shit together. He really understands. Or else he's just being an obsequious shit-stick telling me what he thinks I want to hear.*

"What's the worst thing that could happen, Zeke? You could be killed, right? But you could get killed driving a truck too, right?

"Right on both counts, Urda, but there's a higher probability of being killed, wounded or captured if you're a Grunt. And the working conditions are pretty harsh," Zeke said with a smile.

"You should go for what your heart tells you to do—what you will look back at with pride many years from now."

Urda was speaking slowly with eyes half-closed like a Zen master. He sounded more articulate and made more sense to Zeke the more Singhas they drank.

Based on Urda's profound advice and his own internal voices, Zeke vowed to find something else to do that would be more exciting, meaningful and more directly involved with the war as soon as he returned to Vietnam from R&R. He was pumped, which made him horny. He jumped into Urda's car and off they went to sample more of Bangkok's delights.

The trip back to DaNang from Bangkok was nerve-wracking. The plane flew over Cambodia and Laos and approached DaNang from the west. The pilot announced artillery fire below and the need for evasive action. This made no sense to Zeke. The plane was five miles high. *Artillery? Nonsense. Does he mean anti-aircraft missiles? Maybe.* It would be quite a coup to bring down a plane loaded with American servicemen. *What an undignified way to die—shot out of the air while returning from an orgy in Siam.* The pilot flew aerobatic maneuvers—sixty degree angle turns, high G-force assents and steep and rapid descents—to avoid possibly being hit. This went on for about ten minutes until everyone was ready to puke. Shortly thereafter, they began the normal descent into DaNang. Everyone was happy to touch down. *Better to die on the ground than be splattered over miles of Vietnamese countryside for the pickings. It would be even worse, to live through the crash and be captured and tortured.*

When Zeke got back to Heavy Platoon, his fellow truckers gave him good-natured guff about his tattoo. "You're a lifer, Zeke. You *love* the Marine Corps. You've bitched about the Corps every day and then you get a Marine Corps tattoo? What a hypocrite."

"Are you aware that the enemy pays bounties for tattoos skinned off servicemen, dead or alive, and you've now made yourself a valuable target? You'd better wear long sleeves. One of these Gooks will cut off your arm for a tattoo like that."

"Wait a couple more days. You'll probably get blood poising or infection; maybe the black syphilis."

And so forth. Zeke had no regrets and only a mild concern about the bounty issue. The words of Corporal Bush came back to him. He could only imagine what would happen when the VC spied his tattoo if he ever fell into their clutches.

✪ ✪ ✪

Zeke picked up the mail that had come to him during his absence in Bangkok. There was no correspondence from Aaron. Zeke had expected a reply to his last letter. Zeke went ahead and sent him a note with the promised pictures from Bangkok. Zeke was still having an endorphin rush from his R&R experience and it was a very spirited letter. He closed the letter by telling Aaron that they should try another attempt at out-of-country R&R together later in their tour or try to arrange in country R&R together at China Beach.

Almost two weeks went by and there was no reply from Aaron. Zeke sloughed it off as a normal byproduct of the distractions of Vietnam and assumed he would hear from him eventually. Finally, Zeke received a letter from Sharon telling him that Aaron had been killed—both legs blown off at the hip. He had run over a land mine while driving in a convoy heading north to DaNang from Chu Lai.

"He was going to look you up and surprise you. Aaron and Fat Sue had talked about marriage when he returned home. She is beside herself with grief. She suffered a breakdown of some sort and had to go to the hospital. It was awful."

When Zeke read those words, he could not stand and could only mumble a few words at a time before running out of breath. All the adventures and misadventures with Aaron flashed through his mind. He sat down on the sand looking up at the sky trying to hold back the tears. *My God, they will send his belongings, including his letters, home to his parents. They'll see the pictures I sent him from Bangkok.*

"You got me back, Aaron," yelled Zeke, still looking up at the sky, "for all the bullshit stuff I pulled on you. Your parents will give the letters I sent you to Fat Sue and she'll probably turn around and let Sharon read them. They'll all see the pictures of those Siamese Charlottes I sent you. Very funny! You're having the last laugh, aren't you shithead?"

Zeke chuckled at the irony and to deflect his attention from the horror. He got on his feet, looked up at a passing cloud, snapped to attention and rendered a slow, precise hand salute. "Go with God, brother. *Semper Fidelis.*"

## 22

# COMBINED ACTION

---

"Because I spent my time with the boys; now I want to serve with the men."

---

"I need volunteers for Sniper School and for the new Combined Action Platoon," announced the company gunnery sergeant. The gunny bore a striking resemblance to Nigel Green, color sergeant in the movie, *Zulu,* with the exact same moustache and the lilt in his voice. At that time there was a push to add snipers to Marine infantry units and men were also needed for CAP as part of a counterinsurgency program whose operational model was "winning hearts and minds" rather than search and destroy. Either one, sniper school or CAP, represented a good opportunity for Zeke to change direction.

After talking to other rank-and-file Marines, who did not know any more about sniping or "CAPing" than he did, Zeke went to see Gunny Green and volunteered for CAP. He figured being a sniper was a virtual guarantee of death or dismemberment, but CAP seemed just the right balance of action and purpose—serving and protecting the good Vietnamese people from the bad Vietnamese people.

Had Zeke chosen sniper school, he would have found himself on Hill 55 in the company of Carlos Hathcock, a.k.a., *Du Kích Lông Trắng*—"White Feather" in English. Gunnery Sergeant Hathcock was the most famous sniper in Marine Corps history at that time with hundreds of *self*-reported kills and 93 confirmed kills, some of which were at extraordinary distances under daunting conditions.

121

Zeke had killed forty seven woodchucks over varying distances on the farm using a Marlin lever-action .22. He was also a Marine Sharpshooter. Aaron had stood near Zeke grab-assing (busting balls) when he was requalifying with the M14 rifle at Camp Lejeune. This jinxed him out of a possible perfect score, just missing the Expert level by a few points. Zeke would have been a good sniper, but CAP seemed more intriguing.

Getting into CAP was the same as applying for a job. Zeke was interviewed by a staff sergeant and a first lieutenant. He was made to stand at Parade Rest while responding to questions about his skills, experience, how his participation in CAP would be received by his family and girlfriend, why he wanted to join CAP and so forth. They asked Zeke if he had kin in the military. He told them about his progenitor who had retired from the Marine Corps two years earlier and his second cousin, Farnam, who was an Air Force pilot and headed the Strategic Air Command. He dug further back in his family history and talked about his great Uncle who had fought with the Fifth Marine Regiment at Belleau Wood during World War I and his great, great grandfather, Amos Moses, who had served as a Hessian soldier in the revolution.

Zeke got his information all screwed up, but it portrayed him as coming from a family with good military and patriotic values. The lieutenant thought he would push Zeke a little on one of his points.

"Hammond, do you realize that Amos fought on the *wrong* side? The Hessians were Germans who fought for the British in the Revolutionary War. They were ruthless, aggressive, barbaric, elite soldiers who put the fear of God in their enemy."

"Yes sir, just like Marines, sir," Zeke blurted out with pride.

The staff sergeant turned to the lieutenant who had asked the question and whispered with a smile, "I guess he got you there, sir."

The staff sergeant asked some additional questions about Zeke's training and to list any special qualifications he might have. Zeke proceeded to reel off his skills and training, which were impressive, but standard in the Marine Corps. The interviewers were amused to hear Zeke talk about his training as if it was something out of the ordinary for Marines. However, when he told them about how he could kill a woodchuck at 500 yards with a .22, his Fifteen Minutes of Fame at the Parris Island rifle range, and his virtual Expert status out of Camp Lejeune, they appeared impressed.

"Okay, Hammond," said the lieutenant, "we'll concede that you're a good shot, perhaps a *great* shot, but tell us why you want to join CAP?"

"Sir, I want to help the Vietnamese people in their fight against Communism and make South Vietnam safe for democracy."

The staff sergeant shook his head and stared directly into Zeke's eyes. "Hammond, cut the shit. You are doing that already in your present capacity as a truck driver. So what is there about CAP that intrigues you? Are you a 'John Wayne' type? Wanna kill Commies for Christ? Tell us straight up, Marine."

Zeke had become more annoyed as the interview progressed. *These assholes seem to think they'd be doing me a favor by bringing me into the CAP. Fuck 'um. I'm doing them a favor by offering them a good hand.* He thought he would just tell them the truth and let the chips fall where they may.

After a pause, Zeke paraphrased a line from Marine icon, General Chesty Puller. He stared back into the eyes of the staff sergeant and articulated his response slowly and firmly: "Why? Because I spent my time with the boys; now I want to serve with the men."

He knew he should have stopped with that sentence, but he couldn't. He was on a roll. "I joined the Marine Corps. That's right, I *joined*. I *enlisted*. I was *not* drafted. No one had to force me to join. I wanted to be a Marine and I wanted to go to Vietnam for one purpose—to help the South Vietnamese people in their fight against Communism. If I can't do that then you-all need to send me the fuck home."

The silence was deafening. Zeke had taken the air out of the room with that bold, salty response. *Now they'll put me in jail for standing up for myself and being a man. Screw it all.* At first, both interviewers stared at Zeke expressionless with jaws clenched.

"You talk to all your superiors that way?"

Zeke did not reply. He stood at attention, eyes front, feet at a forty-five-degree angle, thumbs along the seams of his trousers. He had spoken his piece. After a few moments of tense silence, their expressions gradually turned to smiles as they nodded their heads. Zeke passed the test.

Zeke moved to a CAP site being built on bright white sand northwest of DaNang. He started "making a difference" by filling sandbags, building bunkers and trenches, and running concertina razor wire around the perimeter of the compound. He patrolled and guarded the local ville and the surrounding area with other Marines and Vietnamese Popular Forces (PFs). PFs acted as a home guard or local militia of sorts. They were not part of the Vietnamese Army, but could kick ass, often as well as any ARVN soldier. ARVN was an acronym for Army of the Republic of (South) Vietnam.

Zeke's mother, Naomi, sent Care Packages to Zeke to share with the PFs calling them part of her extended family. Care Packages were boxes of food from home, which usually included baked goods, cigarettes, canned fruit, canned milk and other treats not ordinarily available to Marines. Zeke liked the PFs; they were like having a bunch of little brothers. He would often take pictures of them and have copies made for their families. He once took a picture of several of the PFs and a couple Marines posing together. To Zeke's surprise, one of the PFs in the picture quietly opened the gate one night and let VC insurgents into the compound to wreak havoc. The VC *qua* PF and some of his compatriots were killed and some CAP members were injured, one fatally.

The CAP assignment included infantry work, actively patrolling and sometimes supporting infantry operations in the area. On one of Zeke's day patrols, the group marched to a nearby ville that VC had reportedly infiltrated. As they neared the ville, they observed a gaggle of Navy Seabees grab-assing in and around the hooches. They had driven there from a construction site; obviously for some afternoon delight with Charlotte the Harlot.

As the heavily armed Marines silently took positions around the perimeter of the ville the Seabees became angry. Their fun was over. Zeke took cover near a Seabee truck and brought his rifle to bear on the entrance to one of the hooches. An arrogant Seabee with the name Thomas stenciled on his pocket and wearing insignias that looked like he might have some rank approached Zeke.

"What the fuck is going on? Why are you Jarheads here? These people are friendlies. Why don't you guys go find some real enemy?"

Zeke replied in a tight-jawed manner, staring directly into Thomas's eyes without blinking:

"Everybody in this fuckin' ville is VC or their sympathizers and you and your boys are about to die if you continue to stand there with your thumbs up your asses much longer. I suggest you *di-di fuckin' mau* ASAP!"

Thomas was skeptical and replied with a smirk and real meanness in his voice.

"You Jarheads are some stupid MFs. This ville is secure; VC high-ankled out of here long ago. Typical Marines—overreacting. Dumb shits as usual."

Thomas was laughing contemptuously as he shook his head and turned his back throwing up his hands in mock disbelief. At that moment, an enemy bullet tore through one of his upstretched hands, a bullet that had been meant for Zeke. The hand disappeared in a burst of blood. He spun around and looked at Zeke in terrified disbelief. Maybe he thought Zeke had shot him. Several more shots rang out from an AK-47 rifle opening Thomas up from stem to stern. Zeke returned fire toward the rifle flashes and silenced the AK.

VC popped out of the doors and windows like cockroaches shooting at Zeke and the Marines as they ran. Zeke set his rifle on "rock and roll" (automatic) and wasted two of the cockroaches as they scrambled out of a hooch heading straight for him, AK47s in hand. His shots lifted them off the ground, right out of their Ho Chi Minh sandals. They morphed from fearsome enemy to amorphous lumps. *How different they look when life goes out of them—like balloons without air,* Zeke thought.

As it turned out, the Seabees had decided to take their boom-boom break at the same time as the VC. Two of them had been killed; three were wounded. Marines had killed nine VC and taken three captives. The image of the Seabees and the VC sharing the same women at the same time was enormously funny to the Marines. Their laughter echoed in the distance as they marched away.

## 23

# NHỮNG GI QUÁI!—WTF!

THE MARINES' RESPONSE WAS AWESOME IN THE
CLASSIC AND SERIOUS MEANING OF THE WORD.

New guys, a.k.a., newbies—those who had just arrived in Vietnam— were always a question mark. Although they were well trained in simulated combat settings, they had not proven they could hold the line under stress. That's why "F" (fucking) was added to the new guy abbreviation. FNG was a pejorative.

Zeke was assigned perimeter guard in a sandbagged bunker along with two other Marines, a fellow from Nevada and an FNG named Clifton who had just set foot in Vietnam that morning. He was obnoxiously hyper-vigilant—too many questions; too much random movement. He was wearing his bullet-deterring flak vest and helmet (neither one of which could stop a direct hit) all buttoned up and strapped tight. He continuously swept the area in front of the bunker with his locked and loaded M14 pointed out the opening into the blackness as if he was expecting an attack at any moment. He seemed too scared to notice that he was the only guy acting that way. Everyone else was cool, calm and collected. They were experienced and knew when to worry and when to relax.

"Clifton, where are you from," asked Zeke.

"Kentucky, home of the Flip-Top Dumpster." He was actually proud to be from a place where the claim to fame was garbage dumpsters.

"You drafted or enlist?"

"Drafted."

"Figures. That means you didn't *really* want to be in the Marines; you had to be forced to join," said Zeke with a knowing nod to Nevada who jumped in with his own questions.

"Seriously man, why are you so jumpy? You get off the plane at the wrong stop or something? Didn't you know you were coming to the 'Nam? This is Marine country and Marines don't act like you. It's bad luck. You need to get your head and ass wired together before you kill yourself or one of us. Look at you—you're locked and loaded, your safety's off and your finger's on the trigger. If you even fart, you'll send off a round into outer space and it will drop on one of these kids who come up to the line asking for food. If that happened we'd have to kill you and bury you where the kid died. It's Vietnamese law."

"Really?" Clifton responded with a note of fear.

"No. Fuck no. Can't you tell when you're being played with? Hyperbole, get it? We're exaggerating for effect to make sure you understand things."

By that time, Zeke could see that the ballbusting was taking its toll on Clifton. "Okay, chill out man. Everyone has a first day in Vietnam. We all did. After the first day, you get use to it. No sweat. We've got your six, brother."

"What's 'got your six' mean?"

"Good grief man, don't you know anything? Think of a clock with 12 being your front and the opposite side, 6, being your back. We've got your back; your six. Now, do you know what 'got your back' means?"

"Yea, thanks guys. I don't know what the fuck is the matter with me. Sorry."

With that, Clifton took his finger off the trigger and switched on the safety. He seemed to appreciate Zeke's calming words.

After a few minutes of silence, Clifton asked "bet you guys see a lotta action out here, eh?"

Zeke could not resist.

"You bet. In fact, we have VC sneaking up close to the wire and tossing grenades at us almost every night. If you see anything suspicious out there in the dark just keep your eyes focused directly on it. Don't even blink. If you see movement of any kind, fire as fast as you can and do not stop firing until you hear an 'all clear' over the radio. Keep reloading and firing as if your life depended on it … because it does."

Zeke knew from experience and training that everything seemed to move at night, especially if you kept staring at the object. It was an optical illusion caused by stress, fatigue, fear and failure to scan properly just above the horizon to catch movement out of the corner of the eyes. Zeke knew if this FNG followed his advice he'd "see" an enemy behind every rock and bush. *Who knows, maybe there will actually be a VC out there and he'll have something to write home about.*

Clifton had first watch and seemed to be a nervous wreck despite Zeke's attempt to calm him down. He was sweating abnormally and he kept fidgeting—changing his position, checking his ammunition magazines, taking aim, adjusting his helmet, scratching his ass and other obnoxious things. After an hour or so, Zeke had enough and walked out the opening in the back of the bunker with a cautionary comment to Clifton:

"Don't aim your weapon south in my direction. I'm goin' to take a leak and I don't wanna die with my dick in my hand with pee all over my boots."

Clifton thought that was funny; Zeke was serious.

"Which way is South, Zeke?"

"You're either stupid or a wise ass; I don't like either. Just look out the opening in the front of the bunker. That's north. Aim your damn weapon that way. Scan 180 degrees left to right and back again. If anyone is going to sneak up on you, it'll be from that direction. This is a free-fire zone. If you see anything move, shoot it."

A few yards away from the bunker Zeke turned to judge the distance from his position to the outside of the concertina wire in front of the bunker. He pulled out a hand grenade and limbered up with it like it was nothing more than a heavy baseball. Somehow, he had a special talent for throwing grenades; he could throw them a mile, so to speak. He had learned to do that at Camp Geiger. When he was warmed up, he pulled the pin and threw it, stiff-armed, over the bunker and beyond the concertina where it fell into a drop-off in the sand and exploded. Zeke quickly picked up the pin and the ignition spoon, shoved them into a sandbag and darted back into the bunker.

To Zeke launching the grenade was a slow-motion affair. It seemed to take a long time to reach its destination, but it was only about five seconds from pin pull to detonation. The grenade had exploded with a deafening shock wave and blinding light. Zeke knew that if he threw it just right, the drop-off would absorb the shrapnel. He had considered how Marines in the other bunkers around the perimeter would respond and assumed they would see it as just another minor encounter with the enemy, no questions asked.

The sound of the grenade exploding startled everyone up and down the line. Every Marine responded with perfect interlocking fields of fire designed to "neutralize" any threat that might be out there. Everyone but Clifton. He was doing the "pray and spray"—holding his M14 above his head shooting everywhere without aiming and praying he would hit something. Illumination mortars filled the sky. The M60 machine guns opened up from every third bunker and the .50 caliber machine guns opened up from the towers on each corner of the perimeter. The Marines' response was awesome in the classic and serious meaning of the word.

Coincidentally, a VC all gussied up in his best black insurgent clothes and carrying a sniper rifle that was as long as he was tall, had been out in front of their position, probably 500 yards to the north. He and an iterant water buffalo had been out past the motion detectors. Both were killed in the mayhem. Everyone laughed when they found out about the VC. They imagined him sitting there in the dark thinking he was secure, about ready to do some long-distance damage when a thousand M14 rounds came speeding his way at over twenty-seven-hundred feet per second. His last words must have been *những gì quái!* WTF!

The chain of command examined the hole in the sand left by the "explosive device." They had no evidence that it was a grenade since there was no pin or spoon to be found. They were puzzled, but declared it a *bona fide* sneak attack. Everyone accepted this conclusion except the Sergeant of the Guard. For some reason, he had doubts. Zeke had a run-in with this sergeant the previous day. He had asked Zeke to put out his cigarette after he had just lit up. Zeke made a benign wise crack about wasting a Pall Mall Gold 100 "luxury length" cigarette as he tossed it in the sand and crushed it out with his foot. Zeke had received a carton of those exclusive elongated cigarettes from Naomi and he took one more puff before he tossed it. Something about the extra inhale rubbed the sergeant the wrong way and he upbraided Zeke about his attitude.

After the "attack" the sergeant came to Zeke's bunker to inspect the hand grenade box. It was a meaningless exercise because no one knew how many grenades there were to start with. And it was a wonder they even worked since their date stamps made them older than the guys in the bunker. Clearly, the sergeant felt something was amiss, but Zeke wasn't worried. Feeling harassed by this guy, and since no one else was nearby, Zeke challenged the sergeant to a fight.

"If you've got a problem with me, sarge, take off your stripes and let's settle it man-to-man. Otherwise knock off the petty bullshit and stop being such a ball-buster for no good reason."

"Hammond, I'd oblige, but if I laid a hand on you I'd lose my stripes."

"You'll never lay a hand on me. You'll be the one on the sand cryin' for his mama."

There was some more sputtering at each other and the sergeant left. Zeke spent the whole night worrying what might unfold in the morning. Would the sergeant report him? Would an issue be made about the number of grenades? As he was leaving the bunker at sunrise to return to his hooch, Zeke saw the sergeant walking toward him at a distance. *Oh shit!* The sergeant stopped in front of him, looked him in the eye and said simply, "If you ever act stupid with me in front of the men or play anymore 'take off your stripes' games, I'll have your ass hung from the gun tower, do you understand?"

"Yes, sir. Sorry I acted stupid. I guess I was just shook up because of the close call by my bunker." Zeke was relieved and extended his hand to shake.

"Don't call me sir, I work for a living." The sergeant smiled, shook his hand and walked away.

That was the canned response when an NCO was called "sir," a title reserved for officers. It implied that officers didn't work and enlisted men did. It was a good-natured cliché that told Zeke he was off the hook.

The supposed attack on Zeke's bunker created a buzz among the brass and the enlisted men for several days. How had VC gotten that close without detection? How did they get away given the Marines' quick and deadly response? What did they use, a grenade? If so why didn't they toss it into the bunker opening and kill the guards? The speculation was endless and fruitless. The After-Action Report portrayed the event as a full-scale VC attack that was thwarted by bunker Marines and an infantry unit that covered the sky with illumination mortars. In the process, a sniper was neutralized before he had a chance to inflict casualties using his Starlight scope.

The Meritorious Unit Commendation ribbon was awarded to all the Bunker Marines, staff NCOs and officers, whether or not they were present during the "attack" and response thereto. The incident gave everyone something to brag about to their friends. Zeke made up a story that one of Clifton's bullets had killed the sniper and he would now be entitled to a Bronze Star for Valor. Clifton believed Zeke's jive; his eyes opened wide and a big smile came across his face.

"Really, Zeke? You mean I'm a hero?"

"Clifton, you did well last night. You didn't shit your pants, roll up into a prenatal position or show cowardice, but you did show weakness by shooting all over the place instead of maintaining your cool. I hereby declare that you are no longer an FNG, but you have got to get your head and ass wired together, okay?"

"I really like you, Zeke. Thanks for taking me under your wing. I may make it through this whole Vietnam shit after all."

Clifton was goofy, but likable. He reminded Zeke of Aaron; he even resembled Aaron.

"We got your six, Marine. Don't worry about it. You may end up being a hero before you get out of here. You got thirteen months ahead of you. One day at a time."

24

# GOODBYE LITTLE DOT

SHE WAS CONSIDERED "COLLATERAL DAMAGE" AND
WOULDN'T BE COMING HOME WITH ZEKE.

During the day, it was relatively peaceful along the bunker line except for occasional sniper fire from somewhere way out in the dark hills covered with trees and vegetation to the north or west. Occasionally a bullet would hit its mark and do some damage, but few Marines were killed.

At dusk, when Zeke and the bunker Marines showed up to assume their positions at the perimeter a group of kids would greet them just outside the concertina wire waving and begging for "chop-chop," a term they used for food. The kids spoke Pidgin English; they were charming, cute and usually well mannered. Zeke always had something from his C-ration box to give them. He sometimes pulled pogey bait out of his Care Package from home. He did not know about Operant Conditioning theory at the time, but he was applying it every day by using food to shape and reward begging behavior.

The youngest of the bunch was a cute little girl. She was shy at first and wouldn't reveal her name. The other kids chimed in and told Zeke that her name was Dot. It was something else in Vietnamese, but it sounded like Dot; that was close enough. She was adorable. When they saw her picture, Zeke's three little sisters wrote back asking him to bring her home. They were serious. *Great. Another urchin to live at 240.* He chuckled at the idea. *Always room for one more, I suppose.*

Every evening at the same time, the kids stood in front of Zeke's bunker on the outside of the wire, waving and calling to him with delight. Zeke would wave back, banter with them and hand out food to each one. As the

133

sun went down, the kids knew they had to *di-di* because they were in a free-fire zone—anything moving after dark was fair game.

Things broke down when one of the boys decided to sneak into Zeke's bunker during the day, when it was generally unoccupied, to help himself to an extra ration of chop-chop. The kid snaked his way through the concertina wire, hopped over to the empty bunker and dug up the care package that Zeke had hidden under some sandbags. When Zeke and the guys showed up they found the remains of the care package and small footprints through the concertina leading to the bunker. It was an amazing feat to have negotiated the razor wire … and unnecessary. All the kid had to do was show up as usual and he would have gotten his share. Instead, he got greedy and risked losing his life.

Zeke stormed out through the gate, gathered all the kids in a School Circle and raised holy hell with them. Had the tower guard spotted them their little bodies would have been shredded. Marines manning the corner towers were under strict orders to open fire with their .50 caliber machine guns on anything or anybody that attempted to breech the wire at any time, day or night, no exceptions. Zeke told the kids that they were little thieves and stealing from his bunker was "Number 10," meaning very bad, especially after he had been so kind to them.

More worrisome was how anyone could sneak through the concertina and enter a bunker, sight unseen. If a kid could do it then so could the VC. Zeke wanted to know which boy was the thief and insisted they fess up. A boy named Tan raised his hand timidly; tears were forming in his eyes. Zeke took a picture of him and threatened to send it to the QC. He did not intend to do such a thing; he just wanted to scare all of them and discourage such a thing in the future for their own good.

QC was shorthand for *Quan Canh*, a.k.a. White Mice, the South Vietnamese Army's Military Police. They wore white helmets, white gloves and other white accessories, hence the nickname. Just the threat of QC involvement scared Tan. He promised to be good, blubbering through a stream of tears. He seemed more upset about losing Zeke's friendship than anything else. Zeke hugged Tan and the others gathered around for some hugging as well, especially Dot. She was very upset about the whole affair and had tears running down her cheek. Zeke wiped her face and gave her a kiss on the forehead.

Having made his point with the kids, Zeke was about to hand out Ham and Lima C-rations he had squirreled away in the bunker when a Vietnamese man beamed up behind him. He was wearing what looked like a black bamboo vest over a black shirt, black shorts and the customary coolie hat. He looked like a VC poster boy. His presence out of nowhere startled Zeke.

"Marines, never let anyone sneak up on you under any circumstances. The enemy should never catch you by surprise; it could cost you your life."

That had been a constant refrain in training. Zeke had been so preoccupied with the kids that the man had slipped up behind him undetected.

"Dừng lại!" yelled Zeke, signaling him to stop as he slipped his rifle off his shoulder and flipped it to the ready in a quick circular motion. Practiced Marines could perform the slip-and-flip maneuver in less than one second. The man stopped short and looked terrified.

"You give me chop-chop?"

The man held his hand out, palm up. His face was weathered and his smile revealed a gold tooth sparkling in the sun.

At the same moment, Dot yelled "cha" (daddy) and ran toward the man with a big smile on her face, a .50 caliber round from the nearby corner tower struck the man squarely in the chest. The sound of the impact was extraordinary as was the result. The bullet went straight through him and came out his back leaving a hole the size of a softball. There was blood and tissue all over Zeke and the kids. The man was knocked flat turning the white sand red as he bled out. The kids started crying and screaming uncontrollably. Zeke threw himself on Dot to protect her, but it was too late; the big .50 caliber bullet that tore through the man's body had hit Dot in the throat, nearly decapitating her. Both *Cha* and Dot were dead before they fell to the ground. Zeke and the other guards nearby had hit the deck with rifles at the ready. *What the fuck?! Why?!*

For a second, Zeke aimed his M14 at the guard and wanted to shoot him for killing his little Dot. Someone loudly yelled, "cease fire" several times. Zeke threw down his rifle and picked up Dot's lifeless body, her blood dripping over his hands onto his clothes and boots. He couldn't believe what had just happened right before his eyes. Zeke laid Dot's little body on the sand and vomited as a gaggle of officers and enlisted men rapidly converged on the scene. Zeke was in shock. He couldn't stand or walk; he just sat down next to her, expressionless. He couldn't talk or hear anything anyone was saying to him. His ears were ringing. He felt like going absolutely crazy, but didn't. It was as if he had a built-in circuit breaker that automatically tripped to prevent overloads and protect him from melting down.

The tower guard had seen the VC-looking man approach and became suspicious so he watched him through his binoculars. He mistook the shovel strapped to the man's back for a weapon and when he saw Zeke flip his rifle as if to defend himself, he lit him up, as the expression went. As it turned out, the man was not an enemy soldier; he just looked like one. He was Dot's father.

The guard was "held harmless." Killing is not murder in a war zone if a clear and present danger is perceived. He was just doing his job, it was said, even though it was broad daylight and there were other Marines and kids in the line of fire. Dot was considered "collateral damage" and wouldn't be coming home with Zeke. Her family was compensated for her death and the death of her father by the U.S. government and the incident was closed. The kids took off never to return, their "hearts and minds" lost to America forever.

# 25

# THOUSAND YARD SQUINT

IT CONSISTED OF NAUSEATINGLY BRIGHT WHITE SAND;
A BAD COPY OF THE GREAT SALT LAKE DESERT.

During Zeke's time away from Heavy Platoon, the war escalated. The Marine Corps juggled people and units to put more manpower in the northern part of South Vietnam, at or near the Demilitarized Zone (DMZ), to deal with increasing threats from the NVA. The DMZ separated North and South Vietnam just south of the 17th parallel and was an area of intense fighting and heavy casualties on both sides throughout the war. Experienced truckers like Zeke who were already in country were in short supply; he was one of those juggled. He was recalled to Heavy Platoon to resume Day Trippin'.

Zeke was glad he had volunteered for CAP. It had opened his eyes to other aspects of the war and provided some unforgettable experiences, both good and bad. He had lost weight, "adopted" kids at the bunker, killed and captured a few goblins and matured considerably in the process. But he was also glad to be returning to Heavy Platoon. The timing was right. The murder of Dot and her father, which is how he saw it, *murder*, was fresh in his mind. He had lost enthusiasm for "winning hearts and minds" and wanted to vomit at the sound of the slogan.

Zeke had also witnessed too much "chicken shit," a term for excessive or unnecessary regulation, which constricted combat effectiveness and undermined morale. Zeke had *wanted* to go to Vietnam and had been willing to give his life for his country if need be. Now all he wanted to do was get out in one piece. He was more worried about going to the Brig for some inadvertent violation of the Rules of Engagement than being killed. *I'd rather be dead than in jail*, he thought. Ironically, within the year he would not give either one of those options a second thought in his quest for vengeance.

✪ ✪ ✪

The bunker Marines saw Zeke packing his seabag and wondered what was up. Nevada and Clifton were concerned and started asking questions.

"Zeke, where you going, man? You look like you're gettin' ready to *di-di* on out someplace. You leavin' us?"

Zeke saw the question as an opportunity to be a wise ass and have some fun. *Everybody could use a few laughs right now.*

"Yup. I've been selected for a secret mission with the CIA because of my demonstrated effectiveness in working with the indigenous people."

"Hammond, you are so full of shit it's coming out your ears. What the fuck is going on?"

"Okay, here's the truth: I'm going to be a member of the Dogpatch Town Council representing circumcised rank-and-file-Marines. I'll be your collective bargaining agent and fight for lower prices and cleaner working conditions."

The guys laughed as though that was the funniest thing they ever heard. They hadn't had much to laugh about recently and seemed to be making up for lost time. They loved the double-entendre about cleaner working conditions. "Come on, Zeke, enough bullshit, what's going on?"

Zeke became serious. "I'm going back to Day Trippin'. They need truckin' fuckers like me to help the Grunts win the war. Listen up, if you guys need anything—anything at all—just get in touch with me. Truckers have ways of granting wishes," he said with a smile. "And for God's sake, take care of yourselves. I don't want to read about you as KIA or some other bullshit in *Stars and Stripes*. The Marine Corps, the Vietnamese and the protestors back home won't give a shit if you get killed, but I will!"

They stared at each other in silence with knowing looks.

"That's an order!"

It was a good-natured order; they were all about the same rank. They laughed, shook hands and exchanged sincere goodbyes. Men did not hug each other back then, especially Marines. And they certainly never cried. The handshakes, good-natured shoulder taps and the reserved banter was as much emotion as they were going to show to hide the pain of knowing they would probably never see each other again. Zeke had built a strong bond with those guys and was going to miss them. Well, maybe not all of them. He sure wouldn't miss Wray.

✪ ✪ ✪

Wray was completely *dinky dau*, a colorful term for crazy, whacky, or mentally ill. He would have been a good poster boy for the Marine Corps had he been normal and had a makeover. As it was, he was more of a poster boy for the *Peanuts* character, Pig Pen. Wray showered and shaved only once a week. He smelled bad and left his scent everywhere he went. His actions would have been understandable had he been a Grunt on a long operation in the jungle, but Wray didn't have that excuse. His utilities and cover (cap) were dirty, faded, frayed and unkempt. His hair was long and tousled and his face was generally dirty. Guys avoided shaking hands with him; they assumed he didn't wash after a sit-down at the shitter. They were correct.

When the guard fell out to take their shifts at the bunkers, Wray would bellow out insulting remarks about the Marine Corps and sing songs he made up about Lifers. He would even curse God and flip Him the bird. A couple times a day at random, Wray would assume a pious Jimmy Swaggart-like demeanor, eyes closed and arms raised, and chant "Ooooodin" in a loud, bloodcurdling voice giving praise to Odin, a god in Norse mythology.

Three dogs were attempting to copulate near the mess hall early one morning. They had become locked together and were trying to disengage in different directions. It must have been painful because the dogs yelped, barked and whined at a high pitch for quite a while. The noise disturbed Wray. Something about the pitch and the pain bothered him immensely. He burst out of the hooch with his eyes almost crossed in rage and marched quickly toward the dogs. At about forty yards, he stopped, drew his M1911 pistol and blasted the dogs with all 8 rounds. Every shot hit its mark. The three dogs were dead, still stuck together. Everyone in the area had hit the deck and assumed tactical positions thinking they were under attack. It became eerily quiet as Wray replaced his ammo magazine and holstered his pistol. Considering it was "just Wray" and considering the dogs really were a nuisance, everyone stood down and went back to their business.

It was remarkable how much Wray did with impunity. He didn't seem to be attached to any unit or report to anyone. He was in total violation of most every rule in the book, yet he was left alone. There was a clear double standard when it came to Wray. Zeke did not appreciate Wray's madness at first, but in time the shock wore off and his antics became funny. It was good to be friends with Wray. During the monsoons when it was cold and damp, Wray got Zeke a lined field jacket, an item that was otherwise virtually unavailable to the rank-and-file Marine. Even truck drivers could not get field jackets. Only his god, Odin, knew where he got them. On the other hand, if Wray didn't like a guy or felt slighted or disrespected by someone he'd urinate, perhaps defecate, on their racks, usually under the pillow.

Wray sold American dollars on the black market. The enemy would pay a premium for American greenbacks because the dollar had more value in purchasing weapons from suppliers who were sympathetic to the Communist cause. A VC or VC go-between would transact the exchange with Wray who would then send his profits back home to his grandmother. She would stash the money and send him more greenbacks to sell. Wray and grandma made a lot of money, as did others. What Wray was doing was immoral and illegal. In effect, he was helping fund the enemy. He was outed somewhere along the line, court martialed and sent to the Brig for aiding and abetting the enemy. Zeke wondered if Wray's money exchange had anything to do with why he got a pass on his outrageous behavior. *Were higher-ups benefiting in some way? Nah.*

Heavy Platoon had been placed under the auspices of the 1st Marine Division. Their regimental name had been changed and the unit was relocated to a big white sand lot called Red Beach a few miles west, as the crow flies, from where Marines first stormed ashore in South Vietnam over a year earlier. Red Beach looked like a bad copy of the Great Salt Lake Desert and was bounded on the north and west by high hills and mountains making it an easy target for rockets and mortars. Zeke thought it was a dumb place to build an encampment, but he hadn't been consulted.

The white sand was blinding, sometimes debilitating, on a hot cloudless day, especially without sunglasses. Officers were issued sunglasses, but enlisted men had to obtain them from local peddlers or arrange to have them sent from home. There was a catch: because the glasses were not standard Marine Corps issue enlisted men found themselves in violation of the UCMJ, Section 6, Paragraph 4, "Wearing Unauthorized Shades in a Combat Zone," and deemed "out of uniform," the consequences of which were Office Hours. Marines who forwent sunglasses developed a "Thousand Yard Squint." Most of them probably developed premature cataracts in later life from their eye-melting time at Red Beach. Zeke, on the other hand, weighed the tradeoffs between blindness and Office Hours and sent Sharon some money to get him a nice pair of extra dark Ray Charles Edition wrap-arounds. Nobody noticed.

Zeke reported in to Heavy Platoon wearing a helmet and carrying his M14 slung over his shoulder and weighted down with ammunition and hand grenades. He had other junk in his seabag: canteen, thermos, mess kit, first aid kit, rain poncho and Peter Pan green underwear. He had a carton of Pall Mall Gold 100s from home tucked under his arm. He was dirty, hungry and tired. Top Sergeant Singer greeted him with a scowl, the same angry look he showed to everyone he outranked. That schmuck had not changed a bit.

"Well, well, look who is back with us. It's the speed demon—Zoomin' Zeke. You got Office Hours a while back for drivin' crazy, didn't you?"

Instead of rehashing the whole speeding-in-a-combat-zone fiasco and risk saying something he shouldn't, Zeke replied, "No, Top, that wasn't me. That was another guy named Zeke; he rotated back to the states."

"You're full of shit. You're that same Zeke. I'd know you anywhere."

Singer's silly scowl and pseudo-gruff voice amused Zeke—so much, that he had to suppress a laugh by pretending to cough.

"What the fuck is so funny, Marine?"

"Nothing, Top Singer. It's just a cold I caught from being out in the Monsoons without a blanket, field jacket or anything to stay warm except C-Ration heat tabs. I sure never expected Vietnam to be cold, but the monsoon season is a bitch."

"The Marine Corps never promised you a rose garden," said Singer as he turned to walk back to his air-conditioned office.

*Holy shit, the dumb ass turned my harmless comment into a negative. What a complete jerk-off! How did this fool ever become a first sergeant? He must have kissed a lot of ass; looks like the type.* Top Singer turned to look at Zeke as if he had read his mind. *Oh crap, did I say that aloud? What is he, a mind reader?*

"Oh, by the way, Hammond, you'll be on night duty until further notice. Tomorrow, get your license endorsed to drive a BAT. I want to see you on the road dusk till dawn every day, beginning tomorrow night."

"Will do, Top," replied Zeke, but one question, if I may?"

"You may not," responded Singer.

Zeke ignored Singer's response and asked his question anyway. "Top, what's a BAT in the context of our conversation?"

"You'll find out, in the *context* of driving one, Hammond. Now go find yourself a hooch and settle in. Number 240's got some empty space."

*Oh, come on; 240 again? It can't be. What's with this number? Why does it keep coming up?*

"Top Singer, did you really say 240? I'm superstitious about that number; just want to make sure."

"Two Four Oh, Hammond, that's 240 in English. Get your ass moving."

✪ ✪ ✪

The Red Beach living quarters consisted of numbered ten-man buildings called "hooches." The derivation of the term hooch was unclear. Zeke assumed it meant "not quite a house." The term applied to both Vietnamese and military abodes. Marine hooches were rectangular tin-roofed wooden structures with doors at both ends and screened all the way around. They rested on wood supports a couple feet off the sandy ground. Hooches were built a few feet above the white sandy ground in neat rows. Esthetically pleasing, but defensively inadequate foxholes were constructed adjacent to each hooch. They were too shallow and too exposed to be useful in the event of a firefight or rocket attack.

Zeke trudged a couple hundred yards in the deep, hot white sand and found Hooch number 240. He dropped his gear, fell to the floor, leaned his head back on his seabag and closed his eyes; he was exhausted. A couple Marines in the hooch set up a cot for him up in a vacant space. He thanked them by tearing open his coveted carton of cigarettes and throwing a pack to each man. One of the guys opened a bottle of stashed whiskey and passed it around as they smoked Zeke's obscenely long Pall Malls and told war stories. *I think I'm gonna like Hooch 240.*

# 26

# BAT MEN

The escalating war increased the need for logistical support. Heavy platoon and other motor transport units were called on to carry more, travel further and move quicker. Speeding in a combat zone was no longer an issue unless it was truly excessive or reckless. Heavy platoon ramped up their efforts to support the war by traveling further from Red Beach and doing so with higher capacity trucks. They were put on convoy duty taking war materiel directly to hotbeds of fighting.

To meet demand, Heavy Platoon attached long flatbed trailers to the back of the 5-ton trucks by means of dolly converters. This new 26-wheel configuration boosted carrying capacity to more than thirty tons. The 26-wheelers were nicknamed BATs—Big Ass Trucks. BATs were slow on take-off, took longer to stop, required more load and unload time, took more finesse to go around corners and make turns, and were maddening to back up. Because they carried more cargo, BATs were more susceptible to confrontations with the goblins, ranging from hooking cargo off the tail end of the long trailer to hijacking at the point of a gun. Truck driving became significantly more dangerous.

The next morning, Zeke practiced driving a BAT around the motor pool. The greatest challenge to driving a BAT was backing it up. The BAT configuration had two pivot points, one at the trailer hitch on the back of the truck and another at the point where the trailer connected to the dolly converter. Rather than turning the front wheels of the truck in the opposite direction the wheels had to be turned in the *same* direction, but at a slow enough speed to avoid discombobulation ... and embarrassment. Truckers that could not maneuver a BAT around the crowded streets of DaNang, back into a loading dock or up a ship's loading ramp were disqualified from driving them.

Zeke was deemed qualified to drive a 26-wheeler and received a stamped endorsement on his military driver's license. He had joined the small circle of BAT Men, as they called themselves, and was happy, despite his concerns about adding complexity and potential trouble to his life. BAT driving was a character builder and prestigious, at least among motor transport types. It was said that any Marine could shoot a rifle, but few could take a 26-wheeler through its paces. BAT drivers half-seriously thought they should get a special badge in recognition for their skills. They joked that if they ever got a medal it would be a Purple Drive Shaft with a Barbed Wire Cluster in the shape of the Batman TV character.

Top Singer was trying to teach Zeke a lesson of some sort by turning him into a night BAT driver, but the lesson was lost on Zeke. He was grateful to Top Singer for the assignment. It was a challenge and he loved it. It was not as hot, it was less hectic in terms of people and water buffalo and there were fewer micromanagers to interfere with the mission. As a result, things were done quicker and better. There was a greater chance of encountering the enemy at night, but that did not concern Zeke. For him the drawback was the circadian rhythm thing. Night truckers took off near dusk and returned at dawn. Trying to sleep in the sweltering open-air hooches during the busy, noisy daytime was difficult, sometimes impossible.

Zeke heard there was an exquisite Charlotte selling services in one of the fancy French-built structures near DaNang's main street. He took advantage of the time it took to load his BAT at the harbor to pay a visit to the lovely woman he had heard so much about. It was his first visit to a Charlotte in Vietnam and he thought it appropriate to find the best one he could. He felt guilty about it since he knew Sharon would not be pleased, but he was sure she would understand under the circumstances.

He made arrangements with one of the other BAT drivers to take care of his truck if he wasn't back before it needed to be moved, then hailed a cyclo cab—a three-wheel bicycle taxi—and off he went. Zeke took his rifle and tucked himself tightly inside the cyclo. He did not want to be caught by the MPs or meet up with VC. About half way to the house, it occurred to him that his size 11 Jungle boots, prominently displayed on the footrest, might reveal his identity as a big-footed American. He turned his feet inboard to make them look smaller.

To Zeke's surprise, when he arrived at the house he found Charlotte sitting in a large open room with five young Vietnamese men sitting at a table. There was a canopied bed with dark privacy curtains on the opposite side of the room. It looked like a comfortable copulation kiosk. Zeke suspected the guys might be VC even though they were friendly and talkative. He thought it prudent to play along and not start trouble. Charlotte tried to convince Zeke to remove his clothes and put his rifle away. He did neither. Instead, he made a loud display of cycling his rifle for action. As he and Charlotte disappeared behind the curtains, he pointed the weapon toward the men at the table and put his finger on the trigger. It was becoming clear to Zeke that the whole thing was a bad idea, but he had gone this far and didn't see a graceful way out.

Zeke was distracted by the loud Vietnamese jabber coming from the nearby table. It was hard to focus and took more time than usual. As Charlotte and Zeke saw stars together, he jerked the trigger sending a 7.62 round into the back of one of the guys at the table. Zeke pulled out, jumped up and plowed through the curtains, tearing them off the canopy. The other men at the table were scrambling, yelling and screaming like banshees. It looked as though one of the men had a weapon. Zeke had his M14 set on "rock and roll" for automatic fire and opened up in their direction as he backed out the door.

When Zeke returned to his BAT at the harbor, he was a mess. The other truckers wanted to hear the dirty details, but Zeke just mumbled and said it was nothing special; not worth the risk. As he began to think more clearly, he began to see that he had put himself in harm's way, big time. The men at the table could have been VC, but they also might have been South

147

Vietnamese military or police. Everyone seemed to be armed and they all looked alike. He vowed to himself that he would never, *ever* be that stupid again … at least for a while.

# 27

# THE BOYS IN HOOCH 240

HOOCH 240 HAD CHUCKS, SPLIBS, AN ASIAN-AMERICAN
AND A PUERTO RICAN. ALL WERE MARINE CORPS GREEN.

There were no boys or kids in the military in Vietnam yet the media and anti-war moment kept referring to them as such. Marines and other fighting men in Vietnam hated that expression. It was a demeaning and transparent attempt to create an image of them as children to be pitied for antiwar purposes. The ages of the men in Hooch 240 ranged from 18 to 25. None of them were *boys.*

Hooch 240 was a tribe unto itself. The men blackened the seams that ran vertically down the back of their jungle boots with a magic marker to show they were part of 240.

"It's a 240 thing; you wouldn't understand" was their reply when asked why they all marked their boots that way.

Rank played a part in how the hooch was run, but generally the School Circle system was used to discuss issues and solve problems. In boot camp, the School Circle was called and controlled by the Drill Instructor. In Hooch 240, anyone could call a School Circle and everyone had an equal voice. Once an issue was discussed, a vote was taken and the matter was dealt with in accordance with the majority wishes of the hooch members. It was a democracy in its purest form.

Hooch 240 did not have issues with skin color or differences, *per se.* Unfortunately, the majority of splibs that arrived at Heavy Platoon in 1966 and early 1967 were draftees, many with chips on their shoulders. The Marine Corps began conscripting men for the Vietnam War in late 1965.

Marines who enlisted considered themselves a step above draftees because they self-selected to join the most challenging branch of the service on their own volition rather than forced in through the induction process. Enlistees *wanted* to be Marines; draftees did not, it was assumed. While there were exceptions, it was a common perception that the draft introduced riff-raff into the Corps that would not have otherwise been there causing dissention and weakening mission effectiveness.

Splibs self-segregated, just as they had done at Camp Geiger. They were hostile toward non-blacks, chucks in particular, and failed to step up for dangerous or unpleasant jobs the way other Marines did. Their attitudes and behavior created tensions that undermined teamwork and camaraderie— essential aspects of what made the Marines special. Some splib draftees loudly proclaimed that the white man was their enemy and not the yellow man. There were rumors of fragging (killing) of white Marines by blacks, which caused white Marines to watch their backs in mixed settings. It added to everyone's burdens to worry about whether a growing number of knot headed draftees would fight *with* them or against them in a combat situation. That was not supposed to happen in the Marine Corps, but it did.

There were ten Marines in Hooch 240: six chucks, a couple splibs, a Japanese-American and a Puerto Rican. All ten were Marine Corps green and discounted color or any other characteristic that was not germane to their role and mission in Vietnam *if* it was reciprocated. FNGs that showed up and didn't feel the same way were encouraged for find lodging elsewhere.

✪ ✪ ✪

Each of the ten men had interesting stories, backgrounds, predilections and idiosyncrasies. Their names were Redbone, Sergeant Bear, Gyp, Buford, Jorge, Gums, Tom, George, Wilber and, of course, Zeke. A few were particularly interesting.

Redbone was a splib and had enlisted in the Corps. He came from the Watts section of Los Angeles and went through the riots of 1965. He was not particularly race sensitive and did not play the race card. Like a true Marine, his allegiance to God, Country and Corps came first. Redbone would have put his life on the line for the men in Hooch 240, as they would have done for him.

Sergeant Bear was also a splib. When Bear reported to Red Beach, there had been no space for him in the sergeants' hooch so he was referred to Hooch 240. Bear had an easygoing way and a smile for everyone. He showed respect and was friendly with everyone, although he was quite capable of being assertive when it mattered, but without being an asshole. Marines didn't even think about Bear's skin color. He was a Marine Corps sergeant they would follow and support in any situation.

Gyp was an okay guy most of the time, but had a habit of defecating on persons, places and things that displeased him. It was his way of communicating ultimate contempt and disrespect. He was nicknamed Gyp, short for Egypt, because his *modus operandi* was a prominent pile of leavings in the shape of pyramids wherever and whenever he felt the need to "make a statement," as he put it. He suspected all Vietnamese as being VC or NVA, if not actively then tacitly. He disliked most officers and staff NCOs as well. He liked Zeke and a few others, but that was all.

Gyp snuck into the staff NCOs' office one dark night, squatted over the gunnery sergeant's electric coffee pot and added a long, smelly pyramid to the remains of the coffee from the previous day. He then added water, moved the pot's setting to "bold gourmet" and turned it on. He could imagine the conversation in a few hours when dawn broke: "Hummm, coffee tastes kinda shitty this morning, gunny. Bold gourmet?"

It didn't take much for Gyp to change over from prankster to killer if the conditions were right. A civilian Vietnamese handyman hired by the Marine Corps came around one day to nail loose boards on the hooches— tap, tap, tap. Gyp was a night driver and had just fallen asleep. He ignored the incessant tapping as long as he could, but finally broke. He rushed out of Hooch 240 completely naked, which was an acceptable way of sleeping given the daytime heat, grabbed the handyman's hammer from him and proceeded to beat him with it—tap, tap tap. Other night truckers who were also trying to sleep whistled and clapped in support.

"You are an annoying VC hammer-fucker. *Mau lên, di di mau*—get the fuck out of here. If you come back with that goddamn hammer and lay down even one tap, I will strangle you and run over your body with my truck, *hiểu không*? Understand?"

Problem solved. No more tapping. No backlash. Nobody saw nothin'.

Gyp discovered a Vietnamese boy on the bed of his truck one night trying to steal something. He put a stop to the thievery with one blow to the kid's head with a tire iron. Gyp had snuck up so slowly and quietly the boy never knew what hit him. He had not meant to kill him, he said; just scare him. When Gyp came back to the motor pool, he pulled up next to the officers' shower vat—a large open container of water on a tall stand—and threw the body over the top with a gentle splash. When the vat was refilled, the tanker driver just stuck the hose up over the top and never looked in.

"Sure are a lot of minerals in this Vietnamese water" he heard an officer say.

Another officer replied, "smells like sulfur or something. Hard to get clean."

Gyp wondered if they would ever check the vat. Until then, he laughed whenever he saw an officer heading for the shower.

Buford, a chuck from Tennessee, presented himself as a badass; a tough guy. He was a little taller than most and believed his height was a proxy for physical prowess. He spoke white trash jive, a language unto itself, and seemed perpetually and obnoxiously angry. He had a bug-eyed crazy look, missing teeth, a cauliflower ear and a deviated septum, all of which punctuated his image as someone to avoid.

Buford didn't have a lick of sense when it came to Charlotte the Harlot. He contracted some form of STD—Sexually Transmitted Disease—because he took no precautions; no *post*-cautions either. He did not have the self-discipline to forego "riding bareback," as they called it. Marines in Hooch 240 had told Buford that the "secret" to disease-free sex in Vietnam was a prophylactic (even a sandwich baggie would do) and a post-coital douse of alcohol or, absent that, gasoline from the truck. No lips, no tongue, no fingers and, for sure, no back-door entrances. Unfortunately, he interpreted all the "don'ts" as "do's" and sampled every possible form of sex imaginable with some of the most frequented and least hygienic Charlottes in Dogpatch. Once the Marines in Hooch 240 got wind, literally, of Buford's predicament, they gave him a lot of guff about being careless and stupid.

For the Marine Corps, contracting an STD was *ipso facto* evidence of violating a lawful order to stay out of the villages and Dogpatches unless on patrol or other official business. Even a hint of the smell of Dogpatch on a Marine's utilities or breath was enough circumstantial evidence to be found guilty of violating the order. Office Hours and STD were a steep price to pay for three minutes of pleasure.

A garbage truck came around to the hooches periodically to pick up trash, clean out the pit where Marines burned their letters from home and sanitize the French Drains used as open-air urinals. The driver was a black lance corporal named White. He had a sidekick, a Vietnamese civilian who wore an ill-fitting pith helmet. Everyone called the civilian "Pith" which correlated with his function and his hat.

White and Pith stopped to pick up the garbage and clean the piss tube adjacent to Hooch 240 one day and Buford felt compelled to make a noise like a jungle bird. White interpreted that noise as a racial slight and came across the sand in a huff wanting to know who made the call. Buford walked up to White and Pith and made another bird call, this time directly in White's face. The fight was on. Buford danced about nimbly with a style and demeanor reminiscent of 19th Century gentlemanly fisticuffs. White cleaned Buford's clock in two minutes giving him a bloody nose and black eye. Marines that witnessed the fight let out yells and catcalls aimed at Buford followed by derisive laughter. "Way to go. You sure showed him, Buford."

"You're the man, Buford. Where'd you learn how to box, from the Women Marines?

And so forth.

The next day, Hooch 240 held a School Circle around Buford and made him an offer he couldn't refuse.

"Don't bring unwanted attention on the hooch by being a jerk, getting STDs, and picking fights with fellow Marines. We don't tolerate that racial shit from splibs and we sure as hell don't want to hear it from chucks either, especially from Hooch 240."

Buford had disrespected the hooch and his fellow chuck Marines. It could not happen twice. Buford began to protest, but the matter was closed. Zeke had grown disgusted and reinforced the group decision, "Get your head and ass wired together, bro, or we'll trade you to the VC for something we can use." This brought some mild laughter from the guys, but Buford didn't laugh. He knew Zeke spoke for everyone in Hooch 240 and he wasn't kidding.

Tom was a Marine of Japanese ancestry. His father had served with the U.S. Army's famed 442nd Regimental Combat Team in Europe during World War II. Fellow marines kidded Tom about being a VC spy and spoke to him in pidgin Vietnamese, which he accepted as good-natured ballbusting and just part of being a Marine. However, when Vietnamese assumed he was one of *them* and began talking to him in their language, Tom clarified his citizenship and nationality aggressively with a string of curses and epithets bordering on assault.

Tom's claim to fame was performing ventriloquist shows with his penis (covered in his skivvies, of course). He would move his penis and say funny things in a strange little voice that gave the appearance of a real person or thing talking under the skivvies. He had a real talent. Zeke told Sharon that he was going to put on a show like that for her when he got home.

Mickey was only twenty years old, but had lost most of his teeth and did not wear dentures. Fluoridation of public water to reduce tooth decay became a policy of the U.S. government back in 1951, but Mickey's community had opposed it, calling it a Communist plot to poison the population. As a result, everyone in his hometown had bad or missing teeth, which gave them a Zombie-like appearance. Mickey's nickname was Gumster; Gums for short.

Gums was very military—always clean, pressed and squared away as if stationed at the elite Marine Corps Barracks in Washington, D.C. Singer and Tennille loved it and awarded him *Truck Driver of the Month.* The rank-and-file truckers were unaware that such an award existed and wondered what Gums had done to receive such a distinction. They made some jokes about how he might have put his gums to good use on Singer and Tennille to get the award.

Most truckers thought of themselves as equally proficient and did not want to receive any such award or recognition that would put them at odds with their fellow truckers, especially based on unknown criteria. They dubbed the award DOM, pronounced *dumb,* to express their frustration with the process. DOM recipients were shunned for being "kiss-asses" or "lifers. The DOM process, created without much thought, introduced a level of competitiveness and divisiveness that undermined unit cohesiveness. It was phased out in a few months.

Senior NCOs and officers appreciated Gumster; he was promoted to corporal. Hooch 240 *really* gave Gums hell then. Some were envious, but most were happy for him. They continued to deride him for a while in a friendly sort of way, accusing him of being Singer and Tennille's House Mouse (servant). It was all in fun for most. He ignored the remarks and responded with a laugh and a friendly quip. Everyone liked Gums even though they did not appreciate the basis of his success.

Gums knew his DOM award and promotion to NCO did not sit well with Hooch 240 and he had enough sense to avoid becoming a "junior jerk-off," as the rank-and-file called new corporals. He was diplomatic and knew how to handle people. Men felt they were working *with* Gumster and were appreciated. He was one of the few among the NCO or officer ranks that showed them respect and acted as though their existence mattered. In a short time, Marines in Hooch 240 addressed Gums by his rank and acknowledged the legitimacy of his promotion. Like Bear and like Clifton, the newbie bunker Marine, Zeke and everyone in Hooch 240 would have his six if the situation arose.

Jorge occupied the space across from Zeke in Hooch 240. He and Zeke were assigned a truck run to a Navy base called Tien Sha, a frequent destination across the river east of DaNang. Dusk was looming and Zeke and Jorge were standing by their trucks near a warehouse grab-assing as their trucks were being loaded. Without warning, the whole world seemed to blow up right in front of them. There was a colossal explosion with a blinding orange light that clouded their vision and made their ears ring with pain. It swept them up like helpless dolls and threw them to the ground. They couldn't move and thought for a moment they were dead. They could not see or hear and were disoriented for what seemed like a long time, but was only a few seconds.

Shots rang out from the Navy guards walking a post around the warehouses. The shooting brought them to their senses. The guards seemed to have a bead on the source of the explosion and were all firing at the same spot in the adjacent ville. Jorge stared at Zeke with a puzzled look.

"Get your shit," meaning grab your rifle and join the fray.

"No, the Squids got it covered," said Jorge.

Zeke could not believe Jorge's reaction. *Didn't want to fight? Worried about the Rules of Engagement?* Whatever Jorge's reason, it seemed cowardly for two Marines to hunker down and let the Navy guys do all the work.

Zeke grabbed his M14 and dashed toward the fence line using the front of the warehouse for cover. He saw the Navy guards' direction of fire and spotted the muzzle flashes of the enemy's return fire. The guards were firing down from their elevated wooden walking post. They had no cover and were sitting ducks. Zeke set the selector switch on his M14 to rock and roll and emptied a twenty-round magazine in a matter of seconds. He executed a combat reload, replacing the empty magazine with a fresh one, switched the selector back to semi-automatic and took careful aim at any remnants of resistance.

As things were dying down, Jorge came trotting up on Zeke's flank with rifle in hand ready to engage. The guards were still shooting sporadically, but the skirmish was over. Jorge never fired his weapon. He froze at the Moment of Truth—that nanosecond when a man has to take the life of another human being. It was the worst possible thing a Marine could do in a combat situation and grounds for expulsion from the Corps.

Jorge and Zeke received accolades from the guards for coming to their aid. Their commander expressed appreciation and promised to send a note about the action to Top Singer and Captain Tennille. A squad searched the ville and found only blood trails. It was a hit-and-run, a typical VC tactic. The enemy used civilian hooches for concealment and women and children for cover to show they could engage and disengage at will, when and where least expected.

A forty-pound box bomb had been planted and detonated near one of the guard towers. The orange flash, the eardrum-breaking sound and the concussive effect were nauseating. A couple hooches had been leveled and the warehouse was heavily damaged by large pieces of shrapnel. Two Navy guards were dead and three others were wounded. Two civilians had been killed; one was a little boy. It was a mess. *Hope it wasn't my bullets that killed the civilians,* Zeke thought, as the words of Sergeant-of-the-Guard Watkins came back to him about how collateral damage (accidentally killing civilians) could be used against Americans in the propaganda war. At that moment, Zeke did not care about propaganda.

Jorge appreciated the Fifteen Minutes of Fame from the Navy commander and began thinking there might be a medal in it for him.

"Zeke, do you think we rate a Purple Heart for our cuts and bruises?"

Thinking about a Purple Heart in this situation was sinful in Zeke's mind. "Are you kidding? That was bullshit; it was nothing. We'd be the laughing stock of the Marine Corps for even suggesting our scratches are Heart-worthy. You should get your ass kicked for even thinking about such shit. By the way, where the fuck were you when the shit hit the fan anyway, under your truck pissing your pants? Some Marine you are!"

Jorge looked dejected. Zeke was disgusted.

When they returned to Hooch 240, Zeke called a School Circle around Jorge and recounted the action. Jorge had showed reluctance to engage the enemy and failed to support a fellow Marine and hooch-mate in a combat situation. Both offenses were intolerable.

"Imagine if that happened with cops back in The World? They'd be fired! I recommend a vote of 'No confidence in Jorge and move for displacement."

Displacement was a sanitized term meaning Jorge was "fired" from Hooch 240 and needed to find another home. The question was called; it

157

was unanimous. Jorge had turned out to be a shitbird and knew he had no choice. It was an offer he couldn't refuse.

After Jorge left Hooch 240, he was selected for Mess Duty. Word came down that a giant roll of Saran wrap fell onto his hand severing the end of his pinky finger at the last joint, clean as a whistle. Jorge had lost his pinky during the Second Indochina War while helping make South Vietnam safe for democracy. He would probably wear a store-bought Purple Heart when he got home.

George looked like Dennis the Menace's father from the television series. His gift from God was the ability to draw and paint exact images on canvas of whatever came to his mind, or whatever anyone suggested. He never took an art lesson. He was a natural illustrator. He didn't draw caricatures either. He could make *exact* reproductions with nothing more than paper and a pencil.

George helped Zeke with a special art project. It was monsoon season and impossible to stay dry for any length of time. Some of the canvas tops on the trucks were missing and it was like driving a convertible with the top down in a hurricane. Zeke was particularly annoyed that his jungle boots were so porous. A wet body was one thing, but wet feet were particularly exasperating. His feet were constantly wet, which made him empathize with Grunts who continuously sloshed around in rice paddies and sometimes got emersion foot, a.k.a., jungle rot.

Zeke could not remember his feet ever getting wet back home on the farm when he wore his "Sears' Best" rubber hunting boots with the thick soles, not even in the winter when the snow was deep. He sent a letter to his grandmother, Velma, asking her to send those boots to him in Vietnam. Velma thought the request was a bit odd ("Don't they give you boots to wear?"), but dutifully boxed them up along with some pogey bait and sent them across the ocean as requested. When Zeke received the boots, they did not look as rugged as he remembered. They were pea green with a one-inch yellow stripe around the sole and heel. *Oh well. Anything to stay dry*, he thought.

Zeke asked George to draw a set of toes on the end of each boot, which he did with perfection. George noticed a small puncture on the top of the right boot and drew a band-aid over it as if to cover a wound. *God, what talent!* Everyone in Hooch 240 admired George's artwork and dared Zeke to wear the boots to Heavy Platoon's evening formation.

"I'll wear them one time if you guys don't call a School Circle and banish me for disrespecting the hooch or give me any shit about it."

"Come on, Zeke, we won't give you any shit. It would be a hoot. Besides, Singer and Tennille are so dense, I'll bet neither one notices," said Gyp.

At first Zeke balked, he knew it was a dumb-headed thing to do, but decided to wear them to send a passive-aggressive message about the inadequacy of government footwear.

As they stood in formation at attention, feet at a 45-degree angle, Sergeant Bear spied Sears' Best on Zeke's feet and did a double take. Bear resided in Hooch 240, but had not seen the artwork until then. He understood Zeke's penchant for making foolhardy passive-aggressive "statements" when something about the Marine Corps pissed him off. Bear sauntered over to Zeke and said in a low voice, but with command presence, "Zeke, get your ass back to your hooch and take those fucking things off; don't ever let me see you wear those boots again."

Zeke made a weak attempt to explain, but Bear cut him off in mid-sentence. Zeke left unusual tread patterns in the sand and made squishing flip-flop noises with the boots all the way back to the hooch. Once again Sergeant Bear earned the appreciation and respect of Hooch 240. He handled Zeke's lapse of judgment without overreacting.

Zeke took the order literally and made sure that Bear never *saw* him wear the boots again. He wiped off the magic markered toes and band-aid and wore them only when the monsoons hit hard and when he was far away from meddlesome NCOs. Within two weeks, the boots were ruined. They had slices and punctures galore; they were no better than going barefoot. He tossed the boots into the garbage. A few days later, he saw Pith wearing his boots. They were all patched up and Pith had a big smile on his face.

Wilber was the oldest Marine in Hooch 240. He was twenty-four, five years older than the average age of a Marine in Vietnam at that time. Marines called him "old man" and made good-natured fun of him for his antiquated name. Wilber thought they were jerks and said so, but always with a smile. The guys in Hooch 240 showed their affection for Wilber a couple times by placing unflattering signs on him after he fell into deep sleep. They took special delight in making jokes about the name of his hometown—the Village of Intercourse in Leacock Township near Lancaster in Pennsylvania Dutch country. It was an accepted fact in the Marine Corps that the more kidding a man received, the more he was liked. Wilber got a lot of crap; he was well liked.

Wilber wrote to his hometown deejay requesting a tape of one of his shows. A couple weeks later, Wilber received the requested tape along with a personal message from the deejay. In a classic radio voice, he said America supported and appreciated Wilber and his fellow Marines and prayed for them to be careful and come home in one piece. It was a sobering message—the first time the guys had heard appreciation for their presence in Vietnam from anyone outside of their families.

Wilber's tape was interspersed with commercials, weather reports and news, the sounds of music and life from America—a welcome touch of home. Music had changed since they left the states. They cringed at *Snoopy and the Red Baron*, *Winchester Cathedral*, and such, but *really* liked Merle Haggard's *I'm a Lonesome Fugitive* and Frankie Valli's rendition of *Can't Take my Eyes off You*. It made them homesick. There was a dark side to the tape and the news blurbs they had been sent. The Marines learned about the anti-war movement and heard their Baby Boomer counterparts were now calling them all "baby killers." Apparently, a growing segment of America was protesting the war and against *them.*

"Good God, did you hear that?" said Wilber. "Those cock-sucking bed-wetters are opposing us. Wait till the enemy hears that. A lot more guys are going to get killed because of that shit."

## 28

# FOX IN A BOX

---

THANKS TO THE GUYS IN HOOCH 240 SHE'D PROBABLY
BE ON THE INJURED RESERVE LIST FOR A WHILE.

---

When Wilber turned twenty-five, the guys in Hooch 240 really razzed him. He was already considered old at twenty-four, relative to them, but twenty-five made him grandfatherly, or so they said. Hooch 240 held a School Circle and decided to give him a special present for his birthday, one that he would never forget—a date with a Charlotte known as Dogpatch Diva, jokingly said to be voted Most Enthusiastic Boom-Boom in Quang Nam Province—all expenses paid and delivered right to his cot.

Zeke volunteered to pick up Diva on his evening BAT run, put her in one of the cargo boxes and haul her back to Red Beach around midnight. He would be seen as returning for night rations at the mess hall and there would be no suspicion about his being back on base with a fully loaded truck at that hour.

Diva lived in one of the Dogpatches off the beaten path. Zeke knew he would have some explaining to do if he was stopped by the MPs. They would want to see his Trip Ticket and he'd have to explain what he was doing so far from his assigned destination. But the thought of the look on Wilber's face was enough to motivate Zeke to take all the risks necessary. Diva was beautiful and her unique moves and sounds were so unusual and satisfying that she was in high demand and commanded a premium—double the going rate.

Zeke knew where she would be, assuming she wasn't copulating at the moment. Sure enough, there she was sitting at a table sipping a Singapore

Sling. She was wearing a nice dress and flashed Zeke a big smile. Most Charlottes were skinny; Diva was plump in all the right places. Zeke motioned her to come to the truck. She pretended to be reluctant, but then strutted over to him in too-high heels sucking her drink through a straw.

"What you want, Marine?

Zeke had forgotten how hot she was and choked up for a second. "I take you to Red Beach. You boom-boom birthday boy and his friends."

"How many prends?" she asked in her broken English.

"Five or six" replied Zeke as he held up six fingers.

"That make me sore she said, rubbing herself between her legs. How much you pay?"

"How much you want?" Zeke knew it was going to be a costly transaction and was hoping she would be reasonable.

"Okay, twenty dolla for birfday boy and ten dolla for each he friends. You gib me eighty dolla; I come boom-boom all you prends long time."

"Too much. I give you fifty," said Zeke.

"You go fuck *yourself* for fifty dolla, GI," Diva snapped, using the old generic abbreviation for American military men—Government Issue.

Under normal circumstances, Diva might have paid a price for talking to him that way, but it was important that everything go right. Zeke knew he had screwed up the bargaining. His counteroffer was too far below market value, at least for *that* Charlotte.

"Okay, eighty dolla. You douche and we *di-di*" said Zeke, annoyed at having lost the negotiation.

*Douche and di-di; sounds like a rock group*, thought Zeke with a smile.

"You give me money now" Diva insisted.

"Okay Diva, but if you disappear on me, I'll burn down your hooch and kill you," he said with a smile.

Diva was salty and not intimidated. She gave Zeke a bored look and held out her hand for the money. Zeke told her that she would get an extra $20 as merit pay—an even $100—if she pleased everyone. They would take a vote. She flashed him a confident, knowing smile.

Diva was not kidnapped or coerced. She came of her own free will. She was an entrepreneur and had the best product. She knew how to attract and retain customers. Zeke had to admire her spunk and her courage. Other girls would have been afraid to come into Red Beach for fear of being arrested or worse, perhaps being turned over to the QC. Zeke assured Diva that she would be protected.

He helped her up on the trailer and into a half-full box of body bags that would be used to encase KIAs and other deceased en route to Graves Registration for processing and shipping back home for burial. He told her to crawl inside one of the body bags and stay quiet. He put the top back on the box and away they went. This would be a birthday to remember. When he pulled into the main gate at Red Beach, the guard motioned him through. Zeke parked along the road in front of Hooch 240, checked to see if the coast was clear, then popped Diva out of the box and ran her across the sand to the door of the hooch.

The first order of business as they entered the hooch was to give Wilber his birthday present. Unfortunately, Wilber had quaffed mass quantities of *Ba Moui Ba* (Vietnamese "33" brand beer), a liter of Tiger Beer and a couple shots of whiskey in an earlier celebration; he was out cold. Zeke tried to wake him, but to no avail, so he told Diva to boom-boom Wilber in his sleep. Zeke even made her sit on Wilber's face thinking that might work like smelling salts to snap him out of his alcohol-induced coma. No dice. Wilber was limp—body, mind and spirit. Zeke took a picture to show Wilber how he spent his twenty-fifth birthday then introduced Diva to the other customers. He didn't participate. He thought it best to refrain and just take pictures to show Wilber what he missed.

Diva was happy to accommodate, one or two at a time, until Moby stepped up to take his turn. Diva said "too beaucoup, numba ten. No can do."

She couldn't accommodate him easily, but it was funny (and noisy) watching her try and listening to him laughingly complain as the Marines in the hooch sprayed beer on the loving couple.

After that final exchange, she was ready to *di-di* on back to her Sugar Shack. Thanks to the guys in Hooch 240 she'd probably be on the injured reserve list for a while.

Zeke took Diva back to the truck a sorer but richer woman. He gave her the extra $20 for accommodating Moby and for giving him her panties as a birthday present for Wilber. Zeke had placed the panties gently over Wilber's face on their way out of the hooch. They skipped over to the waiting BAT, but this time she refused to get back into the box. Diva had realized that she had cuddled up in a body bag on the trip to Red Beach. It scared her and she saw it as a bad omen. She was ready to throw a fit if she had to do it again.

Zeke weighed his options. He needed to avoid noise and commotion or they would attract attention. He told Diva to get into the cab on the passenger's side. He put his helmet on her head and took off his utility shirt for her to wear. Zeke was wearing a Peter Pan green undershirt and that would be okay for night driving, even though he was technically out-of-uniform. Diva hid her long black hair inside the helmet and they proceeded slowly toward the exit gate.

The guard started to motion Zeke through then suddenly raised his hand telling him to stop. Zeke brought the BAT to a complete stop and the MP climbed up on the running board.

"What's up?" said Zeke nonchalantly.

"I noticed you had a Marine riding shotgun in the passenger seat wearing a helmet and I didn't get any word about being in Condition Red."

"How you doin' Marine" the MP asked Diva.

Diva mumbled in return.

"He's from Guam. His English isn't too good. Guam's a U.S. Territory but they speak mostly Chamorro over there and he's embarrassed," said Zeke.

The MP shined his flashlight at Zeke's shotgun rider, slowly passing the beam over a bare leg.

"Nice legs for a Marine. Are all Guamanians built like that?"

"Okay, I give up. She's Captain Tennille's girlfriend. I'm just the driver. You know how it is, right?" Zeke was surprised he had thought of such a bullshit explanation so quickly.

"Would you like a taste?" Zeke added.

"You asshole," the guard barked at Zeke, "this shit is so out of whack; they'd hang us both from the yardarm. For all I know she's been passed around to everybody. Sure smells like it. Get your ass out of here," he said in a commanding voice, motioning with his flashlight for Zeke to proceed.

Zeke breezed through the gate and gave the guard a salute. "I owe you brother. *Semper Fi.*"

Diva took off the helmet and folded up Zeke's shirt to sit on to make the ride more comfortable on her aching hindquarters and to absorb the residue of the night's adventure. After Zeke dropped off Diva, he put his shirt back on and headed down the road to deliver his cargo. As he was driving, something smelled strangely familiar. He sniffed his shirt. *Holy shit!*

Zeke received a gag gift from his hooch mates—a metal Bush Wing Badge—"for going above and beyond the call of friendship by bringing a Fox in a Box to Hooch 240 at considerable personal risk to himself and his BAT." At first glance, the Bush Wings looked like an aviator's badge or jump wings, but upon scrutiny, it was a set of spread eagle legs with wings.

165

# 29

# NIGHT MOVES

The VC used the night to their advantage. They fired at the trucks or drivers, sometimes for harassment, other times to kill. They had a special penchant for using grappling hooks to steal cargo. It took a special kind of *Chutzpah* to lasso a big heavy box on a moving truck at night, but they did it with amazing proficiency and usually without the driver even noticing. The 26-wheeled BATS were long and the noise from the engine and the clattering of steel as they bounced over the rough roads made it difficult to hear inside the cab. VC loved the 26-wheelers; they were easy pickings.

One night Zeke heard something unusual and caught movement behind him in his side mirror. He brought the big rig to a stop, emerged from the cab with his rifle, and was confronted by three heavily armed Vietnamese men dressed in black. Zeke aimed squarely at the man with the grappling hook who appeared to be the leader and yelled out commands in Vietnamese and English.

*"Dừng lại!"* yelled Zeke. He motioned for them to lower their weapons, and yelled *"di-di* fucking *mau!"*

They did not comply.

"You no shoot. Give truck or *cắt cổ họng của bạn,"* he said as he ran his finger across his throat.

Zeke did not intimidate them. They had only intended to steal some cargo, but now they meant to have his truck. There was no way out. No more palaver. He squeezed the trigger of his M14. The bullet creased the VC's ribs, which spun him around and knocked him to the ground.

Now *di-di mau* or I *cắt cổ họng của bạn* all you mother-humpin' cock-suckers," Zeke yelled at the top of his lungs.

The two horrified companions grabbed their wounded accomplice. As they turned to run, Zeke shot a stream of bullets into the ground all around them as they high-ankled down the road out of sight. He wanted to make sure they were no longer a threat by scaring them as far away as possible. If they'd hesitated, he would have killed all three.

Upon returning to Hooch 240, Zeke called a School Circle to tell the guys what had happened. It was a serious threat to all truckers and raised everyone's hackles. They debated whether to report the incident or handle the matter internally. Most felt that Heavy Platoon brass would not have their backs and might even turn on Zeke as they did with his speeding in a combat zone caper. After much discussion, Gyp volunteered to handle the situation—"in a timely, discreet manner," he said with a scary smile. He provided no detail. Everyone had an idea of what "handle" meant.

"All in favor say aye," said someone.

The ayes had it. Gyp was tasked with sending a message to the transgressors about fucking with Marine truckers.

Gyp was a master at using his truck as a weapon when necessary. He had a reputation of being able to flip the steering wheel of his BAT hard to one side then whip it in the opposite direction a few degrees, then back again causing the long trailer to turn almost perpendicular to the back of the 5-ton truck creating a lethal scythe effect on anything or anyone it encountered. It took some finesse, but Gyp knew what he was doing. Zeke had given Gyp all the information he needed to identify his target—the location of the incident and the exact hooch the three guys had come from. There had been suspicious activity around that hooch in the past. They needed to put a stop to the grappling hook thefts and threatening behavior once and for all before any Marines got killed.

As Gyp drew close to the target, he pulled over to double-check his M14 and make sure it was locked and loaded and to put on his flak jacket. As he picked up speed, he turned his headlights off and switched to night convoy mode, which gave him all the light he needed. The hooch was immediately in front of him just off the road about a hundred yards ahead. It was well lit indicating that it was occupied. He had just started his night shift and his BAT was empty, just the way it needed to be to execute a proper trailer whip. He wound the truck through the gears building up speed. As he got closer he could see moving shadows and outlines of people inside the hooch.

At about twenty-five yards from impact and traveling fast, Gyp turned the steering wheel sharply to the left. When the trailer slipped to the left, he turned the steering wheel sharply to the right causing the trailer to whip back around like a slingshot hitting the house at a ninety-degree angle to the truck. The noise of the impact sounded like a train wreck. The trailer took out the house and everyone in it like an old-fashioned farm mowing machine cutting through hay. Gyp straightened out the truck and trailer and then methodically backed over the rubble several times. He could back up a BAT blindfolded. For good measure, he got out of the truck and left his calling card—a nasty pyramid—on the chest of one of the dead men. Message sent … loud and clear.

As Gyp high-balled the BAT down the dirt road away from the scene of the payback toward his assigned destination to pick up a load, he saw lights behind him approaching fast. *Oh shit, now what?* He thought. *That couldn't be MPs or QCs that quickly, could it?* In a flash two Jeeps flew by him raising blinding clouds of dust. The Jeeps were full of what appeared to be American military men driving erratically, whooping and cheering. Someone in the first Jeep threw a beer can in Gyp's direction as he flew by. The second Jeep cut in front of Gyp and hit the driver's side fender with a loud clank. Gyp blew his horn, flashed his lights and brought the BAT to a stop as the Jeeps stopped and backed up toward him at a fast clip coming to a halt a couple feet from the front of the truck. *Seabees,* thought Gyp. *Of course; who else? They're all fucked-up drunk. Perfect. They'll be my scapegoats.*

Seabees were good at construction, but were seen as obnoxious shitbirds. Gyp recalled Zeke's story about the time they swept that village near Red

Beach looking for VC and found the Seabees and the VC pumping the same women. That led to a dead Seabee. He heard that a few weeks later three Seabees had been captured and tortured along Liberty Road near An Hoa after they were caught patronizing the same whores as the VC. They had been hung upside down with their stomachs cut open and their intestines dripping on the ground. That would have made quite a picture on the front page of American newspapers.

The ranking Seabee, a master senior chief something-or-other, sauntered over to Gyp who was standing by the bumper examining the damage. The chief had a smile on his face and asked what happened.

"You ran into me; *that's* what happened," said Gyp.

"No, *you* ran into me," the chief replied.

It was an awkward situation. Gyp had never been involved in an accident involving a Marine Corps vehicle, neither in training nor at any permanent duty station.

Gyp was facing two Jeep loads of drunken Seabees who would certainly lie for their chief.

"Let's contact the MPs and let them sort it out," bluffed Gyp, knowing that the MPs would quickly see that the Seabees were drunk and at fault.

"By the way," said Gyp in his best commanding voice, "I need all your names, ranks, serial numbers and unit designations," as he filed the chief's name and the Jeep identification number in his memory bank.

The chief balked and implied that Gyp was out of order since everyone there outranked him. "All you guys are fucked up; you're drunk as skunks and you-all ran into me. Under the circumstances, I outrank all of you ass-holes put together and have the right under the Geneva Convention, section 28-B, to relieve you of duty and arrest you."

The chief was stupefied and looked worried. He had no idea that Gyp had just made that up on the spot, citing the first set of numbers that came to mind.

Gyp paused for effect, but knew he had to put closure on the situation. A few more words exchanged and it could turn into a lose-lose situation.

"Chief, we're sitting ducks standing in the middle of nowhere in front of the headlights. We're going to get our asses killed if we don't *di-di* on out of here. Tell you what I'll do. I'll give you a break if you fix the fender right here and now. Put a couple of your guys on it and push it back in place. It'll still have a crease, but maybe nobody will notice."

The chief and a couple rank-and-file Seabees grunted, groaned, and slowly folded the heavy fender back into place, or at least enough so that only a crease and some missing paint showed.

"No hard feelings, right?" said the chief, offering Gyp a warm beer.

They shook hands and parted ways. The Seabees resumed hooting and hollering down the road as Gyp punched a hole in the top of can making sure the foam fell on the road and not him. He did not want to smell like beer when he got back to the motor pool and told Top Singer how he had seen a couple Jeeps full of drunken Seabees deliberately run into a hooch full of law-abiding Vietnamese civilians, wantonly and willfully killing them all, and then taking a dump on the remains.

# 30

# WHO KILLED THE ROADMASTER?

---

HIS CLOTHES, WEAPONS AND JEEP WERE GONE.
HE DIED AN UNNECESSARILY PAINFUL AND HUMILIATING DEATH.

---

The Roadmaster was a cherubic, pink-cheeked overweight sergeant whose job was to monitor the comings and goings of the Red Beach truckers. Although the truckers did not like being monitored and saw the Roadmaster function as just another job impediment, he was considered generally fair and reasonable in the exercise of power. Unlike Singer and Tennille, he could distinguish between serious and frivolous matters and appreciated the truckers' role in the war.

The Roadmaster wore a starched cover, shiny boots and a Colt M1911 pistol in a shoulder holster. The pistol was spotless; it had never been fired in anger—that is, in combat. He was the personification of a Garret Trooper. He would "beam up" in *Star Trek* fashion when least expected, looking clean and squared away, which caused some natural resentment among the truckers who were always unclean and usually not squared away given the work they were doing. The truckers called him Garret behind his back.

Garret's most irritating and dangerous monitoring behavior was sneaking up on truckers when they were nodding off as they waited for their trucks to be loaded or unloaded. He would jump up on the running board and scream out a Marine Corps war cry. That tactic almost cost him his life once when a trucker, thinking he was being attacked, knocked him off the running board and stuck the barrel of an M14 in his face. The trucker's response was ruled justifiable and Top Singer ordered Garret to knock off the bullshit before he ended up dead by "friendly fire," meaning being killed or wounded by your own side.

Garret had a clunky red wooden sign strapped across the front of his Jeep with the word Roadmaster printed in big yellow letters. Just for fun, Zeke cajoled George, Hooch 240's resident artist, into painting over the sign to change "master" to "bastard." He did such a good job that it took a week or more before Garret noticed. He probably wondered why people laughed and pointed at him everywhere he went. Rather than trying to track down the man who defaced his sign, Garret had a new one made without a fuss and went about his business. Zeke liked the way he handled the situation and felt guilty. The word went out that Garret, like Sergeant Bear, was one of the good guys, despite his rank, and was to be treated with respect in the future.

Garret was said to frequent a Sugar Shack located along an obscure road that meandered through thick trees and a hodge-podge of exotic vegetation and rice paddies. It was rumored that he had a special girl there and frequented the place often. The idea of Garret, a by the book, straight-laced teetotaler, having sexual needs was funny and repulsive at the same time. The truckers didn't begrudge him his affair; quite the contrary. It showed he was a regular guy and they hoped it would keep him out of their hair.

During an interlude with his Charlotte one afternoon, the VC killed Garret. He was found in a rice paddy wearing only a t-shirt. His clothes, weapons and Jeep were gone. He died an unnecessarily painful and humiliating death. He had been castrated; his testicles had been tamped down his throat. His body was recovered thanks to a passer-by who happened to see his pink derrière bobbing in the water. Had his remains not been spotted, Garret would have been classified MIA—Missing in Action and his disappearance would have remained forever a mystery.

The atrocity shocked and enraged everyone in the regiment. Hooch 240 Marines took particular offense. Garret was a pain in the ass, but he was *their* pain in the ass. They were surprised the VC had the temerity—or stupidity—to commit such a heinous act right under their noses, knowing the payback would be harsh.

Sergeant Bear called a School Circle with all the Marines in Hooch 240 to discuss the matter. The majority did not trust the Marine Corps to tell the truth about what happened or to administer justice to the perpetrators. Too many times, the enemy or their sympathizers seemed to get a pass because the American government did not want to offend the South Vietnamese government. Politics trumped everything, it seemed.

At the School Circle, Bear asked rhetorically, "Why not let the Marine Corps handle the matter? They'll get to the bottom of it, right? Maybe they'll sic the QC on 'um. Those White Mice play by their own rules and could put a big hurt on those nasty little VC maggots. Better yet, we could ask the Korean Marines to take a walk in that neighborhood. They waste every living thing in their paths."

*Waste* was a more dramatic way of saying *kill* because it implied more widespread devastation.

After much discussion, Wilber summed up Hooch 240 Marines' decision:"The Marine Corps' not going to do anything about one guy getting whacked. They'll box him up and ship him home with a sad letter from Captain Tennille telling his family what a hero he was and that will be the end of it. And, those White Mice QC cocksuckers are corrupt; they won't do shit either. They might even be the ones that 'did' Garret for all we know. As for the Koreans, it's true that they're even more barbaric than the Communists and they're our ally in this fuckin' war, but we have no standing to ask them to do anything for us and we'd get our asses in the wringer if we tried. So, it comes down to administering justice ourselves as we've done in the past."

Gyp was again asked to take the lead on the matter because he was effective and because he enjoyed the challenge. He was told to *only* gather information and report back to determine next steps. He was *not* to take unilateral action and try to avenge Garret's death. It was far too dangerous to go it alone.

"Thanks guys. I appreciate your confidence in me. I'll find out what I can and then we can go from there."

Gyp cracked open a bottle of whiskey and poured each man a shot in a paper cup.

"A toast to Garret," Gyp said as he lifted his cup. "He could have fucked us over many a time, but didn't. Any shit we got from him we deserved and we all know it. *Semper Fi* and rest in peace, sergeant."

"*Semper Fi*," they repeated in unison as they all raised their cups in a show of respect for their mutilated Roadmaster.

31

# JELLYBEAN ROAD

---

"Yea though I walk through the Valley of the Shadow of Death, I will fear no evil because I am the meanest MF in the Valley"

---

As Gyp drew his BAT closer to the Sugar Shack, he recited that line loudly and with conviction. He loved the sacrilegious bastardization of Psalm 23:4 so much that he paid $25 to have it tattooed on his arm when he went to Kuala Lumpur on R&R several months earlier. He always recited it to bolster his confidence when he sensed danger. The road to the scene of Garret's demise was dark and desolate, but Gyp had no fear; he was flushed with adrenalin. He thought about what Zeke and the others had said about just gathering information and not taking action, but he had become more worked up and irrational by the mile. He thought it might be a good idea to deal with the issue while it was still fresh. He wanted to send a message to the enemy and their sympathizers that if they fuck with Marines somebody dies. If you kill one of us, we kill a bunch of you, period.

When Gyp drew up to a halt by the Sugar Shack, he could smell the heady mix of fish, shit, crotch rot and incense. Every Dogpatch smelled like that. A couple bow-legged girls waddled over to his truck to greet him. They were waving, smiling and holding up their dark-tipped mammary glands as if they were selling ripe melons. One of the girls, an attractive young woman wearing a dress and gaudy knee-high socks, jumped up on the running board and started to palaver.

"My name Socks. What you name? You like my socks? You want Boom-boom? Phive dolla."

"That's three questions, Socks. How 'bout we start slow and talk about it?"

Gyp opened the front of his trousers and put Socks' hand where it would do the most good. He let her massage for a few minutes then gently moved her hand away.

Gyp had "liberated" a large can of Jelly Beans from a shipment slated for the Officers' Club. Officers received such delicacies courtesy of Uncle Sam. Most truckers took samples of the goodies they carried as a form of tax. That was acceptable if the liberator took enough to share with his peers. Gyp had gotten several cans for Hooch 240 and decided to use one of them to bribe Socks into giving him information about Garret.

He showed her the jellybeans and gave her a handful as he began asking questions. As Socks was loudly munching the jellybeans in Gyp's ear, still standing on the running board, she gestured toward the men inside the hooch.

"They tra tấn (torture) you phrend berry bad."

"Why?" Gyp asked with a scowl.

Socks pointed to one of the men inside the hooch. "That one with beard no want him boom-boom here. You phrend boom-boom he galfriend."

"They VC?" asked Gyp.

"No VC; VC numba ten," replied Socks.

"Bullshit. You all VC," said Gyp through tight jaws. He gave her the jellybeans and told her to *di-di*.

Socks jumped off the running board to the ground and suddenly became angry. She had given a free sexual favor and information to an unknown Marine and now he was telling her to go away without even a thank you or a few piasters for her trouble. She was also upset at being called a VC. She yelled some hostile sounding gibberish at Gyp in Vietnamese, which made for a very awkward situation given that Garret's killers might be within hearing distance.

City Charlottes were sophisticated and were trained on the finer points of customer relations. Country Charlottes, like Socks, were unsophisticated and undiplomatic. With a soft voice and his best smile, Gyp motioned to Socks to come back up on the running board. When she did, he pulled her halfway into the cab, covered her mouth with his hand and snapped her neck, clean and quick—snap, crackle, pop. She never had time to make a fuss. She snorted a couple times like a pig; it was all over in seconds. Jellybean mash and blood gushed out of her mouth as she crumpled off the running board and onto the ground with the rest of the jellybeans.

The men inside the hooch were indeed VC. They were pimps and used Sugar Shack proceeds to fund their war effort. Ironically, a large portion of the money that the U.S. military and its allies, including contractors and civilians, spent on sexual favors throughout South Vietnam indirectly supported the Communist war machine.

The VC had been keeping an eye on Gyp and had become suspicious because he had been sitting in his idling truck so long. When they saw Socks' lifeless body drop off the running board they sprang into action and charged toward the truck. Gyp jumped down from the cab, M14 set on rock and roll, and let loose with twenty rounds of punishing 7.62 mm Full Metal Jacket directly into their midst. They dropped to the ground in a pile, dead or near dead. Gyp executed a perfect combat reload, dropping the empty magazine to the ground with a press of the release button and replacing it with a full one in a nanosecond, just as he had practiced so many times. He sprayed another dozen bullets into the pile. When the screaming stopped and the shooting ended, Gyp found himself standing alone in dead silence. The surrounding jungle had become quiet. He was the only living soul.

In a few minutes, the silence was interrupted by the sound of a revving engine and grinding gears as Gyp drove his BAT into the hooch and then backed over it several times until it was nothing but broken bamboo poles and scattered thatch. In the process, sparks from the cooking fire in the hooch jumped onto the thatch and, "poof," the whole place went up in flame. Gyp squatted down over the face of one of the dead VC and dropped a sizable pyramid as he watched the hooch disintegrate. Message delivered. Gyp *di-di mau'ed* down the road irreverently humming the *Marines' Hymn*. He was exhausted.

## 32

# A RUSTY SCENARIO

THE DRILL INSTRUCTORS WERE RIGHT:
"WITHOUT MY RIFLE I AM USELESS."

Zeke formed an attachment to one of the old salts in the platoon during his first days in country, a senior PFC named Rusty who was slated to rotate home in five days. As his time to leave Vietnam drew nearer, he would walk around and call out to fellow Marines: "Ask me how short I am."

Marines would smile and give the obligatory response.

"We give up. How short are you, Rusty?"

"I'm so short I have to look up to put on my socks."

Then he would recite other corny one-liners about how little time remained on his Tour of Duty. The bantering would make everyone laugh and wish they too were short-timers.

Generally, short-timers, particularly guys like Rusty with less than a week or so left on his tour in Vietnam were removed from harm's way as much as possible, but he was only a PFC and rather nondescript. Instead of letting him stand down during his last week, he was sent into what was unaffectionately referred to as Indian Country—a synonym for enemy-infested territory. He would be helping with construction of Liberty Road, a long, winding dirt track from DaNang to the Song Thu Bon River near An Hoa, and at night no less. Rusty was to haul dirt in a dump truck back and forth along that shooting gallery from dusk until dawn.

When Zeke heard about the assignment he told Rusty that he was going to speak with someone, even Top Singer if need be, and volunteer to go in his place. Zeke was livid. He could not believe the fools would send a Marine who had already served twelve months and three weeks of a thirteen-month Tour of Duty on such a risky assignment. There was no shortage of Marines with lots of time left in country who would have been happy to go in Rusty's stead.

Zeke understood that all Marines are required to go anywhere and do anything they are told to do regardless of their personal situations, but that was not the point. The goof balls in charge were going against generally accepted practice and that was a bad omen.

"Construction of Liberty Road? Give me a fuckin' break! That's a dirt cow path. They could have those Seabee assholes make a few passes with their bulldozers and call it good. Put our guys' lives on the line to haul dirt to and from a cow path? LHM!"

LHM—Lord Have Mercy—was an expression from Zeke's Calvinist past that he found himself using with some regularity when he couldn't find just the right curse word to fit the occasion.

Rusty appreciated Zeke's feelings, but told him not to intervene.

"I'll be seen as a whiner and a coward if I don't go. Things happen for a reason and we mortals are not privy to those reasons, but must follow their destiny wherever that may lead. Besides, if you went in my place and something happened, I'd never be able to live with that."

"It sounds like you're singing the words to *Baby the Rain Must Fall*. Don't give me that hocus-pocus shit, Rusty, let me go instead," Zeke implored.

"Fuck no," replied Rusty. First of all, that's *your* song so don't lecture me about hocus-pocus. You think the same way I do so cut the shit. I love you brother and appreciate your concern, but I can't and won't sidestep this or anything else that comes my way."

The third night out on Liberty Road with two more days before his 13-month tour of duty was complete, it happened—PFC Rusty was singled out to die. At about 1:30 in the morning, a sniper's bullet slammed through the door of his truck and into both of his legs. Rusty reached for his M14 and tried to defend himself, but to no avail. He was badly wounded and his rifle did not work. The After-Action Report noted that his M14 had "malfunctioned due to excessive rust."

The drill instructors were right: "without my rifle I am useless." The encounter was a test of combat readiness and Rusty had failed, which felt awful to think about let alone verbalize. *What the fuck—did he think he was so short in country that he didn't need to worry about keeping his weapon squared away? How could he have been so stupid?* Zeke was again numb with pain and confused, but no tears came. He was too angry with Rusty for allowing himself to be killed.

The assassins, a suicide squad it was reported, had walked up to the truck, enjoying the sight of a helpless Marine with a useless rifle. Based on the after-action report, they tied him to his dump truck and gutted him. The more he screamed, the more they laughed ... and cut. Vietnam's heat and humidity caused rapid decomposition. Rusty's mangled body became infested with maggots by the time it was delivered to Graves Registration.

The term "suicide squad," sounded implausible to Zeke and everyone else. Those VC were not out to commit suicide. If they were, they would have charged a full complement of Marines somewhere killing as many as they could before the Marines wasted them. On the contrary, they were just a pack of wolves looking for an easy target. Rusty met their criteria.

"He gave his life for his country," Top Singer said.

Rusty's parents were heartbroken, but proud to receive a posthumous Purple Heart and tri-folded American flag at his funeral ... from a grateful country. The Marine in dress blues saluted slowly as Rusty's remains were lowered deep into the ground, followed by taps played at a distance.

Heavy Platoon named the motor pool after Rusty and erected a prominent sign in his honor. It was a remarkable sight and gratifying to the rank-and-file. Zeke wrote a letter to Rusty's parents telling them how brave he was and enclosed a picture of the motor pool sign.

Nine years later when America "bugged out," a term with special meaning in a military context, the North Vietnamese Army swarmed over South Vietnam like ants, razing and killing with impunity. DaNang, Tien Sha, Red Beach, An Hoa and all of Zeke's haunts were "liberated" by the Communists. All the CAP units were overrun. Every CAP Marine, PF and *bác sĩ* (Navy Corpsman) was massacred. They were no match for the hordes of NVA that swept over them. Rusty's motor pool sign was destroyed along with the rest of South Vietnam.

# 33

# HAPPINESS IS A WARM GUN

"IT WILL COME IN HANDY; MIGHT EVEN SAVE
YOUR LIFE SOMETIME." INDEED.

Zeke maintained his rifle in a state of combat readiness locked and loaded and easily accessible whenever he was on the road. He kept himself in a state of Condition Orange ready to shift to Condition Red in a heartbeat. Despite his preparation, he still felt something was missing. He needed a handgun. Truckers were not issued handguns, at least not the rank-and-file. Officers and Staff NCOs had them, generally tucked into shiny leather shoulder holsters, but not the Marines who *really* needed them—those like Zeke who traveled the far-flung back roads, individually or on convoys, or traversed the city streets at night.

Zeke was not going to let what happened to Rusty happen to him. No sir! He told the Marines in Hooch 240 that he wanted a pistol and, *voilà,* one morning the opportunity arose; like magic. After a long night's work Moby and a friend of his from another unit awakened him.

"Zeke, this is Guy. He's a Frenchie and pronounces his name Gee. Him and me were with 26th Marines when we came over. He's got something you might want to look at."

Gee had a 6" pre-Model 10 Smith & Wesson (S&W) .38 Special revolver for sale, complete with plenty of bullets and a tie-down black western style holster with loops enough to hold 18 cartridges. At first, Zeke thought the cowboy looking rig was too flamboyant, but the more he looked at it the more appealing it became.

"Guy, or Gee, that must have been a hard name to have in boot camp, eh? I can just imagine how the DIs messed with you every time they called your name," said Zeke with a smile.

"That was a hundred years ago," replied Gee, not pleased at the reference to his name.

"Zeke, I'm rotating back to CONUS in a few days and understand you'd like to buy a gun.

CONUS was military-speak for Continental United States.

"I'll give you the S&W and all the accoutrements for $100. Consider it a discount because you're a friend of my buddy, Moby. The holster, belt and bullets are worth that much by themselves."

Zeke looked over the weapon, opened the chamber to make sure it was empty, cocked the hammer and pressed the trigger a couple times. He liked the short, light trigger pull; it was perfect for serious shooters. He knew Gee could not take the gun with him because it would be confiscated as unauthorized ordinance before he left Vietnam. This gave Zeke some negotiating leverage.

"Seventy dollars take it or leave it," said Zeke, as he nonchalantly counted out the money in MPC.

Gee needed to dispose of the weapon and seventy dollars was better than nothing. "Okay, deal. It will come in handy. Might even save your life sometime, like it did mine."

*Indeed,* thought Zeke.

Zeke mumbled "*Semper Fi*" to Gee as he left the hooch counting his $70, then dropped back on the rack and closed his eyes. He was feeling more secure already.

Zeke cleaned and oiled the weapon and dry practiced quick draws from the holster. He had enough ammo to fill every loop on the belt and a couple fifty-round boxes left over. At a sparsely populated area in the boonies, he practiced failure drills, one-handed shooting with both the right hand and left hand, simultaneous threats, shooting from the hip and simulated "Rusty Scenarios" where he had to defend himself while inside the truck cab. He practiced drawing the weapon from concealment—inside his trousers or under a utility shirt—and got so he could draw from his holster and make a kill shot in less than one second. He practiced speed reloading by hand, which took a great deal of manual dexterity and concentration. In time, he could use his hand and fingers like a Speed Strip and reload the S&W chamber very quickly.

When he got low on ammo, Zeke asked his mom, Naomi, to replenish his supply, twenty-five rounds at a time, packed inside a box of cookies or some such thing to avoid detection. His mom dutifully complied. In time, he accumulated over three-hundred rounds for practice and self-defense. He became reasonably proficient with the weapon and was more confident and optimistic about his future knowing he had a backup gun if all else failed. As a final touch, Zeke carved an "x" on the tip of each bullet creating what was called a "dum-dum," which caused the bullet to expand upon impact creating a larger and more lethal wound than the traditional Full Metal Jacket round.

Zeke had bought a pair of Akai box speakers a couple months earlier, also from a Marine who was rotating back to CONUS. He removed the front panels of the speakers and stored his gun, holster and ammo inside them—safe from prying eyes and sticky fingers. He carried the S&W in a haversack and strapped it on only after he left Red Beach and only when he was headed to particularly dangerous places. *If Rusty had a gun like this and kept it clean, he would be alive today,* thought Zeke.

✪ ✪ ✪

Zeke was headed back to the motor pool from Camp Tien Sha driving a fully loaded BAT. He was in a hurry and decided to take the Jellybean Road shortcut, bypassing the DaNang air base. It was a dangerous stretch of road, made worse by Gyp's recent firestorm. He knew he probably shouldn't take that route, but disregarded his instincts in the interest of saving time. It was pitch black. Things soon got creepy. *No other trucks are on the road. No one looks friendly. Everyone looks like VC. The fences are made of sharpened bamboo. Sure feels hostile. These VC bastards are vicious animals. I could end up like Garret or Rusty. This was dumb.*

Zeke shifted to Condition Red, meaning flak jacket and helmet on, M14 across the lap and the Smith and Wesson within reach. His prescience

187

paid off. Zeke heard something hit his truck. He looked in the mirror and spotted a shadowy figure trying to lasso his cargo with a grappling hook. Instead of high tailing, Zeke got mad and bellowed, "Cock-sucking VC mother-humper! Fucking with *my* load?"

He brought the BAT to an abrupt halt, skidding all 26 tires. He quick-drew his S&W from the holster as he jumped from the cab with an intense Marine Corps war growl. Zeke thought his display of aggression would startle the man and scare him away.

Zeke's tactic didn't work. The man screamed like a banshee as he charged with a machete, aiming to separate Zeke's head from his body with one quick swipe.

*This is one stupid VC—he took a knife to a gunfight.*

Zeke pulled the trigger four times in rapid succession hitting the VC in the shoulder, chest, stomach and ear. He dropped to the ground writhing in pain and crying out something in Vietnamese. He was not dead. *Why does he have to make all that noise? Why can't he just die? Now I'm really in trouble. I shouldn't be on this road. I shouldn't have stopped to fight. What the fuck was I thinking?*

In a flash, there were two more figures coming toward Zeke at a trot from some nearby trees. Despite all his practice he forgot to immediately reload the revolver and did not remember how many unfired rounds he had left in the chamber. He dove into the cab and grabbed his M14, which he kept set on rock and roll, as did all the truckers in Heavy Platoon. Locking and loading on local runs was frowned upon by Captain Tennille as a safety issue, but most everyone ignored Tennille's frown.

Zeke was not sure why the approaching figures did not shoot. They were both carrying something in their hands. Weapons? All his senses were focused on the two men running toward him. He saw nothing else and heard nothing, not even the sound of his fusillade that brought the two figures to the ground in an explosion of blood, body matter and cries of pain. The first man that had absorbed the four .38 slugs was bleeding profusely in a prone position on the ground and still making hideous animal sounds. Several 7.62 rounds from Zeke's M14 ended his suffering. Zeke jammed a fresh twenty-round magazine into his M14 and scanned the area with his rifle looking for more VC, doing a double take on shadows or any object that appeared threatening. It had become eerily quiet. He could not hear a thing except the ringing in his hears.

The smell was disgusting; nauseating. It reminded Zeke of the time back home when his buddy, Czyk, mistakenly cut the intestines of a deer he was dressing during hunting season. The smell was enough to make a grown man cry. It was just like what he now smelled emanating from the three dead bodies lying on the ground in a casserole of their own blood and guts. Zeke held his nose, trying to breathe only through his mouth as he scooped up his magazine and S&W. He high-tailed down Jellybean Road as fast as a loaded 26-wheel BAT could go, grinding gears as he went. Shifting smoothly was the least of his concerns.

Thoughts kept racing through Zeke's mind: *Was that guy really trying to lasso my load? Was he really going to kill me over a stupid pallet of bullshit cargo? Did he charge me with the machete defensively or offensively? Were the other two guys even armed? Shit, I didn't pick up my rifle brass. Those dum-dum bullets sure did a job on that bastard. Could those dum-dums tie me to that firefight? Fuck it. I don't give a shit! I just had a gunfight; the goblins are dead and I'm alive. I won! That's all that matters.* Zeke yelled at the top of his lungs several times, releasing the adrenalin and expressing his elation. He was on a natural high.

Zeke pulled through the gate, waved at the guard and proceeded slowly to the motor pool, his rig still fully loaded with cargo. He handed his Trip Ticket to the dispatcher and explained how he had been delayed at Tien Sha and that a day driver would need to take his load to its destination. As he slowly shuffled toward Hooch 240, he could see a trace of light in the horizon signaling that dawn was rapidly approaching. He entered the hooch, stowed his gear, fell onto his rack and stared at the ceiling. *After I sleep it will all be over; like a bad dream.*

Days went by without any announcements or scuttlebutt (rumors) about the Jellybean Road confrontation. *Surely, they must have been VC. VC always dragged off their dead and wounded, leaving nary a trace. If they'd been civilians, the bodies would have been recovered and the Marine Corps and the White Mice would have been in a tizzy.* Zeke had experienced a few kill-or-be-killed situations since he arrived in Vietnam, but never so up-close and personal that he could see the enemy's eyes when the bullets hit. He was nauseated yet he did not feel traumatized or guilty. *Would they have had second thoughts about taking my life? Not a chance. Good thing I was wearing my lucky Đồng.*

**34**

# MUSTANG SALLIE

THE POWER AND PRESTIGE OF BEING AN OFFICER HAD GONE TO HIS HEAD.

Jerry Sallie was a "Mustang," the term for an enlisted man who worked his way up to become an officer. Sallie had received a field promotion from gunnery sergeant to second lieutenant a month before he took command of Heavy Platoon. No one knew what he had done to earn the promotion and he did not volunteer information. Mustangs had credibility with the rank-and-file because they were generally older, wiser and better managers of men than junior NCOs and newbie officers. Expectations were high that this new addition to the unit would be a good leader and perhaps a welcome relief from the Garret Troopers with whom they had been dealing thus far.

It was not to be. The power and prestige of being an officer had gone to Sallie's head. He was an abusive, classless bully, even to the most compliant, respectful member of the unit, Corporal Gums. He referred to enlisted men as "peons," and called every Marine in Heavy Platoon "Bo" rather than addressing them by their last name or rank. Mustang Sallie behaved as if Red Beach, Vietnam was a stateside Marine Corps base. He wanted Jarhead (extremely short) haircuts and spit-shined everything.

Sallie conducted a rifle inspection one day and gigged Zeke because the barrel of his M14 was shiny; all the bluing was gone.

"A shiny rifle could reflect the sunlight and give away your position to the enemy, Bo," said Sallie.

"Sir, I am aware of that, but the bluing wore off long before it was issued to me."

"You know what I think, Bo? I think this rifle is too shiny for just being worn. I think you've Brassoed the damn thing for some odd reason. Am I right or wrong?"

"Sir, it got shiny from cleaning it so much," Zeke was proud of himself for coming up with such a good bullshit reply.

Zeke was pissed off about being issued a rifle that was not combat ready and started Brassoing it as a form of silent protest. He came to like the chrome look and retrofitted a selector switch for automatic fire. That feature had come in handy a couple times, most recently at the skirmish on Jellybean Road. Sallie told him to "survey" the rifle, meaning get a replacement from the battalion armory. Zeke "forgot" to survey the rifle, but did not forget to be out on a truck run to avoid inspections in the future.

Mustang Sallie next ordered a Junk-on-the-Bunk (JOTB)—a formal inspection of uniform, boots, weapon, mess gear, and anything else a Marine had been issued (a.k.a., the junk), laid out on a perfectly made rack (a.k.a., the bunk), in a prescribed fashion. Every object had to be spit-shined, clean, folded, and displayed in a prescribed fashion. In Vietnam, it was generally understood that "spit and polish" was minimized and superfluous inspections were suspended. Heavy Platoon had to be the only unit in Vietnam ordered to undergo such foolishness, they thought.

Generally, a JOTB required the inspectee to stand by to be grilled, harassed and belittled for infractions by the inspecting officer. No Marine (except Gums) wanted any part of such a demoralizing time-waster. Most found a way to be on a truck run or otherwise absent for the inspection once the date and time were announced.

Gums looked forward to the JOTB. After he laid out all his junk properly on the bunk, per the *Guidebook for Marines*, he left the Hooch for a moment. As soon as he left, a pair of little red sneakers magically appeared in the middle of Gum's junk, courtesy of Gyp. They were cute and incongruous. Gum's JOTB with the sneakers looked like a Norman Rockwell scene out of the *Saturday Evening Post.*

That evening, no one said a word or asked a question about the JOTB. The little red sneakers were neatly resting on Gums' shelf and his junk was put away. It was assumed that he found the sneakers, had a laugh and removed them before the inspection. The assumption was false. The sneakers were arranged neatly on top of Gums' uniforms when Sallie entered the hooch. He interpreted the sneakers as insolence and disrespect and ordered Gums front and center to explain. Gums was no snitch. He took full responsibility and said it was just a joke. He meant no disrespect. He told Sallie that it was a hot day and thought the inspectors could use a little comic relief. Gums' explanation worked. Sallie patted him on the back, let out a guffaw. He commended Gums for being squared away and having a sense of humor.

Gums chewed everyone out and threatened Office Hours for whoever put the sneakers on his junk. At the end of his tirade, he started to grin and finally let out with a laugh, followed by a warning:

"The sneakers *were* kind of funny. You should have seen the look on Sallie's face. Regardless, never, ever, ever lay hands on my gear or my rack again. Do you knot heads understand me?"

The guys responded in unison as they leaped to attention in mock compliance.

"Yes Sir, Corporal Gumster!"

The Hooch 240 Marines liked Gums, even more so after the way he handled all the nonsense they had just put him through. They appreciated him for his loyalty and respect and his adherence to proper Marine Corps values. He was a role model.

35

# VIETNAMESE CRY TOO

NEVER HAD ZEKE SEEN SUCH PAIN AND GRIEF.
PITH WAS THE PERSONIFICATION OF HUMAN AGONY.

As it became more dangerous to live in the countryside, hordes of Vietnamese men, women and children migrated closer to the cities for the security provided by U.S. forces. If they stayed in their villages, they would be caught between the Americans and the Communist VC or NVA. Both sides suspected villagers of collaborating with the enemy and the consequences could be death or worse, particularly at the hands of the Communists. Americans turned suspected collaborators or prisoners over to South Vietnamese authorities to extract information. The VC or the NVA did their own dirty work.

Refugee camps had sprung up all over South Vietnam and there was a particularly large one a short distance from Red Beach. The refugees built shelters out of cardboard framed with wood from cargo pallets. They flattened empty beer and soda cans into squares and attached them to the cardboard walls as a form of siding. Their ingenuity and skill in making something out of nothing was remarkable. The camp was crowded, smelly and dangerously unsanitary. Zeke felt sorry for the refugees, particularly the children who were perpetually dirty and hungry. They were caught between the proverbial rock and the hard place.

195

In the middle of an otherwise uneventful day, Heavy Platoon got the word that hot coals from a cooking fire had sparked an inferno at the refugee camp and all available Marines were to head there immediately and do whatever was necessary to save lives and property. Hooch 240 Marines burst into action. They grabbed shovels, jumped into an M54, with Zeke at the wheel, and took off for the camp. *Fuck the speed limit.*

As Zeke pulled into the camp, the Marines jumped off the truck before it came to a full stop, just the way Grunts jumped off helicopters before they touched the ground. They spread out, helping people pull their belongings out of the burning cardboard hooches and smothering the flames with shovels full of sand. The Marines were the only fire department and they were doing great, especially as more arrived from other units in the area.

Zeke secured the truck and jogged toward the flames with his shovel when he spotted a man rolling on the ground, pounding the sand, crying and screaming in Vietnamese. It was Pith the garbage man—his two baby sons had been burned alive. Their charred remains were lying nearby. The smell was gut-wrenching. Never had Zeke seen such pain and grief. Pith was the personification of human agony. Zeke empathized, but couldn't cry. Marines needed to keep their cool, fight the fire and lead by example without becoming emotional.

Zeke got down on his knees in the sand next to Pith and tried to comfort him. Pith put his arms around Zeke and cried like a baby—like the babies he had just lost. Pith kept crying and saying the same things in Vietnamese, repeatedly. Zeke spoke to Pith in English, Pidgin Vietnamese and even used the few French words he remembered in an attempt to console him. Neither understood what the other was saying; only what each was doing. Here was a guy Zeke had learned to regard as a potential enemy—to look upon as a "Gook" and maybe kill without compunction—now exhibiting a level of human emotion that he had never seen or even imagined. Zeke threw up.

Pith survived, but his kids had not; neither had his wife. She suffered third degree burns over most of her body and didn't survive another day. Many of the refugees, including several kids and old people died of smoke inhalation. Some Marines had become hard-hearted during their time in country and mumbled "good riddance" when they heard about the casualties.

Vietnam had become a cesspool of blood and pain. Thousands of Americans and Vietnamese had been killed and Pith's two little boys lay silent and unrecognizable … and there was nothing Zeke could do about any of it.

# 36

# INDIAN COUNTRY

---

CONVOYS WERE DANGEROUS. TRUCKERS HAD BEEN
KILLED OR WOUNDED IN HELLACIOUS AMBUSHES.

---

In early 1967, Heavy Platoon was tasked to join convoys on resupply missions to Marine outposts, mainly Phu Bai and An Hoa. Convoys consisted of M54 (5-ton) trucks, semitrailers, lowboys, tankers and BATs that carried food, ammo, water and materiel. They were often a blend of several motor transport units. Heavy Platoon was usually overrepresented because they had most of the few BATs available in their area of operation.

Vehicles would converge southwest of the DaNang air base at first light and then proceed to the edge of Indian Country to pick up a platoon of Grunts as bodyguards. Indian Country was the term used to describe dangerous territory. For additional security, a tank would take the point (front) position and an Ontos would fall in behind the last truck. An Ontos was like a tank except smaller with six long rocket tubes attached. It was sometimes referred to as a "tank killer," which was a good description of its lethality. The trips were relatively short in terms of miles, but were dangerous day-long jaunts each way because of the poor condition of the roads, incessant gunplay and periodic stops to clear landmines.

✪ ✪ ✪

In Vietnam, the "front" was said to be a misnomer because the enemy fought everywhere and often beamed up when and where they were least expected. That was true in general, but there were clearly areas of South

Vietnam that were more dangerous than others, particularly the An Hoa area. Marines knew those areas and referred to them using the military Color Code of Awareness to symbolize threat levels: White (low); Yellow (maybe); Orange (good chance) and Red (guaranteed shitstorm). Truckers knew they would be driving through the color spectrum from white to red as they lumbered along from Red Beach into Indian Country. They also knew that slow moving trucks made easy targets. Many Heavy Platoon truckers had been killed or wounded in hellacious ambushes as convoys to Indian Country became routine.

Zeke was mentally and physically ready for the trek to An Hoa. His BAT was loaded, as were his weapons, and he had plenty of extra ammo. Heavy Platoon truckers had an official allotment of sixty rounds of ammunition—three magazines. Smart truckers carried one hundred rounds in five magazines when driving locally. When heading into Indian Country, any driver with common sense would carry a two-hundred-round ammo box under the driver's seat in addition to the usual five magazines. Zeke had at least that much plus one hundred rounds of .38 Special dum-dums.

*What difference would it make to the Marine Corps if a driver had a thousand rounds? How about two thousand? Was there a shortage of ammo, a shortage of money to buy ammo ... what?*

Ammo restrictions in Vietnam made no sense to Zeke. He ignored the guidelines and carried as much as he thought he needed, just like every other trucker in Heavy Platoon.

✪ ✪ ✪

The evening before departure Gyp and Moby came to Zeke with a request. They said nothing and simply handed Zeke a 7.62 round with Sallie's name marked on the side in bold black ink. They hated Sallie with a passion and wanted him removed ... permanently. Although Mustang Sallie was an irritant, Zeke didn't really *hate* him. He just thought Sallie was neurotic and avoided him as much as possible. Zeke understood the unsubtle request and handed the bullet back to them.

"You gotta be shitin' me! Killing is one thing but murder is another, especially one of our own. Not a chance. You guys are really fucked up!"

At that moment, Zeke saw his two hooch mates differently. They were serious. They were lost. They were no longer Marines in his mind.

✪ ✪ ✪

The sun was rising as Heavy Platoon's trucks—five in all—arrived at the rendezvous point to await the other units. Before long, a gaggle of men, women, kids and dogs from the nearby village beamed up and slowly waddled in their direction. Truckers quickly raised their rifles and aimed at the approaching hoard, not knowing what was going on.

"Shit detail. Stand down," yelled one of the truckers.

The puzzled Marines lowered their rifles as they watched the villagers pick out spots, drop their drawers and squat down to take their morning constitutionals—within sight, sound and smell of each other. They were unabashed. As far as Zeke knew, the Vietnamese did not have toilets or running water except perhaps for a handful of rich people and politicians in DaNang and Saigon. The early morning uninhibited squat was a way of life.

"Holy shit" said Zeke with an unintended pun, "this is their bathroom!"

Sure enough, it was a shit detail, literally, and the air soon turned sour. Zeke began laughing.

"What's so funny?" asked Wilber.

"Look at them ... their asses are all pointed the same way—toward us. And they must all be double-jointed to sit that low to the ground with their feet perfectly flat."

I wonder if they have an SOP about how many times they use the same spots," said Wilber with a snicker.

"Maybe that's the Vietnamese version of Parade Rest," said Zeke.

Zeke got out of his truck, armed only with the Smith & Wesson hidden under his clothes, and walked over to the poop party, giving them all a big smile and waving. They smiled back without missing a grunt. He acted like a Drill Instructor standing before recruits and bellowed out to the squatting throng, "On your feet! Jumping Jacks, one fucking million of them ... ready begin," counting off loudly as he went through the exercise routine.

The squatters did not understand anything he said or did, but the words *dinky dau* could be heard as they shook their heads, finished their business and drifted back to their hooches.

The trucks from the other units had arrived and all the Marines were watching Zeke's skit, laughing, making cat calls and taking pictures. Finally, Zeke walked over to an attractive young lady, squatted down next to her and tried to strike up a conversation. By that time, the onlookers were doubling over with laughter, which attracted the attention of Mustang Sallie who had parked his Jeep out of view talking with another officer.

"Hammond, get your dumb ass back in your truck and stop harassing the indigenous people."

"Yes sir, Lieutenant. I was just tryin' to win hearts and minds."

"Like hell you were. I know what you were trying to do. Now get back here!"

"Good God, they don't even wipe their asses," said Sallie under his breath as he walked back to his Jeep shaking his head.

Mustang Sallie and a captain named Burg positioned their Jeep behind the tank that would be leading the procession. Their driver was a lance corporal wearing a white MP helmet—a nice target for an enemy sniper. All three were wearing flak jackets and carrying M1911s. Leading a convoy through Indian Country was a very big deal. Sallie took the responsibility seriously as evidenced by his wide eyes, pursed lips and tight jaws. On the other hand, maybe he was just scared since only officers rode in Jeeps, which made him the likely first target in an ambush.

"Convoy, fire up your engines. Prepare to move out on my command," yelled Mustang Sallie.

He paused for effect then yelled out something that sounded like "berrip har."

*Forward ho? Was that really forward ho? What the fuck does he think this is, the cavalry? What a jerk*, thought Zeke, as he laughed aloud.

The convoy started slowly then gained speed and moved down the road at a good pace. The lush rice paddies and tree lines contrasted sharply with the red dirt road, the clear blue sky and the purple mountains in the distance. To the south and west, there were hills and mountains. It was picturesque and inviting. Everything was so nice. In some ways, it reminded Zeke of home. For a moment, he lost himself in the scenery and forgot where he was.

As they rolled along, Zeke voiced his thoughts to George the artist who was sitting in the passenger's seat riding shotgun.

"God this is pretty country. Remind me, George, why the fuck are we here? What's this fight really about anyway?

"Well, like they told us in training, Zeke, South Vietnam is a tiny country, half a world away and they need our help to prevent a Communist takeover. Sounds like a good reason to me."

"I use to buy that shit, George, but I'm starting to have my doubts considering that the people we're supposed to be helping seem to hate us. On top of that, the government and the Marine Corps have imposed so many obstacles to winning, it's become ridiculous—can't do this; can't do that. It's nuts! If World War II had been fought like this, you and I would be speaking Japanese or German right now.

"Ours is not to make reply. Ours is not to reason why. Ours is but to do and die. Into the valley of death rides Heavy Platoon." George had paraphrased from *The Charge of the Light Brigade* by Alfred, Lord Tennyson.

"You're an ass, George, that's not what I wanted to hear, but I guess you're right. We're just cannon fodder in some sort of big-time global power bullshit that's goin' on and there's nothin' we can do about it except to stay alive and get the hell out as soon as we can."

✪ ✪ ✪

A few miles down the road, the convoy picked up a platoon of Grunts from the 5th Marine Regiment to serve as bodyguards through the most dangerous part of the trip. They distributed themselves on the beds of the trucks on top of the cargo. Two Duce and a Half (2½ ton) trucks carrying M45 Quadmounts, a.k.a. "Quad 50s," joined the convoy as well, positioning themselves tactically for maximum effectiveness in the event of an attack.

The Quad 50 consisted of four .50 caliber machine guns attached to a turret that could turn 360 degrees inside the bed of a truck. The machine guns could be fired in pairs or all four at once. It looked like an ack-ack gun from an old WWII movie. The operator had a crazed look on his face. He was either *dinky dau* or pretending to be, much like Heavy Platoon truckers did when they beamed up at Air Force and Navy chow halls covered with dirt and dressed in combat gear, eating with their hands and grunting like animals just for show.

A Grunt with a .60 caliber machine gun climbed into the passenger side of every third truck and mounted his weapon through the open front window.

*Lord have mercy,* thought Zeke, *where the fuck are we going, Iwo Jima?*

The convoy was now fully formed. Away they went in a cloud of dust, minus the hearty Hi-Yo-Silver, into Indian Country. The dust kicked up by the hundreds of tires rolling down the dry road made it difficult to see the truck directly ahead or civilians trudging along the roadside. With each mile, every Marine became more at one with the earth until they were completely covered with layers of red dust. They were hot, sweaty, thirsty, and dirty. The convoy had entered the Red zone. Zeke wondered *when*, not if, they would be hit.

Truckers soon morphed into Grunts, which was natural since *all* Marines are trained to be infantrymen, first and foremost. The truckers looked like Grunts, felt like them and began to assume their hyper-vigilant demeanor. By then Sallie and Burg probably wondered what the hell they were doing riding in an open Jeep, wearing their shiny officer insignias and starched covers. No one wanted to be them at that moment.

Bam! Thwack! A sniper round from the west side of the convoy came out across the rice paddy from somewhere in the tree line and hit Mustang Sallie square in the head. The impact blew the starched cover off his head and into the air. The round had been fired from such a distance he never heard the shot that killed him. Blood and brains were everywhere. A tiny piece of flesh flew into Captain Burg's open mouth; he was covered with Sallie's blood. Captain Burg flew out of the jeep and began firing his M1911 randomly toward the tree line. In the fog and shock of the moment, he failed to acquire his target properly and hit two kids, a boy and a girl, who were sitting on a water buffalo in the rice paddy some distance from the Jeep. He killed them both.

The sound of bullets hitting metal, tires and Marines could be heard up and down the line. Within seconds, every man on the convoy was returning fire. Down went the water buffalo with a loud bawl, falling directly on one of the dead kids. There were so many rounds screaming through the air in opposite directions it was a wonder the bullets didn't collide.

The Ontos moved up a small hill and laid down salvos in the direction of the enemy. The tank pounded the entire tree line. Wilber took a picture at the very moment a tank round hit one of the VC and sent him into the air ... without his head. It was a serendipitously gruesome picture. It would be widely circulated with dark comments about what happens to people who mess with Marines. Grunts were on the ground laying down interlocking fields of fire across the distant tree line. The .60 calibers were lighting up everything in sight and the Quad .50 was barking their slower inimitable staccato. The firing from the VC from many positions continued despite the defensive fusillade from the Marines.

Zeke had jumped out of his truck and landed on some hardened mud. It was sharp and painful. Zeke remembered thinking *I'm not supposed to feel pain in the heat of battle.* But he did. He laid down a line of bullets toward the muzzle flashes across the paddy. Every third round in Zeke's M14 magazine was a tracer. It helped with target acquisition, but after one magazine, the enemy followed the tracers back to their source and Zeke found himself under heavy fire. Bullets were coming way too close for comfort, hitting his boot and flattening one of the 26 tires on his BAT.

"Hope they don't hit the gas tank," he yelled loudly to warn others.

Zeke looked behind him and noticed that Redbone, who had been driving the truck ahead of him, had taken cover and was not engaging the enemy.

"What the fuck are you doing, Redbone—shoot!" yelled Zeke.

Redbone shook his head and yelled back, "Don't need to; Grunts got it covered."

That excuse sounded familiar. Like Jorge at Tien Sha, Redbone was hesitating at the Moment of Truth. Zeke reloaded, no tracers this time, and sprayed a hooch that was about halfway between the tree line and the convoy on the edge of the rice paddy. He had seen rifle fire coming from one of the windows when the attack started. He heard a muffled scream from inside the house and saw no other movement or rifle flashes.

The tank and Ontos ceased fire, as did everyone else down the line. The whole shootin' match lasted less than ten minutes; it seemed much longer. It was so quiet all Zeke could hear was the ringing in his ears from the noise and the sound of his own heavy breathing from the adrenalin dump. For some reason, an overpowering sexual urge came over him. *WTF! Can't be. Wish I had a fox in a box on the back of that truck right now.*

The Grunts immediately shifted from defense to offense. They formed a long line, each about ten feet from the other and walked slowly and methodically toward the tree line with rifles, M79s, rocket launchers and machine guns at the ready. Their job was to check out the damage and make sure the VC were no longer a threat. The Grunts were a formidable looking bunch as they sloshed across the rice paddy ready to administer pain and suffering to those who had dared attack a Marine convoy. Zeke was never as proud to have been a Marine as he was at that moment.

*Good God a' mighty they're beautiful!*

As the Grunts disappeared into the tree line, Zeke heard sporadic rifle fire and the thuds of an M79, then silence, followed by a full scale "Madness Minute" that sent chills down everyone's back. A Madness Minute was the term used when all Marines in a group shot their weapons as fast as they could for one minute whether the enemy was present or not. It was designed to kill and intimidate with a demonstration of overwhelming firepower. At the end of the minute, there was silence again. The platoon emerged from the tree line and headed back across the rice paddy to the convoy, apparently more relaxed than they were going in.

It was about then that Zeke noticed that the machine gunner who had been in the truck behind him was on the ground being attended to by a Navy Corpsman. He had been shot in the throat and upper chest within seconds after he opened up with his M60. It was true what they said: a Machine Gunner's life expectancy in combat is just a matter of seconds, on average. They are the greatest threat to the enemy and are number one on the hit list.

Zeke replaced the flattened tire in short order and was thankful there was no more damage than that, other than bullet holes and broken glass.

The truck still ran and that was all he cared about under the circumstances. They packed up, realigned the trucks onto the road and slowly moved out to continue their trek to An Hoa. As they approached the spot where Sallie had been hit, Zeke saw what was left of the water buffalo that had been mangled in the crossfire and the kids who had been shot by Captain Burg. A Corpsman and some others were tending to the kids' bodies and Mustang Sallie's remains. Vietnamese authorities would be notified and families would be reimbursed for the loss of their children and the water buffalo. Sallie's family would soon be organizing a funeral and the world would keep on spinning.

There were no further ambushes as the convoy proceeded. The only action in their path was a two-Phantom team (F4-IIB fighter jets) that swooped in at tree top level to drop napalm on a nest of VC. Phantom 1 dropped its ordinance and then climbed straight up into the clouds perpendicular to the ground. Phantom 2 followed and did the same. The sights and sounds of F4s in combat were awesome and sobering. The sound alone was enough to strike terror in the hearts of brave men, friend or foe. Originally, Napalm was used to torch buildings, but came to be used on people by planes, tanks, riverboats and Marines with flamethrowers. It sucked the oxygen out of the lungs and burned the skin off the body. Being doused with napalm was a hideously painful way to die.

When the convoy came to a halt near the Song Thu Bon River, Zeke overheard a sergeant say that the combat engineers had *not* cleared the road they had just traversed, meaning they had not searched the road for land mines and other booby traps with their electronic detection equipment. The sergeant said, laughingly, that it looked like the convoy had done the engineers' job for them. It was stunning that the engineers had not done their job. It was equally stunning that the sergeant would make a joke about it within earshot of the men who had just driven down that road.

The tank, Ontos and the Grunts from 5th Marines unobtrusively slipped away. Their job ended at the Song Thu Bon. Their mission had been accomplished and in good form. The truckers yelled and whistled at them and gave them the thumbs up sign as a way of saying thanks for the help. Zeke stared at them as they waved back and dutifully moved to their next skirmish.

*I wonder how many of those guys will make it back home alive.*

37

# AN HOA

ZEKE LEAPED OFF THE TOP OF HIS TRUCK JUST AS ANOTHER
BARRAGE OF MACHINE GUN FIRE PEPPERED THE CAB AND
THE CANVAS TOP WHERE HE HAD BEEN LAYING.

Liberty Bridge, the conduit across the Song Thu Bon River to An Hoa, had been destroyed by the VC months earlier so the convoy crossed on a large raft powered by motorboat engines, three or four trucks at a time. It was primitive, but functional. It took three hours for all the vehicles to get across the river. Except for a sniper using the trucks for target practice, the crossing was uneventful. A Marine sniper "neutralized" the irritant with one shot.

Sniping was the norm in the An Hoa area. Shots rang out all the time, some at random to harass; others carefully aimed to produce casualties. Local Marines knew the difference and went about their business accordingly. On the other hand, Heavy Platoon truckers took every incoming shot seriously and hit the deck each time they heard a pop.

Once all the trucks had been ferried across the river, the convoy took a break before moving into An Hoa proper. Zeke, Wilber, Redbone and some of the other truckers went down to the river to wash off the red dirt that had found its way into every nook and cranny of their bodies. They waded into the murky water wearing their boots and utilities to clean their clothes as well. While in the water, a shot rang out from a nearby clump of trees kicking up the dust close to them. At that exact moment, Zeke felt a sharp pain in the back of his head. He thought he'd been shot, but then realized he'd been hit with a golf ball-sized stone. He looked up to see a few local

209

Marines on the riverbank pointing and laughing at him as blood trickled down his neck from the cut.

Zeke slogged out of the water holding his non-military issue red bandana on the wound as he headed toward the stone throwers with a handful of truckers right behind him.

"Which one of you shitbirds threw the stone? Zeke asked calmly, but firmly.

No reply. He looked at one Marine sitting on the ground wearing no insignia of rank on his collar. He had a smirk on his face. Zeke judged him the culprit and looked directly into his eyes.

"What is your major malfunction, boy? Do you have some sort of death wish?"

Zeke pointed to the fresh Marine Corps tattoo he had gotten on R&R in Bangkok several months earlier.

"We're the good guys; we're all on the same side, remember?"

And then, without warning he kicked the sitting Marine squarely in the face with his wet jungle boot while letting out a classic Marine Corps growl. Blood flew from a gash above his eye and one of his nostrils.

Just before they all jumped on each other for an old-fashioned donnybrook, a corporal who had witnessed the whole thing from beginning to end, intervened.

"Stand down, Marines. Cut the shit and get your fucking heads and asses wired together. I saw you guys throw stones at these truckers and I'm going to write your dumb asses up for Office Hours unless you apologize and tell them—loudly and clearly—how much you appreciate all they do for us out here in the middle of Indian country. And you, what's your name … Hammond? Where do you get off kicking a fellow Marine in the face? You could have killed him."

They all reluctantly complied with the corporal's order and shook hands. As Zeke shook hands with the guy he had kicked, the one who had thrown the stone, he pulled him close and whispered with a smile, "Real Marines don't do that to each other. You must be a draftee," he said, as he threw the blood-soaked bandana in his face.

The convoy regrouped and trekked down the road the last few miles to the An Hoa base. Driving through the village, Zeke recognized a Marine who had been at Parris Island with him. He was standing near one of the hooches talking to some Vietnamese men. The DI had nicknamed him Gomer Lurch because he talked like the television character, Gomer Pyle, and resembled Lurch from *The Addams Family*. He was wearing an M1911 on his hip; no rifle. Zeke yelled his name and waved at him as they passed. Gomer Lurch waved back with a puzzled look. Zeke couldn't stop; the convoy was on the move.

Zeke wondered how his other platoon mates from Parris Island were faring, thinking that most graduates of Company S were probably in Vietnam somewhere at that very moment. He knew one of them had been KIA and another had been shot by a fellow Marine over some stupid racial issue. More were probably dead as well. Had Zeke known how many of them had already been killed or maimed he might have cried.

✪ ✪ ✪

Zeke's cargo consisted of 175 mm projectiles, which were used to feed the M107 self-propelled artillery gun. He parked next to two M107s with the words *Vua chiến trường* (King of the Battlefield) painted on their sides. He had never seen a more awesome weapon of war. It weighed over 31 tons and could hurtle its 150-pound projectiles twenty-five miles at a rate of one per minute. One of those rounds could wipe out a whole nest of VC.

After the projectiles were off-loaded, Zeke pulled himself up on top of the truck to take a snooze. The M54's cab cover served as a makeshift hammock and was a relatively comfortable place to sleep sometimes. It was an occupational fringe benefit. As he was drifting into semi-consciousness, the M107s received a fire mission and opened up on an enemy position miles away. The ground vibrated and the sound penetrated Zeke's body right through to the bone. Each discharge shook the truck and lifted him off the canvas.

*That expression, "raining down a shitstorm," must have been inspired by the M107,* he thought.

211

The next morning, Zeke heard an officer yell out "Sergeant Barnes!" with a booming voice. The name caught Zeke's attention. He wondered if, by chance, that Marine might be the same Bubba Barnes he had known in high school—his classmate who had dropped out to join the Marines. When the sergeant appeared, Zeke did a double take; it was Bubba.

Zeke and Bubba had an unusual connection in their senior year. They had competed for the affections of the same girl, which caused a lot of conflict and drama. They almost came to blows many times over that girl, but came to like each other begrudgingly. When Bubba dropped out of school, he did not pick up the class ring he had ordered. It was solid gold with a yellow topaz stone—it was beautiful and unique because no one else had ordered that color. Zeke had the opportunity to buy Bubba's ring and, when he met Sharon, he gave it to her as their "going steady" ring. She was wearing it at that very moment.

Zeke snuck up on Bubba and yelled loudly for the world to hear, "Where the fuck did you get the name, *Bubba*? What the hell does it mean in English?"

Bubba was startled and swung around quickly in a defensive stance. If looks could kill, Zeke would have been dead. Bubba shifted his eyes back and forth a couple times from Zeke's face to the name scrawled on his utility shirt. He started to shake his head and broke out with a smile.

"Zeke Hammond! What the fuck are you doing in this shit hole? This is insane. You can't really be here, can you? Yes, you are. Come here you crazy bastard, let me take a look at you."

They almost did a man-hug, but backed off. Marines did not hug. Instead, they shook hands with enthusiasm and slapped each other on the back a few times.

There wasn't much time to talk. Heavy Platoon was about to head back to Red Beach. Zeke and Bubba exchanged in country mailing addresses and promised to reconnect when they got back home. Zeke heard the call to "mount up" and someone yelling, "where's Hammond?" They said their goodbyes and Zeke turned to jog back to his truck. Bubba yelled out to him at a distance, "Hey Hammond … *Semper Fi.*"

"Do or Die," answered Zeke as he gave Bubba an informal salute.

*This is some crazy shit. Of all the assholes I could possibly meet up with.*

✪ ✪ ✪

Other units that had been part of the convoy had already headed back to the DaNang area in small groups as soon as they were off-loaded. That made no sense to Zeke. He was worried about the prospect of being attacked again and being outgunned.

*Why would we not all be going back together? Is it not just as dangerous going one way as the other?*

He was pissed off about the inconsistencies he kept seeing where Marines' lives were put at risk unnecessarily. It was all part of a pattern that made him pessimistic about the war aim and the prospects for victory. The Marines had already been in Vietnam for two years and things were only getting worse.

*Who's in charge of this bullshit anyway? We shoulda kicked ass and been outta this God-forsaken place by now. What gives?*

Heavy Platoon truckers knew they might get hit again on the return trip, but they hoped the VC were more interested in hindering the *in-flow* of materiel to An Hoa rather than bothering with empty trucks heading back. Except for some harassing fire and maybe a land mine or two here and there, it would probably be a relatively easy ride back to Code Yellow territory. That's what they told themselves.

Mustang Sallie's virtually headless body was shipped back to Graves Registration in DaNang; it was already decomposing. Captain Burg had departed with another group of truckers and left no one in charge of the Heavy Platoon contingent. As the senior lance corporal, Wilber assumed command per military protocol. He had the most seniority and no one else wanted the responsibility anyway. The guys quickly thought up a title for Wilber—SIC, meaning Snuffy-in-Charge. The word Snuffy was a pejorative used by officers and NCOs to refer to privates, PFCs, and lance corporals.

It was dusk and Wilber called a School Circle to discuss the wisdom of heading back to Red Beach in the dark. There would be no escorts and God only knew if the Combat Engineers had done their job and cleared the road of land mines. Worse, there were only five trucks and eight Marines, not enough to hold off a serious assault. It would be suicide to run that road at night.

They drove a few miles and pulled into a 5th Marines base camp for the night. Grunts on guard called out in jest "halt who goes there," as if it wasn't obvious.

"Your mother," yelled Wilber. "Get out of the way or we'll run your asses over."

Wilber was careful that the guards saw he was smiling. He waved at them and they waved back as if welcoming family members. Some of those 5th Marines were the same guys that rode with the convoy to An Hoa the previous day; they were glad to see each other.

The base camp was carved out of a hillside that had sufficient elevation to provide a good view of the surroundings and a tactical advantage. Heavy Platoon parked their trucks in a semi-circle sandwiched between the hill and the concertina wire perimeter ready to interlock fields of fire if attacked. It was all good. With Wilber as SIC they were functioning well as a team and there was a feeling of confidence should the VC attack.

It was a quiet evening except for the soft dreamy sounds and sensations of warm breezes blowing through the trees. Zeke could hear the occasional clink of equipment, low-pitched voices and muffled laughs as the Marines drank C-ration coffee and readied themselves for what the evening might bring. The pitch-black night made the full moon and stars appear even brighter by contrast. He thought of Sharon and wondered if she was looking at the moon at that moment. They had agreed to use the moon to communicate. Zeke had told Sharon in a letter: "Whenever the moon is full, let's both look at it and send positive thoughts to each other. I will say I love you and my words and thoughts will bounce off the moon and back down to you. You do the same. We'll be feeling each other's vibes that way."

He stared at the moon for a while and was sure that he heard her voice and felt the love.

As Zeke thought of Sharon, he realized that he loved her even more for having the patience to stick with him while he went on what seemed to be turning into a fool's errand. He felt he had been deceived about the war. Back in '65, Zeke was "gung ho" about serving his country for all the right reasons. Now, he referred to the Vietnam War as a fool's errand because he saw the U.S. government fighting a war of attrition and not committed to winning. It was also a morale-buster to perceive that the South Vietnamese and the American public did not support the war and did not appreciate or respect the sacrifices being made on their behalf. Ironically, only the NVA voiced grudging respect for American fighting men, particularly Marines, in the same way a serious competitor respects a strong opponent.

✪ ✪ ✪

Marine Force Recons had observed a score of VC making their way down the river and moving toward the 5th Marines' base camp where Heavy Platoon had taken up residence for the evening. Without warning, Marines positioned on the hilltop several yards above the trucks let loose a barrage of 81 mm mortar rounds into the night. Mortars were not loud when launched, but were earsplitting upon impact. The mortars landed with ferocity, lighting up the target area and blowing shrapnel in all directions, surely killing anything within a forty-yard radius of impact and wounding those within two hundred yards, which was its proven range of effectiveness at the time.

There was dead silence for a few moments and then the sounds of automatic gunfire could be heard in the distance through the trees. Marine Recons were engaging the enemy and pulling back to the 5th Marines line, signaling they were the good guys so they wouldn't be hit by friendly fire. Sporadic firing began along the line. *The goblins are here,* thought Zeke.

Zeke was tired, hot, dirty, hungry and dehydrated. He was exhausted. He decided he was not going to let the war nonsense keep him awake any longer. It was a way of life in that area and he needed his rest. He climbed up the side of his truck and plunked down on the cab cover to catch a few winks. He was nodding off when the shooting started again, this time with greater intensity than before. Zeke was so tired he didn't care. With eyes half closed, he lifted himself up on one arm to check things out when an illumination grenade exploded at the nearby concertina wire fence. The

Marine at that position let loose with his M16 rifle on whatever was in front of him. He fired several shots and then his gun jammed. The M16s issued at that time were not good and if they jammed at the Moment of Truth it usually meant a dead Marine. Zeke was glad he was still using an M14. It was reliable and more effective and he could "hit a pimple on a fly's ass at five-hundred yards" with an M14, or so he liked to say.

In the light of a dozen illumination mortars, Zeke could see that the Marine had hit what he was shooting at, but had become preoccupied with clearing his malfunctioning rifle. VC were swarming out of the shadows like cockroaches. They had wrapped their extremities with makeshift tourniquets to slow the bleeding if a bullet or shrapnel hit them. The dope they ingested, perhaps heroin, coupled with the tourniquets, made them hard to stop absent a head shot. It seemed to take half a magazine (ten rounds) or more to drop each one of them. The Grunt with the malfunctioning M16 finally got his weapon to work, but as he raised it to his shoulder to engage the onslaught, his head exploded in a splash of red. He had been hit by several enemy bullets, all at the same time, and was dead before he hit the ground.

Redbone and Wilber, wallowing on the ground under the truck, rifles at the ready, yelled up to Zeke, who was still lying on the top of his truck, to take cover.

"Zeke, you better get down off there; you're going to get your dumb ass killed."

"Oh bullshit! I'm too tired for fun and games tonight. I've gotta catch some shut-eye. Wake me when the war's over."

"Zeke, get down here right now; that's an order," yelled Wilber.

"Stop overreacting, Wilber! You sound like a fuckin' newbie."

Not more than a few seconds later an enemy machine gun opened up on Heavy Platoon's trucks from somewhere out in the darkness. The sound of bullets ripping through metal, blowing out windows and flattening tires was deafening and momentarily terrifying. Zeke leaped off the top of his truck just as another barrage of machine gun fire peppered the cab and the canvas top where he had been laying. Had he hesitated a moment longer, he would have ended up on a slab next to Mustang Sallie back at Graves Registration.

Every driver was using his truck for cover and returning fire—methodically and accurately, just as they'd been taught. Marines were extraordinary riflemen. All of them had been taught to shoot at long distances—two hundred, three hundred and five hundred yards in the standing, sitting and prone positions, respectively, and hit the bulls-eye every time. Heavy Platoon stood their ground; no one holding back. They became as one with the Grunts in the defense of the base camp—Marines all!

The tourniqueted, drugged goblins could not withstand the Marines' fierce defense and pulled back. M107s, helicopter gunships and the Devil Dog mindset won the day, big time. There were three KIA and seven WIA out of a platoon of over fifty men, including the truckers. Redbone was among the wounded. When one of the tires got hit by an enemy bullet, the steel compression ring that secured the tire to the rim blew off with tremendous force and struck him squarely in the back. His spine had been severed and he could not move or talk. He could not even cry from the excruciating pain.

Twenty-three dead VC were left on the battlefield. Blood trails indicated that more had been killed or wounded and dragged off by the enemy. They had left three or four of their WIA lying on the ground groaning, perhaps playing possum, waiting for Marines to get close enough to detonate a hand grenade, killing themselves and as many Marines as possible in the process. Marines had wised up to VC tactics after a couple years of fighting them. The VC used every dirty trick in the book of war and even wrote some additional loathsome chapters. Accordingly, the possums were dealt with at a distance. One by one, they joined their dead brothers in the afterlife, courtesy of a Marine sniper. Better to be safe than sorry. VC that high-ankled were blown to smithereens as 175 mm rounds rained down on their path of retreat. Apparently, their body tourniquets were not much help to them.

The truckers sat on the ground with their backs resting against the wheels. Nobody spoke or moved. The adrenalin rush was exhausting. Zeke's canvas top was in tatters, the passenger side of every truck—the side that faced the enemy—had lots of bullet holes and dents revealing the shiny steel under the paint. There were at least a dozen flat tires too. Bullets that went through the doors also broke the door glass. Many windshields had been blown out as well. Redbone had been seriously hurt and medevacked.

When things settled down, Zeke gave Wilber some good-natured guff about his order to Zeke to get off the roof of his truck and take cover.

"So, you gave me an order, eh? Boy, aren't you hot shit, Mr. SIC?!

"I didn't want you to get killed, you jerk," replied Wilber, annoyed.

"Thank you, man; that was close. I was so tired I couldn't see straight and had no intention of coming down off the truck. I think you saved my life. I may get home to see Sharon after all."

The two of them looked squarely at each other, shaking hands and fighting back emotion.

"*Semper Fi*, Wilber."

"Do or die, Zeke."

✪ ✪ ✪

When dawn broke, SIC Wilber told the truckers to saddle up and prepare to head back to Red Beach in a half-hour. They gobbled down unheated C-rations, quaffed cold instant coffee and were ready before the allotted time. There was no place or time for basic hygiene. They stunk, but didn't care since everyone was in the same boat. It was a welcome change of pace to sport a couple days' growth of beard and smell like a water buffalo without being scolded by officious Garret Troopers.

The Grunts had painted a Purple Heart medal on the side hood panel of Zeke's truck, just a few inches from a couple bullet holes. The Grunts knew the truckers had "really taken some shit," as they put it, and gave as good they got. They also handed Wilber, as SIC, a French Fourragère, a prestigious award bestowed on their regiment by the French government during World War I.

"The Purple Heart on the truck and the Fourragère is our way of saying thank you to you guys—not all truckers, mind you, just to you guys. You are now honorary members of the 5th Marines."

They shook hands all around and said they'd see one another when they came through on the next convoy. Despite the well-intended words, they knew they'd probably never see each other again, but it made them feel good to pretend. The Heavy Platoon trucks departed with a round of applause from the Grunts that turned into friendly cat-calls and assorted hand gestures—primitive symbols of appreciation and acceptance.

When they reached the spot where they had been ambushed and Mustang Sallie and the Vietnamese kids had been killed, they slowed down and were on the lookout for trouble. There was a young Vietnamese guy sitting near the road under a tree. He was dressed in stereotypical VC garb and seemed to be trying to conceal something in his hands. Zeke guessed he had been in the process of setting a land mine, but hadn't completed it before he was spotted. He flashed a sardonic smile; he knew he was busted.

The trucks slowed to a stop and Zeke drew his S&W motioning the suspect to approach his BAT with his hands up. He complied reluctantly and sputtered his innocence in broken English.

"Me no VC. American numba 1; VC numba ten. You no kill me. Me no VC!"

The suspect was not smiling anymore. He dropped his hands and quickly reached for a shiny object on the rope around his waist, perhaps a gun or knife, or maybe a detonator to set off an explosive device. That was enough to convince Zeke that he was a VC and posed a mortal threat. Six shots rang out in rapid succession—so fast that it sounded like automatic fire—each bullet hitting the man center mass, in the middle of the chest. It was unbelievable how much blood came out of six little bullet holes. When they searched him, sure enough, he was reaching for a pistol, an M1911 that he probably took from a dead GI, maybe even one he had killed. As he faded from the world, "burn in hell, VC mother-fucker" were the last words he heard. The man had fallen into the road when he was shot. Each truck crunched over the dead body as they resumed their trek.

✪ ✪ ✪

When they drove through the gate at Red Beach, rank-and-file Marines clapped and cheered as they slowly drove to the motor pool in their battle-scarred trucks. Zeke was surprised at all the fuss. Apparently, word had gotten around that the Heavy Platoon truckers had "kicked VC ass in Indian Country and done some heroic shit." The truckers appreciated the recognition, but knew it was out of proportion to what had happened. The Iwo Jima slogan "Uncommon Valor was a Common Virtue" was the norm. Routine skirmishes like An Hoa were considered inconsequential, but since there were few "attaboys" in the Marine Corps, Zeke and his fellow truckers accepted their moment in the limelight with humility and gratitude.

The trucks proceeded into the Rusty (memorial) Motor Pool at the north end of the base. Top Singer, Captain Tennille and assorted Staff NCOs were waiting for them with their usual tight ass demeanors. The only one smiling was Sergeant Bear who was happy to see that most of his Hooch 240 guys had made it back safely.

It was business as usual—annoyed looks and comments about their appearance and the condition of the trucks. There was no sense of concern about the near-death experiences of their men. There was no mention of the stunning shot that left part of Mustang Sallie's head back on the An Hoa road or poor Redbone who would be a paraplegic for life. Of course, if Sallie had still been alive and seen the condition of the trucks he too would probably have had a conniption. He would have also disciplined the truckers for using up their ammunition allotment (and then some).

As the truckers walked to their hooches with their gear, Zeke looked back at his truck. One of the Garret Troopers was removing the Purple Heart with a rag and paint remover. It was not SOP to paint Purple Hearts on government vehicles.

# 38

# SHARP, WESTMORELAND AND HAMMOND

---

"WHY ME? OF ALL THE OTHERS WHO CAN DRIVE THOSE
LITTLE GODDAMNED JEEPS, THEY PICK ME?"

---

A few weeks later at an evening formation, Captain Tennille announced that 4-star Admiral of the Navy with the pretentious name of Ulysses S. Grant Sharp, Jr., Commander-in-Chief, United States Pacific Command, and 4-star Army General William C. Westmoreland, Commander of all U.S. forces in Vietnam would be visiting the area. Heavy Platoon would be providing a jeep and driver/bodyguard for the two commanders and Zeke Hammond had been selected for that duty.

"WTF," Zeke exclaimed in a too-loud voice that earned him disapproving looks from everyone that outranked him, which was almost everyone. He could not believe his ears. On one hand, it was a big deal to be entrusted with such responsibility. On the other, it was the last thing he wanted to do. *Why me? Of all the others who can drive those little goddamned Jeeps, they pick me?*

Zeke was salty from time-to-time as most Marines came to be as they acquired more time in Vietnam, but he did his job and kept a low profile. His adventures and lapses of judgment were not widely known and, notwithstanding the toes-on-rubber-boots and speeding in a war zone capers, Zeke was regarded as a good Marine with a colorful personality.

All the rank-and-file Marines high-fived Zeke and told him what a great thing it was to have been selected for such special duty as they patted him on the back and praised him. It would be the next best thing to chauffeuring the Commander-in-Chief, President Johnson. Zeke appreciated the accolades and the attention, but he had a serious problem: he didn't have the proper clothes to wear. His utilities were worn and faded and his jungle boots were badly worn. Sallie had brassoed his rifle, but only Mustang Sallie had cared about that. He was dead so that was no longer an issue. The black paint had chipped off his collar insignias and he had brassoed them as well until they became a shiny gold color that resembled a 2nd lieutenant's bars at a distance. The Marines in Hooch 240 pitched in and scrounged the unblemished clothes, boots and equipment he would need. Truck drivers could get most anything. Bear loaned Zeke his M1911 for the day, complete with polished holster and Brassoed ammo.

Zeke loved his Brassoed collar insignias. It was amusing when enlisted Marines saluted him thinking he was an officer and then cursed and sputtered when they got closer and realized he was just one of them. Staff NCOs were the most fun because once they realized they had saluted a junior enlisted man they went into contortions to pretend they hadn't. He had been told to get new insignias but never did, insisting they were not available.

Then the ballbusting and bantering began. Bantering among Marines was an art form that required finesse in delivery to avoid a violent reaction by the ballbustee. They told Zeke, in hushed tones and feigned concern that the VC knew all about the dignitaries' planned visit and it was a virtual certainty he'd be killed or captured in an attempt to target his high-value passengers. They reminded Zeke of what happened to PFC Robert Harwood, a fellow motor transport guy, who had been captured by the VC a couple years earlier when chauffeuring a high-ranking general. Zeke knew it was all in fun and sort of enjoyed the banter as a form of comic relief.

A day or two before Sharp and Westmoreland were to arrive at Red Beach, Hooch 240 organized a dress rehearsal for Zeke which involved donning his chauffeuring get-up, practicing protocol and responding to hypothetical questions. They also discussed actions that should be taken if the VC attacked and took them hostage.

"Never happen. I'm a short-timer. I'll use those two muckety-mucks for cover and let *them* handle things," he replied with a laugh. Zeke knew the score. He would have to put himself between the enemy and the generals to protect their lives and would do just that if the goblins beamed up.

The first order of business was to know whether to kiss their ring, kiss their ass or just salute them.

"They have more brass than all the officers at Red Beach put together," said Zeke, half-serious.

The guys reminded Zeke that based on their collective shitter burning experience, officers shit stank too; therefore, they were no better than anyone else. Zeke shook his head in disgust.

"Thanks for the visual. I'll remember that when I meet them; might quell the jitters. Hope I don't break out laughing."

When Zeke first got word that he would be Jeeping Sharp and Westmoreland around the Red Beach neighborhood, Zeke sent a note to his mother and to Sharon. They thought it was a big deal and told all their friends and family. He had become an overnight sensation back home. He was enjoying the limelight and the good feeling that his existence mattered to someone in the Marine Corps besides himself. Captain Tennille even deigned to chat with him about the upcoming honor and big responsibility. The transformation from not wanting to chauffer the two top military men on the planet to being proud and happy about the assignment felt good; a natural high.

✪ ✪ ✪

The day before Westmoreland and Sharp were to arrive, Gums burst into Hooch 240 with a disappointed look and bad news.

"Don't worry about the tour Hammond; Sharp and Westy aren't coming after all. There was a change of plans. Sorry, Zeke. You know how it is."

Everyone and everything at Red Beach had been spit-shined for the visit. Zeke had detailed the Jeep, inside and out and Brassoed his rifle ammo like a classic Garret Trooper. Even the omnipresent dogs had been removed to avoid distasteful displays of copulation for which Vietnamese dogs were notorious. Zeke was not angry; he was disappointed and disgusted.

"What a time-waster, just like this whole fucking war, you know that Gums? It's a metaphor for the whole goddamned clusterfuck."

Hooch 240 gave Zeke a few more minutes of fame as they took back their borrowed clothes and passed around a bottle of whiskey that had been slated for the Officers' Club but got "rerouted."

Zeke's mom wrote *c'est la vie*—so goes life, her reaction to most disappointments. Sharon wrote "you're still my hero." Naomi, Sharon and the Marines in Hooch 240 still liked Zeke anyway. Some of the guys, in typical Marine Corps fashion, began bantering and calling him "Almost"—almost a bodyguard. It felt good to laugh.

## 39

# DARKNESS

"... THIS IS THE HARDEST LETTER I HAVE EVER HAD
TO WRITE TO YOU. BRACE YOURSELF ..."

Zeke went to the motor pool at dusk for formation, as usual. He listened to Captain Tennille's spiel and picked up his Trip Ticket and mail before heading out. He saw a letter from his mother but nothing from Sharon. He was disappointed. He had not heard from her in a while and was missing her light-hearted words on perfume-scented pages. She would always put on a heavy coat of lipstick and kiss the back of the envelope, leaving a perfect imprint of her lips. She would draw Zeke + Sharon hearts too. The mail clerk always gave Zeke a knowing look and a smile when he delivered her letters. It was a bit embarrassing, but when he thought about the alternative—not having Sharon in his life—he didn't mind the embarrassment at all. Without her, being in Vietnam would be that much more onerous and his life would be empty.

Sharon would always close her letters with a countdown of the number of days until Zeke returned and a reminder of how happy they were going to be when they got married after he got back. Zeke was due to rotate out of Vietnam in less than six weeks and was gradually allowing himself to get more excited about being reunited with her with each passing day.

According to his Trip Ticket, two M54s were needed at an ARVN compound on the other side of DaNang. It was an unusual assignment. Heavy Platoon trucks were never used for direct support of ARVN operations. All the dispatcher knew was that a request had come from "higher up" and the purpose was TBD—to be determined. That made Zeke and the other trucker, a PFC named Bader, uncomfortable; they did not like mysteries. They also did not appreciate the ARVN who were generally regarded as ineffective and unreliable by rank-and-file Marines.

The Vietnamese Marines, on the other hand, were go-getters modeled after the American Marines. They were regarded as South Vietnam's military elite—motivated, effective and fearless. When America pulled out of Vietnam in 1975, ARVN soldiers were sent to reeducation camps and not executed. Vietnamese Marines, on the other hand, were considered too tough to tame and not reeducable; they were murdered outright. The consequences of their bravery and tenacity in opposing the North Vietnamese Communists were horrific.

Bader played the guitar, drank whiskey, and was a good average Marine. He bragged about being the only person in the world to have his Social Security Number tattooed on his arm. Marines gave him some good-natured ballbusting about what the numbers meant—IQ, body parts, his class standing in high school and so on. He had a good sense of humor too, saying that his goal was to work himself up to master sergeant so he could call himself Master Bader. That was good for a laugh the first time, but Bader repeated it a lot and it became obnoxious. Zeke thought he might have been serious.

Bader fell in love with a Dogpatch Charlotte, which confirmed that he had never been laid before and he wasn't quite right in the head. He caught another Marine poking what we saw as *his* sweet Charlotte and threatened to kill them both, brandishing his M14 from one to the other while they lay naked. Rank-and-file Marines who witnessed the outburst subdued Bader. They tied him up and had a "come to Jesus" with him—a minor ass-kicking followed by a candid lecture about whores, love, threats to fellow Marines and related issues. He got his head and ass wired together, admitted the error of his ways and laid off the Charlottes, literally, for the duration of his tour in Vietnam.

Bader and Zeke arrived at the ARVN compound, their M14s locked and loaded and set on rock and roll. Zeke's S&W was concealed beneath his waistband in a holster he had made from a spare pocket from his utility trousers. The compound consisted of a large, impressive white stone building surrounded by a wall of the same material and color. The French had built it during the First Indochina War. They were waved into the compound by the guards, parked and walked to the main door with rifles at sling arms ready to slip-and-flip in a heartbeat.

Inside, they found a score of ARVN officers and senior enlisted men eating at picnic tables. One of the officers, a lieutenant, directed a question to them in Vietnamese, which Zeke thought was rude since he and Bader were Americans and would be unlikely to understand what he said. Zeke responded in French, "*Quoi de neuf?* "(What's up?)

The lieutenant's demeanor changed immediately. "*Venir manger avec nous,*" (Come eat with us) he replied with a smile pointing to the table.

Many Vietnamese spoke French. Zeke had taken French in high school and often found the few words he remembered helpful in connecting with the Vietnamese. Even if his pronunciation was faulty or he used the wrong words, they appreciated his effort.

The food looked and smelled like road kill and it made them sick to their stomachs, but Zeke and Bader knew they needed to be polite, especially since the room was filled with officers. Marines were told to treat Vietnamese military officers the same as they would American officers. That was a hard sell to rank-and-file Marines and most of the time they didn't comply.

Bader summed up the consensus: "I ain't salutin' those assholes. They should be salutin' *me* for bein' here in their sorry-ass country and fightin' their battles for them."

Zeke bit down on a piece of something that looked interesting. It was awful and much too spicy. It was water buffalo *ear,* which tasted like uncleaned tripe that had not been cooked properly. It was pure gristle. Zeke had once eaten a monkey meat hamburger, which induced the Green Apple Quick Step, a.k.a., acute dysentery. Another time he had an exotic meal in the home of a Vietnamese Air Force pilot in the bowels of DaNang. Zeke had also sampled Vietnamese gobbledygook as part of his CAP experience.

He wasn't a stranger to Vietnamese food, but *nothing* had ever looked or smelled as nasty as that water buffalo ear. Zeke and Bader did their best to choke it down.

Zeke heard the lieutenant say *"mauviettes"* (weaklings), in a muffled voice; everyone laughed. Zeke's lips formed a smile, but his demeanor registered anger as he stared directly into the lieutenant's eyes and said "schmuck" in a respectful voice. Bader did not understand French and the lieutenant did not understand Yiddish, but everyone laughed along anyway, looking puzzled.

After enough ear, the lieutenant told Zeke and Bader to go to their trucks and wait. They meandered out and climbed into their respective cabs wondering why they were there and what their assignment would be. Maybe it was a mix-up. It was puzzling and aggravating at the same time.

✪ ✪ ✪

The ARVN compound abutted a cemetery and the light from the moon reflected off the white tombstones, the building and the stone wall. Zeke pulled out his L-shaped military flashlight, hooked it on the canvas just over his shoulder, as usual, and opened the letter from his mom that he had picked up before he and Bader left the motor pool.

"Dear Zeke, this is the hardest letter I have ever had to write to you. Brace yourself, my son, I have bad news ... Sharon was killed in an accident. She was thrown from a car. The ambulance rushed her to the hospital, but her neck was broken upon impact; all attempts to save her failed. She only lived for a couple of hours and never regained consciousness. She died on April fifteenth. At her funeral, just before they closed the casket, her mom, Helen, placed your high school ring in her folded hands and tucked your letters next to her shoulder. What happened was…"

Zeke put the letter down without reading any further. He turned off the flashlight and sat in silence staring into the black night not caring if goblins snuck up at that moment and killed him. He half-hoped they would. Reading news about death while sitting next to a cemetery in the dark of night was surreal to Zeke.

*Did I really read that? It didn't really happen, did it? This is a bad dream. Where am I? What the fuck is going on? I'm off balance. Am I awake?*

He read the letter again to be sure he wasn't dreaming.

*She was in awful pain. My God, she must have been scared. And I wasn't there with her. If I had been there instead of in this goddamned place, she'd be alive. I should be with her now.*

After some time, he didn't know how long, Zeke began to recover his wits. He wanted to get down on the ground and tear out his soul the way Pith had done when his sons were burned up in the fire at the refugee camp, but he couldn't. He thought he would explode and blow into a million pieces if he didn't suppress his emotions and redirect himself quickly. He took a drink of water from his canteen and did some tactical breathing as he weakly stumbled out of the cab of the truck.

Bader came over to Zeke's truck with a worried look on his face.

"Why the fuck are we here? These asshole ARVNs don't need us. This place gives me the creeps. I think we should *di-di* on out of here before we find ourselves in a world of hurt."

Zeke could not respond at first. His chest was hurting and he felt dizzy. He took some more deep breaths and forced himself to reply.

"I agree. These fuck-sticks don't have a clue. Almost seems like a set-up or something. Got any grenades under your seat?"

"Grenades? Zeke, are you nuts? What the hell for?"

"I want to play catch with that wise-ass ARVN lieutenant."

Bader noticed that Zeke seemed to be in pain, but did not press the matter. He knew something was wrong, particularly when he implied fragging the lieutenant. That was not like Zeke at all. He seemed disoriented and different.

Just then, the door of the compound swung open and the ARVN lieutenant walked briskly toward their trucks, still wearing his wise-guy expression, to say they wouldn't be needed after all. Zeke and Bader looked at each other in disgust. They just nodded and said nothing. They did not salute the lieutenant as they turned toward their trucks to leave. They both wanted to say and do some bad things to him, but maintained their composure. As they pulled out, Bader backfired his truck as soon as the engine built up sufficient compression. The sound was deafening, amplified by the echo off the walls of the compound and headstones. The ARVNs hit the deck or scurried for cover, maybe shitting in their pants in the process.

When they arrived back at Red Beach, Zeke parked his truck in the motor pool and staggered to Hooch 240 feeling as though he'd been drugged. He didn't have the energy to walk up the three steps to the door so he rolled into the foxhole in front of the hooch and sprawled out on the sandbags.

After lying there motionless for a few minutes he clasped his hands together as if readying to pray, fingertips pointed at the moon, and cursed God: "Thanks again, God. No shit. Is this another test? What the hell for, God? Trying to see how long it takes me to break? Don't you know I'm not very good at tests? Why the fuck did you allow Sharon to die? You couldn't exercise a little divine intervention for *her,* one of your best and brightest? You work in mysterious ways all right. BULLSHIT!"

He shook his head, closed his eyes and covered his face with his helmet and poncho.

The guys heard Zeke yelling from the foxhole and piled out the door to see what was going on. They realized that Zeke was not playing around. Something serious had happened and he was in a world of hurt. He looked like he'd been wounded, but there was no blood. They sat down around him on the sandbags and tried to find out what was wrong. Zeke did not utter a word; he just handed Wilber the letter from Naomi. Wilber read the letter aloud for all to hear.

"Holy shit, man. This is really fucked up," said Wilber. "What a kick in the ass. And you being almost a short-timer and all."

Everyone echoed variations of Wilber's sentiments. Some just said "sorry man" and put a hand on his shoulder. Others said nothing; they just hung their heads, eyes averted, as a sign of shared pain. Brothers are like that. They cleared the area to give him some space. Wilber brought Zeke's gear into the hooch and put his revolver in its hiding place.

Most Marines had girlfriends back home; a few had wives. They all related to Zeke's situation and imagined what it would be like if the same thing happened to them.

"Well, now the Marine Corps will be happy," said Zeke bitterly, "They don't want us havin' wives and girlfriends anyway."

The Corps felt that having a wife was a distraction and compromised combat effectiveness. Unmarried men made better cannon fodder. They would take more risks and die more willingly without such emotional ties. "If the Marine Corps wanted you to have a wife, they would have issued you one," was the refrain. Whether married or not, a Marine in Vietnam was assumed to be more vulnerable to danger, death and injury than the folks back home. Ironically, after nearly a year in Vietnam, Zeke was alive and Sharon was the one who was dead.

The next morning Zeke awoke early with the day truckers. He wanted authorization to use the Military Auxiliary Radio System (MARS) to call home and get a reality check on what he had read in the letter. MARS was a form of short-wave transmission from Vietnam to somewhere in the U.S. where it was then patched into the mainstream phone system. There were no cell phones or laptop computers at that time. MARS was restricted to emergencies for rank-and-file Marines. It was rumored that the call standard for officers was more relaxed.

Zeke needed approval from everyone in his chain-of-command, starting with Corporal Gums, before he would be allowed to use the MARS. Gumster said yes, as did Sergeant Bear. Next in line was a new gunnery sergeant named Potter. He had replaced Gunnery Sergeant Green, the mustachioed Staff NCO who had called for CAP and sniper volunteers, which now seemed long ago. Potter was a humorless gray-haired fellow. He was all business and never smiled. *He must be Calvinist*, thought Zeke.

Zeke timed it to catch him just as the morning formation broke up. He approached the gunny determined to keep his emotions in check. Zeke's sentences were choppy; he had difficulty catching his breath as he talked. He kept his head down and eyes averted to hide his discomfort as he made his request to call Long Island over the MARS network. The gunny could feel Zeke's pain and agreed with the need to use the system to help him return to normal as quickly as possible. He said he would clear it with Singer and Tennille and send someone for him as soon as the communication link was set up. There would not be any waiting list for Zeke. *Gunny's a good guy despite his rank,* Zeke thought.

Zeke waited on his rack in a trance smoking the Pall Mall 100s his mother had sent to him. As he blew smoke rings into the air, he thought he would tell her how much he appreciated her keeping him stocked with those unique cigarettes for the past many months. He reflected on his ability to take one painful emotional punch after another and still keep his head and ass wired together. The punches began with the death of his grandfather only days after he arrived in Vietnam. They continued with the death of Marine comrades and Vietnamese kids. Even his dog, Tip, had died. Tip had been Zeke's best friend since he was five years old.

*And now Sharon's gone; sealed in a cold dark coffin deep in the ground with nothing to comfort her but my ring and letters. This must all be some kind of mistake. This can't be happening. It's insane. That's it? Gone? Nothing more? Fuck this! I'm in Vietnam and she's the one that dies rather than me? Impossible! Gramp said to be a man. Stone face. No tears. Pain is weakness leaving the body. Others have dealt with worse. I can't.*

Each emotional punch put him in a temporary fog, what psychologists would call "affective flattening." With that came the loss of sensory acuity, particularly hearing. It would last for a while and then he would snap out of it, always a little stronger for the experience. Up until then, his psychological "circuit breaker" had worked well—the fuse, or whatever it was, seemed to break before it caused serious damage to his whole system. But the impact of Sharon's unexpected death felt different. His circuit breaker was not working and he wasn't sure he could come back from the precipice this time … or if even wanted to.

At about 14:00 hours, 2:00 p.m. in normal time, Gums burst into Hooch 240 to get Zeke to the dispatch office immediately for his MARS call, reminding him there was only a narrow window of time to use the system once they logged in. A master gunnery sergeant who resembled Perry White, the editor of the *Daily Planet* in the old Superman television series, would be monitoring Zeke's communication in an adjacent room. White had served on Guadalcanal at the start of WWII, the Chosin Reservoir in Korea, and now in Vietnam. He was an "old" guy in his mid-forties but still tough as nails. It was hard for Zeke to believe he was still in the Corps at that age.

White's job was to eavesdrop on MARS conversations to ensure that nothing inappropriate was said in terms of military secrets, salacious comments, threats, foul language and so forth. He also verified that calls were, in fact, urgent and not just cases of homesickness. Zeke found this humorous and ridiculous at the same time. Anything he might know, the enemy knew too and probably long before he did. However, that was protocol and Zeke was glad he could still muster a little humor under the circumstances.

Master Gunny White did all the button pushing and rigmarole to reach Long Island. It was a more complex process than Zeke assumed. The call was placed at 2:45 p.m. Vietnam time, which was zero dark thirty in Area Code 516. Naomi groggily answered the phone. Master gunny told her that her son was calling from Vietnam and that he would be monitoring the call. He instructed her to say "over" at the end of each short transmission. "Yes sir, over," she said. Naomi understood that a master gunnery sergeant is the highest enlisted grade in the Corps, co-equal to sergeant major, and deserved respect.

There were no hearts and flowers. No emotion. No small talk. Just direct questions and answers in a crisp businesslike "just the facts ma'am" tone.

"Mom, what happened? Over."

"She was thrown out of a car. Over."

"Where and when? Over."

"Near the grade school, around that uphill curve on Creek Road. Sharon's friend, Donna, was in the car, a convertible. The car flipped. Sharon and Donna were thrown out. Sharon died, although not immediately, and Donna had a broken pelvis and other injuries. Over."

"When? Over."

"April fifteenth. In the afternoon. Over."

"Who was driving the car? Over."

Zeke did not recognize the name.

"To me he's just a mope with no name. That's what I'll call him—Mope. Over."

Without thinking about who was listening to the conversation or where he was, he said in a low, calm tone of voice between clenched teeth, "I'll be coming for Mope. Make sure the word gets out so he can sweat about it until then. Over."

"Zeke, it wasn't like that. Don't you..."

"Over and out," he said as he cut his mother off in mid-sentence.

Zeke thanked the master gunny for his help and gave him a thumbs-up as he got up to leave. Zeke could not tell what he was thinking and did not really care. His Perry White face was an enigma.

"Hammond, did you just threaten to kill someone?"

"Not me, master gunny, I'm not a violent guy."

White beckoned Zeke into his eavesdropping room and said with command presence, "Sounds like a bad situation, son, but you best get your head and ass wired together or I'll guaran-goddamn-tee that you'll be in a world of shit if you follow through on what I just heard."

White put his hand on Zeke's shoulder in a fatherly fashion and said with a gentler demeanor.

"Listen Marine, you'll get over this. It may take many years but the pain will fade. Exacting revenge for something that was an accident will not bring her back. You'll be in the brig for the rest of your life, if they don't fry your ass in the electric chair for being felony stupid."

Zeke appreciated White's sensitivity and advice, which he thought was extraordinarily out of character for a Marine Staff NCO.

✪ ✪ ✪

That night Zeke did not have an assigned truck run, which was unusual. Unbeknownst to him, Master Gunny White arranged to cut him some slack given the circumstances. Despite the night off, Zeke felt like crap. Although he appreciated the condolences, he felt uncomfortable about being the center of attention with everyone feeling sorry for him. He was also annoyed with himself for being such a jerk with his mother. His last words to her—an unsubtle vow of retribution toward the guy that caused Sharon's death—must have upset her a lot. Most of all he felt like crap because he was done with God for allowing this to happen. Sharon was a beautiful, delightful person and her death was painful and pointless.

His last thought struck him as ironic. That same thing could be said of the war—painful and pointless. It was all one big cauldron of insanity now—the war, the pain, his life. It was as if someone else was experiencing all those things and he was just looking on at a distance like he was watching a movie.

Once again, Walter's advice to "be a man" came to mind. Zeke understood his trials and tribulations paled in comparison to the misfortunes of many others around the world, but knowing that did not lessen the pain for him. Velma would say, "God doesn't give us any more than we can handle." Zeke always dismissed that line as one of her cryptic Calvinisms. *If that was true, then why do people commit suicide? Maybe this is my test for God for a change. If I can't hack it and kill myself, then God failed and Grandma Velma was just blowing smoke.*

Some Marines in Heavy Platoon brought whiskey over to Hooch 240 and passed around the bottle. Bader strummed a guitar and sang some sad songs. No one spoke of anything too serious or tried to comfort Zeke with platitudes. They just drank and talked among themselves in hushed tones. Like a family, they were there to give Zeke moral support and it was working.

Much later that night, Zeke went out to the bunker and sat down on a sandbag. He lit up a cigarette and stared at the full moon looming bright and low in the dark sky. *She was afraid of the dark; thunder and lightning made her cry. I should be there with her, somewhere in the ephemeral universe, to comfort her and be with her.* Zeke pulled his ka-bar knife out of the sheath and for a moment considered the possibilities. He could hear a song coming from Armed Forces Radio inside the hooch. It was Herman's Hermits' *There's a Kind of Hush ... all over the world, tonight.* Indeed.

Zeke received a letter from his mother. She expressed great concern about his state of mind and cautioned him not to do anything stupid when he came home. She knew her son well enough to know what he might do, especially given the way he ended the MARS conversation.

"Think of your little brother and sisters; they wouldn't want a big brother who is a murderer," she wrote.

Her strong statement redirected him to his siblings, then ranging from 4 to 11. *What would they think? I don't know. A man's gotta do what a man's gotta do. What the hell was she doing in that car? Why were they heading up that particular road? Was she cheating on me? Why did the Mope drive like a jackass? Why wasn't she wearing a seatbelt, particularly in a convertible? Why were Donna and Sharon thrown from the back seat and the others left unscathed? That Mope must have been driving wild. It was his fault. He killed her and maimed Donna. He's gonna die ... slowly, just like she did.*

After serious consideration of the pros and cons, Zeke decided there was no other course of action possible. Mope needed to pay for his crime regardless of the consequences, regardless of what anyone would think, regardless of anything. *He took what was most precious to me; I'll take what's most precious to him—his life.*

It wasn't long before Zeke called a School Circle for the guys in Hooch 240 to solicit advice about the slowest and most painful ways to kill the man he now called Mope as though it was his real name. They suggested all kinds of gruesome and repulsive ways to extract retribution. Two guys voted to suck it up and let God and the law sort it out. Gyp suggested kidnapping and torturing Mope, making sure no one else was involved, and disposing of the body in a tree mulcher. He even volunteered to do the job himself when he got back to the states ... for a nominal fee.

"You're not that violent, Zeke, to just shoot that guy or do some other crazy shit. You don't have it in you to just *murder* someone. I could save you a lot of trouble by taking care of the matter for you."

"Violent? Murder? Killing? Hell Gyp, those words aren't relevant; they don't describe what's going to happen. What I'm set on doing is administering *justice* and doing so in a calm, dispassionate manner, the same way a murderer is executed by the state. We've had to administer justice here in Vietnam, right? Of all people, you should know what I'm talking about."

Gyp smiled and nodded, sensing Zeke's agitation.

"I guess you're right, Zeke. You'd be 'administering justice' and that's something only you should do in this case," said Gyp.

Zeke thanked them for their input but decided to stick with the original plan—to use his S&W, up close and personal, with five shots to the extremities and the last shot between the eyes after Mope had suffered enough and understood why he was leaving the Earth under those circumstances. He neither considered nor cared about the aftermath—the legal consequences, his family or his soul. He was on a pathway to hell and did not give it a second thought.

# 40

# WE GOTTA GET OUT
# OF THIS PLACE

---

"HAMMOND, FALL OUT OF VIETNAM, ON THE DOUBLE,
AND DON'T COME BACK!"

---

Zeke's thirteen-month tour in Vietnam would be ending soon. It was time to get things squared away for the transition back to The World. The first order of business was to mail his S&W and holster rig home so it would be waiting for him when he rotated. He had important work to do with that weapon and did not want anything to go awry. He heard that outgoing mail was x-rayed so he crisscrossed metal tent pegs over the pistol with tape to distort the outline of a gun and then mailed it to his rum-dum, but trustworthy friend Flaco back in Pennsylvania. Zeke included a cryptic unsigned note using code-talking nicknames and shorthand, essentially telling Flaco to keep the gun under wraps until he got back.

He sent the holster rig separately, minus the bullets, and phonied up a foolproof return name and address to make the package untraceable. He also wiped the fingerprints clean. He assumed everything would work out fine if he acted nonchalant when he handed the package to the postal clerk with the contents listed as "Gift for friend (metal wall hanging)."

Zeke had thought about extending his tour of duty to stay with the guys in Hooch 240 and continue to help South Vietnam in their struggle against Communism. Marines who voluntarily extended their tours for six months received thirty days' R&R to any place in the free world as well as a substantial cash bonus. It was tempting, but thirteen months was enough; anything more would be bad luck in Zeke's mind.

Zeke had soured on Vietnam. "Fighting for your country," "making Vietnam safe for democracy," and "stopping Communism" based on the Domino Theory put forth by the government were empty slogans; they had no meaning given the totality of the circumstances. He was not going to risk being a casualty of war unless every young man in the country shared that risk and unless there was truly an existential threat to the country.

By 1966 the song, *We Gotta Get Out of This Place* by Eric Burden and the Animals had been adopted by American servicemen as the tongue-in-cheek national anthem of Vietnam. Zeke found it ironic that the song now had deeper meaning given one of the lyrics: *"Now my girl, you're so young and pretty...you'll be dead before your time is due..."*

It was time to "get out of this place."

Zeke had two worldly possessions that he willed to Hooch 240—his "Cambodian" fan and a lawn chair. The fan did not have a safety frame. Its four sharp steel blades were exposed and sliced anyone who inadvertently came too close. At the time, Cambodia was not friendly to the U.S., hence the connection. Zeke kiddingly told them to use it as a weapon if they were overrun. He had found the lawn chair somewhere and had used it in his guard bunker. Lawn chairs were rare commodities for rank-and-file Marines. It was probably against some rule to have one. Zeke willed the chair to Moby who was slated to be next to rotate out of Vietnam. He gave it to him on the condition that he would pass it to the next man out and so on down the line until the chair wore out or the war ended, whichever came first.

It was common for Marines rotating back to the states to make promises about sending booze, cigarettes, condoms and other necessities back to their former hooch-mates. Most never followed through. They had completed the defining experience of their lives and then neglected the Marines who went through it with them. Zeke hated that and vowed to be different. He promised to send each man in Hooch 240 a bottle of their favorite booze.

"Do you want the money now?" asked Buford.

"Fuck no. I'm buying, packing and mailing."

"Would you get beer if we don't like whiskey? I'd give anything for a 6-pack of Coors."

"Beer? You must be shittin' me, Buford. First, that's a lot of extra weight. Second, Coors is impossible to get outside of Colorado. I said *booze*, one bottle, not beer and other shit. Take it or leave it."

"Okay, Richard's Wild Irish Rose wine. You said *bottle* and didn't specify size. I'd like a gallon bottle."

"Fuck you, Buford, figure it out and get back to me before I leave or you'll get nix." *What a dolt.*

✪ ✪ ✪

When the day came to depart, it was an emotional goodbye. They shook hands and said some profound things to each other, trying to sum up everything they had gone through and everything they meant to each other. It was not fashionable to say, "love ya brother" back then, but that's what they meant. They knew they would never see each other again, except by chance. They also knew that as long as they were in Vietnam anything could happen and some might not make it back. No one cried. Marines never cried, it seemed, at least not in front of one another. Crying was a sign of weakness reserved for pussies, the DIs use to say. Zeke had one full carton of Pall Mall Gold 100s left. There were now nine Marines in the hooch; he put a pack on each of the racks and kept one for himself.

Gums pulled up to Hooch 240 in a Mighty Mite, a small Jeep-like vehicle, to take Zeke to the "Transient" facility at the DaNang air base. Transient was where service members were "processed out" then put on a Freedom Bird back to The World by way of Okinawa. The Freedom Bird was either a commercial airline—TWA, Pan American or the like—or a military plane, one of the variants of the C130 Hercules transport. Everyone hoped to get out on a commercial flight. Civilian stewardesses treated servicemen with respect and class; military personnel did not.

"Hammond, fall out of Vietnam, on the double and don't come back!" Gums yelled with a big smile.

241

It was customary to give a final order to that effect, unofficially and in fun, of course. No officers or staff NCOs were present to bid *adieu* and say thanks to departing men. Marines like Zeke were nobodies to the brass. Their existence did not matter; they were easily replaced. It was up to the rank-and-file to muster their fellow Marines out of the country. Zeke rendered a crisp hand salute to Gums and to his hooch mates.

"Aye, aye, sir. High-ankling out of Vietnam as ordered."

"Oh yea, one more thing, here's your lance corporal stripes."

"For God's sake. Now? Wow, that's a nice going away present, Gums, are you just making this up? Is it official?"

"Would I shit you, Zeke? replied Gums. "Do what you want with them. They're yours. You sure as hell earned them."

Zeke grabbed his seabag and made his way across the deep white sands of Red Beach for the last time. He could hear the Marines in 240 singing *We Gotta Get Out of this Place.* He tried to block out the song; it was too emotional for him. *God that sun is blinding.*

# 41

# BAD MOON RISING

"... NEARLY 1,500 SERVICEMEN HAD BEEN KILLED
ON THE LAST DAY OF THEIR TOUR OF DUTY."

"Transient" was a large hooch that abutted the DaNang air base. It was staffed by Marines and Air Force enlisted men who were more obnoxious than they needed to be. They were curt and disrespectful to everyone regardless of rank. They had power over those rotating out of Vietnam—they knew it and those rotating knew it. They could delay a man's departure, divert him to a military aircraft instead of a commercial plane or "misplace" paperwork.

In addition to verifying orders to leave, they searched sea bags for contraband. Some fools tried to sneak weapons, ammo, grenades, bayonets, ka-bars and even marijuana out of the country with them, although drug use was only a minor problem at the time, at least with Marines. *Such dumb asses*, thought Zeke, shaking his head, *they could have sent some of that stuff home by mail.*

When Gyp rotated a couple weeks earlier, he packed a live hand grenade, intending to smuggle it all the way home to the states. He changed his mind when he got to Transient fearing it would be found, so he dropped it in a shitter never giving a thought to what might happen when the brew was set on fire by the shit stick detail the next day.

Late that afternoon Zeke was standing in line on the tarmac ready to board the 707 Freedom Bird that he could see in the distant sky entering base leg and then turning on final approach. There were a couple hundred service members, 98 percent men, from all branches of service wearing all kinds of different uniforms, from kakis and dress uniforms to utilities, red, green and black berets, piss cutters, and barracks covers. Some guys were spit-shined; others were filthy, having just come out of the field in a chopper still looking wild from having been extracted from hell less than a few hours earlier. Those were the men that saw action every day, sometimes even having to fend off the goblins to get to the helicopter to take them to Transient.

Zeke followed the plane intently with his eyes and for some reason began humming the music to the song, *More*, the wonderful theme from *Mondo Cane*, as the majestic Freedom Bird descended slowly toward the runway. He saw the flaps retract to forty degrees and then a puff of blue smoke as the wheels contacted the pavement. Zeke touched his 10-Đồng piece—*wow, lucky me. Finally getting out of here and on a commercial plane no less.* That meant American stewardesses, decent food, air conditioning and maybe a beer or two … or six.

The aircraft stopped about fifty yards from where the passengers were waiting as the jet engines shut down one-by-one. A mobile stairway was pushed up against the fuselage. *That's the stairway to heaven,* Zeke thought. Out came the stewardesses looking dapper in their tight-fitting airline uniforms. Truth be told, they were not that hot. Stewardesses assigned Vietnam duty were second-stringers. The first string flew to the desirable destinations catering to civilians. It didn't matter though. They were a welcome sight because seeing them meant going home.

Zeke noticed a handful of guys, mostly Air Force officers, with handfuls of papers trotting up to the front of the line waving their arms. They had been authorized emergency leave and, as such, could bump other passengers from the flight. The flight officer began selecting bumpees. After about six or seven names were called and Zeke got close to the stairway he thought *all clear; I'm outta here.* Then he heard his name called.

It was hard to describe the feeling—first, anger at being singled out then self-pity. *Why me?* Two of the eleven bumped were Grunts from up north near the DMZ. They had probably paid their dues more than most and certainly did not deserve the setback, yet they were not complaining. *Fuck it. I really don't have a problem. What's the hurry anyway? It's not like anyone is waiting for me.* Like other Marines, Zeke believed in luck, omens, signs and so forth. He believed that a change in trajectory, as he called it, always had an upside and a downside. Wonder what's going to happen now. *Be a man, you jerk; roll with the punches like you always do,* he said to himself.

Tight-jawed and forlorn, Zeke and his fellow bumpees watched the Freedom Bird wind up its engines preparing to taxi for takeoff. He imagined his mom saying *c'est la vie.* He felt the need to say something to take the edge off.

"Well, what the fuck, those guys had to go home on emergency; probably have to deal with some serious shit. I'd rather be me than them. Besides, those stewardesses were so ugly they were *oogly*."

A few bumpees smiled and nodded in agreement, but no one spoke. It was a humorless thing to be bumped—*very* humorless at many levels.

Back at Transient, they were told their sea bags had been sealed which meant they had been wired closed and were tagged as having been searched and cleared. If they broke the seal, they would again be subject to search. Zeke left his bag sealed, appreciating the excuse to let his beard grow and get funky. He imagined what he would say to an officer or Staff NCO if questioned about his appearance: "Why do we look grungy, sir? Well, after thirteen months of fighting to prevent the spread of Communism in Southeast Asia, I was summarily bumped without even so much as a "Sorry 'Bout That," as in Nancy Sinatra's new song. So, go fuck yourself."

The cots they had slept on the night before inside the Transient hooch were now being used by a new batch of servicemen that had arrived and were being processed out. There were no cots, blankets or ground cover of any kind for Zeke and the bumpees, so they propped themselves up against their sea bags and rested on sandbags or pieces of cardboard—anything they could find—to keep them from direct contact with the ground and all the creepy, crawly critters that slithered around in that part of the world.

Zeke and a few Marines took refuge under the Transient hooch for the night. It would be a good place to be in case it rained … and it did, so much so that rivulets of water seeped under the hooch and soaked their makeshift beds. Ignoring the elements, they talked about where they would be at that

245

moment if they had not been bumped, the first thing they were going to do when they got back to The World and similar diversions. It was comforting and pleasant to share stories.

Zeke played along with the game: "I'd sleep in a real bed, take a hot bath, have a twelve-egg omelet, drink a case of beer, and then go have a *ménage à trios* with two big fat women. No more skinny-Minnies like these Vietnamese Charlottes, ever again!"

It would have spoiled the moment had he told the truth—that he was going to shoot his girlfriend's killer before he reported to his next duty station. It was all light-hearted stuff with the expectation that tomorrow they would be "out of this place," as Eric Burden had sung about.

✪ ✪ ✪

Zeke was agitated about the bumping and had a sick feeling in the pit of his stomach. That feeling had always been a reliable early warning that something bad was going to happen. He could sense it; he could smell it. Credence Clearwater's song *Bad Moon Rising* came to his mind.

About midnight, a series of powerful explosions could be heard in the distance. These were not the usual nightly sounds of distant artillery; this was different. It was closer and *incoming*. In short order, they could see the rockets and mortars dropping on Red Beach from the nearby mountains to the west. Scores of them, in rapid succession, were hitting with devastating accuracy, causing deafening secondary explosions and earth-shaking concussions. The death and destruction was heading directly toward the Transient hooch. The enemy was scoring hits by successive approximations—dropping one rocket ahead or near the last, like walking, until the target was found. The enemy had picked that night, of all nights, to rain down an unprecedented shitstorm. *Bad Moon Rising indeed,* thought Zeke.

The enemy scored a direct hit on the Transient hooch, probably taking delight in killing Americans on their last day in country. The explosion was blinding and deafening. The concussion was bone-breaking. Splinters of wood and gobs of mud hit Zeke and the other Transient Marines as they braced for death. Zeke was hit by a piece of shrapnel squarely on his left dimple. It was a hot, stinging feeling. It burned his flesh as blood seeped from the small wound. He could hear guys screaming in pain, cursing, crying … and dying. It was a nightmare of blood, broken bones and severed limbs. The rockets walked past the Transient hooch onto the air base hitting a fully bomb-loaded and gassed F4 Phantom, killing and wounding dozens. The entire area was being hit; the casualty toll was heavy.

Then the shitstorm ended as suddenly as it had begun. *Thank you, God,* Zeke said to himself as he touched his 10-Đồng coin, squeezed it and closed his eyes. He was still under the hooch, where he had been when the shit hit the fan. Drops of blood fell on his hand and his Đồng through a crack in what was left of the floor above him. The smell of death was everywhere. Thirteen Marines in the Transient hooch had been killed or wounded, including two of the ballbusting staff who had played head games with rotating Marines.

Those killed included a couple Grunts who had served their time in hell; they were unarmed and homeward bound. Zeke could imagine the reaction of their families. They had probably been praying every night for their safe return, but would soon receive the news "from a grateful nation" that their sons had been blown to bits on their last day in Vietnam. The funerals would need to be closed-casket affairs. By the time the war ended, nearly fifteen hundred service members had been killed on their last day in Vietnam. The thirteen killed that day were among that number.

Zeke had a small round band-aid over his dimple wound, which probably needed a couple stitches. He was glad to be alive and did not care about stitches or scars. A Corpsman had given the band-aid to him with a smile, a slap on the arm and a smart-assed comment: "you'll live."

"I should get a Purple Heart for this, don't you think?" said Zeke, trying to muster up some humor.

"A Boy Scout award and a lollipop is all you'll get," replied the Corpsman.

"I'd take a lollipop right about now," said Zeke, enjoying the banter.

The Corpsman reached into his sack, pulled out a Tootsie Roll pop and handed it to him. "*Semper Fi* brother."

When dawn broke, Zeke and his fellow bumpees were carted to a C130 military transport plane. They were dirty, tired, hungry and reeling from the midnight wake-up call that had taken the lives and limbs of their brother Marines and other Americans. They felt lucky to be alive and were not complaining. They did not care what plane took them out of Vietnam as long as they left before anymore shit happened.

The C130 airplane was nothing like the Boeing 707 from which Zeke had been bumped. It was cold, austere and functional; no frills. The seats were uncomfortable fold-up units with webbed straps placed shoulder-to-shoulder. They were like little Loden green lawn chairs. The "bathroom" was a piss tube with a lid placed at intervals on each side of the plane. Urinating was not for the modest. Instead of a fancy warm meal and a beer, each received a box of C-rations. The C-130 was indeed a poor excuse for a Freedom Bird.

When the plane lifted off, there were no shouts of joy. It was surprisingly quiet. Zeke looked around and saw faces that were mostly expressionless. There was still a chance of being hit by a sniper as they lifted off and it was bad luck to show emotion before the plane attained enough altitude and distance to discourage sniper fire or a hit from a shoulder-fired missile. When they reached cruising altitude and were miles away from Vietnam, Zeke relaxed and looked around the cabin, pausing to look at each passenger for a second. Most were Marines. They had served their country in Vietnam. Like others before them going back to the Revolutionary War, they had answered the call. They had sworn fealty to God, Country and Corps. Zeke's ambivalence about the Marine Corps faded for a moment and he was proud. He started to hum the *Marines' Hymn:*

*From the Halls of Montezuma to the shores of Tripoli;*
*We fight our country's battles in the air on land and sea;*
*First to fight for right and freedom and to keep our honor clean;*
*We are proud to claim the title of United States Marine.*

It was contagious. Shortly, everyone on the plane, even those who were not Marines, chimed in. Members of each branch took turns singing their respective service songs and everyone joined in loudly and passionately, letting off many months of pent-up emotion. For a magic moment, service distinctions vanished. They were all *Americans*. And they were going home.

# —PART IV—

# HOMECOMING

42

# BACK TO THE WORLD

---

WHO IS CASSIUS CLAY, OR WHATEVER THE FUCK HIS NAME IS, TO THINK
HE'S ANY BETTER THAN ELVIS ... OR US?

---

Before they had left Okinawa for Vietnam over thirteen months earlier, Marines had boxed up their uniforms and possessions not needed in Vietnam and addressed them to their next of kin in the event they were KIA. The first order of business was to open the boxes and recover their belongings. Zeke had been cavalier about going to Vietnam when he sealed his box and made light of what should have been a sobering moment. At the time, war was an abstraction. Training had been like gym class or intramural sports—fun, competitive, rigorous and character building. Now that he had "been there, done that," he understood things differently. Zeke stared at the shipping label; he had addressed it to his grandmother. He patted the box lovingly and fought to hide his emotion.

Zeke's grandmother, Velma, his "other mother" who raised him during his formative years was gone too. While Zeke was fussing about chauffeuring Westmoreland and Sharp, she had slipped and fallen on the kitchen floor. Walter was long gone and she lived alone on the farm with a middle-aged Beagle named Tweed. When she fell, her hip shattered. She could not move and was in no shape to crawl to the phone for help. The coal fires died out and it became colder as the hours passed. She laid on the cold linoleum, praying hard, calling for help occasionally ... and crying. Tweed sensed her pain and curled up next to her to give her warmth. Two days later, they found Velma dead, still lying where she fell. Zeke had saved Tweed from being euthanized years earlier and she had given aid and comfort to Vel-

253

ma during her final hours. That little dog had repaid her debt. When they removed Velma's body, Tweed bolted out the door, never to be seen again.

When he received the news about Velma, Zeke thought of the time she saved his life when he was a little kid. His grandfather, Walter, had fallen asleep at the wheel of their faded 1939 Ford as they crossed a bridge high above a river. The car flew off the bridge turning in mid-air before landing upside down on the riverbank. Walter and Velma were badly injured and the car was totaled. Zeke was unscathed thanks to his grandmother using herself as a shield to protect him. Walter and Velma were the greatest. Their deaths hurt almost as much as Sharon's did—too much to cry.

They were next ordered to dump the contents of their sea bags onto a table and submit to a shakedown. Samples of contraband from previous shakedowns were on display: knives, bandoleers of ammo, rifles, pistols and even a Claymore land mine. Hand grenades seemed to be the most popular item. Also on display was an array of drugs ranging from marijuana to heroin. It was not clear how these items managed to slip through the Vietnam screening and make it to Okinawa. Zeke suspected maybe a rogue Transient clerk in Vietnam could have "overlooked" the items … for a price, conveniently "forgetting" to say that there would be a second screening in Okinawa.

The Corps liked its Vietnam Marines to return to CONUS looking clean, squared away, and sanitized after doing their part to make South Vietnam safe for democracy. They were ordered to get Jarhead haircuts, whether they needed them or not, "shit can" (discard) their Vietnam clothes and don their khaki dress uniforms. The makeover included going to the Post Exchange to purchase service ribbons. The NCO in charge of the group called cadence as a signal to march in step with precision as Marines ordinarily did. No one complied; instead, they ditty-bopped out-of-step. They had just left Vietnam. It was way too soon for marching.

Presence in Vietnam for *any* period merited the Vietnam Service Ribbon (VSR). No distinction was made between those who served one or more full tours and those who served one day. That did not seem fair to Zeke.

He assumed service members had to be in country for at least six months to earn the VSR. It also bothered him that those serving in the military anywhere in the world and those serving in Vietnam were all categorized the same—as Vietnam *"Era"* Veterans. That did not seem fair either.

Zeke suspected that he and many others rated additional awards depending on their circumstances, but they were told that for the time being, everyone would get the same ribbons for purposes of uniformity: the VSR, the Republic of Vietnam Campaign Medal and the National Defense Ribbon if they had not already purchased the latter. Marines were required to buy the awards with their own money. Apparently, a "grateful nation" did not have the funds to provide *real* Vietnam veterans with real Vietnam ribbons. Then Zeke snapped out of it. *You dumb shit; you got out of Vietnam in one piece. What the fuck do you care? None of these things are problems; they're just annoyances. Fuck the ribbons—it don't mean nothin'.*

Most of the Marines were young and new to the Corps and felt "decorated" with their three ribbons and shooting badge, assuming they had qualified with the M14 rifle. They were eager to get home and show them off. Families would beam, girls would swoon and baby boomers that had "opted out" of the war would be envious when they saw their decorations … or so they wished to think. They did not realize how pervasive the anti-war sentiment had become back in The World. Nearly half of Americans were opposed to the war at that point. Service members returning from Vietnam were seen as willing instruments of that war and many were treated badly, ranging from apathy and disdain to name-calling and violence. Some servicemen said they were reluctant to appear in public wearing their military uniform and wished they could wear civilian clothes, but the airlines required active duty personnel to wear their uniforms to qualify for military travel discounts. Zeke had heard about all the trouble back in the states, but was not intimidated. In fact, the common sentiment among Marines was "bring it on." They had been killing Commies for God, Country and Corps in Vietnam, a few more at the airport wouldn't matter.

Off they went, into the wild blue yonder. This time Zeke flew in style—no pissing in a tube or eating C-rations. They looked sharp and so did the stewardesses; they were first-stringers. Most Marines had not seen an American woman for 14 months, maybe longer, and appreciated being greeted by those charming, respectful ladies as they boarded the Pan American 707 and took their plush seats. Ten hours later the plane stopped in Honolulu where Zeke bought another token for good luck—a lead tiki god on a chain to dip into his beer to "test for poison," he would say. His silly routine was always good for a laugh. Five hours later, they landed at Norton Air Force Base in San Bernardino, California. They were again processed—queues, paperwork, and the usual bullshit. Zeke wondered aloud why they landed at an Air Force base, but was glad to touch down on American soil and didn't make a fuss.

After being processed for what seemed like the tenth time in some form or fashion since leaving Hooch 240, Zeke was officially released on leave to go home. He and some other Marines piled into a cab and off they went to Los Angeles Airport (LAX). Soon after they left Norton, the taxi driver pulled into a liquor store and bought a pint of Thunderbird wine for his passengers.

"Cheap but good," he said, laughingly paraphrasing the T-Bird advertising jingle: "What's the Word? Thunderbird. How's it sold? Good and cold. What's the price? Sixty twice."

Thunderbird was a fortified wine with an alcohol content of almost *18* percent. Zeke remembered that wine from his high school days. It was powerful. He never forgot the strong taste and smell of that brew, but it was cheap and made girls less inhibited.

The Marines were on leave and the clock was ticking. Every minute mattered. If the passengers had their druthers, they would have passed on the sidetrack to the liquor store. They were anxious to get home, but figured the driver meant well and tossing back a couple shots might be just what the doctor ordered, they thought. They passed the bottle around, each taking a big slug, shrugging and shaking their heads, not wiping off the mouth of the bottle. Considering that the driver was a splib, Zeke thought the wine was an exceptionally nice gesture given that the passengers were chucks.

Zeke had grown disgusted with black Marines pissing and moaning about being oppressed and "fighting the white man's war against the yellow man," *ad nauseam*. He never heard that crap from other minority groups; only splibs, with few exceptions. Maybe they had a point, but the message was lost in the frequency and hostility of the delivery. He thought the taxi driver might be different until he started running his mouth about how he praised Muhammad Ali for refusing induction into the Armed Forces. It became clear to Zeke that the taxi driver's Thunderbird gesture was more about his own taste for cheap wine than patriotism or appreciation of Vietnam veterans.

Zeke was in the front seat next to the driver and quietly cautioned that he and his passengers had been in Vietnam for a long time and were out of touch with all the anti-war and racial horseshit going on in the states.

"Marines don't appreciate cowards who use their elevated status to beg out of their obligations to their country. Elvis Presley got drafted and *he* served. Who is Cassius Clay, or whatever the fuck his name is, to think he's any better than Elvis ... or us?

"Bet you wouldn't say that to his face," said the driver with a sardonic smile.

"We shoot draft dodgers on sight, don't we guys," Zeke said, tongue-in-cheek, assuming his best crazy-man smile.

"Up close or a mile away; don't matter any day," came a reply from the backseat Marines, parodying Ali's penchant for rhymes.

All four Marines in the back seat then let out with their best boot camp growls in affirmation. The driver got the message and went silent. Zeke flipped on the radio to a country music station and turned it up loud. After a while, he flipped to a rock station for a change of pace. They passed around the Thunderbird among themselves, excluding the driver, until it was gone and listened to some guy named Jimmy Hendrix singing *Are You Experienced*? He looked at the driver and nodded his head, "Indeed."

At LAX, Zeke sat for beers with some other Marines—splibs and chucks—while they waited for their planes. They were all wearing the same uniforms with the same ribbons and badges. There was no overt animosity; no racial nonsense. They were all Vietnam Marines and linked to each

257

other through their shared experiences. They talked about what they were going to do when they got home, where their next duty stations would be and exchanged war stories. Some people looked in their direction, but no one really seemed to care about them. There were no protests, no spitting and certainly no "thank you for your service" greetings. Nothing. As they would all learn, apathy and benign neglect would be the primary reactions to their Vietnam service for the rest of their lives.

✪ ✪ ✪

Five and a half hours after takeoff from LAX, Zeke arrived at JFK Airport in New York. He was carrying his seabag with his jungle boots secured to the outside strap as a subtle way of showing the world that he had been in Vietnam. He soon discovered that most people that crossed his path did not know or care about the funny looking boots with green canvas. Instead, they just felt sorry for him for "having to go" and participate in an "immoral and illegal" war.

Zeke walked out of the terminal and approached a cab full of men—business types heading into New York City. One of the occupants told the others to make room for him. Zeke squeezed in the back seat and off they went. The passengers seemed respectful and curious, assuming correctly that he was returning from Vietnam.

"What's it like over there?"

That was the first time anyone had asked Zeke that question and he was not prepared with a good answer. It was a very broad question and a hundred images ran through his mind. They thought anyone in Vietnam was knee-deep in the shit; they were all poised to hear a lurid anecdote.

"Well, it's hot, very hot; hot and humid ... and sometimes very rainy. The kids are cute; the women are frisky. There's free food, cheap cigarettes and the South Vietnamese appreciate our being there about as much as Americans do. Guys who don't go to Vietnam are missing the definitive experience of the 1960s."

The men in the cab just looked at each other not knowing whether to pursue the question, laugh or shut up. They smiled, made light of his response and changed the subject.

At the time, the well-meaning people genuinely wanted to know what was happening and what it was like "over there." They were aware that the war had been going on for more than three years and wanted to hear about it from those directly involved. Thousands upon thousands of American men had already been killed and thousands more wounded. Vietnam was on everyone's mind and affected the entire country directly or indirectly.

The taxi driver took Zeke as far as the Southern State Parkway and dropped him off at one of the entrances. No charge. Zeke thought it would be easy to hitchhike to his family's house at 240 from there. The passengers and driver waved goodbye and made saluting gestures. As Zeke walked down the entrance ramp he stuck out his thumb. A pickup truck sped by him then slowed to a stop. The driver backed up very fast and told Zeke to throw his seabag in the bed of the truck and jump in the cab. After asking Zeke where he was going and made some small talk, he asked what it was like in Vietnam.

"Well, it's hot, very hot; hot and humid, and rainy. The kids are cute ..."

The line that he had first spieled to the men in the taxicab at JFK would be his standard response to questions about Vietnam for the rest of his life.

The driver took Zeke all the way to 240 Central Avenue, which required him to get off the main highway and meander around the neighborhood. Zeke appreciated the favor and the show of respect.

"My dad was killed on Iwo Jima in 1945; I was just a few years old. Good luck to you, Marine."

"Well thank you, Zeke replied, "God bless your dad in heaven and you too."

# 43

# BEHIND THE GREEN DOOR

---

WALKING THROUGH THE GREEN DOOR WAS LIKE WALKING
THROUGH ALICE IN WONDERLAND'S LOOKING GLASS.

---

The side door was still that obnoxious green color that Midge had painted back in 1956. Zeke remembered how his friends poked fun at him because of that stupid door. Jim Lowe's, *Green Door* was popular in '56 and they would sing that song whenever Zeke came around. The recollections were agitating. For a second, he wished he were back in Vietnam.

Zeke knocked on the door as he hummed *Green Door*. He had to knock because the doorbell stopped working back in 1958 and had never been repaired. No one answered. Zeke was getting out of sorts. He continued knocking and began yelling at the inhabitants to "answer the goddamned door." Finally, his mother appeared and peered through the door's glass windows.

"Why didn't you just come in instead of acting wild out there? The door wasn't locked. In fact, there is no lock at all. It broke two years ago and Midge is looking for a replacement. Why didn't you tell me you were coming?"

"Hell of a greeting, mom. How about welcome home Zeke, we missed you?" he said with a smile.

She teared up as she hugged him while showing a level of emotion that Zeke had seldom seen. Naomi was a sensitive, loving person, but kept her emotions bottled up ever since Zeke's progenitor, Dan, had hurt her so badly during her first marriage.

Walking through the green door into the house was like walking through Alice in Wonderland's looking glass; it was surreal. Midge was in the living room watching television—his hobby, avocation, passion and addiction. Zeke could hear the sounds of a quiz show at excessive volume that echoed throughout the house. When Midge realized that Zeke was there he came and shook hands and said "how youse doin'?" in his classic Queens, New York accent. He didn't know what else to do or say so he went back into the living room to see how the contestants were doing. Aunt Lena from next door came over and shook hands, made small talk and spouted some platitudes. She had met Sharon before Zeke had left for Vietnam. She had encouraged them to use her bed before he went. She felt awkward given everything that had happened. She didn't know what to say except goodbye and good luck in Gaelic as she disappeared.

Zeke's three little sisters and little brother greeted him with screams of happiness and hugs, jumping up and down and going wild. They dragged out pictures, toys, school things and other stuff they were proud of and had been waiting to show him. He was their big brother. He loved them, they loved him, and they didn't hesitate to show it. Zeke had sent a child-sized Vietnamese *Ao dai* (traditional long dress) for the 4-year old and a jacket with a map of Vietnam embroidered on the back for the 11-year old. Zeke had planned to send Vietnamese dolls to his other two sisters, but it was said that VC sabotaged the dolls with drugs, poison or explosive devices, consistent with their war of liberation, and he didn't want to take the chance.

Not including the five-hour flight from Vietnam to Okinawa, Zeke had been on three different planes flying for over twenty hours, excluding several-hour stops between legs of the trip. He was tired; very tired. There was only one place for him to sleep and that was in the converted sunroom about a hundred square feet in size. He did not realize until then that he had claustrophobia, which he probably acquired when he became trapped in a sleeping bag in the bunker one night. While sleeping, he got catawampus inside the bag. When he was awakened by a skirmish, he found himself trapped and had to use his ka-bar to cut his way out. The little sunroom gave him that same panicky feeling.

After sleeping for 18 hours straight, Zeke got up and began to get acclimated to his new surroundings. Even though he was home, he wore his utility trousers, a Peter Pan green t-shirt and Jungle boots out of habit. After all, he was still in the Marine Corps. Besides, he didn't have any other clothes. The four young siblings were waiting for him to get up. They had even brought their neighborhood friends into his bedroom to look at him while he had been sleeping.

"That's our big brother. His name is Zeke. He's been a long way away somewhere helping people," they said, along with a lot of other kid babble.

Zeke started the day by getting rid of all the letters and pictures he had sent to his mother and that Sharon had sent to him before she was killed. Naomi could understand his wanting to dispose of Sharon's letters, but not hers.

"I want to keep those letters that you sent; they're special to me."

"Mom, I've seen too many cases where someone's died and a bunch of strangers read their letters and pawed through their most personal stuff. I do not want that to happen to me. My letters were for your eyes only. Sharon's letters were just for me. I don't want anyone to read any of this shit, not ever."

Zeke started a fire in a 5-gallon steel can in the basement and began tossing in letters, envelopes, pictures and memorabilia. The central oil furnace had been removed, but the grate was still there. Anyone could look down into the basement through that grate and vice versa. The smoke from the fire rose through the grate and wafted throughout the house. Zeke's mom ran down to the basement to see what was going on.

"You didn't say you were going to *burn* the letters. The whole house is going to be smoke damaged."

"Mom, this is *240*. No one will notice. Besides, this is the way we did it in Vietnam; it works well."

She told Zeke to "open the basement windows and don't burn the damned house down" as she stomped back upstairs, clearly not pleased with Zeke's approach to waste management. Sharon's picture dropped out of one of the envelopes and onto the floor. Zeke picked it up slowly and carefully as if it were fragile and would break. He stared at her smiling image for a few moments then read the words of love she had written to him on the back. He always liked the way she wrote the first letter of his name—so fancy and feminine. He closed his eyes, mouthed a prayer and kissed her picture before tossing it into the fire.

Naomi was treating Zeke with kid gloves. She was trying her best to deal with his frustrations, which were compounded by the state of 240 where everything was broken, half-finished, fell if you touched it, disorganized, messy, or needed painting. The only thing that did not need painting was the green side door. Zeke opened the refrigerator and a frozen gallon block of ice cream fell on his foot and smashed a toe. He tried to slide the large closet doors in the hallway open and they fell off their tracks. He couldn't get them reattached because the closet was jammed full of junk so he threw the doors into the living room, which scared and upset his little sisters. When he opened the back door to leave, there was so much junk jammed behind it that it sprung back and hit him in the face, at which point he tore it off its hinges and threw it in the back yard. Everything he touched seemed set to break, fall, disintegrate or malfunction. Whenever that happened, which it did with regularity, he would punch or throw (or both) the offending object and curse and bellow like a nut case. Clearly, 240 was driving him crazy, especially falling on the heels of all that he had recently experienced.

Zeke became angry about virtually everything and everybody. He went into tirades about Vietnam War protestors, draft dodgers and shirkers, as he called them, and people in general. Naomi had been very patient with Zeke since his return from Vietnam, but decided it was time to give him her side of the story. She could be as tough as a Marine, which she was about to demonstrate.

"Zeke, sit your ass down; I've got something to say."

Her tone and demeanor derailed his tirade and he begrudgingly sat down to listen.

"You weren't the only one who went through crap over the past 13 or 14 months; I did too. You know I teach in a community of left-wing anti-war liberals. You wouldn't even begin to understand how much grief I had to take from my fellow teachers because you volunteered to go to Vietnam—and with the Marine Corps no less. You *wanted* to be there; that was horrible in their eyes. They asked me how my son, in good conscience, could be participating in an immoral and illegal war and it went on from there."

"I'll tell you another thing: every day that went by I dreaded getting the mail, worrying there'd be a letter from the government telling me you'd been killed or wounded. That's right, *every* day. It was a long nightmare for me and for the whole family if you want to know the truth. So stop pissing and moaning and get it through that thick head of yours that you being over there was stressful for me too."

Tears flowed down Naomi's cheeks. Zeke's being in Vietnam was a very emotional issue for her, one that she had not shared with anyone until then.

"Mom, I had no idea you took crap because of me. It never occurred to me that your friends and colleagues would be such assholes, especially to *you* and especially for nothing you did. That's awful! How about we take a little ride over there and introduce me to the ones that said all those things."

"Oh for God's sake, Zeke, don't be a fool. Are you going to have a fistfight with everybody that's opposed to the war or behaves badly? What makes you even think that way? You could get your butt kicked in the process and end up in jail. Cut the crap. I'm just trying to make you understand that you Vietnam guys aren't the only pariahs; we parents and family members were too. We are not going to my school and you are not going to confront any-one. You're still an active duty Marine so act like one and watch your step."

✪ ✪ ✪

Zeke's next task was to follow through with the promise he had made to the Hooch 240 Marines to send them some booze. When he went to the liquor store to fill the order he found that he didn't have enough money. *Why did I promise to send booze to all those guys? What was I thinking? I should have known it would be expensive back in the states.* Naomi showed her patriotism by footing the bill for all the vodka, rum, whiskey, and schnapps he needed. She even paid the postage. He decided to put in a pint of Thunderbird for Gums and Wilber just for fun. Zeke's only respon-sibility was to pack everything in foam rubber, paper and a bunch of old yellowed undershirts from Midge's underwear drawer to keep the bottles from breaking on their long trip over to Vietnam. Technically, sending booze through the mail that way was not okay with the postal service. However, the clerk ignored the glugs from all the bottles when he saw where the package was headed.

Wilber reported to Zeke that the box arrived from Long Island to Hooch 240 in good order and every guy in the Hooch and a few of the "good guys" from other Hooches had drank to Zeke's health and God-blessed him all night long. Zeke never received a thank you, but those guys had no sense of etiquette; they were just young Marine truck drivers. He was happy that he had kept his promise to his brothers and forgave their lack of social graces. He rather wished he could have been there with them when the party started.

✪ ✪ ✪

A few days later, still on leave, Zeke made ready to take off to Pennsylvania to visit the deserted farm and take care of business. He wanted to see his rum-dum friends, visit Sharon's grave and take possession of his S&W that he had sent to Flaco. Walter's Buick LeSabre had been languishing at the farm ever since he died over a year earlier. Naomi arranged to have it made roadworthy for Zeke when he returned. It was a thoughtful "welcome home" gift, made even more meaningful because it had been Walter's car.

Zeke threw his essentials into the trunk of the LeSabre and stashed his Jacksonville Bowie knife under the seat, positioned for quick access, "just in case," as he said.

Before he left, Naomi said she needed to tell him about "one more thing." She had a pained look on her face. "It's about the farm and the Lobacter Tribe. I didn't want to tell you until you got home."

People in that area referred to the Lobacters as a tribe rather than a family to differentiate them from the rest of civilized society. They were a pack of local degenerates that had roamed the area for years breaking most of the Ten Commandments, causing pain and suffering among the law-abiding folks in the community.

"Good Lord, here comes another bomb; I can tell. Somebody else die or get killed?"

She proceeded to tell Zeke about the robbery that had taken place at the farmhouse after Velma died on the kitchen floor and left the house deserted.

The Lobacter Tribe got wind of easy pickings and went on a rampage. They smashed through the front door with an axe. Whatever they didn't steal they broke or defaced. The upright piano was too big and heavy to carry off so they set it on fire—right in the living room. Thankfully, they didn't burn the house down. Many precious and important things were missing—things that had been in the family for generations and were irreplaceable. When Zeke heard all that, his pent-up anger and frustration spilled out in a flurry of curses and bloodcurdling threats.

"Where the fuck did those troglodytes get the balls to do that shit to *our* farm? How dare they? Gram and Gramp were always kind to those worthless bastards and they repay their kindness by ravaging their house like wild animals?

The Lobacter Tribe's rampage was more than a crime to Zeke; it was a *sin*. Like the good Calvinists they were, his grandparents had always shown kindness and respect to everyone, including the Lobacters when the occasion arose. And Zeke saw the farmhouse as something sacred, not to be trifled with, especially not desecrated in that way. It stuck in Zeke's craw that the Lobacters knew, or should have known, that if they messed with *that* house they were messing with *him* and would suffer the consequences.

"Maybe they forgot who I am, mom; I'll pay them a visit and give 'um a subtle reminder. I'll carve my name on their chests with my Bowie knife; then they'll remember. Those animals have run wild for years and nobody's done a damn thing about it. They always get a pass. Well, no more!"

"Zeke, don't you dare take the law into your own hands. No good will come of it. They were arrested and are out on bail. They will stand trial for robbery and probably go to jail. Stay away from them. Leave things up to the court. Your grandparents would not want you to get into trouble over this. It's just not worth it."

Zeke kissed his mother, hugged the siblings and waved to Midge who was lying on the couch watching television with a miniature dachshund named Gretel curled up on his chest. He sped off in the LeSabre in dramatic fashion. *Damn, I have a lot to do in a short time.*

**44**

# THE GREEN, GREEN
# GRASS OF HOME

THE HOUSE HAD A SOUL. HE COULD FEEL THE
PRESENCE OF GOD AND HAD NO FEAR.

Zeke had looked forward to setting foot on the farm again. He wanted to rub his hands in the dirt, smell the hay and see the trees. He wanted to stand in front of the house and soak it all in. He wanted to climb the old apple tree next to the house, the same tree he had climbed so often as a child. Most of all he wanted to go into the house, even though nobody lived there anymore and all the dogs, cats, cows and horses had vanished from sight and sound.

He had waited a long time to once again sit at the kitchen table, drink some of that pure, sweet ice-cold water that had continued to run to the house from a spring atop the hill. He visualized lying on his old bed, closing his eyes and listening to the sounds of silence. The best years of his life had been spent in that house and he needed to be there, to sit and think and to feel the spirit of his ancestors who had lived there over the past 150 years. He had a picture in his mind's eye of just how things would look, feel, taste and smell.

Zeke had played Tom Jones' song, *The Green, Green Grass of Home*, repeatedly in his mind for months. The time had finally arrived. As he drove up the old dirt road and neared the house he noticed that things were not as he remembered. The "green, green grass of home" had grown into tall weeds. The paint was coming off, the tar paper roof had holes and several windows were broken, including the picture window, which someone had replaced with cardboard. The window in his Grandfather's old room on the second floor was hanging open and ready to fall to the ground. The shock and disappointment was overwhelming. Naomi had not given him a "head's up" about how the house had been left to rot.

He made his way through the tall grass to the porch and sat down looking way out across the road to the woodchuck hole. He use to shoot woodchucks from the porch or sneak up through the meadow, hiding next to the blackberry bushes waiting patiently for a head to pop out of the hole. Zeke smiled as he thought about killing woodchucks versus killing human beings—no difference at a distance; big difference at close range. He laughed out loud remembering how he played the "woodchuck card" as a qualifier for the Combined Action Platoon during his interview. No more. He'd never go hunting or kill anything again except in self-defense.

Zeke could hear the familiar sounds of the birds and insects and felt the warm breeze against his skin. He smelled the rich earth and the perfume of the perennials that Velma planted long ago. He could almost hear the cows out in the pasture and see the horses standing in the shade of the Black Walnut tree. He could feel Tip nuzzling his hand wanting some attention. He remembered how he and Sharon sat together on the same antique settee he was sitting on at that very moment. He sensed his grandparents and his ancestors around him. Many of them had been born and died there. The house had a soul. He could feel the presence of God and had no fear.

"God damn it!"

He snapped out of his bittersweet melancholia and his mood changed to anger—anger toward his mother and all of his kin for letting the house and the property decompose. *They all have plenty of money, why hadn't they taken care of the homestead? This place was supposed to be a special sanctuary and they let it rot like this?* The Lobacter Tribe had added insult to injury by robbing the house and doing so much unnecessary damage in the process. Robbing the house after it was deserted was like kicking someone who was already down.

Zeke walked into the house through the unlocked front door and looked around. Most of the old furniture was still sitting in the same place it had been when he left for Vietnam except for the antique tables and chairs and his great-grandfather's cherry wood desk. Those pieces had been stolen. There was a pile of ashes, metal strings and ivory keys in the living room where the piano had been burned. He proceeded slowly up the steep narrow steps to his room. His single bed with the green vinyl headboard and the desk and chair he had made in shop class were destroyed—smashed with a sledge hammer and cut with a knife. His clothes, high school papers and pictures were still there except for a few shirts that had been stolen. He lay down on the floor, flat on his back and stared at the ceiling. He listened to the quiet and was alone with his thoughts. The Beach Boys' song, *In My Room*, came to mind and brought a smile. He had listened to that song many times on his record player in that very room.

After a while, he snapped out of his trance. He got up and checked out every room in the house then walked to the barns and looked around. He noticed many other things were gone, presumably part of the Lobacter heist. Although the Lobacters had been arrested for the robbery, nothing had been returned. *I can't believe those bastards had the balls. I really need to say something to them face-to-face. If they give me shit, I'll deal with it. If they're not sorry or don't take me seriously, well, I'll see about that.*

✪ ✪ ✪

Zeke felt the need to protect the house from further incursions. He drew on his Marine Corps experience and made booby traps, some of which were fake and designed as deterrents; others were real and designed to cause pain. He learned about these booby traps from SERE training and from seeing and hearing about their effectiveness in Vietnam. He found an old dried out bamboo pole in the barn and built a non-functioning Malayan Sling on the steps leading to the front porch. He attached razor blades to the window screens so that if someone tried to unhook them they would slice their finger open. He also dug holes and put Cartridge Traps near possible points of ingress. Cartridge Traps were made by placing a 12-gauge 00 Buckshot centerfire shotgun shell on top of a nail inside a small wooden support just below the surface of the ground. The trespasser's foot would push the shell down onto the nail and trigger serious damage.

Zeke made a warning sign to let the world know that the family property was off-limits. He painted the sign white and used large red stick-on letters to create his message. He was proud of his sign and posted it on the front yard for all to see. The message was clear:

WARNING!
THIS AREA IS BOOBY TRAPPED
WITH LETHAL EXPLOSIVES
TRESPASSERS BEWARE!

✪ ✪ ✪

Zeke remembered that he had parked his defunct cars behind the house in a clump of Sumac trees. He walked toward the Sumacs and spotted the black and white Riviera, sitting right where he had left it over two years ago, along with a couple other cars he had junked during that special summer of '65. He walked slowly around the Riviera examining it carefully like a jeweler grading a diamond. His mind was flooded with memories of past adventures—the drive-in movies with Sharon, the drunken cruises with his rum-dum friends, the late-night road races and the daily trips to school. He laughed to himself when he thought of all the loud muffler tickets he had gotten as well. The car represented the best of times and the worst of times, certainly a more innocent time.

He thought back about the day he totaled the Riviera and hauled it to its final resting place in the Sumac grove. He had committed to attend his twin cousins' high school graduation. He was going to clean up in the farm pond, get dressed and pick up Sharon. She wanted to go with him to meet his family. He donned his Sunday clothes, plastered on a handful of Top Brass hair cream to hold his Little Richard hairdo in place and raced over to pick her up. She looked and smelled positively glorious. He wished they had time for a quickie, but he was already late. He had to avoid being *very* late.

As they got further from home, radio reception became weak. They couldn't hear Scranton's Mighty 590 on the AM dial. As Zeke fiddled with the selector the Riviera strayed over the center line at the crest of a blind hill at the same moment a Ford Edsel coming in the opposite direction did the same thing. The Riviera and the Edsel met virtually head-on in a gut-wrenching, deafening crash. Both cars had been traveling at least sixty miles-per-hour, the net equivalent of running into a stone wall at 120 miles-per-hour.

Zeke brought the Riviera to a stop alongside the road about fifty yards from the point of impact. It had all happened so fast … in the blink of an eye. Zeke could not believe it. Sharon was curled up and crying.

"Sharon, you okay?"

She shook her head indicating yes, then no. Zeke held her tight. "I'm so sorry babe. I am so sorry. I can't believe this happened. Are you hurt?"

He saw that she was shook up, but not injured. Zeke remembered how distraught he was. It was all he could do to keep from exploding into a fit of anger at himself, the Edsel driver and the fates, all at the same time. Then he remembered what Sharon had said to him at that moment as she kissed him on the cheek and embraced him firmly.

"Think how lucky we are to be alive. Can you imagine if we died today? I would never want to die in a car accident. It would be so painful, especially if I wasn't killed outright." She teared up again.

Zeke painfully remembered his response: "Don't worry, kiddo, you'll never die in a car accident. We're going to live forever … together."

He remembered how he had hugged her and held her close as he whispered those words in her ear.

✪ ✪ ✪

Zeke pried the Riviera's rusty, battered door open and slid in behind the steering wheel. He closed his eyes and took a deep breath. Sharon frequently sprayed her perfume into the heater vents to enhance the ambience. He thought he could still smell a trace of her dizzyingly seductive perfume even after all this time.

Zeke was "back in the saddle" again as the Marines called being in the driver's seat behind the steering wheel. It was intoxicating. He rocked the steering wheel back and forth, pushed the buttons on the radio and read the love notes that Sharon had written all over the white upholstery. She had locked herself inside the car, wrote "Zeke and Sharon forever," and drew heart symbols on the headliner, front and back seats—everywhere she could. She also wrote a couple embarrassingly suggestive notes and poems about what they had done in that car. Zeke looked at the faded hearts and love notes and could see the whole episode vividly in his mind's eye. The tender hands that had done all that mischief were now holding his high school ring inside a casket buried deep in the ground.

After daydreaming in the car and rubbing his hands over every nook and cranny of the Riviera from the engine to the trunk, Zeke loaded all the stuff that remained in his room into the front and back seats. This included his letters for track and football, school notebooks and papers, love letters, records, *Playboy* magazines, pictures, certificates, his high-cut Italian shoes, track shoes, clothes and keepsakes. He then emptied a 5-gallon can of gasoline inside the car distributing the liquid evenly in the front and back seats. He took one last look at his past, breathed deeply and lit a match.

"And so it goes," he said, as he tossed the match into the car.

The Riviera burst into flames with a powerful "whoosh" incinerating the interior and boiling the paint off the roof in a matter of minutes. Zeke stood staring at the flames for quite a while holding a 45 RPM record. He looked closely at the label where Sharon had written their names inside a heart. He touched it, smelled it, held it to his lips then tossed it into the inferno. He watched the record melt and wondered how different things might have been if he had never heard that record, *Baby the Rain Must Fall.*

Zeke slept all night sitting upright in Velma's old rocking chair. It was pitch black and completely quiet. If there were ghosts in the house, he was sure they would be friendly. He was not skittish about being there; on the contrary, he welcomed the absolute peace. He closed his eyes, rocking quietly and thinking about his life. He thought about Velma and Walter. Those were not common names anymore. He thought about the dogs, cats, horses, cows, aunts, uncles and cousins that had made things so lively and interesting there. It had been a special time and place—warm, comfortable, loving, secure and sunshiny—where he never wanted for anything and couldn't have been happier. He knew he was romanticizing, but that was how he wanted to remember that part of his life that was now gone forever.

# 45

# HEY JOE

The .38 Special S&W and holster rig had made it to Flaco's house, tent pegs and all. Zeke had not told Flaco about the shipment ahead of time. He was aghast when he opened the packages. Flaco had a bad feeling that Zeke intended to use the gun in a way that had something to do with Sharon's death; Flaco wanted no part of it. Zeke had expected Flaco to do his bidding and keep the gun until his return, as instructed, but instead he freaked-out and took the weapon to Sharon's mom, Helen. Zeke was thoroughly disgusted with Flaco and told him so. Helen would surely have her suspicions too and it would make the reunion with her even more awkward.

Helen started to tear up as soon as she saw Zeke. He would have been her son-in-law and she loved him. She hugged him and held the hug for a full minute.

"Welcome home, son. God, we missed you!" she whispered.

The sight of Zeke brought back the agony of Sharon's death. She began to sob uncontrollably. He tightened his jaws and tried to block out her pain as he hugged her. He wished he were deaf so he couldn't hear her cries. Zeke did everything he could to hold back his own emotions. He had not cried in such a long time he didn't know if he still could, but he knew for sure that if he started, he'd never stop.

After things settled down, Helen made some coffee and they chatted about superficial matters for a while, avoiding the topic they both needed to talk about—Sharon. Zeke grew impatient and steered the conversation to what she called "the accident" and what he referred to as negligent homicide. Zeke wanted to know exactly what happened from beginning to end—did she suffer, was the Mope driving stupidly, why was she even in the car, why weren't Sharon and Donna wearing seat belts, where was she buried, where was the Mope now and a hundred other details. Helen told Zeke everything; it was a difficult couple of hours for both of them.

Sure enough, Sharon had *not* been cheating; she had just gone along for the ride. The driver, the guy Zeke called Mope, was a nothing-burger from some jerk-water town in the next county. Zeke's buddy, Dex, from back in First Grade, was the lead singer in a local band of rum-dums that played everything from Buck Owens to Jimi Hendrix in all the bars between Binghamton and Scranton. Dex knew the Mope and had invited him to a party in Dinglebury. The Mope had a new Pontiac GTO convertible and wanted to show it off to Dex and his fiancée, Donna. Sharon was Donna's best friend so she went along for the ride. Sharon and Donna sat in the back seat; the top was down. The Mope pulled some stupid high-speed racing stunt while going around a sharp corner causing his GTO to slide out of control and overturn. Sharon and Donna were thrown from the car. Dex and the Mope survived without a scratch; Sharon and Donna did not. Donna's pelvis was broken and she suffered massive internal injuries. Sharon's neck was broken, but she didn't die immediately. She suffered horribly, dying hours later, crying softly for Zeke.

It was hard for Zeke to hear all that and probably harder for Helen to tell him the story. Helen cried and convulsed as Pith had done when his little boys burned to death in the refugee camp. Helen slowly regained her composure, took Zeke's hand in hers and looked him squarely in the eyes.

"What are you going to do with that gun you sent to Flaco?"

Her question asked at that moment and in that manner, caught Zeke off guard. He hemmed and hawed and his face turned red.

"Nothing, really. It's the gun I had in Vietnam. It's just a keepsake. Who knows, a genuine Vietnam gun might be a collectable someday, maybe worth some real money. I also need it for protection. I don't feel comfortable without a weapon anymore. I have my Bowie knife, but that's not enough."

"Don't try to bullshit me, Zeke Hammond. I've known you too long. I can tell when you're not being straight. You always blush when you're bullshitting."

Zeke looked at her with feigned indignation trying not to blush. "Whadd-aya mean, Helen, you don't believe me? What are you gettin' at?"

Helen stared into his eyes again; she did not blink. "I heard you were going to shoot the guy you call Mope, the one who was drivin' that GTO. You blame him for Sharon's death and you're planning on killing him or doing something horrible, aren't you?"

"Not me. It was just an 'accident,' right? I'm sure that Mope didn't intend to hurt anyone. Shit happens, right?"

Helen caught Zeke's sarcasm and felt his underlying fury. She did not want him to get in trouble and became more assertive. "Zeke, it was an accident and killing or hurting that guy won't bring Sharon back. You know that." Zeke clenched his teeth in anger. He could not hold back any longer.

"Accident? Accident, my ass! It was *gross* negligence; negligent homicide. There are few true accidents, Helen. Most of this shit happens because of incompetence, stupidity, negligence or choice. And where did you get the idea that I was going to do such a thing, anyway?"

"Flaco implied. And I know *you,*" she responded.

*Stupid fucking Flaco. If he'd done what he was told I wouldn't be going through all this crap.*

Now Helen was getting angry and *her* teeth were clenched.

"Zeke, I understand how you feel. How do you think I feel? She was my baby girl, my only daughter. She was everything to me. You know how close we were. If someone was going to declare a vendetta, it should be me; not you."

Zeke persisted, "I loved her more than you knew. If she were alive, we would be married at this very moment. That's how close we were and that's what we wrote to each other about all the time I was gone."

"I know," replied Helen, "I saw the letters." Zeke turned red-faced from embarrassment.

"Oh great," said Zeke, with annoyance.

"Did you really think I didn't know what you guys did, where you went, how you felt about each other?" You are naïve, Zeke Hammond, but don't worry. I approved then and I approve now. I put your letters to Sharon—*all* your letters, your first one from Parris Island to your last one from Vietnam—into her coffin so your words would be with her in heaven. I also folded her hands around your class ring just before they closed the coffin. She wore your ring faithfully. As far as she was concerned—and as far as I'm concerned—that ring meant you were already married."

"I can't talk anymore," said Zeke.

He sat back in the chair with his eyes closed, rubbing his temples. The emotion was overwhelming.

"I'm not giving you back that gun, Zeke. I know it's your property, but I think you really want to shoot that Mope and I'm not going to give you back the means to do it. Things are bad enough. I could not live with anything else. I lost Sharon; I don't want to lose you too. And you know what? He just might kill *you*. Did you ever think of that? You're not the only one that knows how to use a gun, just 'cause you're a Marine."

Helen sounded adamant. Zeke knew her well too. He had to handle this situation carefully or he would never see the gun again.

"Look Helen, I'm not going to do anything at all with the damn gun. It's been six weeks since Sharon was killed and I've had time to process the whole thing. It was an accident, as you said. Accidents happen. I am still in the Marine Corps. I would not risk a dishonorable discharge from the service, jail time and the electric chair over an *accident,* would I? That would be insane."

"I thought you just said it was negligence and there was no such thing as an accident," said Helen skeptically.

"I just want to get my pistol, do some fun shooting around the farm and then take it to my mother's house before I go to Cherry Point, my next duty station."

"Where's Cherry Point? I thought you were getting out of the Corps after Vietnam."

"It's a Marine Corps Air Station—fighter jets and all that jazz. It's located in eastern North Carolina, Havelock to be exact, and I've got more time to do; my enlistment isn't over."

"So what would you have done if Sharon were still alive?"

"I'd have married her while I was home on leave, maybe even today, and asked her to wait for me until I got out in a few months or maybe taken her to Cherry Point with me. Hey, you wanna hear something crazy? My progenitor was stationed at Cherry Point after he and my mother got married. He cheated on her and ruined everything. If Sharon and I were at Cherry Point together, that kind of crap would *never* have happened. We would have been true blue and lived happily ever after down there.

There was a long silence. Helen had no more questions. She disappeared into what was once Sharon's room and returned with the S&W along with the fancy black holster and ammo belt. It was an intimidating rig even without the shiny bullets in the belt loops.

"Promise me you won't do anything stupid," she implored, tears forming in her eyes.

"I promise," Zeke said, forcing the words.

"Do you really mean it?"

"No sweat. The only thing I'm going to kill with this Smith and Wesson is the raccoon that invaded the attic at the farm while I was gone and maybe that fat woodchuck that took up residence under the porch," Zeke said with a smile.

Helen seemed relieved as she handed him the weapon.

"If you break your promise to me, Zeke Hammond, I'll kick your ass, so help me I will," she said, as she looked him straight in the eye. She meant it.

Zeke decided that he and Helen had both had enough of each other for the moment. He was exhausted and he was sure that she was too.

"I'm going to *di-di* on out of here and will see you later.

"You're going to what?"

"*Di-di.* It means 'leave' or 'get out' in Vietnamese, at least that's the term we used."

As Zeke got into the LeSabre and threw his holstered S&W and gun belt onto the back seat, Helen studied the car with a furrowed brow. "That car looks familiar."

"It should. It was the one I had when I came home on leave before I left for Vietnam."

"When you took Sharon out for the last time, right?"

Zeke nodded. Helen touched the car ever so gently as her eyes filled with tears.

✪ ✪ ✪

Zeke drove slowly down the decrepit driveway to the highway then peeled out, heading straight to the Dinglebury hardware store, charmingly named, "A Country Store for Country People." He bought a box of Winchester .38 Special ammunition from Swede, the owner. Zeke was not old enough to vote or legally drink. He was not quite old enough to purchase ammunition either. But Swede had known Zeke since he was born and had gone to the same Grange and Calvinist Church as his grandparents; he didn't ask questions. Swede knew that Zeke just gotten back from Vietnam and that made him old enough for anything.

"Do you have any dum-dum bullets?" he asked Swede.

"Dum-dums will make a hole as big as a quarter going in and a wound the size of a softball coming out the other side," Swede responded. They're illegal, but you can make your own by …."

"Never mind, Swede, I know how. Thanks anyway."

A haunting line from a Jimi Hendrix song came to mind: *Hey Joe … where you goin' with that gun in your hand?*

# 46

# THE MOMENT OF TRUTH

---

"WHAT IN THE FUCK ARE YOU CRYING ABOUT?
ONLY WEAK, WORTHLESS GIRL-KILLERS LIKE YOU CRY!"

---

Harley, Sharon's brother and Zeke's best friend, suggested they take a ride to the main bar in Dinglebury. He said Dex and his band were playing there and they were really good. Zeke hadn't yet seen Dex and wanted to have a few words with him about his culpability in Sharon's death. He felt that Dex was partially responsible. Had he not brought the Mope to Dinglebury in the first place, Sharon would still be alive.

"Zeke, you won't believe this, but do you remember that name you called his band in the old days—Buster Hymen and the Zonites? Well, that's now their official name. Some shit, eh?"

"Zonites?" Where the hell did I get that word?"

Zonite is a brand of bottled douche, remember? Probably not around anymore so people don't know what it is," replied Harley.

"Jesus, what a douche bag Dex turned out to be, pardon the pun," said Zeke with a laugh. "That name was a put-down and he adopted it? Hey, that's what I'll call him and his band now—Dex and the Douche Bags. Let's write that on the marquee on the way in."

"Hey wait," said Harley starting to enjoy the foolishness, "let's call his band The Nocturnal Emission. Wouldn't that be funny? Everyone would understand *that* name 'cause everyone's had one. And the dumb shit will probably adopt that name too."

Harley thought that was the funniest thing he had ever said and guffawed all the way through the door of the bar.

As they walked through the bar to the table area and the stage where Dex and his band were playing, Harley turned pale and stopped in his tracks.

"Holy Christ, that's him," motioning toward a fellow sitting alone nursing a drink at a table near the stage.

"That's who?" asked Zeke.

"That's the guy that was drivin' the car," replied Harley.

This was the first time Zeke had seen the Mope. He was dumbstruck and just stared at him. Dex had again invited a few of his friends to hear him play and the Mope was among them.

"Dex invites the son-of-a-bitch back to Dinglebury after he killed Sharon and damn near killed his fiancé? That mother humper doesn't learn from his mistakes, does he, Harley?" I'll have to have a talk with him.

Harley had a bad feeling.

"Hey, Zeke, fuck it. Let's just blow it off and go to Smitty's; his bar's more civilized anyway."

Zeke did not respond; he just stared at the Mope. The Mope was a nondescript guy, average in every way. Zeke didn't know his name, nor did he want to know. Mope was good enough. *How fortuitous. The Moment of Truth.*

Mope felt Zeke staring at him. People have a sixth sense about such things. He looked at Zeke and did not recognize him, but he identified Harley and suspected that Zeke might be "the boyfriend" he had heard about—the Marine, just home from Vietnam. His worst nightmare. The blood seemed to drain from his face. He turned white as a ghost and his eyes darted furtively around the room as if looking for the exit. Neither Zeke nor the Mope expected to meet that evening, but it was inevitable.

Zeke walked over to Mope's table, slowly and dramatically for effect, never taking his eyes off him, never blinking and remembering Helen's line about how he might know how to use a gun.

"Mind if I sit down?" Zeke asked with a strong voice intended to intimidate.

Mope looked up at him and stared for a moment. Before he could respond, Zeke pulled out a chair and sat down.

"Thanks, I knew you wouldn't mind."

This was the meeting that Zeke had thought about for what seemed like a long time. He was savoring every moment. He stared into the Mope's eyes without blinking. It was an intimidation tactic he had practiced for such occasions.

"You know, if I killed someone, I'd never have the chutzpah to come back to the scene of the crime," Zeke said in a casual, matter-of-fact way.

Mope's eyes got big and seemed to change color. He looked like a cornered animal. Zeke motioned across the room to Harley to get him a beer then slowly lit a Marlboro. He took a long drag on the cigarette and blew the smoke in the Mope's face.

"Do you know who I am?" Zeke asked.

Mope nodded, but did not speak.

"Who am I, what's my name?"

"Are you Sharon's boyfriend?"

"Boyfriend?" What a quaint word. Fiance would be more accurate. And do I look like a *boy*? I am a United States Marine and Marines are not boys; we are *men*. I have spent the last 13 months in Vietnam. That makes me a *super* man. While you were grab-assing back here in the states with your lightweight friends and showing off with your fancy car, I was killing Commies for God, Country and Corps. Maybe you should salute me? Whaddaya think?"

Mope did not reply or move.

"Guess you don't think do you? Not even a patriotic courtesy, eh? Okay, one more time, Mope, do you even know my name?"

Mope looked puzzled and shook his head. "I, I can't remember," he stuttered.

Zeke had been calm and even-toned, but he interpreted that answer as a sign of indifference and disrespect.

"You can't remember? It's *Zeke*, you dirty mother-humpin', low-life cocksucker. You can't remember? Your name is Mope, with a capital M. How come I know your name and you don't know mine? What the fuck is wrong with you? Do you remember the name of the girl you killed? How about the other girl, the one you crippled for life?"

285

Zeke sounded like a Joe Pesci character. He had gotten loud and people were beginning to stare.

Harley came over with a couple of beers, one for himself and one for Zeke, and sat down at the table ignoring Mope as if he did not exist. Zeke grabbed a bottle and pointed the long neck toward Harley.

"Here Mope, this is Harley, Sharon's brother. You know him, right? Say hello to him."

Mope nodded and stared at the drink he had been nursing before Zeke and Harley arrived.

Zeke grabbed Mope's glass, lifted it up and looked at it. "So you drink whiskey eh? Do you drink when you drive? Do you get aggressive when you drink? Never mind. Just making conversation. How about a toast to Sharon—RIP, gone, but not forgotten, right?"

Zeke and Harley raised their bottles and hit the long necks together as hard as they could without breaking them.

Mope flinched at the sound of the bottles clacking together.

"Aw, come on, surely you owe her that, don't you?" Zeke said as he glared at the Mope. "Sharon sends her regrets; she can't be with us. Do you know where she is today, Mope?"

Mope looked into Zeke's eyes with a pathetic, agonized look; he was frozen.

"You don't know? Well, I do. She's lying in a six-foot hole in the ground covered with dirt with my high school ring in her hands. Guess what happened to her? *You* killed her!"

Mope said nothing; tears welled up in his eyes and he looked as though he might pass out. Zeke looked into the depths of Mope's soul and bellowed in his best imitation of a Drill Instructor, "What in the fuck are you crying about, maggot? *I'm* the one that should be crying, not you. But I'm a Marine; we don't cry. Only weak, worthless girl-killers like you cry!"

Mope looked pathetic. He seemed genuinely upset. It was not an act. Having killed an innocent and maimed another through sheer negligence might really be bothering him—maybe nightmares or some form of post-traumatic stress. The idea that Mope could have a conscience or regrets never crossed

Zeke's mind until then. He had dehumanized Mope to make killing him easier. He had learned that trick in the Marine Corps.

Mope's tears saved his life. Had he responded in a less remorseful way or if he had been flippant or pushed back, no matter how slightly, Zeke would have ripped out his eyes, drove his nose into his brain and beat him to a bloody pulp before anyone could have intervened. That was the depth of Zeke's rage and pain. It did not matter if Mope was bigger or stronger or knew martial arts or anything else. It was a simple case of mind over matter. Had Zeke chosen to do so, he could have killed Mope with his bare hands. The Marines had taught him how, mentally and physically. He wouldn't have needed a weapon.

Mope started to get up to leave. It was surprising that he sat glued to his chair for as long as he did. As he arose, Zeke kicked the chair out from under him. Mope collapsed on the floor like a spastic rag doll and reacted as though he was going to spring back up and do something. Zeke motioned to him to stay where he was as he subtly revealed his Bowie knife strapped inside his shirt, the way he had carried it when he and Sharon went into New York City that one time long ago. It was a formidable looking weapon and made the desired impression on Mope.

Looking down at Mope still lying on the floor and having shit his pants, Zeke lifted the death sentence he had imposed on him. He made sure that Mope understood and appreciated that fact.

"I won't kill your sorry ass like I planned, but I will never forgive you. Nobody will. I just take more comfort in you living with the image of that beautiful, loveable, carefree girl lying there with a broken neck, gasping for air and writhing in pain. I want you to think about her every fucking day and reflect on the pain you caused and the fact that you will be going to hell when you die. Hopefully, sooner or later, you'll kill yourself to even the score. I recommend hanging, it takes longer and you can get a buzz as the lights go out."

Zeke clenched his jaws and whispered slowly with perfect enunciation, "Now *di-di fucking mau* before I *cắt cổ họng của bạn* your pathetic goblin ass.

Mope looked puzzled.

"That means get the fuck out of here, pronto, before he kills your ass," said Harley, glancing at Zeke to confirm he interpreted correctly.

Mope was gone in a flash. He looked miserable and did not say a word or look at anyone as he ran out of the bar. It bothered Zeke that Mope never said he was sorry. But it was over. God had given Zeke a loud resounding Marine Corps slap on the side of the head, figuratively speaking, reminding him that killing Mope was not the answer. Zeke got the message. Gyp was probably right; Zeke could kill, but he could not murder.

Dex had been singing Doors, Stones and Hendrix, along with some Hank Williams and Buck Owens during Zeke's tête-à-tête with Mope. He had caught glimpses of the intense interaction between the two from behind his microphone. At break time, Dex put down his guitar, meandered over to Zeke and asked sheepishly what had happened.

"Your friend—I named him Mope—is off the hook. And you're off the hook too. Good thing or you'd both be dead at this very moment."

Dex went pale.

"That's right cocksucker. Don't give me any dumb looks like you don't know what I'm talkin' about. If you had not brought that Mope here to Dinglebury, Sharon would still be alive. You are just as guilty for her death as Mope. But since I lifted my death sentence on him, you get a pass too. Just stay the fuck away from me for as long as you live. I don't care about any bullshit friendship we had in First Grade or anything like that. We have been connected for a long time, but that's all over now. If we ever come in proximity and I see you even glance my way, I'll put your eyes out with this," motioning to the Bowie knife. "Just say thank you to Jesus that you're still standing there in one piece. Do you understand me, boy?" Zeke yelled with classic drill instructor inflections.

Dex understood and averted his eyes to the ground; this was not a good time to debate the issue with Zeke given the size of his knife and the fury in his eyes.

Harley was emotional as he walked out to the LeSabre with Zeke. Somehow, neither of them felt any better. They were both sick to their stomachs.

Harley sat in the front seat of the LeSabre and cried like a baby. Zeke felt like crying, puking, screaming and destroying something all at the same time. He vomited in a large paper cup, filling it almost to the top, and splashed the contents on the front door of the bar. That was his primitive and unsubtle way of communicating his feelings about the bar, everyone inside and the whole world at that moment.

# 47

# THE LOBACTER TRIBE

WITHOUT WARNING, HE RIPPED THE SCREEN DOOR
OFF ITS HINGES AND THREW IT INTO THE YARD.

The next item on Zeke's "to do" list while on leave was to visit the Lobacters, specifically Henry and his two brothers, and have words. Henry, the ringleader, resembled the dueling banjo kid in the movie, *Deliverance*. The two brothers, JO and Moore, were bad copies of Henry. JO had no real first name; only initials.

The Lobacter Tribe subsisted on government welfare programs and proceeds from pimping out their sister, Ima for "ten dollars-an-hour to all comers," a pun they liked to use when advertising her services. Ima enjoyed the experience and the popularity; she was a willing victim. The more the merrier. She was a bottomless pleasure pit that never ran dry. She had no teeth, which made her all the more popular. Moore took 8mm videos of Irma's performances through holes in the wall or the ceiling. He sold copies to a porno shop in Scranton and charged admission to show the films at bars in smoky back rooms.

The three brothers had been thieving all their lives. They had committed countless burglaries and served time in jail, but jail was clearly not a deterrent. Upon release, they immediately resumed their outlaw ways. Zeke knew that being arrested was not a big deal to the Lobacters, which is why he felt a face-to-face conversation would be more effective. He did not intend to do violence; just have a no-nonsense talk. He figured if they knew he was back from Vietnam maybe they'd think twice about ravaging the place again.

Zeke slowly drove up to the house in the LeSabre. Henry, JO and Moore were hiding behind the curtains peering out the windows as Zeke and Harley got out of the car.

"I'll bet these troglodytes are getting Irritable Bowel Syndrome about now, don't you think?" said Harley with a laugh.

"I got your six. Just holler if you need help."

"I got my six right here, replied Zeke with a laugh, as he grabbed his crotch "and here" tapping his S&W secured inside the waist band of his jeans. After he tapped his gun, he thought it might be best to leave it in the car. He strapped on the Bowie Knife instead. It seemed to scare people more than a gun.

With a cherubic demeanor and a non-threatening gait, Zeke approached the front of the house. The door was open, but the screen door had been hooked shut. Zeke knocked and rattled the screen door.

"Henry, it's Zeke Hammond, he called with a cheerful voice. "I'd like to talk to you for a minute if you don't mind."

Henry yelled back from somewhere in the bowels of the house, "Ima ain't here. She's gettin' her ass reamed down in town. She'll be back later."

That imagery almost made Zeke gag. *Maybe he doesn't remember who I am.*

"I'm not here for Ima; I came to see you and your brothers. I want to talk to you," Zeke responded, again in a cheerful, deliberately unthreatening tone.

Henry came to the door. As soon as he saw Zeke, he understood the situation and replied in a white trash dialect that was almost undecipherable.

"I ain't comin' out Zeke Hammond. I ain't talkin' to you or lettin' you in. Get back in that big old ugly car of yours and get on outta here and leave us alone."

"Big old ugly car? Now that's not a very nice thing to say to a Marine who just served his country in Vietnam. Show some respect, please, if not to me then to the car at least."

"You don't scare me none, Zeke Hammond, I don't care if you are a Marine or not. Don't mean shit to me. All you guys who go to Vietnam think you're hot shit and better than anyone else."

"Well, Henry, that's because we are."

"You go to hell, Zeke Hammond" and get off my property, right now."

"Henry, my boy, why do you use my first and last names every time you say something to me?"

Zeke did not wait for an answer. Without warning, he ripped the screen door off its hinges and threw it into the yard. He bolted through the doorway and unleashed overwhelming force, growling in Marine Corps fashion as he struck. Henry tried to fight back to no avail and found himself stumbling toward the only window in the room. Zeke took advantage of the momentum and pushed him completely through the glass and onto the dirt yard. He laid there sprawled out, blubbering, cursing and gasping for air trying to say something.

At that moment, JO huffed and puffed and jumped onto Zeke's back. Zeke reached over his shoulder and flipped JO through the air followed by an upward thrust to his nose with the heel of his hand, just the way he had been trained at Parris Island. JO was flat on his back with a broken nose and streams of blood pouring from his nostrils. *This is getting out of hand; it's like Vietnam—escalating out of control.* He had not intended to throw Henry through the window. He had not intended to break JO's nose or do anything but talk to them. Had Henry been the least bit remorseful and manned up, things would not have unfolded the way they did.

Harley had been sitting on the front fender of the LeSabre casually puffing on a cigarette listening to the commotion and enjoying the thought of Henry and his brothers getting their comeuppance. When he heard the glass break and saw Henry come hurtling out the window, face first, he couldn't believe his eyes. He started laughing uncontrollably. He jumped off the fender and ran over to Henry telling him to stay on the ground if he wanted to live while laughing in his face.

"If you go back in, Zeke will kill you."

Zeke dragged JO out of the house by his shirt, threw him on the ground next to Henry and told them slowly and articulately, enunciating every word between clenched teeth, what would happen to them if they ever set foot on his family's property again—that he would gut and skin them alive and leave them out in the field for the crows like so much carrion. He unsheathed the Bowie and lightly ran the tip down Henry's chest, slowly for effect.

"I think they got the message," whispered Harley to Zeke as they walked to the car.

Just then, Moore Lobacter beamed up from out of nowhere with a formidable looking rock in his hand. He was fussing, fuming, and threatening to throw it through the back window of the LeSabre. He was highly agitated and seemed to be frothing at the mouth like a rabid dog.

"Get outta here or I'll do it; just see if I don't," he squealed in an excited childlike voice. Moore seemed believable and was stupid enough to do such a thing without evaluating the immediate consequences of his actions.

Zeke came breath smelling close to Moore and, with his best Marine "war face," made him an offer he couldn't refuse. "Moore, if you throw that stone, I'll kill you dead as a doornail, here and now on this very spot, no ifs, ands or buts, and I'll leave your smelly dead ass on this road for the crows to pick at." Zeke liked the crow-eating-carrion imagery. People in rural areas knew what that looked like.

Moore was stunned by the intensity, tone, and seriousness of the threat. There was no question that Zeke meant what he said. Moore dropped the stone as if it suddenly burned his hand and backed away, pacing around, cursing and making idle threats at a distance. Zeke was glad that Moore had not called him on that one. That stone was large enough to have broken the back window of the LeSabre or Zeke's head. He was getting tired and had made his point. Things had gone too far and he did not want to escalate the situation any further. Moore must have been the smartest of the three brothers. He walked away unscathed with only a bruised ego.

"We'll get you for this, Zeke Hammond, you'll be sorry, you'll see."

Zeke turned to look at all three Lobacters, locking eyeballs on each one individually for a moment, and then let out an intense Marine Corps growl. When they took off, Zeke did a colossal peel-out with the LeSabre, spinning its back wheels and stirring up a massive dust cloud that blew all over the Lobacters' grungy clothes hanging on the line.

A warrant was issued for Zeke's arrest the next day. The Pennsylvania State Police (PSP) came to the Everly house; the Lobacters told them Zeke might be there. Helen phoned Zeke to let him know he was a wanted man. Zeke had an uncanny knack of finding humor in every situation no matter how bleak. He started humming Merle Haggard's song, *The Fugitive,* to her. She did not think it was funny that her almost son-in-law was in big trouble.

"I thought you promised me you'd behave," she scolded.

She advised him to turn himself in to the PSP and explain the situation to them.

Zeke never considered that his visit to the Lobacter Tribe would have legal repercussions. He assumed the confrontation would be an internal matter and soon forgotten, the way conflicts were traditionally handled in that neck of the woods. Instead of taking their comeuppance like men, the Lobacters had ratted him out to the cops. Zeke considered ignoring the whole thing, but he was still in the Marine Corps and worried about double jeopardy—that if he got into trouble with the civilian law, he would also be in trouble with the Corps for violations of the UCMJ related to the same crime. He decided to go talk to the PSP.

He had trouble thinking that the situation was as serious as it was being portrayed. *All I did was create a little excitement in the lives of three criminals. Why such a big deal?* The desk officer at the PSP substation was a nice fellow. He was a sergeant named Krupke and he was a mirror image of the Sergeant Phil Esterhaus character from *Hill Street Blues* in appearance, height and manner of speaking. Krupke knew Zeke's family and knew that the Lobacter Tribe was the scourge of the county. He knew the whole situation, including Zeke's status as an active duty Marine who had just returned from Vietnam. Zeke was surprised: *How the hell does he know all that?*

Krupke was sympathetic and treated Zeke with respect. No handcuffs, no jail cell.

"Well Zeke, you are under arrest so you should have a seat. I hope you won't try to throw *me* through a window."

Zeke did not see the humor and replied that he had no reason to do that, which implied that he would if there was a reason. Zeke started to clarify, but Krupke just waved his hand with a laugh.

"So, I guess I don't have to worry then?"

Zeke had turned red from embarrassment at that point and just said "no sir."

Zeke and Krupke sat around drinking coffee while they waited for another PSP officer to come to the substation to escort him to a Justice of the Peace (JP) to post bail. Krupke asked what Vietnam was like. Zeke gave the usual weather report—"hot and dry; hot and wet ..." and asked Krupke what it was like to be a PSP officer. Zeke told him about his plans to join the PSP when he got out of the Marines. Krupke shook his head and told him that vigilante justice was no way to go about it.

"You did know that those Lobacters had been arrested for robbing your grandparents' house and a lot of other houses in the area and were out on bail pending trial, didn't you?"

"Yes, sir I did, but that's never been a big deal to them; it never deterred them from being repeat offenders. They just don't give a shit about law and order and never have. I felt the need to make an impression on them. What they've done to people all their lives has been awful and I figured I'd have a chat with them to see if I could straighten them out."

"Well, said Officer Krupke, you sure made an impression on them. They are pretty messed up, physically and mentally from what you did. If you believe in law and order, the next time you have a problem with someone I suggest you do not go to their house, tear off the door, throw them through a window and threaten to wipe them all out. It is our job to knock the bad guys around, if necessary, not yours. I understand why you did it; Lord knows, we would like to have done that to them a hundred times, but that's not how things work. You're in serious trouble, Marine, and it was all unnecessary."

"It was a nasty job, sir, but somebody had to do it," replied Zeke adamantly, almost defiantly.

About that time, PSP officer Crawford arrived to escort Zeke to the JP to post bail.

"Do I ride with you?" Zeke asked.

"No, just follow me in your own car. Once you post bail you will be free to go until your trial. Now, my young Marine, if I look in the mirror and do not see a green Buick LeSabre directly behind me, you will be in a world of shit. We are giving you a break; do not screw it up. Get my drift?"

*This guy sounds like a Drill Instructor. Looks like one too in that Smokey Bear hat.*

Crawford pulled out in his green and white PSP patrol car with the LeSabre following close behind. Zeke thought it was cool to be riding around on the heels of a cop car. He enjoyed watching the reactions of other drivers along the way.

At the JP's office, they rendezvoused with Zeke's uncle James, a man of character and a devout Calvinist, who pledged a portion of his farm in lieu of cash for the $300 bail. Uncle James, the JP, Crawford and Zeke had a nice chat over coffee after the paperwork was completed. Crawford reminded Zeke that he was under a peace bond and to stay away from the Lobacters and let the law handle the matter.

"You know, Zeke, they would have been justified in using deadly force when you ripped off the door and entered the house. He could have easily said that he feared for his life. You're lucky you're alive."

Zeke looked directly into Crawford's eyes and, without blinking, cracked a knowing smile.

"You don't know the half of it, sir."

# —PART V—
# NON SEQUITUR

# 48

# CHERRY POINT

---

"THE MOST IMPORTANT THING I LEARNED AT
CHERRY POINT WAS HOW TO USE A CHAMOIS."

---

Being in the Marine Corps seemed to have lost its luster after Vietnam, especially at Marine Corps Air Station, Cherry Point, North Carolina. It was anticlimactic; a *non sequitur*. Zeke had the "been there, done that" feeling. It seemed that there was nothing new and exciting to look forward to; just SOS-DD—Same Old Shit-Different Day. It seemed to Zeke that it had all been downhill after Parris Island. Boot Camp was a natural high. It brought out the best in him and others.

Everyone was "proud to claim the title" then, but now it all seemed different. He had seen the best and worst sides of the Corps and was disillusioned, not because of the physical or mental challenges, but because of the petty bullshit and disrespect for the rank-and-file. It was maddening to feel the indifference shown by the Marine Corps toward its own Vietnam veterans regardless of medals won, Purple Hearts earned or suffering endured.

On his way to the chow hall, Zeke heard someone call to him.

"Marine, see here."

It was a gunnery sergeant who was walking with a captain. The captain noticed that Zeke was wearing jungle boots and told the gunny to call Zeke to account for being out of uniform. The gunny assumed his best Staff NCO pouty-face and marched right over to Zeke. He reminded Zeke of Top Sergeant Singer back in Vietnam.

"Marine, why are you wearing jungle boots? Don't you know jungle boots are not SOP stateside?" The gunny had a voice like a Munchkin from the *Wizard of Oz* and his anger seemed all out of proportion to the transgression. It was hard for Zeke to not smile, but he was contrite and responded respectfully.

"Gunny, I earned these boots in Vietnam. I've been wearing them since I arrived at Cherry Point and no one said anything to me until now. I didn't realize I was out of uniform."

The gunny did not want to hear an explanation. "I don't give a shit if you were in Vietnam or not; never wear those goddamned boots again. Do you understand?"

Zeke stood there, dumfounded. *He doesn't give a shit if I was in Vietnam. I gotta hear that from a fellow Marine ... and on a Marine base, no less? My God, what next? He couldn't just say, welcome home or thank you. No, that would be asking too much. What a typical POS.* Zeke loved to use the abbreviation, POS. It meant Piece of Shit. He used the term liberally to describe people, places and things. Back in Vietnam, the Marines in Hooch 240 would refer to their rank as POS instead of PFC or lance corporal. It was funny, but it was also a commentary of how their superiors made them feel.

Technically, the gunny was correct, but countless Vietnam veterans wore their jungle boots at stateside Marine bases with impunity. Jungle boots were an important status symbol among the Vietnam veterans on base. It signaled that the wearer was a member of the subgroup of Marines that had been to Vietnam and, therefore, deserved respect. *What the fuck is the matter with this captain and his flunky gunnery sergeant? Are they jealous?* Sidestepping the gunny, Zeke turned toward the captain and rendered a passive-aggressive hand salute.

"Yes sir, I will never wear jungle boots again, sir."

*Indeed I won't, you disrespectful shit-sticks. Next time I'll wear Sears' Best hunting boots with magic markered toes and a band aid.*

At an infantry tactics refresher, a staff sergeant who had never been in combat talked about how one Marine could handle two VC at the same time in a bayonet fight.

"Of course, being Marines dealing with more than one enemy at one time would not be a problem because we know that any one Marine is equal to two or three of those VC bastards."

The Vietnam veterans just shook their heads. The bravado and hyperbole rang hollow. The newbies ate it up and thought they were invincible; the Vietnam veterans knew better.

That same staff sergeant selected a lance corporal, a recipient of the Silver Star and Purple Heart, earned in Vietnam, to be a communications runner between units for war games. The Silver Star is America's third highest military award after the Medal of Honor and the Navy Cross. To the Vietnam veterans in the tactics refresher it was appallingly disrespectful to require a Silver Star recipient to be part of such mundane training in the first place let alone being designated as a lowly runner. The instructors seemed out of touch with reality and with the young Vietnam veterans under their command.

✪ ✪ ✪

Zeke was assigned to drive a school bus to transport the children of officers and enlisted Marines living on base. Like BAT training in Vietnam, he was given cursory instruction, had an orientation run and then soloed—all in the same day. After he sped by a batch of kids waiting to be picked up, missed a stop or two and got lost a couple times, he was transferred to limousine duty.

The most challenging part of limousine duty for Zeke was keeping his shiny new black sedan spit-shined, inside and out with the aid of a chamois that he always carried with him. Years later, Zeke would tell people, only half-kiddingly, that the most important thing he learned at Cherry Point was how to use a chamois.

He carted senior officers (majors, colonels and generals) to various places on base and off. He enjoyed driving them around and chatting with them as if they were normal people. Senior officers liked Zeke to be their driver and asked for him by name. He was gaining a good reputation. He began to feel valued and appreciated ... even important.

The downside of his job was carting *junior* officers (lieutenants and captains), particularly to and from the Officer's Club. Junior officers were generally arrogant, obnoxious sorts when they were sober and became particularly abrasive when inebriated. His most memorable pick-up was when he was dispatched to pick up a second lieutenant, an LT, and his female companion. Zeke pulled up to the front of the Officers' Club with his shiny sedan and spotted his passengers immediately. They could hardly stand and were leaning on each other for support, laughing and pawing one another like animals. Zeke saluted the LT, opened the rear door and they dove in, falling on top of each other.

"Where to sir?" asked Zeke.

"No place in particular at the moment. Just drive around for a while, Private."

"I'm a lance corporal, sir; name's Hammond, Zeke Hammond," he replied respectfully.

Within a few minutes, the LT and his lady friend were naked from the waist down with the intention of copulating right then and there. Zeke could see it, hear it and smell it. One or both of them had crotch rot. It was nauseating. He was not sure how to proceed. He tried to redirect the unfolding situation with some levity.

"LT, you might be interested to know that I received the coveted Bush Wings for helping win the hearts and minds of the Vietnamese women. I have this badge to prove it."

With that, Zeke pulled out the silver Bush Wings he had received from Hooch 240 for the Fox in a Box caper.

"Based on that award I call dibs on creamy seconds," he chuckled.

It was a lighthearted comment expressed in classic Marine Corps crudity, something Zeke thought the LT would appreciate, but he had no sense of humor. He became incensed and, in a slurred voice, accused Zeke of "disrespect, bordering on insubordination." He cursed at Zeke and upbraided him, calling him a dumb shit and an enlisted low-life peon almost in the same breath. Zeke gritted his teeth and maintained military bearing. Backtalk was out of the question. Zeke drove without further comment while his passengers pawed each other and made strange noises. He rolled down the window to keep from gagging.

# 49

# DEVIL WITH A BLUE DRESS ON

"TRY AND KNOCK THE DERBY OFF ME, MOTHER FUCKER!"

*Z*eke really liked the song, *Devil With a Blue Dress On* by Mitch Ryder and the Detroit Wheels. Every bar played it loud and the dancing girls went wild to the beat. He was never able to shake off the image of the enormous, *oogly* girl who danced to that song, half-naked at the Jarhead Bar and Grill just outside the base in Havelock. The bar scene in towns around any military base were filled with servicemen and devoid of women. Drinking, fighting, smoking and bullshiting were the main off-duty pastimes. There were probably Marines that went to the library and attended cultural events, but Zeke did not know any.

Lance Corporal Fink and PFC Pablo were both Irish although the name Pablo did not fit. He said he was half Mexican and half Irish. When asked which half was Irish or which half was Mexican, he would say "the good half" depending on the individual or group he was addressing. They happily conformed to their ethnic stereotypes, meaning they liked to drink and fight. Both had served 13-month tours in Vietnam. Fink had received a Bronze Star and Purple Heart for being shot in the back while saving the life of a helicopter pilot whose craft was downed by enemy fire on Operation Hastings. Pablo had an MOS of 0331, Machine Gunner. That was all anyone needed to know. Zeke, Fink and Pablo had all fired their weapons in anger, as the saying went. They shared a common bond despite their disparate occupational specialties.

Fink and Pablo gave Zeke something to look forward to—drinking and fighting. Every Wednesday and Friday, sometimes more frequently, the three of them would jump into the LeSabre, *di-di* on out of Cherry Point and hit all the bars in the area. They would limit themselves to one or two beers at each bar and then move on to the next one repeating the cycle until they found a bar they liked, at which point they'd get down to serious drinking.

Fink was an angry guy. His anger attracted and instigated trouble. Every time the trio was granted an evening or weekend pass to leave the base, they found themselves in a fight, usually the result of Fink's troubled attitude. He always wore a brown derby, one size too small, which looked ridiculous perched on top of his head. He wore it for the sole purpose of instigating fights. No sooner would the trio get to their first bar stop and order a round of Falstaff beers when someone, usually another Marine, would make a comment.

"Nice hat," followed by laughter.

Right on cue, Fink would respond with a challenge, "Try and knock it off me, mother fucker!"

With that, the fight was on. The irony of it all was that Fink and Pablo had been very brave in Vietnam, but were not too proficient in hand-to-hand bar combat. Fink never won; Pablo sometimes did. Inevitably, Zeke and Pablo would have to rescue Fink from defeat most of the time.

One weekend, the trio decided to drive up from Cherry Point to Washington D.C. to try out a cool nightclub they had heard about. After a couple drinks, Fink, wearing his too-small derby, became rowdy. When the bouncer came over to calm him down, Fink moved his chair to block the bouncer's approach. When the bouncer politely asked Fink to move his chair, Fink bellowed out "make me," at which point the bouncer picked up the chair with Fink still in it and bounced him out of the club, chair and all. Pablo and Zeke would have intervened, but they were laughing too hard and felt Fink had that one coming.

After disposing of Fink, two bouncers came back to the table and the laughter soon turned into an argument, followed by some pushing which turned into serious fighting. The bouncers were taller and heavier, features that were meaningless to the two Marines, but Pablo was not faring well, as usual. Zeke saw an opportunity to end the fight in dramatic fashion by using the naked strangle, a judo move he had learned in hand-to-hand combat training at Parris Island. The alcohol had affected his aim and he did not execute the lethal move properly, although he put that one bouncer out of commission temporarily. As they fought their way toward the exit, evading death or dismemberment, they could see others in the club starting to fight. The cacophony of breaking glass, flying tables and chairs, and the screams of the patrons was bloodcurdling. Zeke and Pablo came rushing out the door, faces bloodied and clothes torn.

Both Zeke and Pablo burst out the exit door at the same time, grabbed Fink who was waiting for them, and jumped into the LeSabre.

They cruised around DC for a while without much talk. Zeke spotted a parking place in front of an old hotel, which turned out to be the *Mengier* Annapolis, the place where he and his classmates stayed on their class trip to Washington three years earlier. He parked the LeSabre and went to the trunk for some beer and blankets. They quaffed some more beer and toasted to their exciting evening as they faded into sleep where they sat, doors locked, clothes torn and faces bloodied.

✪ ✪ ✪

On the way out of the Enlisted Men's Club one night, Fink spotted three Marine reservists standing nearby talking to each other. Fink saw reservists as second-class Marines, like draftees. He pushed their buttons and the fight was on. Fink and Pablo were quickly knocked to the ground. Zeke looked at the third reservist who was a bit larger than he was and knocked him down before he knew he was in a fight. Zeke hit the guy sitting on Pablo in the nose with the heel of his hand—one of his trademark moves—then gave the guy sitting on Fink a Thunder Clap—a simultaneous flat-handed hit to each ear. As MPs descended on the scene with lights and sirens all six took off in different directions. Somewhere in the melee, Zeke broke his cherished Seiko watch, the one he had bought in Bangkok on R&R from Vietnam. He was angry with himself and his two companions. The constant fighting had become more frequent and more violent. It was getting old.

The trio brawled on and off base, anywhere and anytime. Looking back, some would say (in hushed tones) that they were suffering from Post-Traumatic Stress Disorder (PTSD), but that term hadn't yet been invented so their behavior was explained, laughingly, as IGS—Irish Gene Syndrome. Marines at that time would not have embraced the diagnosis of PTSD. They would have thought it stigmatizing—a sign of mental illness or weakness, something to be hidden and not discussed.

✪ ✪ ✪

Returning to Cherry Point in the LeSabre late one evening, Zeke saw a roadblock ahead as they neared the main gate. MPs were directing all cars into one lane with their flashlights. There had been a serious hit and run accident—a green car had hit a pedestrian and taken off. MPs ordered any suspicious cars, particularly green ones to pull over for a more thorough look. The LeSabre fit the profile. As Zeke was showing the MPs his papers and explaining where they had been that evening, Fink stuck his head out the back window and began to wail loudly and belligerently about being pulled over. Zeke and Pablo tried to quiet him but to no avail. MPs did not tolerate any guff from anyone, regardless of rank. Within seconds, they yanked Fink out of the car and tossed him into their patrol Jeep. The consequences for back talk, particularly in the context of a felony investigation were serious. Fink had bought himself some unnecessary trouble … as usual.

As the MPs continued to examine Zeke's car for damage that might indicate an accident, Fink bolted out of the Jeep and disappeared into the night. That put Zeke and Pablo on the hot seat. Zeke tried to explain that the whole situation had been a misunderstanding, but the MPs were not having any of it and ordered them to recover Fink by any means and bring him back to the MP office at the main gate posthaste or they would all be in the Brig by midnight.

Fink used his Marine training to "escape and evade" his way back to the squad bay and was in his rack feigning sleep. Pablo rousted Fink, but he refused to come along peaceably. In the process, Fink took a swing at Pablo and called him some nasty names. Pablo and Zeke decided that it was time to escalate and take Fink by force. There was no choice. Failure to bring him back would guarantee Brig time for all three of them.

As Pablo tore the blanket off Fink, they saw that Fink had taken off all his clothes except his shoes and socks. Pablo and Zeke started to laugh.

"Is this really happening?" Zeke asked rhetorically.

"What the fuck are we going to do with this guy?" asked Pablo, now at his wit's end.

"I've got an idea. Remember that blue dress that Fink grabbed as he was leaving that last bar we were at? It was folded and sitting on a table by the door and that fool swiped it. I'll get it from the car and we'll use it to cover his doggy dick."

At that point, Zeke and Pablo were laughing so hard they could barely stand. Zeke dragged Fink off his rack, got him in a bear hug and held him in a viselike grip while Pablo put the dress on him as well as he could. Once "dressed" they carried him kicking and screaming out of the squad bay and threw him into the trunk of the LeSabre.

The Provost Marshal was shocked and amused when Pablo and Zeke helped Fink out of the trunk and into his office wearing a dress and in their firm custody. The contrast of the hairy legs, white socks and loafers with the blue dress presented a funny picture. It was even funnier that he was naked underneath. Zeke felt the need to offer some explanation.

"Sir, this man is a transvestite. I don't know how he got in the Marine Corps, but somebody should look into this and get him some help with his identity problems."

Fink stopped struggling and cursing and had the good sense to recover his military bearing, but if looks could kill, Zeke would have been dead after that introduction.

By that time, the real perpetrator of the hit and run had been found. Zeke, Fink and Pablo were released with some stern words. Fink would be slated for Office Hours for his belligerence and disrespect. He would also be cited for "wearing inappropriate civilian attire." Pablo and Zeke would be commended for their cooperation. Fink was furious, but it became clear to him that it was best to shut his mouth and accept the consequences. The next night the trio went out to celebrate, renew their friendship and marvel at their ability to skate through such tribulations. They laughed and drank for hours cherishing the moment and the camaraderie.

**50**

# BLOODY RED SNEAKERS

---

ON'T MEAN NOTHIN'."

---

In late summer, Zeke received another letter from Wilber, this time with bad news. Rockets and mortars had hit every area of Red Beach including the Heavy Platoon living area. Two rockets hit Hooch 240, one landed in the bunker in front of the hooch and the other hit the roof almost directly above Gums. He was mangled beyond recognition. The little red sneakers he had kept from the infamous Junk on the Bunk inspection were covered with blood; one was shredded from the shrapnel. There wasn't much left of Gums either. It was hard to identify his remains. Everyone who had been in the hooch at the time had been killed or wounded; the double hit was devastating. Most of the hooches had been hit. The attack wiped out half of the Heavy Platoon in one fell swoop. Hooch 240 no longer existed.

The one positive, according to Wilber, was that Clifton, the scared newbie from Zeke's bunker, had been a hero and received the Bronze Star with Combat V for valor. When the shit hit the fan, he dragged a lot of wounded to safety at extreme risk to himself. He was hit with some shrapnel, but managed to save eight or nine men by pulling them into the bunkers and, in some cases, covering them with his own body. Zeke was proud of Clifton. The draftee had turned into a Marine after all.

To add insult to injury, Wilber said that Marine infantrymen—the Grunts—were gleeful that Red Beach had been rocketed. Grunts saw themselves as fighting the war all by themselves, up close and personal. They did the bulk of the killing and dying while non-infantry had it easy,

311

or so they believed. They liked the idea of Red Beach getting a "taste of war," as they put it.

Most of the truckers were aware of what infantrymen experienced and held them in high esteem. Unfortunately, that regard was not reciprocated. Non-infantrymen were called "pogues," a term intended to derogate. Ironically, the so-called pogues respected the Grunts and supported them in every way possible. They would ride through shit-storms to bring a load of ammo or a tanker of water to them when they were suffering more casualties from heat exhaustion and dehydration than from enemy bullets. It was as if there was a bifurcated Marine Corps. The schism between blacks and whites multiplied the complexity. All the talk of brotherhood, teamwork and such that Zeke had been taught in boot camp seemed to be bullshit.

Zeke put Wilber's letter in his pocket, got into the LeSabre and drove off base to a small park near Havelock. He could see the faces of each man who had been killed in Hooch 240. He knew their stories and regarded them as family. Zeke locked the car doors, pulled down his cap and stared at the dashboard. *What a fancy set-up, he thought. I'm very lucky to have a car like this with the freedom to come and go as I please.* He was hoping the small talk with himself would calm him down so he could regain his composure. Zeke wondered about his bunker kids, the ones that had disappeared after Dot had been killed. *Aw fuck it, I don't want to know. They probably all ended up like Dot.*

Try as he may, he could not shake the image of the bloody red sneakers Wilber described. He tried to make himself laugh or redirect his thoughts to something normal and mundane. It just did not work. He felt tears running down his face, which he thought was odd since he wasn't crying. He suddenly hit his steering wheel and dashboard with such force that he cracked them both and thought he had broken his hand. The knuckles were bleeding and his left hand was numb—no feeling at all. His outburst ended as suddenly as it began. He crossed his arms and closed his eyes; he was exhausted.

After an hour or so, he opened his eyes, blinked a few times and rolled down the window to smell the fresh air. Then he remembered Wilber's bad news. He yelled out to the world as loud as he could, "Hey everybody, all my friends are dead. They died for God, Country and Corps and none of you bastards gives a shit! I could use some help here!"

No help came. A couple of people in the park looked at Zeke sitting in the LeSabre and hurried off thinking he must be drunk or crazy. He could not blame them. He was on his own and he knew it. Nobody cared.

Zeke always discounted his own emotions by reminding himself that compared to those suffering around the world at any given moment, his pain was insignificant: *What if you'd hit one of those land mines and got your legs blown off? Then you'd have something to piss and moan about. Get a grip, boy. All the Marines in Hooch 240 were enlistees. They knew and accepted what they were getting into. Would they cry for you? Stop being so fucking dramatic.*

He wanted to use the phrase commonly used in Vietnam, "don't mean nothin'," but he could not force it out. The deaths of his friends meant something. *Everything.*

# 51

# JUSTICE FOR ALL

---

GOD INTERVENED AGAIN. OR MAYBE IT WAS
WALTER PULLING STRINGS FROM HEAVEN.

---

Zeke got word from his mother that he needed to return for trial in the Lobacter case. He had requested a few days' leave for a "family situation." He confided in his platoon sergeant and received a sympathetic and supportive send-off. The sergeant reminded Zeke that if he were found guilty he would be in serious trouble with the State of Pennsylvania *and* the Marine Corps. Zeke put up a solid Calvinist front—stoic, confident and contrite.

"God wouldn't let that happen to me," he replied as he clutched his 10-Đồng coin. He has always looked out for me. I'll be back at the end of the week."

Zeke entered the courthouse wearing his Marine Corps dress blues with his service ribbons and Sharpshooter Badge neatly attached. Everyone was impressed except the Lobacters who were sitting in the court wearing prison garb looking like the in-bred dogs they were. They had been sentenced to jail time for their robberies a month earlier. The Lobacters had received their just desserts—the "wages of sin," as Velma use to say. Zeke should not have taken the law into his own hands but, then again, he hadn't intended to; shit happens.

"How does the jury find in the case of Lobacters vs. Hammond?" the judge asked the jury foreman.

"Your Honor, the jury was not able to reach a verdict in this case. In viewing the totality of the situation, it was not clear that Mr. Hammond is guilty of the charges brought against him by the criminals sitting in this courtroom whose actions brought about his reaction in the first place. We are a 'hung jury' your Honor."

The judge calmly thanked the jury and dismissed them. He ordered a retrial and Zeke was dismissed for the time being. The Lobacters shuffled back to their jail cells with their heads down. Zeke and Henry caught a glimpse of each other as they were leaving and Zeke gave him a big, happy smile and waved at him.

Zeke's situation had touched a nerve with the jurors. They were members of the community and had either been victimized by the Lobacters themselves or had known for years about their thievery. They also respected Zeke's grandparents, supported the war in Vietnam and admired the Marine Corps. They knew Zeke and his family and felt bad that his fiancé had been killed in a car accident—a point that was objected to as immaterial by the DA when raised by Zeke's attorney. Case closed.

Zeke made it back to Cherry Point a day early.

"Told ya, Sarge. God's on my side," he said with a half-convincing look.

He had gotten through this part of the Lobacter mess successfully, but was concerned about the prospect of a second trial. He was convinced that a second trial would be bad luck.

About three weeks later, Zeke received a letter from Naomi. He had developed some ambivalence about her letters; so many had contained bad news. He took a deep breath and opened the envelope. Naomi had laid it all out in detail. There had been an election. The District Attorney was elected to become the new judge and Zeke's attorney was elected to be the new District Attorney. That "musical chairs" situation presented many legal problems especially in view of the hung jury.

It was said that the court had a tête-à-tête with the Lobacters who agreed that it would be in their interest to drop the charges against Zeke. The case was dismissed; no second trial. Zeke took another deep breath and closed his eyes. *God had intervened again or maybe it was Walter pulling strings from heaven.*

**52**

# NAVY CROSS

---

Zig killed him, rallied his Marines, beat back the enemy and saved the day—all on his 21st birthday.

---

Marines used bunk beds in their enlisted squad bays. One man slept on the top rack, the other man slept on the bottom rack. They were called bunkies. At Cherry Point, Zeke's bunkie was an acerbic corporal named Zbigniew, Zig for short, who did not warm up to people easily and took some time to befriend. Zig's parents were immigrants from Poland and he had joined the Marine Corps to gain his citizenship. During his tour in Vietnam, he had received some serious wounds. His hands and face were badly scarred. He had suffered disfiguring body wounds as well. In time, Zeke and Zig became friends, sharing stories, talking about home and hearth and remarking, tongue-in-cheek, how lucky they both were to have names that began with the last letter of the alphabet.

Zig had been assigned to the motor pool and did menial office jobs. He had trouble using his left hand and he walked with a limp. Sometimes he would drop things or trip over objects. He often seemed to be in pain. His superiors labeled him eccentric and antisocial. They called him "klutz" behind his back. The disrespect was particularly galling since Zig had "served his time in hell" and those who made fun of him had neither been in Vietnam nor ever fired a weapon in anger.

Zeke learned that Zig had been in the deep shit in Vietnam one night when hordes of NVA troops tried to overrun his position. Zig had been hit by a grenade and then an NVA soldier jumped into his foxhole, aimed point blank at him and pulled the trigger. The soldier's rifle went "click" instead of "bang," meaning it was out of ammunition or malfunctioned.

He then jumped on Zig and tried to strangle him with a rope. Zig killed him, rallied his Marines, beat back the enemy and saved the day—all on his 21st birthday. After months of recuperation, he received a Purple Heart for his trouble.

One day, unexpectedly, Zig told Zeke that he got word of an award that he was to receive. He did not know what award it was and did not seem to care. When it came down that he might receive a Silver Star, everyone at every level began to see him as a real person, perhaps even a hero. They began treating him nicer and stopped using the word "klutz" to refer to him. A week later, it was announced that Zig was to receive an even greater honor—the Navy Cross, the country's second highest military honor, one step below the Medal of Honor. Zig became an overnight sensation. Everyone at Cherry Point, from the commanding general on down, took pride in Zig's Navy Cross. It was seen as a positive reflection on Cherry Point and the entire Marine Corps. Zig appreciated the respect he was being accorded and enjoyed how those who once derided him were now fawning over him.

Zig confided to Zeke that he was worried about the award ceremony because his parents were going to attend and they were not fluent in English. He thought they might not respond appropriately because they could not understand the language and might be laughed at by onlookers.

"If anyone laughs at them I'll kill them, I swear to God; I don't care who they are."

Zeke was alarmed; he knew Zig was not kidding. His state of mind was such that he just might do it.

"Come on Zig, surely you wouldn't do such a crazy thing. If anyone did snicker or make fun of them, it wouldn't mean a thing and you should just blow it off. Don't mean nothin,' remember? Don't fuck things up by landing in the Brig the same day you receive the nation's second highest military award. That's an order, goddammit," said Zeke, even though Zig outranked him.

After the ceremony, Zeke asked Zig how it felt to be a hero. He just smiled and said in Polish, "*dziękuję, bracie*—thank you, brother—as he shook Zeke's hand.

"It's an honor, sir," Zeke said, as he snapped to attention and rendered a slow, respectful hand salute.

# 53

# ALMOST A LIEUTENANT

---

"DYING FOR SOUTH VIETNAM OR AN UNGRATEFUL,
UNSUPPORTIVE AMERICA IS NOT AN OPTION."

---

Zeke's active duty time was almost over and he would be released to
the 4th Marine Division for reserve duty. The government had sunk
a lot of money into Zeke and Marines like him. To get a return on their
investment it was important to convince as many Marines as possible to
extend or reenlist. Zeke was called into Major Haupt's office for a "shipping
over" talk, the purpose of which was to convince him that staying in the
Corps was a good career move and a much better option than going back
out into the cold, cruel world of civilian life. It was SOP to offer a Marine
slated for an honorable discharge a chance to reenlist in the Corps, but it
was unusual for a major to be doing the coaxing to a junior level enlisted
man. Sergeants or staff NCOs usually dealt with the rank-and-file.

Major Haupt unloaded his sales pitch, "As a Marine you are part of a
family. The Marine Corps takes care of you. Where else but the Marine
Corps can you get "three hots and a cot" (free food and housing), wear dress
blues, and be part of the finest fighting force in the world?"

The shipping over lecture went on for forty-five minutes itemizing all the
positives of military service in general and the Marine Corps in particular.
Zeke interrupted a few times to ask Haupt to explain some inconsistencies
just to see what he would say. He noticed Haupt was not wearing a Vietnam
service ribbon on his uniform and found that his take on the war was shallow. The major spoke in clichés and was not convincing. He just wanted a
feather in his cap for inducing Zeke to ship over.

Zeke was a high school graduate and he had scored high on the various tests he had taken during the first week of basic training. Being a high school graduate with high scores made him eligible to become an officer. Major Haupt promised Zeke an immediate promotion to corporal, free college and a 2nd Lieutenancy at the end of the journey. All he had to do was sign on the dotted line for six years of active duty, maintain a good grade point average in college and satisfactorily complete officer training at Quantico, Virginia—yada, yada, yada. Zeke was pleased that the Marine Corps, through Major Haupt, was finally acknowledging his potential. He was flattered, but he did not trust the Marine Corps to follow through on their commitment. He declined the offer without a second thought.

Zeke had sampled Marine Corps life; it had been a multidimensional character builder. He had developed a profound sense of accomplishment and enough self-confidence to last a lifetime. And to be offered a chance to go to college and become an officer of Marines, by a major no less, was a particularly heady thing, especially for a young man not yet 21. Had there been more Chesty Pullers, a Marine icon, and fewer Mustang Sallies and had the war not been so politicized, Zeke might have accepted the offer, but it was not to be. The Corps had taught Zeke what he did *not* want to do or become. It was time to bid adieu and start a new chapter in his life.

"Major Haupt, I see from your ribbons that you haven't yet been in Vietnam. Let me give you my take. The war in Vietnam shows no signs of abating and there is no hope of winning under the rules of engagement and the leadership I have experienced. It seems to me that the South Vietnamese military, except for the Vietnamese Marines, do not have the fortitude and mindset to win their own war. I am also getting the impression that the American people are against the war, more so every day. Dying for South Vietnam or an ungrateful, unsupportive America is not an option for me."

Zeke was not going to tempt the fates a second time. He was not going to risk death for South Vietnam's newly elected President, Nguyen Van Thieu, President Johnson ... or anybody.

Major Haupt was silent. He seemed to be trying to decide whether to call Zeke down for being disrespectful.

"Hammond, you'd have made a good officer. You speak and think well and you could pass every test we would throw at you. Between you and I—and I do mean that Marine, just between us—the war is going to get bigger and bloodier before it is over. I believe 1968 will be a high point in terms of troop commitments and casualties. It's a mess. We could have taken care of that situation in two years had we been allowed to do so. Hell, the Marine Corps could have done it by itself. But, politics being what they are, that's not going to happen. I worry that if we do not take the gloves off and give our men full latitude and support we might just lose this damned war or be seen as losing it. Hammond, I suggest you go to college and make something of yourself. And never forget, once a Marine always a Marine. *Semper Fi*, Zeke."

"I will never forget. Thanks, sir, and God bless you. *Semper Fi.*"

They both stood up at the same time and departed with a handshake and a respectful nod. Zeke walked out of his office with a sense of complete closure. No regrets.

## 54

# EOD

---

"BE A MAN, ZEKE, BE A MAN." "I WAS GRAMP; AND
I AM ... WHEN IT MATTERED."

---

Then came EOD—End of Day; End of Watch. It was time to pack up
and get out of the Marine Corps. Zeke clutched his Đồng and looked
up as if praying.

"Lord get me out of here. Do not let me do anything stupid. No tricks.
No screw-ups. Please don't test me today; you know how I fail your tests,"
he said aloud.

Zeke packed his seabag, the one with all the places he had been, neatly
magic-marked, one after another: Parris Island, Camp Geiger, Montford
Point, Camp Lejeune, Camp Pendleton, Vietnam and Cherry Point, with
stops at El Toro, Wake Island, Hawaii, and Okinawa, not to mention an
orgy in Siam. *Lord Have Mercy. It was a time.*

He snapped out of his reflections when he heard someone call his name.

"Hammond, whatcha gonna do with them jungle boots you got hangin'
from your seabag?"

It was Monroe, a splib lance corporal who bunked on the other side of
the squad bay.

"I'm gonna wear them for huntin' when I get back home. I had a pair
of Sears' Best rubber boots but they got tore up in 'Nam and I got nothin'
else," replied Zeke.

"I'll give you twenty bucks for them clodhoppers. You don't wanna be
seen wearin' that shit at home. People think you be a baby killer. That's
what them newspapers say we are," said Monroe.

"You know, Monroe, maybe you got something there. I told a captain here at Cherry Point that I would never wear jungle boots again. I should keep my word. You can have the damn things. Keep your twenty dollars and just give me a pack of cigarettes for them. All I want in return is for you to tell your splib 'bros' to knock those chips off their shoulders and understand that most of us chucks are good guys ... just like me. Right?"

"Fuckin' A, said Monroe. You got it."

They slapped hands, gave each other a *"Semper Fi"* and Zeke was on his way.

"Good luck, brother," yelled Monroe.

Zeke smiled, gave Monroe a friendly salute and walked out of the squad bay for the last time.

Zeke had accomplished his goals: he had tested his mettle. He had done his job in Vietnam and done it well. He held up. He had not faltered. He had not run away. He never hesitated at the Moment of Truth. And he never cried. But he had done some crazy things, took foolish chances and literally dodged a few bullets and brushes with death in various forms. It had been a lottery; returning in one piece meant that he had won.

Too bad the Baby Boomers' war was becoming catawampus. Vietnam was being poorly managed and controlled by the "Best and the Brightest" in the White House; specifically, the President and his circle of advisors that David Halberstam would write about five years later. They had painted the picture of a poor little country needing America's help in their fight for freedom against Communist aggression. Vietnam was actually a proxy war between the U.S. on one side and the Soviet Union and "Red" China on the other. It was an extension of the post-WWII Cold War between the good guys and the bad guys. Of course, each side thought *they* were the good guys. People got hurt—lots of them and in many ways. Aside from platitudes and generalities, it was the war that nobody won.

As Zeke slowly walked to the LeSabre wearing his civilian clothes and with his seabag over his shoulder, the Cherry Point automobile permit on the inside of his windshield caught his eye. *My permit expires today,* he thought. He peeled it off as he got into the car and tossed it into the glove compartment. He was a civilian, at least for the time being, assuming he was not recalled as a reservist. He looked forward to getting back to a normal life, wherever and whatever "normal" might now mean without his grandparents and Sharon. He knew that nothing would ever be the same ever again. The kid that joined the Corps at eighteen was long gone. He was older now, much older.

Zeke could hear his Gramp's voice in his ear just as plainly as if he was standing right next to him: "Be a man, Zeke, be a man."

He replied aloud as he looked up to the heavens. "I was Gramp, when it mattered, and I *am*.

As he drove out of the gate for the last time, he flipped on the radio. An oldie but goodie was playing; it was *We Gotta Get Out of this Place*. He turned up the volume full blast, as he headed north for home … with tears in his eyes.

# ABOUT THE AUTHOR

Timothy C. Hall served with the Marines in Vietnam in the 1960s, after which he earned an Associate's degree from Nassau Community College, a Bachelor's degree from Adelphi University and a Master's degree from the University of Memphis. In the 1970s, he was an analyst with the governor's office in Virginia and the U.S. Department of Labor in Colorado. He also worked as a consultant with Booz Allen Hamilton, one of America's oldest, largest and "best" management consulting firms, according to Forbes.

In the 1980s he was director of the (Denver) Mayor's Office of Employment and Training and the (Colorado) Governor's Job Training. Tim was also Director of Finance, Administration and Membership Development at the American Numismatic Association.

Through the 1990s and 2000s, Tim was Executive Director/CEO of Laradon Hall, Colorado's first school for children and adults with developmental disabilities. Concurrently, he was an Adjunct Professor in the Management and Human Resources areas at Webster University Graduate School and Chapman University. He rounded out his career as the Deputy Executive Director of the Colorado Department of Human Services where he headed Veterans and Disability Services programs, retiring in 2009.

Tim has published numerous professional and technical articles and has also contributed to magazines and journals related to his pastimes, which include vintage cars, competitive pistol shooting and flying. He is an honorary lieutenant with the Denver Police Department and is active in military veterans' activities and causes.